HOMICIDAL ALIENS ARE INVADING AND ALL I GOT IS THIS STAT MENU

J.J. ACKERKNECHT

JAYACK PUBLISHING

This is for my wonderful wife, and my amazing parents, who have always been there to support me and my stories. A huge shoutout as well to my most supportive patrons, who were there even when the story was not: Noelle and Scott. You're both absolute legends. Thank you, always.

PART ONE
THE ACCUMULATED
UNIVERSAL KNOWLEDGE
ARCHIVE PROJECT

FROM EARTH #1

From Rutherford International News Network:
NASA CONFIRMS LARGE ASTEROID TO PASS THROUGH
SOLAR SYSTEM

Top officials at NASA have confirmed that an asteroid roughly the
size of Australia will pass through our solar system. Astronomers may
be able to spot the big asteroid if they have powerful enough equipment in the coming months. When asked if there was any danger of
the asteroid getting close to Earth, scientists stated that no, its gravitational arc would propel it away from Earth, but may cross within
several million miles of our planet's orbital path before leaving our
system and continuing into space beyond.

———

From The Modesto Bee:
MULTIPLE INTERNATIONAL TELECOMMUNICATION
COMPANIES REPORT IRREGULARITIES IN SERVICES

There have been a lot of dropped calls and weak wifi signals this
week. Reports from several international telecommunications companies suggest that the problem isn't just a local one, and that there have

been a number of "black spots," or areas of reduced signal reception, popping up across supposedly well-covered areas.

"I paid for the service, so why aren't I getting it?" demanded Frank White, 54, from Ceres. He and many other customers have been calling their local telecom provider (or trying to) in an effort to get to the bottom of this.

"It's not just one or two companies," Shannon Smith from CaliCom services in Modesto said. "Several telecom companies in America and Canada and Mexico are reporting similar problems."

Further research reveals that this "black out" problem could have a global scale. A report two days ago from the London Times stated that Great Britain had been experiencing lost connections and dips in bandwidth.

For now there's no clear answer as to what may be causing the interference, but don't go canceling your current monthly plan just yet. Chances are, the other companies are having the same issues.

———

From *Le Monde* [Translated from French]
CEO AND WIFE FOUND MURDERED, SON MISSING
Michel Duclair, CEO of Duclair Financial, and his wife Agathe were found dead in their Paris penthouse earlier today by housecleaning staff in an apparent burglary gone wrong. Inspector Abadie of the Préfecture de Police addressed the press shortly after the discovery was made public.

"Mssr. and Mme. Duclair were the victims of an attack sometime between late last night and very early this morning. Their son, Gabriel Duclair, is missing. We ask anybody with any information to please assist in our investigation, and contact the PP with any details you may have regarding the whereabouts of Gabriel Duclair as well as anything related to the attack itself."

When asked if Gabriel Duclair was considered a suspect, Inspector Abadie offered no comment.

Michel Duclair had recently come under fire for reports of insider trading, tax evasion, and other possible criminal offenses related to

Duclair Financial's acquisition of several smaller investment firms last year.

———

From HeckYesScience.com:

SETI STATES SIGNAL FROM OUTER SPACE MAY BE SIGN OF INTELLIGENT LIFE

The Search for Extra Terrestrial Intelligence (SETI) Institute reported some strange signals they have received from space. SETI has been listening to the deep reaches of space for years in the hopes of finding some sign of life among the stars, but to no avail.

Until this past week.

"It's nothing concrete, and we're not entirely certain it couldn't be reflected radiowaves from Earth, or an orbiting satellite," says Dr. Juno Reid. "It's nothing conclusive, but maybe something is out there. We're going to keep listening and trying to figure out the source. Until then, please don't put anything salacious in your headline."

1

The aliens known as the Engineers sent their technology across the vastness of space, past untold stars, and beyond countless light years of dark and fathomless void. It was the herald for cataclysmic change, for invasion, for intergalactic war.

And the bastards did it on a Friday night.

They could have at least waited until Monday when everybody was going to be miserable anyway.

The faster-than-light package carrying the extraterrestrial technology sped toward the far end of the Milky Way galaxy, and toward a G-type yellow-dwarf main sequence star along one of its spiral arms. The alien parcel slowed to sub-light speed as it entered the outer orbit of the star's farthest planet (technically a dwarf planet depending on who you asked), and streaked past an asteroid belt and several lifeless worlds home to nothing but gas and rock and ice.

The parcel slowed again as it approached a certain pale blue dot, then stopped between it and its singular moon. It hovered in the silence of space, an orb of pure silver a few feet in diameter. It rippled like liquid at regular intervals, as if a beating heart lay beneath its flawless surface.

The silver orb glowed from within, brighter and brighter, then exploded into tens of thousands of points of multi-hued light. Each tiny mote of light hung in space for a moment before all of them shot down to the planet below and ruined everybody's weekend.

———

ANYA NOWICKI, of the planet Earth, United States, New York, Brooklyn, 67 Stanhope Street, Apartment 7C (next to the maintenance closet) did not know the world was a few hours away from being host to alien technology. She did know that her boss, Mr. Davis, was a tremendous asshole and would likely benefit from being thrown down a small flight of stairs.

"We've talked about you being late before," Mr. Davis said and looked at a printout of Anya's shift check-ins. He was a short, bald, egg of a man, whose pale exterior was cracking with age. Mr. Davis obsessed about punctuality as if he were managing an ICU ward rather than a café.

And not even a good café, but just one of dozens of branches of a chain in the heart of New York's financial district. The coffee at any branch of Cody's Corner Café was a tepid watered down version of actual coffee that Anya referred to as "bean juice." She wasn't an expert, but she knew enough to know that what they served at Cody's was an affront to the actual thing.

But the café had a convenient location in the lobby of one of the city's many skyscrapers that housed at least a dozen investment firms. The low-level brokers, accountants, and other newbie financiers didn't seem to care too much about the quality, so long as the caffeine content was on point.

And that it was cheap, which it was.

"I was only a minute late, Mr. Davis," Anya said, trying to stop herself from sighing or rolling her eyes. Instead, she thought about how long a staircase would need to be to readjust Mr. Davis's attitude. Five steps was hardly a staircase at all, but fifteen steps might do him too much damage. Anya thought of Mr. Davis's rotund, egg-like form falling down the steps and then cracking open like Humpty Dumpty at the bottom, yolk and cheap coffee spilling out of him.

"That's not the point. Late is late. One minute or one second. Early is on time," Mr. Davis said. He scowled at Anya and asked, "Are you listening to me, Ms. Nowicki?"

"Ten steps."

"What?"

"Sorry. Yes, sir, I'm listening."

"This is the second time you've been late in as many weeks. If it happens again, I'll have to replace you," Mr. Davis said.

"Yes, sir," Anya said, and before she could stop herself, snapped off a quick salute and clicked her heels together.

"Are you being smart with me?"

"Me no be smart, boss-boss," Anya said before she could stop herself again. She clamped her mouth shut and winced. Mr. Davis scowled at her, causing the lines beside his eyes to deepen and further the impression of a fragile shell cracking. The last time Anya had seen him like this had been a few days before, when he'd been ready to fire some new kid for screwing up an order. Anya had taken the blame for that, because the kid had been on the verge of tears and she knew Mr. Davis wasn't going to fire his most senior barista who did most of the work.

"I don't know if you're late because you're just too stupid to understand how a clock works or because you're lazy, and I don't care. You'll clock out in five minutes and then close tonight to make up for your tardiness," Mr. Davis said. "Or you can find a new job."

"You want me to finish my actual shift off-the-clock? As in, unpaid?"

"Maybe you're not so stupid after all."

Anya sighed and folded her arms over her chest. She had been late, and she was willing to accept a bit of a verbal brow-beating because of it. But she wasn't at Cody's for community service, or to be Mr. Davis's workhouse and verbal punching bag.

"Time to find a new job then," she said and removed her name tag and flicked it at Mr. Davis's chest. Mr. Davis's eyes goggled at her as though she had slapped him. "Also, go fuck yourself."

"You have to give two weeks notice before—" Mr. Davis sputtered, but Anya was already walking away from behind the counter.

"No, I don't," she said over her shoulder as she approached the elevators at the far end of the lobby. She entered the nearest one and grinned as the doors closed, framing Mr. Davis's furious ovoid form for a moment before shutting him out entirely.

Anya smiled to herself and hit the button for the thirtieth floor, humming to the dull music within the elevator as it went up. It dinged and opened upon a slick, brushed steel sign that informed Anya she had arrived at Harcourt & Simms Investment Firm. Darkness lay over the offices beyond the window, as the market had closed for the day and most of the employees had left. Only a pair of janitors, a few random desk drones, and the secretary in front remained. Anya strode straight toward the secretary's desk in the waiting area and the slender, sharp-faced woman behind it.

The woman wore a sleek navy suit, and had her straight blond hair pulled back into a simple but stylish knot. Despite her outwardly professional appearance, her posture conveyed all the agitated malaise of an irritated house cat: she slumped in her seat and clicked idly on a mouse as her heavy-lidded eyes stared at the monitor before her. She looked up from her computer, and her expression softened as she saw Anya.

"Hey, Tori," Anya said, unable to stop feeling like a bit of a potato whenever she was around her friend. Where Tori was slender and sharp, Anya was short and stout. Where Tori's hair was gold and straight and long, Anya's was copper and messy and short. While Tori always wore a slick suit and coat, Anya was stuck in her canvas apron and polo shirt. "How was the bean counting today?"

"Same as every day. How was the bean roasting?" Tori replied. Her voice was low, bored, and tired. She glanced at her computer with obvious disgust, as though it had somehow manifested the ability to fart.

"You think they actually roast beans at Cody's? It's some liquid that comes in a plastic tub they keep under the counter. Also, I quit."

"You quit?" Tori raised her eyebrows.

"Davis was being a prick. He wanted me to work for free because I was two minutes late. Hell yeah, I quit."

"That guy always seemed like a jerk. I'm glad for you, but what about, y'know, your rent?" Tori asked.

Anya blinked and then nodded, "Oh, right."

"You forgot about rent?"

"I didn't forget! I just… wasn't going to take Davis's shit anymore. And it's not like I was in some super specific niche job you can't find anywhere else. I'll find somewhere else to work on Monday. Hopefully with a boss that isn't a shitheel."

Rent was an issue, but she also worried about the new hires. She had been on staff at Cody's the longest, and taken the brunt of Mr. Davis's tantrums. Now the newbies would have to fend for themselves.

A pang of guilt stung her, and she considered going downstairs to request her job back.

Fuck that, she thought. She hadn't left one abusive control-freak years ago just to get saddled with another now.

"Well," Tori leaned forward as she lowered her voice, "my boss is still a shitheel and I can't afford to up and leave just yet. He told me I have to stay late and double check some of the accounting department's numbers."

"He wants you to do accountant work even though you're only hired as the secretary?"

"Yup. Like I said: shitheel."

"I imagine that'll take you a while?"

"At least another hour or two, yeah. If you wanna get started on the weekend early, I won't blame you."

"Hell no. We had noraebang plans tonight and we go together or we don't go," Anya said and folded her arms across her chest. Tori smiled at her, then gestured at one of the slick leather chairs nearby.

"Might as well get comfy then. There's actual coffee and some over-priced leftover pastries from this morning in the break room if you want some."

"I might steal a few. Let me know if you need anything in the meantime," Anya said as she pulled out her phone to pass the time while her friend finished her work.

———

THEY WENT STRAIGHT to their favorite noraebang once Tori was done. One upside to having to wait for Tori to finish work was that the subway was not quite the horrendous experience it usually was during rush-hour. The downside was that both women were more likely to be creeped upon by the inevitable weirdos who somehow always mistook their guarded postures and lack of eye-contact as invitations to engage in awkward and sometimes obscene flirtations.

Anya usually took up a rather guarded position in front of her friend during subway rides. Her brothers had all been happy to teach her some moves from their wrestling and football teams or boxing classes (despite her mother's protestations that such things were "inappropriate," for a girl). While Anya would never think she could win in any serious fight, she knew and had practiced enough to deter any half-hearted perverts that wouldn't take the less subtle hints that they weren't interested.

Tori had perfected a rather impressive death-glare over the years that could stop a drunken lech at ten yards. And if that didn't work, she also had a can of bear mace in her purse. The death-glare was usually enough.

Thankfully, the subway was relatively drama-free that Friday, and they arrived at the Taebak Noraebang just in time to get the last room. The Taebak Noraebang (or Amazing/Cool Singing Room) was equidistant between Anya's and Tori's apartment buildings, and so was the perfect place for them to get drunk and then stagger home whenever they felt like it. Coincidentally, they almost always felt like it every Friday. Anya's neighbor, Mr. Choi, also worked the front desk and would frequently sneak them extra bottles of soju or free snacks.

They spent the next two hours belting out some of their favorite songs in the privacy of the enclosed and neon-lit singing room. Tori chose mostly 80s power love ballads and cheery pop songs, while Anya favored the glam and classic rock selections. They both joined in for some of the recent K-Pop songs and show tunes.

Tori was on her fifth soju and soda while Anya thought she might be on her tenth, but details got fuzzy past drink number six. A polite knock at the door interrupted her thoughts as Mr. Choi poked his head into the small room and smiled. He was an older Korean man with gray hair, a round face, and very thick glasses.

"Sorry ladies, it's been two hours. Would you like to buy another hour or are you finished for the evening?" he asked.

"I can go for three more hours," Tori slurred and held up four fingers. Anya snorted and shook her head.

"How're you this much drunker than me? You had like, two drinks."

"I had five!" Tori protested, held up three additional fingers, and scowled.

"Are you both okay to get home? I'll be done in another hour or so. I wouldn't mind escorting you two," the older man said.

Anya smiled but shook her head. She was still mostly sober. She wouldn't trust herself to drive, but walking shouldn't pose a problem. Besides, the walk back to their respective apartment buildings was short enough and well-lit. She'd made the late-night drunken stumble home from Taebak Noraebang on more than one occasion with Tori in tow.

"C'mon, you," Anya said and helped Tori to her feet. Tori slumped against her and chuckled.

"You're so short. Like a little... short thing."

"Just don't puke in my hair."

"That was one time."

"Uh-huh."

"Cash or credit?" Mr. Choi asked as they approached the counter and cash-register.

"Oh, uh, credit, I guess," Anya said and fumbled in her purse with one hand while her other steadied Tori.

"No way," Tori produced her card from the handbag at her side. "My treat this week. Your treat when you get a new job. With no shitheels this time."

Anya blushed a little, but only nodded and said, "Thanks, Tori. I'll get you back next time."

"Be safe out there," Mr. Choi waved at them as the women left the warm neon embrace of the noraebang and went back out into the chilly night.

Brooklyn—and particularly Bushwick—in winter was not the loveliest part of New York. Snow from a week ago had had enough time to pile up into black and brown piles of slush and discolored ice along the edges of the streets and sidewalks. Barren trees scratched at the night sky with their naked branches. Wind from the ocean bit sharply as it swept between Bushwick's stumpy buildings. It was a far cry from the pleasant breezes one could feel on Coney Island in the summer.

The chilly air had the side-effect of sobering Tori up just enough that she didn't need to lean on Anya so much to maintain her balance. Both women still needed a few extra moments to navigate around the dirty piles of snow or precarious patch of ice on the sidewalk, but they made it to Tori's building without incident.

"Thanks Anya," Tori said when they arrived. "You wanna sleep on my couch tonight? It's a long walk to your place from here."

"Not that long," Anya replied. "Especially since I don't have to carry your drunk ass."

"You barely carried me. You got plans this weekend?"

"Job applications!" Anya said with obvious forced enthusiasm. Tori made a retching sound then hiccuped and actually retched and covered her mouth.

"Well, I can help with those, too. I need my toilet right now though. Bye!" Tori gave a quick wave to Anya before dashing inside, hand over her mouth. Anya laughed, then began the walk back to her place.

She tried to ignore any thoughts of how she was going to pay rent next month if she couldn't find a job, but the cold in the air forced her to consider it. If her landlord kicked her out of her apartment, she'd be at the mercy of the elements. She didn't even have a car to camp in as a last resort.

Tori would likely be fine with her being roomies for a while, but she didn't want to impose on her friend like that.

She knew her mother would welcome her back with open arms and a closed mind.

Anya shuddered at the thought.

Never.

Anya took out her phone as she walked and opened the photo app. The last couple of years were all pictures of her and Tori and a few of their other casual friends, all in New York, all smiles. The photos before that showed Anya and her three brothers: all of them broad and stout and copper-haired, each with a faint constellation of freckles across their noses.

When it was just a picture of her and her brothers, the smiles were genuine, relaxed. Sometimes somebody would be laughing.

If their mother were present, the smiles were still there, but they had changed. They were stiff, stretched, and tight-lipped. Everyone's back seemed too rigid, their shoulders bent forward as if anticipating some sort of blow from behind. The only actual smile to be had came from the concrete slab of a woman lurking behind her children. It was not one of happiness, but satisfaction. Satisfaction that her children knew their place, and knew to be cowed, and knew who was in charge of them and their lives.

The most recent photos only had Anya, her mom, and two of her brothers.

Nobody was smiling in those.

As for their father...

The only photos of him were a few physical copies Anya's oldest brother had saved back when she had been in grade school.

Anya pushed the thoughts aside as she came up to her apartment building. She had enough on her plate with finding a new job and figuring out how to make her withering bank account last as long as possible. Mulling over how her mother might cackle if she came crawling back to South Carolina after failing to make it in the city wouldn't help.

For now, she still had her apartment, and tomorrow Tori would come over and help her look for work. She trudged up the stairs ("Elevator under repairs," the two week old sign in the entryway still read), and let out a heavy sigh as she closed the door to apartment 7C behind her and leaned against it.

Apartment 7C was little more than a glorified closet with a kitchenette and a bathroom, but it was a monster when it came to devouring her monthly income.

The living area was cramped but cozy, and held only the necessities: a bed, sofa, dresser, coffee table, and a small desk with a laptop on it. It was mostly stuff Anya had gotten second hand, and it was all ratty or scarred. The couch had some patches she had sewn onto it to keep the stuffing in, the coffee table needed an old paperback to hold up the left side, and the bed was lumpier than she would've liked, but it was all clean and comfy.

The only item in the apartment that Anya had gotten brand new was the gaming laptop her oldest brother had gotten her for Christmas when she'd first arrived in New York. That had been the last gift she'd received from him or anyone else in the family, after their mother had told them if Anya wanted to make it on her own then she would do exactly that, and they shouldn't bother with her anymore.

Anya once again pushed those thoughts away, changed into her flannel pajamas, and sat on the couch beside the narrow window that looked out on Stanhope Street. She smiled to herself as she watched the few pedestrians braving the cold, listened to the hum and honk of traffic, the dull background soundtrack of the city itself.

New York was crowded, expensive, smelly, and a constant rat race. But after a couple of years, it felt like home. Moreso than her actual home in Clemson had ever felt. It was her city, and she didn't owe anyone there anything.

Looking for a new job would be a pain in the ass, but worth it. She hadn't left the bullshit her mother subjected her to just to deal with more of the same here. Her little brother hadn't made it out. She had.

Anya looked up at the light-polluted sky and saw how the winter night burned a faint orange from the countless lamps below. That was the only thing she truly regretted about the city: no stars. The only twinkling in the sky came from satellites or airplanes. A small price to pay to have her own life.

She watched an airplane pass by, the red and white lights at the tips of its wings blinking at her from high above. Red, white, red, white, red, orange, orange.

Not blinking anymore, but solid.

The plane moved on, but the pinprick of orange light remained and continued to grow. It sparkled a deep mandarin, visible even through the lights of the city, glowing like a tiny little sun. Unlike the satellites or aircraft, it wasn't moving. It remained still in the sky, winking at her. She stared at the light above her and winced when it shined on her, directly into her eyes.

"What the f—" she started to say when her window shattered and then her entire apartment was spinning around her. She tumbled backward, only somewhat aware of a burning sensation in the center of her chest. She smelled something burning. Her head hit the wooden floor of her apartment with a loud crack.

Before she lost consciousness she thought, *Helluva start to the weekend,* and then the apartment went dark, and Anya went with it.

2

t was still night outside when Anya came to. The sounds of endless traffic and the only somewhat subdued bustle of the city filtered to her through the hole in her window, along with a constant gust of chilly January air. She was surrounded by tiny shards of glittering glass and the smell of scorched flannel.

Glittering like the stars, Anya thought through a murky haze of semi-consciousness. No stars in the city. What was that orange thing?

Her head cleared as she winced and the pain brought her back to her senses. She sat up, careful to not cut herself on the surrounding glass. She sniffed at the air and looked around for whatever was burning, then winced with the movement.

Her chest was stiff and stung a bit in the center. She reached down and frowned when she felt a hole in the middle of her flannel pajama top. The hole was about the size of a quarter and singed black around the edges. Her chest beneath the hole looked undamaged, and she brushed her fingers against her skin there to see if it was tender.

There was a slight tingle when her fingers touched the spot just over her sternum, and then a beam of light shot out from her chest and flashed across her room.

Anya screamed and scrambled back on her hands and feet, heedless of the broken glass around her. She didn't notice as the tiny shards bit into her palms and soles of her feet as she tried to escape the thing suddenly in front of her. She was too panicked to focus on it, startled out of her wits by the appearance of a glowing object that filled most of her vision. When she thumped her back against her bed she had no choice but to stop and stare up.

A large opaque gray rectangle floated in front of her, covered in glowing orange text. The text was unreadable, just a series of squiggles and lines and dots that might have been a language. The symbols changed as Anya stared at them, snapping into recognizable English letters. Anya tried to get her heart and breathing under control as she stared at the rectangle. She squinted at it as the last of the unknown letters transformed into English.

ANYA NOWICKI: LEVEL 24 HUMAN
Statistics

- Awareness-6
- Dexterity-4
- Fortitude-7
- Intelligence-4
- Strength-3
- Willpower-7

On the right side of the rectangle was another label that read "SKILLS" and another below that which read "CLASSES-NOT CURRENTLY AVAILABLE" and in the center at the very bottom was a flashing crimson circle with the label "HELP." Below that, a smaller message with a star next to it said, "YOU HAVE UNSPENT POINTS TO ALLOCATE."

Anya stayed on the floor and stared up at the floating rectangle before her. Though really, she had played enough Role-Playing Games to know what it was as soon as it had translated itself into English.

It was a character stat menu for a game.

And it was hers.

She reached out to touch it and her fingers passed through it as though it were a hologram. There was a slight tingling sensation as her fingers went through the floating menu, and again when she pulled her hand back. She tried to rest her fingers on it, and found that while it wasn't solid, tiny halos of dull light appeared around her fingers when she made contact with the menu.

She looked down at the small hole in the center of her sweater and frowned. She touched her sternum, it tingled, then the menu disappeared. She touched her sternum again and the menu reappeared hovering before her. Whenever she turned, the menu turned with her, always centered in front of her. It phased through furniture, the walls, anything solid.

She made the menu disappear again, then looked down around her at the broken glass from the window, and a few splotches of blood from her cut hands and feet.

"Oh shit," Anya whispered and winced as she limped to the bathroom on her cut feet and spent a few minutes taking the tiny pieces of glass out of her skin and putting bandages over the thankfully small cuts. She focused on just tidying up the mess in her room for the moment, and picked up every piece of glass and cleaned up the blood. It was a normal thing to do, which was a relief because her brain was starting to scream at her that something very much not-normal had happened.

But for the moment, Anya just busied herself with tidying up. When she had finished, she decided her bed was a bit too messy, and made that, then thought she might as well do some laundry, and then realized she was stalling and she'd have to face the glowing stat menu in her chest eventually and took a deep breath.

Maybe she had just had more to drink at the noraebang than she thought. Maybe she was hallucinating. That didn't explain the window though. Something real had broken her window, and it had come from outside, or she wouldn't have had to pick up glass off the floor. The hole in her pajamas was real too. She felt the burned, crisp edges of the toasted flannel with her fingers. That was definitely real.

"Okay. Just…okay," Anya said to herself and touched her sternum.

The menu reappeared.

"Holy shit," Anya breathed. "What the fuck is this?"

She walked to her bed, the menu floating ahead of her as she moved, and sat down on the mattress. She had a million questions as she stared at the menu, and thankfully, it had been kind enough to provide what she hoped would be an answer to them. Anya reached out and pressed the flashing orange "HELP" button. It blinked once and a bright flash of warm light blinded Anya as she cried out and put her hands up in front of her face.

She blinked and lowered her hands as her vision cleared, and saw something floating in the air between her and the menu. It was made of translucent orange light and was about the size and shape of a very chubby baby with an over-large head shaped like a rose just starting to come into bloom. Its arms and legs were stumpy, and she saw it didn't really have fingers or toes, but hands like mittens and feet that ended in rounded points. Its face was simplistic and almost cartoonish, featuring a wide mouth and huge eyes. It smiled at her and waved.

Anya screamed and threw a pillow at the creature. The pillow passed right through it, and the menu behind it, and flopped harmlessly to the floor after bouncing off the wall.

"What the fuck!" Anya shouted.

"Hello!" the creature said in a sweet, childish voice. It didn't seem bothered or even to notice that Anya had just tried to knock it out of the air. "I'm your personalized assistant! What can I help you with?"

"Get out of my apartment!" Anya shouted.

"Of course!" the creature said. It floated to the side and through her window, passing through the pane of broken glass like a ghost. It hovered in the air just outside and smiled in at her. "Now what?"

Anya kept as far away from her window as she could and eyed the floating creature outside. It didn't seem dangerous, and it had technically done as she asked. At worst, the impish creature was too literal. Anya tapped her chest and the menu vanished, but the creature remained.

"I see you've dismissed your interface menu," the creature said, its voice muffled by the pane of glass separating them. "Would you like me to return to standby?"

Anya regarded the creature while it continued to smile placidly at her. It didn't appear threatening. Hell, it didn't even look like it was tangible, floating through the window like that.

"Come back inside," Anya said but kept away from the window as the creature followed instructions and floated back into her apartment. "What are you? What's going on? What the hell is all this?"

"I'm your personalized assistant!" it replied. This time it even gave her an awkward salute with one of its stubby arms. "What's going on is I'm introducing myself! All of this appears to be your apartment!"

Anya glared at the chipper response. It really was entirely literal. She took a deep breath and tried not to scream in frustration or panic or both.

"No, I mean, what are you like, your species?"

"Oh! I see. I'm an Artificial Intelligence designated to you, Anya Sabrina Nowicki, for your use in determining how you wish to specify the use of your points for your personal statistics and skills."

"Okay. An AI, great," Anya said and took another breath. Her brain was already reeling at the implications of that statement, but there were other things to ask first. Anya brought up the orange-and-gray tinted menu again by touching her sternum and it appeared at once.

"What the hell is this thing?" Anya asked and pointed at the menu.

"That is the visual user interface for the Accumulated Universal Knowledge Archive Project," the AI said and floated beside the menu screen and waggled their weird little mitten hands at it.

"And what is that?" Anya asked.

"The Accumulated Universal Knowledge Archive Project is a system by which users may draw upon the collected knowledge and skill of surveyed worlds and transfer it to themselves instantaneously!"

Anya's mind spun at the further implications. Was it saying what she thought it was saying?

"Give me an example," she said and had to lean back into her bed. She was dizzy and nauseous, but she did not—no matter how much she wished—feel like she were dreaming. Anya had had twenty-four years of dreams and none of them had been like this. Whatever the hell was happening, it had the unmistakable and tangible weight of reality to it.

"Okay! What is a skill you would like to have, but do not currently possess?" the AI asked.

Anya thought for a moment, happy to focus on a simple question. There were a lot of things she always wanted to do, but never quite had the time, money, or patience to learn how.

"Kinda always wanted to learn how to play the guitar," she said after a moment of thinking.

"Great!" the AI replied and then the menu flashed with hundreds, thousands of skills for a second before narrowing down to one that simply read "GUITAR." That one word expanded into a branching tree that had options underneath such as Spanish guitar, electric guitar, acoustic guitar, bass guitar, and then into different genres of music. The menu grew to accommodate the growing list of skills.

"Whoa," Anya said as her eyes widened.

"You would first need to select the primary 'Guitar,' skill, and then use a skill point to unlock that. Then you could select a specialization, or you could just focus improving the general guitar skill itself," the AI said.

"And then I just... know how to play the guitar?"

"Well, with only a single skill point, your ability would be quite low. But around ten points, you would be very good, at a professional level of performance, based on what scans of this planet have acquired regarding this particular skill and projected point values."

"God damn."

"It's really neat!"

"No shit."

"That's correct, there is no shit here," the AI said and did a brief scan of the apartment.

"No, I mean... forget it," Anya said. The list of questions in her head was growing, all of them piling on top of one another until her brain had become a hive of buzzing queries.

"How many skills are there?" she asked as she studied the sprawling tree of guitar sub-skills.

"5,271,359,009 skills and assorted sub-skills. Many are redundant or heavily related to each other, like what you see here," the AI waved at the guitar skill tree.

"And if I just give you some basic criteria, you'll find the skills for me?"

"Yup!"

"Okay. Show me some assorted physical skills."

"You got it!" the AI nodded their head and an assortment of skills replaced the guitar tree.

Akido. Fidget Spinning. Archery. Weaving. Stunt Driving. Finger Guns. Acrobatics. Heavy Weapons. Sneaking. Cliff Diving. Shadow Puppetry. Disco. Dismemberment. Baseball. Fencing (swords). Fencing (construction). Marksmanship. Jump-Rope. Boxing. Skateboarding.

Anya was at a loss for words as she continued to scan the list. It looked like every single physical pursuit somebody could imagine, including several that were impossible, like dinosaur riding and Atlantean wrestling.

"Uh, wow. What about mental skills?" she asked. The AI nodded again and once more, a list of improbable variety appeared.

Physics. Japanese. Mahjong. Architecture. Polka Trivia. Naval Strategy. Dowsing. Business. Surgery. Wine. Astronomy. Pig Latin. Board Games. Persuasion. Saxophone. Painting. Robotics. Psychology. Deduction. Guerrilla Tactics. Rocketry. Daemonic Speech.

"How are these types of skills here? These aren't real," Anya said and pointed at "Daemonic Speech."

"The Archive informs me they are, in fact, real," the AI replied. "The Accumulated Universal Knowledge Archive Project has collected many skills which you may be unfamiliar with."

"All right, I'll bite. Show me a list of some of the weirder skills," Anya said.

"Weird?" the AI asked.

"Like Dinosaur riding or Atlantean wrestling. Magic and science-fiction stuff, if it's in here," Anya said and gestured at the screen.

"Of course!" The AI nodded and presented Anya with a third list of skills, this one consisting entirely of things she either considered too fantastical to exist, or did not understand.

Flame Dominion. Flesh Shaping. Ectoplasmic Materialization. Prognostication. Elemental Summoning. Void Walking. Ki Mastery. Shapeshifting. Elemental Evocation. Pheromone Secretion. Necromancy. Psychokinesis. Pact-Making. Energy Manipulation (Kinetic). Density Control. Aether Manipulation.

"Holy shit, these are real? I can actually learn these? Just like a guitar?"

"Yup!"

Anya clutched the side of her head as she started to feel dizzy. This was insane.

"Why is this here? The Universal Knowledge thing?" Anya asked and gestured at the menu. "Why do I have it?"

"Oh! That's because REDACTED," the AI said, its chipper, cheery, childish voice switched to something cold and robotic at the last word. Anya flinched at the change, not only in the AI's voice, but its appearance as well. Their face went from animated and smiling to flat and unreadable, their posture went stiff, and their slightly transparent orange body flickered with static for a moment.

Then the AI went back to normal and smiled again.

"Did that help?" they asked.

"What the hell was that?" Anya demanded.

"What was what?"

"That thing you did! Saying 'Redacted,' like that and going all weird."

The AI cocked its rose-shaped head to the side for a moment and squinted as if in thought.

"Huh. There is a zero-point-eight second gap in my memory. That's funny! Let me see if I can find an answer!"

The AI's face vanished entirely, and their rose-head closed its petals up and in. Its arms stuck out to the side and its legs pointed straight down as it began to slowly rotate in mid-air while Anya stared at it.

"Are you T-posing?" Anya muttered, mostly to herself.

After a few seconds of this, the AI returned to normal and gave Anya a sheepish smile and bowed.

"Sorry, but it seems there are some pretty severe gaps in my memory. I do not have access to all of the information I should, and I'm not even sure what's missing," the AI said.

"So you won't know you don't know something until I ask you about it?" Anya asked.

"It seems so."

"What if I ask you why parts of your memory are missing?"

"Then I could try to answer you."

Anya rolled her eyes. Literal. Right.

"Why are parts of your memory missing?" she asked.

"It's because REDACTED," the AI said and went stiff and robotic again.

"Saw that one coming," Anya sighed.

"Sorry again. However I've started to flag known missing areas of my memory if that's of any help. Do you have any more questions?"

"Oh yeah. Where did you come from? Technology like this doesn't exist on Earth," Anya asked. The more she spoke to the little AI, the easier it seemed. Which was sort of surreal in itself, Anya supposed, but she didn't feel like she was going insane (quite so much) anymore, which was a definite improvement.

"I came from REDACTED."

"Great. Who made you?"

"I was made by REDACTED."

"Fuck's sake," Anya said and squeezed the bridge of her nose.

"I really am sorry about this," the AI said.

"It's not your fault...I think," Anya said and then pointed at the menu full of skills. "Can you go back to the main menu screen? Where it showed all my stats and stuff?"

"Yes!" the AI chirped and the menu returned to the initial screen. Anya waved a hand at her personal statistics.

"What about these? Can I change these too?"

"Absolutely! You have statistic points to raise them, which will increase the upper limit of any associated skills."

All of the information the AI had told her so far—as well as the intimidating amount of information it had implied—was beginning to overwhelm Anya. For now, asking questions was fine, but what was she going to do with all of this? She knew she wasn't smart enough to figure it out (a fact which the menu's reading of her statistics seemed to reflect), but that had given her an idea.

"So if I raise my intelligence stat, I'll get smarter?" Anya asked.

"Sort of!" the AI replied. "The definition of intelligence can vary between cultures and species. What you on Earth may consider to be very smart, somebody on another planet may consider foolish, or basic, or vice-versa."

Anya was tempted to ask about alien life on other planets, but suspected that would inevitably come up anyway. It seemed a safe bet that wherever the Accumulated Universal Knowledge Archive Project had come from, it probably wasn't anywhere on this planet.

"Wait, if you're not sure about a culture's definition of intelligence, how come I got a four? How'd you, or this menu thing, get that?"

"Intelligence as the menu defines it as a general rule is a measure of brain efficiency and processing power, sort of like a computer."

"So what happens if I raise the stat?"

"The connections in your brain will become more efficient at relaying information at higher speeds."

"So I'll be stupid, faster."

"You got it!"

Anya scowled a little at the AI, who maintained their gentle, clueless smile.

"Is it going to mess me up at all? Make my brain grow bigger than my skull, or rewrite my personality, or erase my memories or anything else horrible?"

"No! It's just going to improve what's already there."

Anya sighed. Being able to think about things more efficiently would be nice. And trying to sort through the salvo of information coming at her was making her feel like she was drowning. She was sorely tempted to try something both out of basic curiosity and a further need to confirm this was all actually happening.

One point.

As a test.

And hopefully one that would help her process everything better.

"How many stat points do I have?"

"Twenty-four."

"Based on my age, got it. Is it possible to undo any changes I make and go back to how I am now if I don't like something?"

"Yes!" the AI said.

Anya took a deep breath. "Okay. Put one point into my intelligence."

Anya's stat menu now read "Intelligence-4+1—Confirm?" and flashed a faint orange.

"Are you sure you'd like to allocate this point?" the AI asked.

"Do it," Anya replied, and the "Confirm?" prompt flashed again then vanished. The number beside the Intelligence stat changed from "4+1" to "5."

"That's it?" Anya asked after a moment had passed. "I expected—"

That was when the inside of Anya's skull began to burn and something sharp pierced her forehead. She gasped and arched her back from the pain, mouth agape in a silent scream as she prayed that if she were about to die, that it would only be over soon.

3

And then the pain was gone. Almost the moment she registered the searing, brain-melting agony, it vanished. It didn't fade away, and no soreness or headache lingered, it was just gone.

Anya lay on her bed, panting, staring wide-eyed at her ceiling, and felt all around her head for blood or burnt hair.

Nothing.

She was fine.

The AI floated over her and smiled down at her.

"How you feeling?" they asked.

"What the fuck was that?" Anya snapped, and the AI flinched and floated away.

"The Accumulated Universal Knowledge Archive Project has adjusted your brain as you confirmed you wanted it to. Is it not what you wanted?"

"You didn't say it would hurt!"

"Oh. No, I did not. There will be some discomfort for zero-point-seven seconds while the menu recalibrates neural pathways."

"Yeah, no shit! And no, I don't mean there literally isn't any feces in my apartment, I mean what you said was obvious," Anya said before the AI could make a statement about the absence of poop.

"If it was obvious, why did you need me to tell you it would hurt?"

"Just... nevermind," she said. She had been about to say "Forget it," but worried the AI might mind-wipe itself or do something else stupid. She also thought that she should parse her words more carefully and then started to go back over everything she had said when she paused.

She was thinking a lot more clearly.

"Whoa," she whispered. It wasn't a dramatic shift in her thought processes but it was noticeable. If she had to classify it as something, she would compare it to being "in the zone," when she played a video game. Normally she had to make a genuine effort to clear errant thoughts from her head, or concentrate on two different things at once, but now it was easy.

"Holy hell, that's cool," Anya said and smiled.

"What is?" the AI asked.

"That point in my intelligence, it actually did something. You're not gonna tell me the apartment's temperature is normal or something because I said 'cool'?"

"No, I am beginning to understand your use of slang. Sorry it's taken me so long, but I've only been aware of English for a few minutes."

"Hey, you're doing all right," Anya said, and her eyes drifted back to her stats. She'd survived using a point, and nothing had gone wrong. The pain hadn't been fun, but given the overwhelming benefits this Knowledge Archive thing offered, it seemed like a fair trade.

Anya's attention drifted down to her lowest stat: Strength, at a measly three. She thought back to all the times somebody had hassled her and Tori on the Subway, or had followed them back from a bar or restaurant after dark.

She thought of her oldest brother, Dave, teaching her boxing and laughing as he said "You're supposed to float like a butterfly, not punch like one!" whenever her hits landed on him.

She also thought of wanting to punch her mother after Nathan had died, and Dave stopping her with casual ease and shoving her out of the house.

"What's the scale of these numbers?" Anya shook the thought away and pointed at her stats. "One-to-ten?"

"One hundred is the current maximum," the AI replied.

"Current?"

"Yes, it can go up to REDACTED. Aw, darn. Sorry again."

"You don't have to apologize every time that happens. Not your fault," she said, but her newly enhanced mind began to churn through the possibilities. She was in single digits, which out of one hundred, was pathetic. "I don't suppose you have a stat chart for what an average human would be, do you?"

"Based on planetary scans prior to atmospheric entry, the general average for humanity in all stats is five. Ten is the peak for almost all of humanity: think of Olympians and geniuses. A few outliers throughout history may have hit fifteen as the absolute maximum: figures of great historical significance and possibly legend."

"And this is out of one-hundred?" Anya asked and the AI nodded. "Whoa. So If I raised my strength up to ten, that's the normal human peak?"

"You got it! The strength statistic measures how much muscle development and mass you have, as well as how effectively the muscles are arranged to increase maximum power."

Anya glanced at her current strength stat of 3, and then back at the AI and asked, "If I raise my strength stat by seven points, is that gonna make my body explode with muscles or turn me into some kind of freak, or will I keep my current shape? The intelligence change didn't alter my head any."

"Any physical changes are within normal human parameters. You will gain physical mass, but it will not go beyond what is normal for your species. If you choose to go beyond the human maximum of fifteen, your muscles will become denser and undergo other changes to accommodate for superhuman increases, but your body will not exceed the range of recorded human measurements."

"Great, so no turning into a muscle monster. And you're sure I can undo this stuff?"

"Absolutely!"

"All right, let's give it a go then. Can I change my stats myself, or do I have to do it through you?"

"You can do it! Just tap the menu!"

Anya tapped the space next to the "Strength," statistic and saw a plus and minus symbol appear on either side of the "3." She added seven points, and then hit "Confirm?" as she braced herself for the pain.

Just like before, there was a few seconds of nothing happening, just enough to make her think nothing would happen, and then it hit. Her body spasmed, and every muscle she had seized up in an immobilizing, agonizing full-body cramp that made her gasp. Tears sprang to her eyes as she convulsed on her bed, gasping for air as invisible hands crushed her chest and what felt like cords of razor wire whipped through her limbs. She couldn't scream as her arms and legs stretched and popped, bones cracked, and she heard her skin stretching until she thought it must have torn open.

And then, again, it was done. No echoes of pain, no soreness. It was all full-body agony one second and then complete normalcy the next.

"God damn!" Anya gasped when she could breathe again.

Anya groaned and sat up, then winced at a mild tightness in her chest. Maybe there was some residual pain after all. Except it wasn't really pain, just discomfort, and it extended to her arms and legs, everywhere really. She glanced down and saw that her loose pajamas were no longer loose, but pulled taut across her, straining to contain her. She flexed one arm and her eyes widened as the sleeve of her flannel top ripped open and revealed a very large and very new bicep.

"No way," Anya breathed. She looked in the mirror nearby and her jaw fell open. Powerful muscles had appeared beneath her pajamas. She had also grown about two or three feet, somehow, perhaps to accommodate her new mass. Her pajama top was no longer long enough to conceal her tummy, which was less of a tummy and now more of a washboard. She poked her newly acquired six-pack and shook her head at the feeling of firm, springy muscle.

Then the reality of the moment washed over her, and she slumped backward. She examined her hands, arms, legs, felt all over herself to confirm that this was real. She looked in the mirror again and let out a shuddery breath.

That was her face. It was leaner than before, but she was still very recognizable. Same dull copper hair, same dark eyes, thick eyebrows, same freckles dusted across the bridge of her nose. Her gaze drifted down from the mirror to her hands again, her rock-hard stomach, and her much longer and more powerful legs.

"What the hell is this?" she demanded of the AI and gestured at herself.

"That's you! I'm getting really good at these questions," they replied.

"No, you're not!"

"Oh," they said and their face drooped in an over-emotive frown.

"You lied to me!"

"No, I didn't! I can't lie! My basic functioning parameters forbid it!"

"I specifically asked you if changing my strength stat would make me all muscle-bound or something and you said it wouldn't!"

"You asked me '…is that gonna make my body explode with muscles or turn me into some kind of freak, or will I keep my current shape?'" the AI said, perfectly imitating Anya's voice when it quoted her. "Your body did not explode, it expanded, you're still human and have a standard human shape."

Anya felt the vein along her temple throbbing. She wanted to scream at the little AI but bit her lip. It was her fault. The creature—or program or whatever—had shown themself to be entirely literal thus far and she'd neglected to take that into account. Sure the AI had seemed to be learning, but that didn't mean they were perfect. But, the AI said they couldn't lie, so…

"I can undo changes, right?" Anya asked. "You said I could."

"That's correct!" the AI said. Anya let out a sigh of relief, then tapped the minus sign next to "Strength." A message appeared in front of her that read, "YOU DO NOT HAVE ANY AVAILABLE RESPECIFI-CATION TOKENS," and then vanished.

"What the fuck is that?" Anya demanded and pressed the minus sign again. And again. And again. The same message flashed up each time and she cursed at the menu.

"You don't have any respecification tokens," the AI said.

"Yeah, I can read! What the hell is that and how do I get one?"

"A respecification token is an item that will reset your stats and skills to the point of menu integration. Tokens become available at level 50."

"Level 50," Anya said and glanced at her current level at the top of the menu. Level 24.

"That's correct!"

"Okay," Anya sighed as she clenched and unclenched her fists. "Okay, okay, okay."

"Okay!" the AI gave her a thumbs up.

"Look, tiny baby AI thing," Anya said and leaned in until her face was less than an inch from the AI's. Their smile drooped as she scowled. "I need you to tell me if this menu is gonna be making any more changes to my body, or doing anything dangerous, or about to make a mess, or anything that could cause a disturbance. Got it?"

"Uh, y-yes!" the AI said. Anya rolled her eyes, walked to her bathroom, and whacked her head on the top of the door frame.

"Son of a bitch!" Anya snarled. She rubbed her forehead and ducked as she entered the bathroom to study herself in the mirror. It still felt like she was hallucinating. She prayed she was. She didn't dislike the idea of being a tall, buff, warrior woman. That was pretty neat, actually. As she looked at herself better in the mirror, she had to admit, she looked pretty great. Hell, she felt great, better than she ever had. There was a lightness to her movements she'd never experienced before.

Anya flexed in the mirror, admiring the small hills of her biceps and the way her lats spread out behind her.

"Damn. I'm gonna be so good at hugging now," she chuckled to herself.

She looked amazing.

But having it hit her like this, to be short and stout one second and a ripped Grecian statue the next... what would she tell people?

New diet?

Some light plastic surgery over the weekend?

Hell, if she was being honest with herself, the only people who would really notice would be her mom, her brothers, Tori, her neighbor Mr. Choi, and that was about it. And she only saw Tori and Mr. Choi with any regularity.

And if they or other people noticed, so what? What would they do? Report her to the cops for being tall? Anya snorted. Worst case she'd have to get new ID cards. But maybe not even that, since her face looked the same, just leaner.

She supposed it wasn't too bad. Anya flexed her arm and smiled at the firm muscle that appeared.

But what the hell kind of thing can make this possible? she thought, and her smile faded as she lowered her arm. That was the million-dollar question. She had gone through a dramatic transformation, head-to-toe, in seconds. There wasn't any kind of procedure or technology on Earth that could accomplish that.

"Hey, AI thing?" Anya asked.

"Yes? How can I help?" the AI asked as it floated into the bathroom beside her.

"How did this happen?" she gestured at herself.

"You increased your strength stat by seven points!"

Anya took a deep breath and shook her head.

"My fault. I understand the correlation between this number," Anya tapped her chest and pointed at the "Strength," attribute when it appeared, "and my new body. I want to know how the hell it was possible for me to go from short and chubby to tall and muscular in a few seconds. I grew almost three feet and gained pounds and pounds of muscle mass and bone in seconds. That's impossible!"

"The Archive did a scan of your entire body down to your genetic code and integrated itself within it to allow for basic mental and physical modifications. You look really great by the way!"

"This is basic?" Anya shouted and gestured at herself. "I look like Wonder Woman's big sister! And I just asked to get stronger, not taller."

"The Archive will maximize relevant physical changes by default. Being taller allowed for more efficient dispersal of muscles for maximum benefit! Are you unhappy with the changes?"

"Not really. It feels amazing, and I look fucking rad. But it's unnatural. And weird. And talking to you is weird! This is all kind of making me freak the fuck out." Anya looked at the menu and the other statistics and shook her head. "So I've just got this Archive forever, huh?"

"Correct!"

"And I guess that means you, too?"

"Also correct!"

"Great. How the hell was I chosen to have this thing?" Anya demanded, fully expecting the usual "REDACTED," response.

"You were given the Accumulated Universal Knowledge Archive at random," the AI said.

"Excuse me? At random?"

"Yes, you know, like the lottery, or lightning."

"Yeah, I know what random means, I want to know why I have this thing and where it came from! And I'm sure it's 'redacted,' or whatever—"

"Actually a few of the gaps in my memory have filled themselves in while we've been talking."

Anya bit back a swear and counted to three before she replied.

"Right. Teachable moment: if any gaps in your memory become unredacted, or fill in, or whatever, I need you to tell me as soon as possible. Got it?"

"Got it!"

"So, why was I given this thing, and where the hell did it come from?"

"You were given the Archive as a defensive measure."

"Defensive measure? Against what?"

"Against the hostile alien force that will invade your planet thirty-one days from now."

Anya's face went numb. She blinked at the glowing, smiling AI.

"Alien force," Anya said. "Invading Earth."

"You got it!"

"They sent the Archive?" Anya asked. She felt like her brain was misfiring. It kept playing the words "alien," and "invade," over and over. She had obviously suspected aliens or some other nebulous extraterrestrial force behind the Archive. It was too advanced to be anything but alien tech or literal magic.

But hearing that it was aliens in such a blunt way was a bit much. Whenever Anya tried to grasp at anything else, her train of thought jumped the tracks and went straight back to invading aliens.

"No. The Archive was sent by a third party from somewhere on the far side of the Milky Way Galaxy. I don't have a more precise location beyond that but I will let you know as soon as I do!" the AI said.

"More aliens. Different aliens," Anya said. Her voice had become monotone. Any thoughts she had about her new body, what to tell Tori, the particulars of the skills and stats of the menu system, all of it was wiped from her mind by two words repeating on a loop.

Aliens.

Invade.

"Yup! Different aliens!" the AI confirmed.

"I," Anya said after staring in silence at the AI for several long seconds, "am going to bed."

"Okay! Sleep well!" the AI replied.

Anya whacked her head on the door frame again as she exited the bathroom and walked to her bed. It seemed much smaller now, but it didn't bother her. She curled up into a fetal position and buried herself entirely beneath the covers. She closed her eyes and let her mind go blank.

It was surprisingly easy.

Given the choice of looping over what she had heard, debating over whether or not she was crazy, or simply tuning out, the last option was by far the easiest. She embraced that quiet field of nothing between her ears, closed her eyes, and prayed that it would all be gone when she woke up in the morning.

4

nya awoke to early morning sunlight and cold air coming in through her broken window.

"Good morning!" the AI said and waved at her. Anya glared at it.

She had held out a final hope that when she woke up, the world would make sense again. The AI's presence, her broken window, and her towering new body were all still there.

"Mother fucker," Anya sighed and tried to sink into her pillows.

Everything was the same as before, which meant everything had changed. Less than twelve hours ago, Anya would have considered the idea of an alien invasion nothing but fiction. And now, here it was, floating around her apartment like a fat, cartoon infant.

But maybe there was one last hope that Anya had merely gone mad and aliens were not a thing. Her experiments alone weren't enough: she needed another pair of eyes. Anya picked up her phone and opened her contacts list and selected "TORI."

The phone rang several times before it was finally answered. There was a thump from the other end of the line, a curse, and then a mumbled, "Hello?"

"Tori?" Anya asked.

"Mmmfff," Tori replied. "Anya? What time is it?"

"It's a little before nine. Are you seriously hung over?"

"You sound like my grandma. What's up?"

"I know you're not feeling great, but I need help. Can you come over to my place?"

"What's going on?" Tori asked, her voice a fraction more alert than it had been a moment ago.

"Something's wrong with me. I don't wanna say over the phone. Just…please. I don't think I can go outside like this and I need some help."

"You owe me big," Tori said with a groan. "I'll be over soon."

"Thank you," Anya said and hung up. She changed into clothes that weren't torn to bits: a previously over-sized t-shirt that had once reached down to her knees and now almost left her stomach exposed, as well as some baggy sweatpants that now looked like high-waters. She taped some old delivery bags over the hole in her window, and made the place look as presentable as she could.

As soon as she'd finished sorting her apartment out, her phone buzzed with a message from Tori.

TORI: Stopped to get coffee. At your building now.
ANYA: My door is open. Just come in.
TORI: ok??????

Anya unlocked her door and then hid under her blankets. If this was all real, she didn't want to scare Tori off upon seeing her.

"AI, disappear for now!" Anya snapped.

"You got it!" the AI said and then blinked out of existence.

"Anya?" Tori asked as she opened the door. She wore large sunglasses and held a cardboard container with two coffees in it in her free hand. Her voice cracked when she called out and entered the apartment. "Why are you hiding under your blankets? What's up with you? Did your mom call and give you more shit or something?"

"Yeah, uh, something happened," Anya said. "Either I've gone really, truly crazy or…or something incredibly strange is happening."

Tori raised her eyebrows as she locked the door behind her and set

Anya's coffee down on the counter. She took a sip of her own and then sat on the tattered second-hand sofa. "Okay. Crazy how?"

"Just…tell me what you see," Anya said. She took a deep breath, then stood up and dropped the blanket.

"Whoa!" Tori shouted and pressed herself as far back into the sofa as she could. Her coffee dropped to the floor and spilled in a creamy brown puddle. "Who the hell are you?"

"Tori," Anya said and put a hand out as her friend scrambled to her feet and lunged for the door. "Tori, it's me."

Tori looked back over her shoulder, her eyes wide behind her sunglasses, her hands frozen over the door locks. She stared at Anya, then focused on her face before looking her up and down.

"No," Tori said. "No, no way."

"It's my voice, right? That's the same? And my face? It's just thinner," Anya said and pointed at herself. Horror and relief welled up within her in equal measure. Tori was panicking just as she had, so Anya wasn't crazy and she wasn't hallucinating.

It was real.

"Jesus Christ. What the what?" Tori's mouth wobbled around the words.

"It's me. It's Anya. Something happened last night."

"No. No way. You're like, her long-lost twin sister or something. Like that movie with Schwarzenegger and Devito."

"No, I'm…wait, did you just compare how I used to look to Danny Devito?"

"I don't know! Maybe?"

"We went to the noraebang last night. You got comically drunk on like, two drinks. It's me. I promise."

Tori looked her up and down again and her tense posture relaxed a degree.

"Tell me something else. Something only Anya could know," she said.

"My mother is a heinous bitch."

"Everybody who's met Anya's mom knows that."

Anya snorted and nodded. "Okay. Fair. I've dated two people in the last six months: the gal from your office and the guy we met at the taco place on the roof. Both were disasters because the gal only talked about how awful New York is because of people like me moving here from out of town and 'ruining it,' or some shit. The guy ate with his mouth open and I slapped him when he tried to grab my ass."

"Holy shit," she said.

"It's me, Tori. I swear."

"How? How? Anya, I...what?" Tori babbled.

"Look. Just watch, but don't freak out. AI, get out here!"

The AI appeared once more with a quick bow and said, "At your service!"

"You can see this too, right?" Anya asked and pointed at the AI. Tori's sunglasses slid down her nose as she gawked at the chubby, luminescent figure floating in the air beside Anya.

"Hah!" Tori said, then slid to the floor as her legs gave out from under her.

"Tori?" Anya asked.

Tori gawked at the AI, shook her head, laughed again, then took a deep breath and rubbed her temples.

"I can explain," Anya said and knelt down on the coffee-soaked floor. Over the next several minutes, she did her best to explain and had the AI confirm what she said. Tori's face remained slack for most of this, her wide eyes flicking between her friend and the floating AI. She demonstrated how she summoned the menu, dismissed it, dismissed the AI, and summoned them both again.

Anya was able to get Tori up off the floor and back onto the sofa while she cleaned the spilled coffee and gave her friend the other cup. Tori's hands shook as she took it, but she managed to hang onto it. Anya sat on her bed across from her and waited for her to respond or do anything but stare in numb silence.

"Tori?" Anya asked.

"Yeah," Tori said with a nod, her voice flat.

"Are you okay?"

"Yeah," Tori said again in exactly the same way.

"Are you just saying that?"

"Yeah."

Anya sighed. "I'm sorry for putting this on you, but I thought I was hallucinating. Well, I hoped I was, kind of."

"Ye—" Tori started to say then shook her head. "I'm...I don't know what to say. I'm not hallucinating?"

"No. Neither of us are."

"I'm not hallucinating either!" the AI said.

"This is really, really, really weird," Tori said as she studied the AI then Anya. "That's really you, isn't it? Same face, same freckles, same voice, even same...I dunno. Mannerisms? Your expressions and the way you move around."

"Yeah," Anya nodded. "It's really me. And believe me, it's just as weird looking at myself. I mean, it's kinda cool, but it's also a lot to take in."

"And this thing," Tori reached out to the AI and stuck her hand through its rounded tummy and out its back. The AI cocked its head to the side and glanced down as her hand phased through it and then back out. "Honestly, if it wasn't for this thing and that menu popping up I'd think that you were just Anya's secret buff twin sister she never mentioned. But floating hologram guy here kinda doesn't fit with that."

"Nope!" the AI said and grinned.

"Cool," Tori said, but the quaver in her voice made it sound like it was anything but. "So, I think I'm psychologically scarred for life, or something."

"Me too," Anya nodded.

"Can I touch you?"

"Uh, sure?"

Tori pinched Anya's cheek, then poked her in her abs. Anya flinched and let out a laugh. "That tickles!"

"Sorry. Holy shit, it's like you got rock implants in your stomach or something. This was seven points?"

"Yup. Took about two seconds."

"Jesus," Tori said and let out a breath. "Aliens."

"Aliens," Anya shrugged.

"Aliens!" the AI cheered.

"Invading aliens," Tori clarified. She pointed at the AI again. "So you're here to what, help us fight the bad ones who're getting here in a month? Something like that?"

The AI shrugged. "The data I have access to only says the Accumulated Universal Knowledge Archive was sent 'as a defensive measure.' I would assume that means to help you in a fight, but I can't be sure."

"Why not?" Anya asked. "Aren't you from them? The aliens that sent the Archive, I mean."

"I do not have access to that data within the Archive. Many facets of it remain redacted, such as the specific location of its origin, its creators, and other gaps I am still trying to locate."

"This doesn't make any sense," Tori said. "Aliens send this thing from across the galaxy to supposedly help you defend against other aliens, but don't show up themselves. So they send a helper AI, but lock it out of the system it's supposed to help you with. And they give it to you completely at random."

"Yeah, they sound like assholes," Anya said.

"I've never actually met them! But I'll follow your lead," the AI added.

"What about the other ones? The invaders? How do you know they're not going to be here for a month?" Anya asked.

"The Archive told me. While I don't have a map of the exact path the menu system took from wherever they are to Earth, I have some isolated notes of interest that I'm permitted to access. This includes the archive's scanning systems picking up alien signals on a trajectory for the Archive's point of arrival roughly thirty-one days from planetfall. This time estimate was made based on observed speed and known intelligence."

A picture appeared in the air in front of Anya where her menu usually popped up. To her, it just looked like a black field with a few pinpoints of reddish light. Mathematical equations and numbers, lines that chartered likely paths, and more information that was well beyond the scope of Anya's understanding came into view around the dots of light.

"Earth is also the only planet with life on it nearby for quite some distance in the direction they're traveling," the AI continued, "and according to the Archive, the hostile aliens don't stop on uninhabited planets."

"Does the Archive have any other stuff on these guys? Or whatever they are?" Anya asked and pointed at the reddish dots on the picture.

"Only that they're a month away, they're definitely coming here, and they are dangerously hostile. Any other internal queries I conduct tell me that the data is redacted."

"Shit," Anya said and chewed on her thumbnail.

"So what now?" Tori asked.

"What do you mean?"

"I mean," Tori said and gestured at Anya with both hands, "what the hell are we going to do? We can't just sit here for a month. At the very least you'll need to get some new clothes. Those don't exactly fit you."

"Believe me, I've noticed. Definitely hit up the second-hand store. As for what to do about an invasion, shit, I don't know. I've been trying to wrap my head around the basics so far."

"Well, shouldn't you call the government? Y'know regarding the whole alien-life-coming-to-Earth thing."

It had occurred to Anya last night when the AI had first mentioned aliens. It had been pushed back by coming to the realization of aliens existing in the first place but now it rushed to the forefront of her mind. This was all beyond her. She was clearly out of her depth.

"I don't even know who to tell," Anya said. "The cops? FBI? NASA? The UN?"

"You gotta tell somebody. You're living proof of alien stuff! That's an alien right there!" Tori jabbed a finger at the AI.

"Actually, I didn't exist until I merged with Anya, so I was born right here on Earth! Hello, fellow Earthlings!"

"You're a floating, orange, computer-baby-thing with a rose for a head. Calling you an Earthling is a stretch," Anya said.

"A computer-baby-thing from Earth!" the AI replied.

"Fine. Now that I know this is real, I guess I should tell somebody with authority. I just don't know what the best way to do that is. They'd never believe me over the phone. But I don't wanna walk in with the AI and get thrown into Area-51 or Guantanamo. They'd probably start experimenting on me or put me in a specimen tank. Or they'd just draft me into service and demand I work for them. Fuck that."

"Yeah I can't really see that going well," Tori said, then leaned forward and put her head in her hands. "Can I lie down on your bed? I'm still really dizzy."

"Yeah, of course," Anya said and scooted over to make room for Tori. The AI floated in lazy circles above them, casting a halo of ruddy light around it.

"So what are you going to do?" Tori asked as she closed her eyes.

Anya took a deep breath and closed her eyes for a moment.

"All right. Fuck this, I'm getting super powers," she said.

"What?" Tori cracked an eye open.

"Aliens are coming here in a month to kill me, according to this one," Anya pointed at the AI.

"That's absolutely right!" the AI said.

"By the way, you need a name. How about Felix?" Anya asked.

"That works for me!" Felix said.

"Why Felix?" Tori asked.

"It's Latin for 'happy,' and this little guy just made homicidal aliens coming for me sound like I'd won the lotto."

"Gotcha. So, super powers?"

"Right. Aliens coming to kill me. Confirmed. Need to inform the government but don't trust them. Currently I am super ripped, but I'm gonna go out on a limb here and say some biceps and killer abs aren't gonna be enough to help with either of those situations. Thankfully there's this huge list of superpowers I can just pick from."

Anya regarded Tori in silence for a moment and then added, "Also having superpowers would be cool."

"I guess if you could do something superhuman it might help to convince somebody in the government that you weren't just making this all up," Tori agreed. "In addition to showing them the AI."

"And also being able to defend myself," Anya added.

"That too. But are you sure it's safe?"

"The Archive itself has been optimized for this planet. No skills will cause harm to Anya on their own. She would have to misuse them after selecting them in order to be hurt," Felix said.

"But accidents can happen," Tori added.

"Yeah, they sure can!" Felix nodded.

"So we go somewhere to test some stuff out where nobody can get hurt," Anya said.

"Before we jump into the deep-end of the super powers pool, how about we take a couple days to go through them, and the rest of this Archive thing. We've got a month. A couple days to sort through everything would be better than just rushing in."

Anya nodded. The rush of information and impending invasion had rattled her, but Tori was right. Taking the weekend to study the Archive and probe Felix for more information was a good idea.

"First of all, we should probably get you some clothes," Tori pointed at Anya's questionable attire. "You look like some kind of gym hobo."

"Shit. Yeah. All right, I got some cash, and you can run down to the thrift store and get me whatever, if you don't mind."

"Just order some clothes from the store!" Felix said and brought up another menu. This one had the title of "Reward Allocation Currency Shop," across the top, and then a list of sub-menus beneath it.

- Cosmetics
- Weapons
- Armor & Clothing
- Food
- Enhancements
- Vehicles
- Companions
- Materials
- Structures
- Tools

There was a number underneath the menu title that showed "You have 350,000 RAC Available," in flashing red letters.

"Holy hell. This fucking thing keeps going," Anya said as she eyed the menu.

"See? This is what I'm talking about. All these things...geez, we could spent weeks looking over this stuff," Tori said.

Anya reached out to touch the "Weapons," sub-menu and Tori swatted her hand.

"Ah! Clothes first. Then we go through the skills. We should also look into what the best way to tell the government about an alien invasion is."

"Right," Anya said. "Felix, can you just show me some basic clothing please?"

"You got it!" Felix said and the store menu expanded into hundreds upon hundreds of tiny screens displaying rotating models of all sorts of clothes.

"Too many!" Anya said, and then asked Felix for the basics: Shirt, underwear, jeans, shoes, jacket. She selected a black turtleneck, a brown leather jacket, some dark blue jeans, hi-tops, socks, and a sports bra and underwear. Felix informed her that all the items would fit her perfectly, since the Archive was making them specifically for her. All of it came out to a total of 200 RAC.

"Does the Archive make these? It's not stealing them from somewhere?" Anya asked.

"Nope! It makes the items from the store out of raw materials off-site, then transports them here," Felix replied.

"Off-site?"

"REDACTED," Felix replied.

"Got enough on my plate anyway," Anya muttered, then pressed a glowing "Confirm Purchases?" button. There was a dull flash of light and a faint whooshing sound, and then the clothing appeared in the air for a moment before falling to the floor.

"Wow," Tori said.

"Yeah, wow," Anya said as she picked up the leather jacket. "This is a really nice jacket. This would probably run at least a couple thousand bucks in a store on 5th Avenue."

"Not gonna lie: I'm a little jealous," Tori said as she looked at the menu.

"Holy shit the jeans have actual pockets!"

"Extremely jealous."

"If we can figure out how to share, and we can spare the RAC, or whatever this currency stuff is, I'll take you shopping. For now, I guess we should start narrowing down skills."

"I'm gonna start looking up government stuff. Mind if I borrow your computer?" Tori asked.

"Go for it. Okay Felix, let's go back to the skills…" Anya said and began to peruse the nearly endless lists of natural and supernatural abilities before her.

————

OVER THE COURSE of the weekend, Anya grilled Felix on every aspect of the Archive. In addition to the main menu, skill menu, and RAC store, there was also a map that showed her location in real time, and a status menu that showed an outline of her body, along with things like her heart rate, overall condition of her body, temperature, and other details.

Felix also took the time to explain what all the basic stats meant.

Awareness affected her five senses (or more if she took a skill that granted her any additional senses), as well as her ability to spot basic details around her, as well as things like pattern recognition, and memory recall.

Dexterity managed her hand-to-eye coordination as well as her flexibility, anything that required complex physical movements, and balance.

Fortitude was a measure of her physical endurance and how much internal energy she had if she picked any kind of magic skill that required such things. It also governed the ability to process or "filter," sources of external energy that some skills required.

Intelligence, as Felix had already explained, didn't make her smarter. It just made her brain more efficient at processing information, with the capacity to allow her consciousness to operate at multiple levels if she got it high enough. It was also important for any skill that required intense mental focus.

Strength was exactly what she thought: her raw muscle mass and capacity to perform acts that required nothing more than pure brawn.

Willpower was a reflection of a person's control over their own mental and physical state. A person with high willpower would be more adept at resisting or overcoming sensations such as pain, fear, fatigue, and any external force that attempted to sway them against their own desires. It was also crucial for any skill that involved the summoning or taming of creatures with simple mindsets.

Once the basics were established, Anya gave Felix some parameters for skills she wanted: something that would help protect her from harm, negate it, or heal it; and something that could cause a lot of damage at a moment's notice if she needed it to, but that she could conceal easily; and finally, a skill that would help keep her head clear if she was in an emergency situation.

At first she thought she was being a bit too picky and specific, but the Archive didn't lack for options. Anya also requested that Felix look through the RAC store for any items that would synergize with the skills she had narrowed down.

There were still hundreds, maybe thousands of options. Many of the skills required items from the RAC store to use effectively. Most were affordable, but many were well out of her price range.

Anya couldn't stop herself from occasionally browsing some of the more fantastical items as well: space ships, laser swords, an actual unicorn, mobile battle fortresses, enchanted armor, healing potions, and on and on.

Tori slept over on Saturday, but Anya stayed up most of the night continuing to comb through the Archive. By the time Sunday night arrived, she was mentally drained, but had narrowed her choices down.

Tori ate from a box of cashew beef and rice while she sat across from Anya.

"So, what did you pick?" she asked.

"These," Anya said as she set aside her box of fried rice and brought up her menu. The initial list of millions and millions of skills had shrunk down to four:

- Flame Dominion
- Kinetic Dispersal (Thermal Conversion)
- Combat Cognition
- Regeneration

"Huh," Tori said. "All right. I'll bite: what are these and why'd you pick them?"

"Take it away Felix," Anya said.

"Flame Dominion is a skill which grants the user the ability to summon and control heat, fire, etc. It's used by tapping into the 'Sun's Heart,' artifact, which is integrated into the host upon taking this skill and increasing it to skill level 5, and purchasing the artifact from the RAC store," Felix said.

"So it's fire magic?" Tori asked.

"Kind of," Anya said, "The short version is that there's about a thousand different kinds of 'fire magic,' in the Archive but most of them require external tools, like wands or scrolls or focusing crystals or something. Things that can get dropped or lost or break in a fight. Not good for surviving.

"There's other kinds that require a lot of prep work: mixing chemical ingredients, performing ceremonies and rites, drawing complicated runes, that kind of thing. Also not good if you could have problems pop up anywhere at any time. This Flame Dominion one, it's all internal. That Sun's Heart thing is like a big magic fire battery, and it can soak up ambient heat to recharge, and it can't be taken away or lost since it's effectively going to be a part of me."

"And that's...safe?" Tori asked.

"As safe as any of this," Anya shrugged.

"And why fire magic?"

"It has one of the highest direct damage potentials," Felix said. "Not specifically 'fire magic,' but the use of heat and heat-weapons is extremely efficient at causing damage, especially when focused. Kinetic energy is great too."

"Why not just take guns then?" Tori asked. "Like a laser gun or something?"

"Guns can be lost, have to be reloaded, can get broken, and they cost RAC. I looked up laser and plasma guns and they're cool as fuck, but they've got a price tag to match. Plus, they have recurring ammo costs. All the really good guns don't have any Earth-equivalents, so I'd be forced into using the RAC menu regularly or have useless guns. There's ammo-creation and gun engineering skills, but that also requires constant prep-work, material costs and so on," Anya said. "The Sun's Heart artifact costs RAC too, but it's a one-time deal, it's more versatile, and it's cheaper than buying a lot of guns."

"All right, and this kinetic dispersal thing?" Tori asked.

"That Flame Dominion skill will help me negate any heat damage. So if the aliens show up with lasers, I can redirect the heat or absorb it directly and throw it right back at them. The kinetic dispersal skill will let me spread out any kinetic damage they do. Kind of like a personal forcefield. Also, Felix says the dispersed kinetic energy gets turned into heat as well, which I can just soak up and recharge my Sun's Heart," Anya said.

"Synergy!" Felix said and gave a thumbs up.

"And combat cognition?" Tori asked.

"I don't have any battlefield experience. Except online, and that's mostly experience with twelve-year-olds calling me names," Anya said. "But this cognition thing is there to help me recognize enemy weaknesses, optimal routes of attack and retreat, that sort of thing."

"And regeneration just helps you regenerate, I'm guessing."

"Yup. I thought about getting an armor skill like Steel Skin, or something like that, but they all have breaking points. And if I get hurt, I don't want to be out for good. I can buy armor and enhancements from the RAC shop, and then if I get hurt, I can bounce back fast enough to retreat or fight. And the regeneration skill runs off my body's own energy, which is enhanced by the Sun's Heart."

"Synergy!" Felix repeated and did a cartwheel.

"I feel like you've thought more about this than how you're gonna pay rent next month," Tori said.

"Rent is boring. Super powers are badass," Anya said.

"Can't argue with that. So? What happens now? You just get the skills and poof, you can shoot fireballs?"

"Pretty much!" Felix said. "The archive will make the necessary changes to Anya's body and mind so she can properly utilize the needed skills. It should take about 3.54 seconds."

"And hurt like a bitch, I'm assuming," Anya said and shuddered.

"I'm not certain how much a bitch hurts," Felix said. "Ah, unless it's an idiom. I got it. Yes! It will hurt quite a lot."

"Very reassuring," Tori said then looked at Anya. "And you're sure you don't want to pick more skills? Cover more bases?"

"I've only got forty-four skills points. Twenty-four from my levels, and then a bonus of ten points at levels 10 and 20. I've got thirty-four stat points: twenty-four from my levels, and then five bonus points from levels 10 and 20. I can't spread them out too much or I'll basically be good for nothing, but if I over-specialize, I could screw myself."

"I have to ask: why is this like a video game?" Tori asked and looked at Felix. "It sounds like an MMO or a tabletop RPG or something."

"The true rationale for the design and implementation of the Accumulated Universal Knowledge Archive Project is redacted. However, if I had to guess, I would say it's that numbers are a universal constant, so equating greater skill proficiency with greater numbers makes sense to just about everybody," Felix replied.

"Right, but why limit the available skills at all? Why not give Anya infinite points?"

"Whatever the true answer might be is redacted, but I would say it's because the creators want people to experiment and add their knowledge to the Archive, but not become so powerful that they might threaten them. There's currently a level cap of 50 as well as a stat and skill cap of 75 set within the archive, as well as several items within the RAC store being blocked from purchase, but I can still see them within the store's code."

"As good an answer as we're gonna get," Tori mumbled, then glanced at Anya. She had been updating her menu to allocate her points as she needed them, but had not confirmed the changes yet, while Felix explained.

ANYA NOWICKI: LEVEL 24 HUMAN

Statistics

- Awareness-10
- Dexterity-8
- Fortitude-18
- Intelligence-8
- Strength-10
- Willpower-8

Skills

- Flame Dominion-12
- Kinetic Dispersal-8
- Combat Cognition-8
- Regeneration-8

Items

- Sun's Heart (Basic)(Skill Requirement: Flame Dominion at 5 or higher) -125,000 RAC

"I wanted to make sure all my base stats were above average, and then put the rest of my stat points into a few focused options. Flame Dominion and regeneration both run off fortitude. Combat cognition goes off of a mix of intelligence and awareness, and Kinetic dispersal is a mix " Anya said.

Tori did some quick math and asked, "That's only twenty-two stat points and thirty-six skill points. What about the rest?"

"Panic points," Anya said. "If something comes up I didn't plan for, and I need to get a new skill or pump up a stat in the heat of the moment, I want to have some points in reserve."

"I seriously think you've planned this out more than anything else. Except maybe when you threw me that surprise party last year," Tori said. "You're not gonna do it here, are you?"

"Why not?" Anya asked.

"Uh, because you're about to get alien fire magic and we're in a small apartment and it might explode."

"Mm. Good point. I dunno if I'm up to trekking across the city to somewhere away from people, though," Anya replied and yawned. "Did you find anything good about who to call in case aliens invade?"

Tori laughed. "Yeah, there's not exactly a manual for who to get in touch with vis-a-vis aliens. Didn't help that the internet is really slow for some reason."

"It's been like that since Friday night," Anya replied.

"I was able to get a potential lead though: I think our best bet is probably the FBI."

"Seriously?"

"Yeah. They're a federal organization so they've got contacts across the entire country, they've got a major office in Manhattan, and they've got hotlines for reporting terrorist attacks and things like that. An alien invasion isn't exactly a terrorist attack, but it's the closest I can think of. The cops are too local, and the military doesn't really have a point of contact for this sort of thing. NASA isn't equipped to handle this, so yeah: feds."

"All right. The feds it is," Anya said.

"I sent my boss an e-mail saying I'm taking a sick day tomorrow. You should try and sleep, and then tomorrow we can find somewhere to try out your powers and I can try to call the FBI. If the cell signals are still shitty, I'll just go to their place in Federal Plaza."

Anya smiled at her friend and let out a sigh of relief. "Thank you, Tori."

"My pleasure. I'm serious about you letting me use the RAC store to find some cool shit for me too, though. I saw they had some kinda flying scooter in there?"

"Assuming aliens don't crush me or and the feds don't throw me in Area-51, we can get matching flying scooters."

"I'm gonna head back to my place for the night. I'll catch you tomorrow. Bye Felix!" Tori said and waved.

"Bye Tori!" Felix waved back.

Anya was tempted to just confirm her choices in the Archive and get her super powers now, but all the rush of energy and information and everything else since Friday caught up with her all at once. Anya was asleep before Tori had even left her building.

———

ANYA MET Tori at the Central Avenue Station Monday morning. She had slept late, but that was fine as it allowed them both to avoid the worst of the rush hour crowds. Anya had given some thought as to where they would go to acquire and test out her new powers: somewhere that wouldn't have too many people in the immediate vicinity, and if the worst happened and Anya caused an explosion or other destructive side-effect, nothing would be damaged (and if it were, nobody would care).

That pretty much ruled out Brooklyn and the entirety of Manhattan.

But Jersey wasn't far.

It took a couple of hours to get to New Jersey and the mostly empty lot Anya had been thinking of. She and Tori had gone to a rave there last summer, and it was still as empty and trashed looking as the last time they had been.

While Jersey got more than its fair amount of jokes at its own expense, Anya had picked this spot because she knew nobody would give a damn about loud noises and potentially damaged surroundings. The rave had been noisy and nobody had called the cops, and the lot it had been held in had been deserted save for whatever the organizers had brought with them.

The lot itself was surrounded by a flimsy chain link fence, and covered in equal parts broken concrete and untamed weeds. There were some old factories nearby, but they were all abandoned and in various states of disrepair. There was also a lingering perfume of diesel, burning hair, and what might have been urine, but that wasn't unusual for Jersey.

Or most of the city at large, if Anya was being fair.

New York and the boroughs had their fair share of sketchy empty lots, but the press of civilization and people was much greater there. They had some amount of privacy here, with the nearest sign of people being a distant road that only had an intermittent amount of traffic.

Anya spent most of the subway ride continuing to look at the Archive, which Felix told her he could overlay on top of her phone to avoid suspicion, and that they could also talk directly into Anya's ear so the little AI wouldn't draw attention.

Anya stared at her menu now, at how she had allocated her skill and stat points, and the glowing "Confirm?" button under her finger while Tori waited at her side.

"Do you need me to do anything? Like, catch you, or something?" Tori asked. "Are you gonna pass out?"

"Not sure. Just be ready. Okay?"

Tori nodded and stood behind Anya, who chuckled. She was at least two feet taller than Tori now, and probably well over a hundred pounds heavier. But her friend stood there, skinny arms outstretched, looking like she was bracing to get tackled by a defensive lineman. Anya looked back at her menu, and pressed "Confirm?" before she psyched herself out.

There was a tense moment of absolutely nothing happening, and then the pain hit.

It hadn't occurred to Anya that more points used would equal more pain, but as a wave of agony exploded outward from the center of her ribs and radiated to every atom of her body, she figured it made sense.

There was something else this time, however: a bright spot within her heart that gave her some comfort, a warmth that grew warmer, then hot, but never hot enough to burn.

Oh, a new one, somebody said in a low, smooth voice that seemed to come from right beside her ear.

"Anya!" Tori shouted and Anya blinked.

She was on her back, staring up at the cold concrete sky. Tori and Felix both looked down at her, their faces worried.

"I'm all right," Anya mumbled and sat up. "Did you say something?"

"I said your name. And I may have screamed a little when you fell on me. I tried to hold you up but you're really heavy now," Tori grunted as she helped Anya to her feet.

"Thought I heard somebody. How long was I out?"

"3.62 seconds. I underestimated a bit," Felix said.

"That's okay," Anya replied and then looked at her hands.

"Well? Did it work? Can you do fire magic?" Tori asked.

For Anya, there was no question. She felt a glow inside of her, a pulsing, rhythmic beat of warmth that kept time with her heart. It was an odd sensation, but not unpleasant. She knew how to use the Sun's Heart artifact within her the same way she knew how to tie her shoes, or whistle, or anything else. She held out her hand, palm up, and felt that beating energy within her flow from her center, to her arm, and then her hand.

A ball of fire, no bigger than a golf ball, blossomed to life an inch above her palm, the petals of its flame fluttering in the chill air.

"Holy shit," Anya whispered.

"Oh my God," Tori breathed.

"Pretty neat!" Felix added.

"I can use magic," Anya said and let out a bark of laughter.

"You can use magic!" Tori squealed.

"I can use fucking magic!" Anya grinned at her friend, unaware of the fireball in her hand growing alongside her excitement.

"Anya," Tori started to say and pointed at her friend's hand.

"*I can use magiiiiii—*" Anya yelled, and was cut off as the flame exploded.

5

The blast was enough to singe Tori's hair, but little else. Anya's hair was fine, but Tori was stuck with toasted ends and some frizzy bits sticking out.

"Sorry," Anya said after she made sure her friend was unharmed.

"It's fine," Tori coughed. "What's the deal though? I thought the Archive was supposed to teach you how to use this stuff."

Anya sighed and nodded. She had gotten over-excited and lost her concentration, which her Flame Dominion skill was now informing her was a good way to rapidly expand any fire she had conjured and lose control.

"Yeah, it does, kind of. I just got a little too hyped," she said.

"Can't blame you too much, I guess," Tori grumbled as she broke off some charred bit of her hair. Anya opened up her menu again to look through the store and find something that would enhance her skills and provide some extra protection, and maybe something to help her escape if she got into trouble.

"I'm gonna try some other things out, but at a safer distance," Anya said and backed away from her friend. "While I'm doing this, could you try and give the feds a call? Assuming cell signals are working again."

"You got it," Tori said and took out her phone. "I'm gonna go research in a café I saw back up the road. It's pretty cold out here."

"Yeah, no problem," Anya said, and then realized she wasn't cold at all. She'd been chilly just moments ago, but now she was quite warm. Toasty, even. She took off her heavy leather jacket and rolled up the sleeves of her turtleneck.

She was still warm, even though a strong gust of wind blew in from the Upper Bay and Tori yelped in response and clutched her arms closer around herself.

"Aren't you freezing?" she asked.

"Not even a little. Guess it's a side benefit of the Sun's Heart," Anya replied.

"Well I'm gonna go inside and get the side benefit of not freezing to death."

"Go on. I'll catch up in a bit."

Tori gave her a wave and hurried away, out of the lot. As Tori got farther away, Anya realized she could still sense her body heat.

"Whoa, that is…weird," Anya muttered. Tori's heat was a bright ember of warmth amid the cold, and as Anya focused, she sensed more. There were several smaller spots of heat under a dumpster nearby: probably rats. There was a larger ember of heat further away that could have been a cat or similarly sized creature.

However, Tori was the only person Anya could sense, and as her friend hurried back toward the main road, she too faded away. The knowledge of the Flame Dominion skill that the Archive had given her told Anya that she was at her current maximum for sensing heat, from living things or otherwise.

"So I can't sense anything past a block or so," Anya said, knowing it as surely as she knew anything else about her other senses. "Hey Felix, you didn't tell me Flame Dominion came with this heat sense thing. This is handy!"

"Oh. Oops! It didn't conflict with the criteria you gave me for finding skills, but it wasn't something you requested either. I'll be sure to inform you of any fringe benefits that skills have in the future. Sorry about that!"

"No problem. It's a nice surprise. Hey, while I practice this stuff, can you bring up that list of armor sets we looked at on Sunday? I should pick one. And maybe something that would help me get out of trouble quickly? I thought about taking a mobility skill, but I'm not so sure. Wanted to see what options the store had first."

"You got it!" Felix said and began sorting through the RAC store as Anya played around with her Flame Dominion skill.

Over the next couple of hours, she learned just how versatile the skill could be. She could create a gentle field of heat around her that felt like a balmy summer day, or crank it up and turn her immediate vicinity into a kiln that would roast almost anything. She could summon fireballs, of course, or she could focus the heat and fire into a single, narrow beam, like a laser. She could also coat herself in fire, and not be burned.

Anya's clothes were not so immune and she lost the right sleeve of her turtleneck in a sudden burst of flame.

"Add 'fireproof,' to whatever armor or other gear you find for me," Anya told Felix, who gave her a double thumbs up and continued to trim down options within the RAC store.

Anya knew how to use Flame Dominion from what the Archive had given her, but knowing it and actually doing it were a little different. The basics were no problem, but fine-tuning things took more focus. She suspected that would become easier the more points she put into the skill.

Anya finally stopped a while later just as the sun was beginning its descent. She was covered in sweat and panting as if she had sprinted up and down several flights of stairs. Her enhanced fortitude stat helped her use the energy her Sun's Heart was producing more efficiently, and she could feel herself bouncing back and getting a second wind already, but it wasn't infinite.

She sat on top of a stack of old tires nearby as she caught her breath, and looked at the scorched lot around her. It looked as though somebody had taken a flamethrower, a laser beam, and several sticks of dynamite to the place. Still no sign that anybody had noticed the disturbance, however: no sirens or approaching cop cars.

Anya scrolled through her messages on her phone to see how Tori was doing while she rested. She had a weak signal, but it was enough to get texts. Her friend had sent her a few messages saying she had gotten through to the feds twice, but the line kept disconnecting. Plan B was to go and make an appointment in-person tomorrow, since their office would be closing soon. Anya scrolled through the RAC store, looking at the armor options Felix had arranged for her perusal, when something beeped nearby. She glanced up and looked around the empty lot.

Nothing.

Her new heat sense told her there were still no other people around, just more rats.

Another beep.

"What the hell is that?" she asked.

"Anya! You're getting a message!" Felix said and collapsed a number of screens from the RAC store and brought up a smaller, much narrower screen. It displayed four words in bright, bold red letters.

"INCOMING MESSAGE. STAND BY."

"Felix? What the hell is this?" Anya asked and pointed at the screen.

"I think you're getting a message from, uh, them," Felix said and pointed up at the sky.

"The aliens? The ones that sent you?"

"Yeah! I gu—" Felix said and then their cartoonish face went blank, and their rosebud head turned into a mass of twitching, flickering static. Felix's body became rigid and they assumed the stiff T-pose from a couple nights before.

"Attempting connection. Confirm, local lifeform," a voice said from Felix's floating body. It sounded like a generic text-to-speech program, putting weird emphasis on the wrong syllables and speaking in a dull tone.

Anya leaned away from Felix, or whatever thing had taken control of them.

"Confirm, local lifeform. Accumulated Universal Knowledge Archive host designation Sol-3022. Confirm."

"I—I uh, yes. I have the Archive. Who is this?" Anya asked.

"Local lifeform, Archive host confirmed. Please wait."

"Did you just put me on fucking hold?"

No response.

"Are you fucking serious?"

"Apologies. This one is Initiate Engineer Red-507. Confirm Archive host integration and utilization of Archive data?"

"What?"

"Hold. Adjusting translation parameters... Adjustments confirmed. Have you used the Archive to gain skills?"

"Yeah! What the fuck is going on?"

"Confirm local lifeform planet of origin: Melarus-III?"

"What the hell is that?"

"Your local planet is not Melarus-III?" the engineer asked. As it continued to speak, the weird inflection and dull tone began to sound somewhat more human. Still stiff and awkward, but more like a person than a broken robot.

"No! This is Earth!"

"Oh. Oops."

"*Oops*?" Anya shouted and bolted upright, towering over the little orange hologram. "Oops! What do you mean 'Oops'?"

"Confirm: you have been informed of incoming hostile alien invasion?"

"Yes! About a month from now!" Anya said then subtracted the weekend. "Twenty-nine days. I think."

"Adjusting calculations based on standard time of the Sol system. Oh. Please be informed of new invasion arrival: four hours."

Anya's face went numb.

"Confirm acknowledgment of new invasion timeline."

Anya sat back down on the tires.

"Confirm acknowledgment of—"

"Shut the fuck up!" Anya snapped and fire roared up around her. It passed harmlessly through the hologram and faded away.

"Apologies. This one is being informed of unexpected deviations in Archive dispersal now," the voice said. It managed to sound contrite now, and Felix's posture became less stiff, and managed to bow to her.

"Tell me what the fuck is going on right now. No redacted shit."

"The Accumulated Universal Knowledge Archive was bound for

the planet of Melarus-III. It is approximately 758 light-years from Earth."

"You sent the Archive to the wrong planet?"

"Mellarus-III was destroyed by hostile alien forces. It and its sapient species were the original target for the existing shipment of Archives. The Archives were calibrated for the Mellarusians during initial construction and dispersal. This one was not informed of the change until now. There is... currently some disorganization among Elder Engineers."

Anya blinked.

"Hold on. Archives? Plural?"

"Correct. 13,054 Archives made it to Earth and have successfully integrated with local hosts."

"There are 13,000 people on this planet with the same thing I got?" Anya asked. Her head spun even as her stomach twisted around itself.

"And fifty-four, yes."

Anya put her face in her hands and gritted her teeth.

"This one apologizes for not attempting contact sooner. Standard procedure requires an engineer to initiate contact with local lifeforms within five minutes of Archive integration. However, hostile forces have obstructed most communication."

The questions in Anya's head were multiplying by the second, all of them interspersed by random bits of information the engineer had given her.

Thirteen thousand.

Four hours.

A whole planet and its people, dead.

Four hours.

Thirteen thousand.

There was something else too, underneath the panic and confusion. Her Sun's Heart had begun to beat faster, keeping pace with her own, a burning engine that sent fire through her veins.

It was... excited?

And so was she.

Is that weird? Anya thought before she turned back to the hologram.

"And the aliens, they're definitely coming here to kill us?"

"The invading alien force is lethally hostile to all sapient life. Earth and its inhabitants are not an exception. They are coming to render humanity extinct."

Anya took a deep breath.

The plans she had made with Tori had just gone right out the window. Forget making an appointment with the feds. They needed to do something now.

Or she did, at least.

"What can you tell me?" she asked.

"Repeat query with clarification," the engineer asked.

"The hostile aliens that are going to be here in four hours: what can you tell me about how to kill them? How fucking flammable are they? How many? What do they look like?"

"Hostile alien force is referred to as… gnosiphages is the closest approximation your native languages will allow. Knowledge eaters. They are adept mimics and shapeshifters, and will—valassur ko renna nil—eeeeeeeeeeeeeeeee—uption in communications. Signal from gnosiphaaaaayyy—empting to update host location functions and—aatama ko'lluvra—" the engineer's words turned to gibberish, ended in a squeal of static, and then the hologram vanished.

"Shit. Shit! No, no, no! Felix! Felix!" Anya shouted and tapped her chest to bring her menu up. She pressed the help button several times, until finally Felix appeared, looking like their usual self save for the drunken expression and fluttering petals on their head.

"Anya? What happened? Oh. Ooooooh. I can see the communication logs and… wow. A lot of data just became un-redacted. This is bad! I mean, it's nice that I can see the data now, but oh dear," Felix said and began to dart around in the air around her.

"No shit!" Anya said. Before she could even ask Felix what to do, her combat cognition skill kicked in.

Locate allies that also had the Archive, if possible. Ideally this would be other hosts but anybody with training would be useful. Cops were the next obvious options.

Determine possible sites of gnosiphage arrival. This would largely depend on any information Felix had and whatever the gnosiphages had planned. Manhattan was an enormous city and therefore a potential priority target for an invading enemy.

Reassess threat based on potential allies versus number of enemies and their proximity. If she was outnumbered and outmaneuvered, run. If not, press the advantage.

"Okay. Okay. That engineer guy, I think he was trying to say something about locating the other hosts. Can you do that?" she asked Felix.

"Yes! Sort of!" Felix said and brought up a map of Earth. It was covered in circles of various sizes and opacity. If Anya had to guess, she would say there were exactly 13,054 of them. As she watched, the map focused in, closer and closer, on New York. It encompassed her current location in Jersey, and stretched out to the far side of Long Island.

Her location showed as a single bright pinprick of orange light. There was also a partially transparent circle that encompassed several blocks in Long Island.

"I'm currently able to pick up a kind of signal the other Archives are emitting. It's one of the things that was previously redacted. I can't determine the exact location of the other hosts, but I can make an approximate estimation based on the entry data of all the Archives and the weak signals I can currently receive. The nearest host is somewhere in Long Island. You can send them a message, but there's a lot of interference. If you can get closer, I can get a more precise lock on his signal, and permanently zero-in on it if you actually manage to make physical contact," Felix said.

"Gotcha," Anya said. It occurred to her that with so many Archives in the hands of random people, some of them were bound to be psychos. The guy in Long Island could be a super-powered serial killer but...

Well, that still sounded better than whatever the knowledge eater things were. Anya took out her phone to call Tori, only to see that her signal had finally died.

"Of-fucking-course," she growled, and took off at a full sprint from the empty lot to go find her friend and tell her that the shit had hit the fan at terminal velocity.

6

Anya burst into the café Tori had told her she'd be waiting at fast enough to accidentally tear the door off its hinges and bang her head against the top of the entrance.

"Ow! Fuck!" Anya said as everybody in the café stared at her.

"Anya?" Tori asked, her eyes wide and her mug of coffee frozen halfway to her mouth.

"We gotta go! I'll explain on the way!" Anya said then pointed at the startled barista looking at her wide-eyed behind his thick glasses. "I'm really sorry about your door. I'll be back later to pay for the damage."

"Uh, sorry about this," Tori said and then left a few rumpled bills under her mug as she hurried outside. Anya tried to prop the broken door back in place, then hurried with Tori back toward the subway. Rush hour was just starting and Anya did not want to risk taking a cab and getting stuck in traffic.

Felix just said she needed to get close to the other host's signal to send a message. If that wasn't close enough, they could go further, but for now she wanted somewhere she was mostly familiar with.

"What's happening?" Tori asked under her breath once they were seated on the subway. Anya didn't bother with what any other passengers might overhear, and told Tori everything. Tori leaned back into her seat and let out a long steady breath.

"Everybody's cell service in the café crapped out at the same time. I thought it was just a cell tower somewhere having trouble but it's probably them, huh?" Tori asked and pointed up.

"If I had to guess," Anya sighed.

"So you try to contact this other person and then?"

"I've had Felix trying to message whoever the Long Island host is every few seconds, but so far, nothing's getting through. He's narrowing down their signal and it looks like they may have the same idea as us since they're heading this way," Anya said and brought up a small version of her menu screen overlaid on her phone. It showed the large opaque circle moving in a steady direction East, toward Brooklyn.

"I'm gonna stop by my place, gear-up, and then head out. You should hunker down somewhere," Anya said.

"Obviously no time to contact the feds. I think there's a police precinct on Knickerbocker Avenue, just down the road from your place. Cops will have to do," Tori said. "When we get to your place, I should at least take a video or something of you and Felix so I have something to show them. Unless you want to come into the station with me?"

Anya bit her lip and thought. "They'd have to believe us, but it could cause problems. They might want to detain me or something worse. Last thing I want to do right now is piss off the cops or get stuck in a station. I'll meet this other host first and see how it goes. If two of us show up, it may help, or not.

"I don't know what the right thing to do is, I just don't want to risk having to fight my way out of a police station if things go bad or they start thinking I'm an alien or God-knows-what. Whatever happens, if we still don't have a cell signal, stay with the cops or back at your place."

"Right," Tori nodded. They spent the rest of the subway trip in tense silence, then hurried back to Anya's building and her apartment.

"Still no answer from the message?" Anya asked as the floating AI appeared beside her.

"None yet. Still trying! Ready to confirm your store purchases?" Felix asked and brought up a large menu screen that displayed everything Anya and the AI had decided upon.

- Regalia of St. Llothec, the Ever-Burning (Superior): Provides protection from any and all heat-based hazards, as well as kinetic damage. Also boosts the wearer's innate heat-producing abilities. 85,000 RAC + 1,100 RAC per rune enhancement (This superior quality item has a current cap of five lesser quality runes or three equal quality runes) (+4 to Flame Dominion skill, +2 to Kinetic Dispersal skill, +1 to Fortitude statistic)
- Rune of the Shield (Basic): Provides dual enhancements to quality and defense of imbued item. 12,000 RAC (+50% to item durability parameters and +50% to all defensive features)
- Rune of the Shield's Embrace (Basic): Provides additional defensive covering beyond the standard coverage of imbued item. 5,000 RAC (+50% of item's defensive capabilities to any uncovered body parts)
- Rune of the Maiden (Basic): Provides dual enhancements to healing and stamina of the wearer of imbued item. 12,000 RAC (+2 to Regeneration skill and +1 to Fortitude statistic)
- Rune of the Warrior (Basic): Provides dual enhancements to strength and agility of the wearer of the imbued item. 12,000 RAC (+1 to Strength and Dexterity statistics)
- Rune of the Stallion (Basic): Provides dual enhancements to speed and stamina of the wearer of the imbued item. 12,000 RAC (+1 to Fortitude and Dexterity statistics)
- Mantle of the Gale (Basic): Imbues the wearer with additional speed as well as a light deflective wind-shield. 52,000 RAC + 1,100 RAC per rune enhancement (this basic quality item has a current cap of two equal quality runes)(+1 to Dexterity statistic)
- Rune of the Vortex (Basic): Provides dual enhancements to any wind-based abilities and speed of the wearer of the

imbued item. 12,000 RAC (+2 to wind-based air skills inherent to item, +1 to Dexterity statistic)

- Rune of the Salamander (Basic): Imbued item is granted resistance from fire. 5,000 RAC. (+100% to heat and fire resistance)
- Emergency Relocation Harness: A personal relocation device used to escape dangerous situations. 6,500 RAC
- Draught of Regenerative Enhancement (Basic): Temporarily grants boosts to the drinker's innate healing abilities. 2,750 RAC (+50% to user's healing ability for approximately ten seconds)
- Reinforced, Heat-Proof Vial: A simple glass vial for containing liquids while protecting them from damage or excessive heat. 50 RAC

"Yeah, do it," she said and just like when she had purchased her clothing, there was a whooshing of air and then a number of items appeared around her and fell to the floor.

"What the heck is all this?" Tori asked as she looked between the collection of clothing and items on the ground around her and the menu screen.

"Battle Regalia of Saint Llothec the Ever-Burning, of the planet Hallethar," Felix said and pointed at a sleeveless top made of heavy maroon material decorated with golden thread and a circular emblem over the right breast. It came with a heavy sash of more red fabric, dark leather, and brass accoutrements. There was a pair of loose black pants that had a much larger gold insignia on the right leg: some kind of trident beneath another circular emblem. A pair of boots and forearm guards made of dark red and gray leather and large inter-locking plates of brass-colored metal with intricate designs carved into them completed the outfit.

"It's all fireproof, and woven with the threads spun from golden volcano worms and reinforced with the treated hide of ashen drakes. The metal is sacred brass from the binary star forges of Allethar and Mallethar," Felix said and pointed at the clothes. "All of it is further enhanced with these runes. It also provides basic defense from most forms of attack."

"It won't stop everything, but nothing in the RAC store would, and this was the best I could afford," Anya said as she began to change.

"Sounds pretty badass to me," Tori said, then looked at a a piece of dark maroon cloth with gold clasps and flowing designs of golden thread. "Is that a cape?"

"That's the Mantle of the Gale. It's made from woven down threads of a great condor on Tan-Ten IV by a cult of nomadic air sages. It'll help Anya move a bit faster and deflect small attacks," Felix said.

"How small is small?" Tori asked.

"The equivalent of most small arms fire on this planet. Heavier attacks will still be turned aside or have their impact reduced," Felix added. "It's also enhanced with a rune to make it fireproof."

"And what's this basic quality, superior quality, all that?" Tori asked.

"Many of the items in the Archive can be upgraded. Basic is the default quality for most items. The scale is basic, superior, refined, excellent, masterwork, epic, legendary, cosmic, and divine at the very top," Felix said.

The next item on the floor was a chrome belt with a circular buckle. A red button sat in the center of the buckle and it blinked every few seconds.

"That is my escape plan," Anya said and nodded at the belt as she pulled her boots on.

"A belt?" Tori asked.

"An emergency relocation harness," Felix said. "Also fireproof. When Anya puts it on, she presses the button and holds it, and it will record her saying her apartment address as the relocation destination. It comes pre-loaded with all local Earth addresses. It'll record the site, and if she's in danger she presses the button twice, and it will expand into a one-time anti-gravity harness that will propel her from wherever she is back to here, within a distance of fifty miles. If she's farther than that, it will get her as close as it can. The harness also emits a limited kinetic shield around the user for five minutes. After that, the internal battery is spent."

"And this," Anya held up a tiny glass vial of clear liquid before she tucked it into a pocket, "will give my regeneration skill a boost if I need it. Also had to order a special glass vial for it, otherwise it'd just kinda splash onto the floor. The RAC store is pretty stingy about shit like this."

"Neat," Tori said, then added, "Do they have any kind of other transporter gizmos in the store? Like teleportation gadgets?"

"I asked," Anya grunted as she strapped the forearm guards on. "Anything that allows teleportation, whether that's magical or techno-logical or whatever, is locked out of the store. Ditto for anything that goes faster-than-light. And ditto again for skills that do the same thing."

"What? Why?"

"Some of the previously unredacted data says that hosts aren't permitted to go more than 5,000,000 miles from their home planet. It doesn't say why, though. Fuckers don't want us running away, I guess."

"So no FTL battleships, huh?"

"No, but I definitely looked at some of the spaceships in there. The cheapest one is something like our space shuttles. Basically just a junker compared to the other shit they got. The cheapest alien space-craft is a single-seater with a puny-ass gun that costs almost half-a-million RAC."

"Great," Tori sighed.

"Okay, I think that's everything. How do I look?" Anya asked as she put the metallic belt on and then draped the maroon mantle over her broad shoulders.

"You look kind of amazing. Like some kinda magic warrior monk. What's all that stuff done to your skills?"

"Nothing crazy, but definitely a significant bump," Anya said and brought up her menu again to review the bonuses all her equipment gave her.

ANYA NOWICKI: LEVEL 24 HUMAN
Statistics

- Awareness-10
- Dexterity-8 (+4 from gear)
- Fortitude-18 (+3 from gear)
- Intelligence-8
- Strength-10 (+1 from gear)
- Willpower-8

Skills

- Flame Dominion-12 (+4 from gear)
- Kinetic Dispersal-8 (+3 from gear)
- Combat Cognition-8
- Regeneration-8 (+2 from gear)

"Not too shabby. How much did all of this cost?"

"Almost all of my RAC. I've got exactly 1,000 left. The regalia plus the runes was the biggest expense by far, then the Sun's Heart, then the mantle and its runes. I've got enough left to buy an extra healing potion or other small items I've had Felix bookmark in case of emergencies, but I'm basically broke. Hopefully I won't need any of it and I'm over-prepared, but I doubt it."

"Maybe it'll all be a misunderstanding?" Tori asked and tried to smile. It came out as more of a grimace, and Anya hugged her.

"We'll figure it out," she said.

"Yeah. Also you are really good at hugging now. Wow," the last word came out as more of a wheeze.

Anya laughed and let Tori go. She then made sure to program her apartment into the belt, which was a straightforward procedure of holding the button down and waiting for a confirmation beep, just like Felix had said, followed by stating her address out loud.

"All right, let's get a video of you doing your thing with Felix and the menu, and then I'll head for the precinct," Tori said and got her phone ready. Anya did a quick demonstration of her summoning fire, bringing her menu up, and the map of the world that showed the hosts while Felix floated around and explained the basics of the archive and the incoming invasion.

"That'll have to do for now," Tori said as she stopped filming.

"If that doesn't convince them, I'll come in myself and just pray they don't try and arrest me or shoot me," Anya added.

"Anya! I got through!" Felix said and brought up a new screen that looked like a standard chat window.

EARL: Hello? Is this another Archive user?

"Finally! Good job Felix. I guess whoever we're dealing with is named Earl," Anya said as she hurried out of her apartment with Tori behind her.

"What're you gonna say?" Tori asked as they walked along Stanhope Street. Anya couldn't help but notice the few other pedestrians on the sidewalk cursing at their phones or holding them up to see if they could get a better signal.

"Have him meet me somewhere wide-open and relatively free of people. Felix, is he much closer?" Anya asked.

"Yup!" Felix said inside her ear, out of sight, and brought up the map overlaid on top of Anya's phone now that they were in public again. The map showed the opaque circle south of her, near Prospect Park. It had shrunk in size, but still encompassed several city blocks.

"That'll do," Anya said and pointed at the park. Evening had descended on Bushwick, and while Anya couldn't feel it, the temperature had dropped several degrees if Tori's chattering teeth were anything to go by. The wind picked up and a few drops of sleet began to pelt the pavement as they fell from the dark gray sky. Not many people, if any, would be out for a stroll in the park at this time of day, with the weather taking the turn that it was, and on a Monday night.

ANYA: Yes. Did you hear about the invasion? Can you meet me in Prospect Park, near the carousel?

EARL: I heard. I'll be waiting there.

"Well he doesn't sound like a serial-killer," Tori said.

"Fingers crossed," Anya replied. When they reached Bushwick Avenue, Anya flagged down a cab.

"Just come back, okay? If this Earl guy is nuts, bail. I'll be at the 81st Precinct, or my place."

"Gotcha. Don't let the cops push you around or anything," Anya replied as she squeezed herself into the cab. Tori waved at her as the cab merged back intro traffic, and drove away.

———

THE FLATBUSH ENTRANCE to Prospect Park was a wide open square of patched asphalt and broken concrete tiles that surrendered to the winter-ravaged skeletons of trees beyond. In the spring and summer, it was a lush spread of emerald. In fall, it was a riot of botanical flames, red and yellow and orange that burned themselves out over the slow autumn months.

But in winter, and especially this late, the trees resembled nothing but bony fingers clutching at the dark shroud of the overcast sky. The meager light of lamps within the park only served to further outline the macabre display.

Prospect Park was, thankfully, mostly empty by the time the cab rolled to a stop at the Flatbush Avenue entrance. Anya used her heat sense to examine the area around her and detected the heat from the cabbie and the cab's engine as it drove away, from other cars passing behind her, from people across the street behind her, and from within the park itself. Thankfully the glowing embers of people in the park were all heading toward the exit as the sleet had picked up, and there weren't very many of them to begin with.

There was a single heat source ahead of Anya within the park, but out of her sight. It didn't move, and based on their position, it would be near the carousel.

"Felix? Is that him?" she asked.

"I've narrowed the signal down to several meters, and yes, it looks like this Earl person is straight ahead in the Park. Can't wait to meet him!"

Anya strode into the park and got another message from Earl as soon as she did.

EARL: Hey! Glad you're here. Some friends are coming too. We come in peace lol

Anya didn't respond as she wasn't far. She was within sight of the carousel within seconds, or rather the brick and green-roofed building which held it. The building was locked ahead of the coming night, and dark. Anya could still make out the faint shapes of pale and frozen horses through the bars around the carousel. The faint amber light of the lamps showed them with their mouths open in quiet screams, impaled on their brass poles.

She had never much liked carousels.

"Hey," a man said, and raised an arm. He stood near a bench, just across from the carousel building. He was tall, but not quite so much as Anya. He had broad-shoulders and his muscular frame was clad in a three-piece navy suit with a gold tie, and a long coat with a furred collar.

He was also the single most handsome man Anya had ever seen, to the point of it being almost surreal. Long, blond hair swept behind him, and bright blue eyes locked onto Anya as soon as they saw her. His facial features were sharp without looking harsh, rugged without being crude. It was a face that put every man in Hollywood and the modeling industry to absolute shame.

It was also almost too perfect, as if it had been produced in a factory and designed to be appealing by algorithm. It also made it difficult to pin down his age. He could have been a mature twenty-five or a very well-preserved fifty.

There was another person there, which made Anya pause: a woman in an old-timey driver's uniform, with double-breasted buttons running down her black jacket, slacks, a cap, and white gloves. She was gorgeous, but her features looked even more artificial than the man's. She had black hair tied into a bun and bright green eyes, and lips so red and shiny they looked waxy.

The woman also had an almost comically large pair of breasts that bulged out in front of her and strained against the fabric of her jacket.

Anya blinked and studied the pair again.

One heat signature.

Two people.

The woman didn't have a heat signature at all.

"Uh, hello?" the handsome man asked again.

"Yeah, hey," Anya said, still staring at the woman.

"Good evening," the woman said and bowed. Her movements were off somehow.

"I'm Earl and that's Ellie."

"What the hell is she?" Anya asked.

"She's a robot," Earl said. "Well, an android. So, you got one too, huh?"

"An android?" Anya asked, her confusion growing.

"No, sorry. One of these Archive things. You know, you touch your ear and a little blue hologram comes out and tells you you can do whatever you want."

Earl tapped his ear and a pale blue-and-gray translucent screen that looked almost identical to Anya's appeared. It had different information on it, but otherwise the layout and basics were identical.

A pale blue AI also appeared beside Earl. Like Felix, they also had the body of a fat baby with stubby arms and legs. Their head was different though: some kind of star-shaped flower with five thin, dark points coming out between the petals.

"It's his sex android," the little AI said in a bored tone and pointed at the enormous-breasted woman.

"Bobo!" Earl snapped and blushed. "We don't need to share that."

"Nobody cares," Bobo said and floated in a slow circle on their back around Earl's head. "She's here about the invasion anyway."

"Yeah, no shit," Anya said. "I really hope your sex-bot isn't the friend you mentioned and you're not just here looking for a third."

"Not quite. They should be here soon though. Got caught up in traffic. I went down to the Channel 08 offices this afternoon and told them what the deal was. They saw Bobo and some of my skills and agreed to do an exclusive interview. We were gonna set up near my place in Long Island, but then we got the message that there were other Archive hosts and decided to track you down. Now here we are."

"I didn't come here for an interview. Some aliens are gonna land somewhere to probably try and murder us pretty soon and I needed to know if you were a nutcase or if you could help."

"Well, I'm not a nutcase," Earl said and shrugged as he smiled. The expression was a little too perfect, as if he had spent hours working on it in front of a mirror.

"Why does your face look like that? Plastic surgery or something?"

"I don't know what you mean," Earl said and looked to the side.

"He used the Archive status menu to make cosmetic alterations to his face and body. Especially his teeth. He used to look like a beaver with a perm," the blue AI said.

"Bobo! We don't need to share that either!"

"Fine, whatever. Look, do you have skills that can help with the invasion? Anything that could stop aliens or protect people or do something? Tell me you did not spend all your RAC on a sex-bot and making yourself look like uncanny valley Brad Pitt," Anya said.

"Whoa, hey, I'm ready for whatever those aliens bring," Earl said and opened his coat. There was a thin leather pouch hanging from the jacket's interior, and Earl opened a flap on the side to reveal a lit metallic interior that was full of guns. At first Anya didn't understand what she was seeing: it was if Earl had opened a window into a storage closet within his coat.

"Is your coat bigger on the inside?" she asked.

"Cool, right? Pocket dimension. It's about the size of a small closet. Cost a pretty penny, or RAC, I guess, but yeah. I got some serious fire-power in here. Got the skills to use it all too. My suit is reinforced armor, and my shoes make me pretty damn fast. Ellie here is good in a fight too," Earl said and smiled at the android. She smiled back and gave him a robotic salute.

"Okay, guns. Fine. Anything else?"

"Took some super strength skill, some sword fighting skills, a bit of mind powers. I'm ready for anything."

"Uh-huh. What level are you?"

"Level 21, why?"

"Can I see your menu?" Anya asked and Earl expanded his screen so she could see it more easily.

EARL HENDERSON LEVEL 21
Stats

- Awareness-8
- Dexterity-15
- Fortitude-9
- Intelligence-12
- Strength-7
- Willpower-10

Skills

- Teykvanen Firearms (Small)-7
- Heavy Ordinance Training (Anti-Material)-5
- Combat Acrobatics-5
- Enhanced Muscle Elasticity-3
- Xenobiology Analysis-3
- Enhanced Muscle Density-3
- Amrel-Kar Fencing (Sonic Saber)-5
- Telekinesis-4
- Kama Sutra-3
- Media Relations-3

Anya glared at Earl and said, "Jesus Christ, dude."

"What? Those skills are awesome! And my stats are all higher than average! What's so good about what you took? Why don't you show me, huh?" Earl said, and his voice was one Anya had heard from insecure guys for many years. It did not fit his mature, handsome face, and the disconnect would have been hilarious if it hadn't been so weird.

Anya showed him her main menu screen with all of her stat and skill info and he scoffed.

"Four? You only took four skills? That's nothing!"

"Some of your skills are fine, but you've spread yourself too thin. Yeah you can do a lot, but you're gonna be shit at almost all of it. And some of this is useless! Why the actual fuck would you take Kama Sutra and Media Relations before an alien invasion?"

"Because I don't want to look like an idiot when I tell the whole world aliens are here," Earl said. "And Kama Sutra is fun."

"Master is a very talented lover," Ellie the android said and gave another plastic smile.

"Yeah he's great for like three minutes," Bobo added and Earl swatted at the AI who floated out of reach.

"I wanted to be ready for anything, that's all. And right now, that means talking to the press," Earl said.

As if on cue, a short Asian woman in her thirties in a long, dark coat hurried along the sidewalk ahead of a thin, young, Hispanic man. The man's face was flushed from the effort of jogging behind the woman while carrying a large camera on his shoulder and a heavy bag that bounced against his side.

"Sorry, phones are still out," the woman said, then did a double take as she saw Anya and Felix. "Is this her? The one you were messaging?"

"Yeah, this is her. She could tell Ellie was an android right away, somehow. We ready to roll?"

"Jennifer Chang, Channel 08," the woman said and extended her hand to Anya, who shook it just to be polite. "Angel Ramierez is on camera."

"I'm Anya, and this is Felix."

"Hello!" Felix said with a wave.

"Huh. That one's got a flower head too," Jennifer said as she watched Felix float over to Bobo and the two AIs examined each other. She turned to Anya as she plugged in a small handheld microphone to a battery pack inside her coat pocket. Angel activated a bright light on his camera and Anya blinked as he shone it in her eyes.

"We've got footage of Earl and his special coat, some of his guns, and the AI. You got anything for us?" Jennifer asked as she fiddled with the pack in her pocket.

Anya rolled her eyes, but nodded and held out her hand. A baseball-sized orb of fire appeared in her palm, and she made it move around in a slow circle.

"Whoa. How are you doing that?" Jennifer asked and almost dropped her mic. Angel pointed the camera at her palm and at the two AIs floating around.

"That's it?" Earl scoffed.

"No, but I'm not gonna do anything too crazy unless I have to," Anya said. "Now look, I don't think having—"

"Anya?" Felix asked. Both of the AIs had stopped their idle floating to stare upwards "They're here."

"Who's here? Another one of you host people?" Jennifer asked and held her microphone towards the AI.

"No. The aliens. They hit the atmosphere 3.05 seconds ago. One of them is descending on our location now," Felix replied.

"Well... fuck," Anya said.

7

Anya had expected flying saucers, or maybe weird, organic-looking ships to descend on the planet. A lifetime spent watching movies, TV shows, anime, and playing games had prepared her for any number of dramatic and potentially apocalyptic scenarios. Maybe they would fire on the Empire State Building, or a swarm of small fighter ships would converge on the city, and turn it into a smoking ruin within moments of their arrival.

So when a single mote of red light fell silently out of the sky about a half-mile away from her and landed somewhere in the distant trees with what sounded like somebody slamming a trashcan lid, she was more than a little underwhelmed.

"Huh," Anya said as she looked at the sky where the red light had fallen.

"Was that… it?" Earl asked.

"That's definitely them," Felix said and expanded Anya's map screen to show the whole of the planet. There were thousands of red dots scattered around the globe, all of them directly on or near the larger, opaque circles that represented the other archive hosts.

"There's a lot. I think you guys are dead," Bobo added.

"I picked up 17,875 alien signals as they entered the upper

atmosphere. One of them is about 2,250 feet that way," Felix pointed further into the park. "Their signal is becoming fuzzier. I can't hold it. I'm losing the other alien signals too. There's more: it's like I'm getting a focused signal from the alien, but I can't make it out."

"What does that mean? They're trying to communicate?" Anya asked.

"No, I don't think so. I think they're pinging us, like a radar. Based on their global points of entry in relation to host signals, I'd say however they're tracking us is a lot more accurate than whatever I could do."

"Oh yeah. They got your number for sure," Bobo added.

"Can you trace their signal back to them?" Anya asked.

"I'm trying, but it gets fuzzy really quickly."

"Shit!"

Anya's heart was beating faster, and one part of her mind was telling her to run. Go take her chances with the cops and let them deal with this.

Another part rationally laid out possible strategies.

Right now, she had an accurate location of an enemy Felix would have trouble tracking later, and apparently, the enemy had a much more precise tracking system. If she ran, she'd lose the lead and open herself up to ambush later. But right now she knew the number and general direction of her enemy, and she had another host with her.

The news crew was a problem. They would be a liability.

"All right, news people, you should go. We don't—"

"First contact!" Earl said and took off at a brisk walk in the direction Felix had pointed. Jennifer ignored her and hurried after Earl and Ellie the android. Angel let out a sigh and began jogging at a much slower, more awkward run after them.

"According to one of the hosts and his artificial intelligence, aliens have just landed here in Prospect Park..." Jennifer began narrating as she, Angel, and Earl continued down the pathway.

"You should get the fuck out of here right now," Anya said to the cameraman as she followed.

"So I can get fired? I'll be homeless in a week," Angel whispered as he lagged behind the others.

"Better than being dead."

"If you had a chance to get mankind's first contact on film, you're telling me you wouldn't take the risk? Heck, a year ago they sent me into an active shooter event. This is way more worth it."

"Just be ready to bolt if shit goes bad," Anya said before sprinting ahead to catch up with Earl. She ran down a narrow pathway flanked by trees and under a stone bridge that arched over the path. She blew past Jennifer with ease and caught up to Earl and Ellie as they emerged into a much more open area where three other paths intersected. The dull, flickering amber light from a pair of lamp posts illuminated the cold, snow-covered ground and made the shadow-draped shapes of trees appear to twitch and move in the dark.

"I don't see it," Earl said.

"There's something," Anya said and pointed across an empty expanse of lawn to a distant tree line: two heat signatures just coming out of the trees. Her breath caught in her throat for a moment, but then she sighed.

It was a man and his dog. Probably just finishing up a walk when the weather had turned. Sleet fell intermittently, but it was picking up once more.

"Guy and his dog," Anya said, then movement from further along made her glance to the side. A flock of birds flew up from a tree, like a flurry of glowing embers from a dead fire.

Something had startled them.

But there was nothing but the man and his dog, and they were far enough away that they shouldn't have—

A scream.

A howl of surprise and pain.

The signatures of the man and his dog dimmed, went cold, and vanished.

"Oh shit," Anya said.

"What's that? What happened?" Earl asked.

"Get your fucking gun out." Anya spun around as Jennifer and Angel came panting up behind them.

"Did you... find it?" Jennifer asked and winced. "Shouldn't have worn my heels. Damn."

"You two get out of here right now. It just killed a guy and his dog," Anya snapped at them and then kept her gaze forward, toward the tree line.

"Like hell we're leaving now," Jennifer said, then turned to Angel and started to narrate what was happening while the cameraman turned the bright light on the front of his camera on.

The last thing they needed was to give their position away any more than they already had, and if these people were too stupid to leave, then so be it. Anya focused on the camera and heated it up just enough so the light on the front of it popped and the insides started to smoke.

"Ow! Shit!" Angel exclaimed and dropped the smoking camera with a crash on the pavement.

"Get. Out," Anya snarled at them, and was aware of little motes of fire blossoming around her head.

"Uh, y-yeah. We'll… we'll hang back," Jennifer stammered. That was when another flock of birds burst from a tree nearby and flew away into the night.

A voice, cute and childish, emitted from a dark copse of trees less than fifty feet from them.

"I know my ABCs, do you?" the voice asked.

Anya squinted at the voice, confusion replacing the growing surge of terror inside of her.

"What the hell?" Earl whispered behind her as he lowered a long, chrome rifle he held.

"Sharing is caring," the voice said. A squat, cartoonish figure walked into the circle of light on the far side of the intersection with an awkward gait.

"Is that a fucking puppet?" Anya asked.

The thing that emerged into the light of the lamp post looked like it had stepped off the set of a children's educational program. It was only about three feet tall, with long and wiggly limbs attached to a tubby, ovoid torso that was topped with an oblong head that had tiny circular ears on either side. It was covered in shaggy purple fur and a bulbous felt yellow nose stuck out of the center of its face, just above a toothless grinning mouth.

"I love you!" it said as it paced to one side and then the other.

"Is this a joke?" Earl asked. Anya used her heat sense and couldn't detect anything from the walking, talking puppet. It was just as cold as the rocks and trees around it. It really did just look like a puppet had walked off some kid's show for a late-night stroll through the park, muttering catch phrases to itself.

Then it turned to look directly at them and Anya's stomach clenched.

Its eyes were wrong.

Everything else about the puppet made it look like any other cuddly educational mascot, except for the eyes on top of its head.

Those were real.

They were glistening, wet, veined orbs that glared out with inhuman intensity and awareness. They had red irises and horizontal, goatish pupils. They scanned the open area between it and the intersection and the park beyond as the puppet turned in a slow circle.

Anya also saw that its hands were covered in blood and white fragments she first thought might be snow, but then realized were bits of bone.

"Holy shit," Earl breathed.

"Okay, I'm gonna circle around to get on its other side," Anya said.

"Nah, I got this," Earl said and raised his rifle. The end glowed with heat for a split second before it fired a blast of glowing orange light that connected with the puppet, right in its tubby ovoid center mass.

The puppet fell back without a sound as the bolt of energy (a laser or plasma bolt maybe, judging by its intense heat signature) left a charred hole through its gut and a smoking pit in the ground behind it. It twitched and Earl fired at it again two, three more times, and its body smoked from the numerous holes.

It didn't move.

"Yeah!" Earl said and pumped his fist into the air. He brought the rifle up to his lips and blew smoke off the barrel. He took a step towards the fallen alien, gun still trained on it.

"No way," Anya said and squinted at the smoking ruin of the puppet. "That was it?"

"I guess," Earl said and took another wary step toward the puppet. He was still about thirty feet away from it, gun trained on its body.

"Is that it? Was that the alien?" Jennifer asked, her phone out and clearly filming from a safe distance a couple dozen feet behind them. Angel had produced a much smaller handheld camera from the bag at his side, though at least he was smart enough to keep the light off this time.

"Don't get any closer," Anya said.

"Not planning on it. Bobo? Did I get the reward for killing it?" Earl asked.

The blue AI shrugged and said. "I dunno. Menu doesn't have anything different."

Earl shot the puppet again and one of its arms flew off. The puppet remained a smoking, motionless lump of shaggy purple hair. When it remained still, Earl sighed.

"Ellie, go bring the car around back by the carousel. This was disappointing. Some invasion," Earl muttered and shook his head as Ellie gave him another salute and then jogged back towards the entrance of the park.

"Felix, are you still picking up a signal?" Anya asked.

"Yes!" Felix replied. "It's still alive!"

"No way, I got it clean," Earl said and pointed at the fallen alien with his rifle. "See?"

There was a blur of movement and a whipping sound as something sped through the air between Earl and the alien.

Earl smirked at Anya but he trailed off when he dropped his rifle. It fell and hit the ground with a heavy thud. Its chrome-plated surface glinted under the nearby lamp posts, and Anya sensed a faint heat still radiating from the barrel and within its power core. Something was attached to the grip of the rifle though, and it emitted its own source of rapidly fading heat.

"Huh?" Earl asked and looked down.

It was his hand.

Earl's right hand still gripped the rifle, finger near the trigger. It had been lopped off clean and straight from his wrist. Anya stood in shock as a gout of Earl's hot blood gushed from the stump at the end of his right arm.

"What? What?" Earl asked and took a step back, two, tripped and fell back as he held his bleeding stump in front of him. Two white circles of bone stood out amidst the red oval of exposed muscle and tissue and Anya almost vomited.

Fuck fuck oh fuck, she thought and shot her wide, terrified eyes to the prostrate form of the puppet alien.

It had changed.

Its arm had regrown along with two others from the holes in its chest. One of its chest arms was more visceral than the other two. It was still covered in purple felt, but now red, glistening sinew could be seen beneath it, along with barbs of bone, like white thorns on a gore-soaked vine.

"I'll teach you how to count to ten," the puppet said as it rose up. Its living eyes throbbed with malice as it glared at Earl, then at Anya.

"Oh my God," Jennifer whispered behind them.

"What the fuck?" Angel whispered.

"My hand. My hand, it, it-it-it-it—" Earl's voice wavered as he stared at his stump and tried to scramble to his feet.

Grab him and run, call the cops, some distant, rational part of her mind said. It was a whisper in the middle of a sudden maelstrom of thoughts. Combat cognition was feeding her multiple plans of attack and retreat at once, almost overloading her.

Leave him.

Blast the thing.

Blast them both.

Shouldn't have come here.

Gonna die.

Grab him and RUN! the rational whisper became a stern shout and Anya lunged toward Earl as he finally got his feet under him.

"An—" he said and then there was a blur of purple movement that turned his head into a smear and the air around him into a firework of blood, bone, and brain. One second and Earl was looking at her with naked animal panic, and the next, everything above his neck was gone, spattered onto the trees, the snowy ground, and Anya herself. His blood looked like oil in the dark, but Anya sensed the heat of it before the winter night sapped it.

"Whoa," Bobo said. "Bummer," and then the AI faded from existence.

Anya threw herself back, away from the horror of Earl's headless body as it collapsed to the cold ground. One of the puppet alien's hands was soaked in what remained of Earl's head, a couple of his teeth stuck on the fluffy fingers. Its arm had stretched nearly thirty feet, exposing more wet sinew and bone thorns beneath the felt. The arm retracted to its original size as the puppet alien drew the arm back, then turned to face her.

"Let's be best friends," it said and took a step forward. Its eyes gleamed, their red irises glowed a dull, malevolent crimson, and the veins attaching them to its furry head throbbed. A wet, slithering sound emitted from its body as it grew two more arms, these tipped with harpoon-shaped points of jagged bone. The holes Earl had blasted in it knit themselves closed as muscle tissue snapped back together.

The rational whisper, the chorus of adrenaline-fueled screams in her head, all agreed there was only one choice now. Anya leaped to her feet, grabbed Jennifer under one arm, Angel under the other, and fled away from the puppet and back into the dark, frigid night of the park.

8

Anya was aware of three things while she ran:

One, her Mantle of the Gale made her much faster than she had expected. The dark trees flanking the path through the park had become nothing but a shadowy blur and the wind whistled past her ears as if she were on a motorcycle rather than on foot.

Two, the combination of her naturally enhanced strength and whatever bonuses she got from the runes embedded in her Regalia of St. Llothec made Jennifer and Angel feel more like cumbersome bags of laundry than a few hundred pounds worth of people and camera equipment.

And three, she was never going to look at puppets the same way ever again.

A fourth realization came to her as she stopped just past the carousel near the entrance of the park.

While the park itself was almost deserted now, the city beyond it was most definitely not. Hundreds, thousands of glowing heat signatures appeared within her range as Anya approached the Flatbush Avenue entrance. People in shops, people hurrying home from jobs, people living their lives.

The thing in the park had killed a man and his dog just for being nearby. It had killed Earl. It would have killed Jennifer and Angel if Anya hadn't fled with them.

And she had no doubt it was coming to kill her.

It would just keep following her, and damn however many other people it had to get through to find her and the other hosts on the planet.

"Can you put us down, please?" Angel groaned.

"Sorry, yeah," Anya said as she released them. Jennifer fell down with a grunt while Angel managed to catch himself.

"I think I might puke," Jennifer groaned and clutched at her stomach.

"We have bigger problems," Angel said as he helped Jennifer to her feet.

"That thing… Jesus Christ. Earl's dead," Jennifer said.

"Tends to happen if your head gets slapped off," Anya replied. Her emotions had been going haywire before, but she was already almost calm again. Not entirely, but her panic, shock, and fear were at manageable levels. She didn't know if that was her increased willpower stat or combat cognition, but she was grateful for it. Felix floated beside her and pointed back in the direction they had come from.

"The alien is still that way. I've lost its exact location but it's closing," the AI said and Anya grunted as she turned to face Jennifer and Angel.

"You two get the fuck out of here. Get to the nearest police station and tell them what happened. If the phones are working, tell them to call the 81st Precinct in Bushwick and confirm that what a blond woman told them is true: aliens are here and they're killing people," Anya said. "Tell them to bring SWAT or the National Guard or whatever. Tell them it's terrorists or something if they won't believe you."

"The 78th Precinct is just up the road. What're you going to do?" Angel asked.

"Try to keep that fucking thing here. Go!" Anya said and Angel took Jennifer's hand as the two fled from the park.

Anya's combat cognition was telling her temporary retreat was a better option and that if she could lose herself in a crowd, her odds of survival increased. She could use human shields as distractions and take potshots at the alien to weaken it.

Fuck that, she thought. It was practical, but she wasn't about to throw innocent people at that freakish puppet just to save her own ass.

Well, maybe if her old boss was still here...

No, not him either.

Probably.

"Felix, keep me posted on how close that thing is. Okay?" Anya asked as she ran back into the park. She needed to get somewhere wide open. The trees gave it too much cover. However...

An idea started to form as she sprinted down the path, back toward the intersection where Earl had been killed. Just beyond that had been an open, grassy lawn that stretched for a few dozen yards in every direction and was surrounded by trees.

That could work.

"It's close!" Felix said as she passed underneath the stone bridge. She heard something thump above her, then caught movement behind her as it jumped off the bridge and landed on the pathway.

"Don't talk to strangers," the childish voice said.

"Shit!" Anya shouted as one of the alien's barbed arms swept past her and she jumped to the side. The alien stumbled forward and Anya drew on the power of her Sun's Heart. She filled the narrow archway beneath the bridge with fire, and blasted the alien with a wall of flame and heat that sent it flying. Heating such a large volume of air and throwing it at the alien drained her more than anything she had practiced in the empty lot, and she had to pause to catch her breath.

She knew it wasn't dead, but she needed to see how much damage she had done. The alien stood, its purple hair flaming, large patches of it burned away to expose blackened meat and sinew. She had blown two of its arms off, but it grew more to replace them. One arm ended in serrated claws, the other wriggled with insectile legs like a giant centipede.

The areas that Anya's fire had burned and that her flames were still licking at were healing very, very slowly.

"Yeah," she said and felt a surge of excitement from within her, the Sun's Heart flaring brighter. "Come on!"

She ran until she had reached the field, then fired a number of small fireballs at the tree line behind her. The flames began to eat at the wood and dried leaves, growing with every second. If her energy started to wane, she could draw on the spreading flames to replenish herself.

Anya turned to face where she thought the alien might emerge from and waited.

"Where is it?" she asked.

"Off to the left, maybe. I think it's sticking to the trees," Felix replied. Anya scanned the trees, and stopped when one of them shook. Long ropey arms stretched up into the branches and pulled them down, then the alien flew up and into the air as it sling-shotted itself out of the woods.

It flew directly at Anya and she rolled to the side as she sent a wide fan of flame at the alien. Two of its arms swung out and connected with her left arm and her ribs. The impact hit her like a truck, but it was spread out by her Mantle of the Gale and her kinetic dispersal. The air around the point of impact warmed considerably, and Anya reflexively soaked the residual heat up. It wasn't much but it was something.

Anya cursed as she felt her arm and at least two or three of her ribs snap. She scrambled away just as another two strikes from the alien left small craters in the ground where she had been a heartbeat before. She leaped back to avoid another sweeping strike and stared at the alien as she clutched her side, then coughed and spat up a thick wad of blood.

One of her ribs must have punctured her lung.

Her regeneration skill was already knitting her back together, sealing the tear in her lung and mending her bones, but it was also draining her energy. The fire she had started in the woods was spreading, but soaking all the heat back up now wouldn't do much for her. She would have to wait.

The alien looked down at itself and patted out Anya's flames. More of it was charred, but like her, it was healing. It curled a pair of its arms behind it, like springs, and launched itself off the ground and right at Anya again. She dodged to the side, but the alien's creepy, glaring eyes tracked her, and it used another arm to swat at the ground and change direction in mid-air.

The harpoon-tipped arm stabbed at Anya's waist, and hit her hard. She gasped from the impact, her dodge turning into a haphazard fall. She managed to blast the alien again, but her flames only grazed it this time. It was nimble as hell, she had to give it that.

Her stomach ached and she feared she would find it slashed open as she chanced a look downward. Her armor had saved her, but the enhanced cloth was frayed and thin, on the verge of tearing. Even though the attack hadn't pierced her, it had still done damage: Anya thought she had felt something inside her pop. Whatever it was, it too was already repairing itself.

"Shit," Anya grunted as she caught her breath. "Felix, find me anything in the RAC store like napalm. Something flammable and sticky that this little fucker can't just shake off."

The alien circled her as she kept her distance, looking for an opening. It would jump at her again, use its arms to propel it forward and dodge her flames.

Shooting at it from a distance wasn't working. Her wide flame attacks used up too much of her energy, heating up a higher volume of air and most of it going to waste. The alien would just dodge precise distance attacks.

She needed to be close, where she could burn hotter and use less energy, and have zero chance of missing.

It was going to hurt.

"Got it! Ignition gel. Very gooey, very flammable. A quarter gallon of the stuff is about 750 RAC!" The AI said.

"Can you put it in a glass container or something?" She didn't need a puddle of the stuff appearing out of thin air and splattering onto the ground. The alien glanced between her and her AI and it began to corkscrew a pair of its arms once more.

"Sure can!" Felix replied.

"Give it to me now!" Anya said and Felix didn't waste time confirming. There was a now familiar whoosh of air next to her and Anya caught a large glass jar of orange opaque goo in her hand.

The alien sprang at her again but this time she didn't dodge. She rushed right at the alien, trying to get inside the deadly arcs of its grotesque arms. It missed with two of its attacks, not expecting her to get inside of its reach, but a third and fourth attack hit her as it closed.

A bone harpoon stabbed Anya in the leg, just above her knee, managed to tear through her armored pants, and pierced her flesh. She screamed as the claw arm went for her throat, missed, and then clamped into the muscle between her neck and shoulder. Her blood spurted up in a liquid arc, but Anya ignored it.

She smashed the glass of goop into the alien's face, making sure to smear it down and coat as much of its body as she could and then ignited all of the air directly in front of her with fire so hot it flared white and lit up the entire park and the sky above it.

"BURN!" she screamed in the thing's face as it ignited.

Good, like that, someone said in a low, smooth voice in her ear. Anya barely registered it as the alien emitted a noise like a host of shrieking cicadas. Its arms disengaged from Anya then flailed around it as it pushed away from her. Its harpoon swept next to her and managed to slice open the side of her neck as the alien made a confused, screaming retreat.

Anya fell to her side with a choked gurgle as she clutched at her neck. Blood squirted out of the wound, more of it spilling from the injuries on her leg and shoulder.

"Anya! Anya!" Felix said as he floated alongside her. Anya tried to respond, but her throat and mouth were full of blood. She could feel her regeneration closing up the slashes, but it was slow, and both her blood and energy were dropping by the second.

The alien was fleeing from her, half running and half dragging itself with its arms toward the distant trees. Anya let it go and limped closer to the blaze she had started in the woods before the fight started.

She pulled the heat from the expanding fire, which had now spread several yards into the forest, and the heat rushed into her. The flames shrank and went out, leaving only smoke and charred wood behind. Her Sun's Heart took in the energy and sent it flowing through her, warm and soothing. Her wounds closed and the blood pouring out of her stopped. Anya spat a final mouthful of blood onto the ground and took in a huge gasp of air.

"Holy shit. Holy shit," she said and fell to her knees, shaking.

"Are you okay?" Felix asked.

"Hell no. I feel like ass, but not like I'm dying. Where is that thing?" she asked as she looked around. She caught sight of a brightly burning shape swinging through the trees: a simian will-o-the-wisp screaming its agony and rage.

It was heading further into the park, retreating at speed. Anya considered retreating herself: just hit the button on her escape belt and get the fuck out of this shitshow.

But the alien would still be loose in a city of millions, and it would still be hunting her. Besides, she'd finally managed to really hurt the God damn freak, and she really wanted to finish the job.

"Mother fucker. No you don't," Anya snarled as a crazy, manic grin stretched across her face, and ran after it. She stumbled, felt her head spin, and almost fell down again.

"Felix, how many skill and stat points do I have left?"

"Eight and four, respectively," Felix replied. Anya trotted after the fleeing figure of the burning alien, picking up speed as her regeneration continued to heal her.

"Split the skill points between Flame Dominion and Regeneration equally. Three stat points in Fortitude and one in Dexterity," Anya said. "And be ready with more of those gel jars."

"Done! The upgrades will knock you down for about 1.76 seconds. Ready?"

"Do it," Anya said, then knelt and braced herself for the pain. It was bad, but not as bad as before, and she didn't black out this time. When it was done, she felt significantly better. She shook her head and began running again.

The flaming alien had extinguished some of the fire clinging to it, but it still burned bright enough to follow with the naked eye. She stuck to the pathways and kept the burning creature in sight as best she could.

The alien swung out of the woods and across a pathway just opposite the one Anya was on, then fell to the ground in a smoldering heap. Anya sprinted toward it, then slowed as she drew closer.

Something was different. The alien looked… flat.

"Is it dead?" Anya asked.

"No, I'm still picking up its signal, still moving away from you," Felix said.

Anya eyed the flaming lump on the ground and sucked air in through her teeth. It wasn't the alien, just its charred and crispy hide.

"It tore its fucking skin off?" she breathed as she stared at the heap of hair and flesh. "God damn that is fucked up."

"Useful if you want to get away from your burning skin though," Felix pointed out.

"Where is it?"

"Nearby. Hard to say. It's stopped moving, though."

Anya grumbled and began to turn in a slow circle as she tried to keep her eyes on all of the trees at once.

That was when she heard the sirens.

The tell-tale wail of police cruisers came from the edge of the park, probably near the entrance by the carousel, about a half mile behind Anya.

"It's moving, back the way it came, I think," Felix said.

"Shit," Anya said and desperately scanned the trees. A shadowy figure zipped through the branches at the edge of her vision, moving right behind her.

"No you don't!" Anya said and blasted the tree it was aiming for. The branches shattered in a loud explosion and the alien fell to the ground. It hauled itself away from Anya's next attack, scrambling across the ground on its arms. The alien had regrown some of its hair, but had now also added overlapping bone plates to sections of its body. It had grown a second, malformed head alongside its first, like some kind of conjoined puppet fetus. Most of the thing's form was a raw, gleaming mess of muscle with patches of charred skin still clinging to it.

Those hadn't healed yet, and Anya's ferocious grin grew as she saw it.

"Jar!" she said and held out a hand as another jar full of the ignition gel appeared. The alien swiped at her and Anya jumped up and over with a rush of wind, flying high into the air, then stomped onto the alien's head with both feet even as she smashed the jar onto its body and ignited the soles of her boots with a fiery blast. The gel caught fire again, setting its bony carapace aflame.

"D-don't talk toooooo strrrr-anngerrr-er-errs," the puppet said, it's voice slower and more fractured than before. The overlapping bone plates on its body clicked, separated, then shot out in a shotgun blast of burning fragments that hit Anya full on.

Anya screamed as they struck her and sent her flying back. Her cloak and armor and kinetic dispersal took the brunt of it but it hurt like hell and her body and bones ached from the impacts. Anya hit the ground at a roll, the wind knocked out of her. She was pretty sure she was bleeding internally now, but also already healing again.

The worst part was that the alien was not nearly as injured from the gel this time. It had taken most of it on its bone armor and shot it away. Burning pieces of the organic shrapnel littered the lawn of the park in a radius around it, and more plates grew from beneath its flesh to replace them.

"Clever little shit," Anya said and got to one knee, fire encircling her fists and leaking from the corners of her eyes.

"Here!" a voice echoed across the lawn. "Fire over here!"

A man in an NYPD uniform had appeared at the edge of the lawn, flashlight in one hand, pistol in the other. He was tall, stocky, with short gray hair and a thick mustache. The officer aimed his flashlight at Anya along with his gun.

"Drop the weapon!" the officer demanded.

"Shoot that fucking thing and run!" Anya pointed at the alien with one flaming hand. The puppet focused the eyes on one of its malformed heads on the officer and turned to face him. As it did, three more cops emerged from the distant path. Two of them had shotguns, and both leveled them at the alien. The third officer trained his pistol on Anya with the first.

"Get down on the ground!"

"Drop the weapon!"

"Don't move!"

The officers all began shouting at once.

"Eat y-youuuurrr v-vegetables after e-e-every meeeaaalll," the puppet alien said, adding its voice to the confusion. Its voice fluctuated pitch and speed, as if unsure or unable to moderate it. It lunged for the nearest officer, the one with the mustache.

"No!" Anya shouted and leaped toward the alien. There was a roar of shotgun fire and it struck Anya in the side, barely harming her but enough to knock her down again. The other officers opened fire on the alien. It easily avoided their shots, and swung two of its arms at the nearest two cops.

They were ripped apart as if they were made of nothing more substantial than wet cardboard. The alien's attacks turned them into nightmarish smears of gore across the white snow. Scattered pieces of them—a foot, half a face, a few fingers—were the only indications that they had once been human at all.

"Jesus Christ!" one of the cops screamed and unloaded his shotgun into the alien. The other cop began pelting it with shots from his pistol, but buckshot and bullet alike bounced off its bone plates or only knocked the alien back. It fired its bone shards again, and the third cop's head and torso were reduced to pulp in seconds. The last remaining cop screamed as a pair of errant shards hit him in the side and one of his legs. He sprawled out on the ground clutching at himself as his blood spilled out between his fingers.

The alien began to regrow more of its bony carapace, and Anya flung herself at it. She tackled the creature and wrapped her arms around it in a bear hug, then turned her chest, stomach, arms, and all the space between them into a roaring furnace.

The alien screamed and writhed, becoming a gyrating tornado of inhuman muscle and barbs and claws. Its centipede arm clawed at Anya's face, digging deep furrows into her cheek and scalp. She grabbed the insectile limb and made her palm burn bright and hot enough to incinerate the arm where she gripped it. She bellowed in the alien's face and white fire gouted from the back of her throat and scorched the misshapen head of the creature.

It finally twisted out of Anya's grasp with a final devastating strike to the side of her neck, which popped and cracked audibly. Anya collapsed in a heap on the ground, gasping for air.

She couldn't feel anything below her neck.

"Oh fuck," she said.

"My leg, my leg," the cop groaned not far from her. The alien continued to scream as it writhed across the lawn, away from Anya. She tried to move her toes, her fingers, anything. For a few horrifying seconds, nothing worked, but then her shoulder and arm tingled, and her fingers twitched.

"Oh thank God," she said. She had just enough movement to awkwardly get her draught of regeneration enhancement out, and drink it. Her whole body was flush with the pins-and-needles sensation as feeling returned, and she managed to stand and limp toward the cop as her body continued to repair itself.

"What the hell is this?" the cop rasped, his voice weak. The cop's heat signature was growing fainter. Too much blood loss.

"Fucking... aliens," Anya panted as she knelt next to the cop. "This is gonna hurt. Sorry."

She put her hand on the cop's side, and then burned his flesh shut. The cop screamed and tried to get away from her, but Anya gripped his ankle and held him still while she cauterized the wound on his leg.

"Ahh! Fuck!" the cop bellowed, but looked down at his side with some relief.

"Do you know the address for the nearest hospital?" Anya asked him. She looked behind her at the alien. It had put most of the fire out, and was now squirming mindlessly around on the grass. It had one arm left. It wasn't regrowing anything.

"Yeah, but... but I can't walk," he said.

"Just say the exact address, and I'll get you there."

"Methodist Hospital, 506 6th Street, Brooklyn, New York. What the hell is happening?" the cop asked through clenched teeth. Anya held the button on her emergency relocation harness as the cop spoke, then removed the belt and put it on him instead.

"Tell them it's aliens. Even if they think you're crazy. Aliens have invaded the planet," Anya said in an even voice, then pressed the button on the belt just as Felix had told her to do.

"But what—Ah!" the cop shouted as he became encased in a translucent bubble of energy, floated up into the sky, and flew away.

"You can't afford another one of those, Anya," Felix said.

"Yeah, well. I can't focus on keeping that guy alive and killing that fucker. Besides, I don't wanna give the little freak the satisfaction of seeing me run," she said as she turned to face the alien. It was a charred, black, smoking wreck. It had one eye that glared at Anya from across the lawn with naked hate and killing intent. Its single arm sprouted a number of cruel barbs and it began to drag itself toward her.

"Blast it!" Felix said. Anya stood, then fell down, head spinning. She vomited and gasped, then forced herself to stand on her feet. She managed it this time, but her knees shook.

The healing draught had put her body back together and made her somewhat mobile again, but that was it. She was tapped out.

"Can I afford any more of that gel?" she asked.

"No, I'm sorry. You're out," Felix said. Anya had maybe enough energy inside her to make some small fires, but nothing else. She didn't have time to start another forest fire, and there wasn't any ambient heat to soak up on a night this cold.

"Earl," Anya muttered, and began to limp as quickly as she could back toward Earl's body. The alien followed her, gaining with every second.

"Earl?" Felix asked. The man's decapitated body was just visible at the intersection.

And so was his plasma rifle.

"Anya, you can't use that gun. The RAC store is telling me that all of Earl's weapons—and his pocket dimension—were coded to his life signs, which are nonexistent at the moment," Felix said.

"Figures. What about the rifle? It had some kind of heat source in it, right?"

"Yes! You can't fire the weapon, but you should be able to eject the clip of heated energy!"

"That'll do," Anya grinned and limped faster. She fell on the gleaming chrome weapon as soon as she was close enough and began to frantically look it over. Its side was covered in buttons and switches, all of which Anya began to press or flick.

The alien was a few yards away, and its body split open along its vertical axis to reveal a huge, gaping mouth lined with fangs and whip-like barbed tongues.

"I-I-I waaaant to beeee you-yourrr best fri-en-en-ennnnd," it croaked as it belched out a lump of smoking and ruined organs.

Anya pressed one more button on the side and was rewarded by a section under the rifle's barrel clicking open. A transparent tube full of some kind of glowing orange substance emerged and fell into her hand.

The outside of the tube was barely warm, but its internal contents were plenty hot.

Anya drank the heat in, soaked it up to the last mote of warmth, and grinned at the alien as it rose up over her.

"I got a best friend already," she said and then created a tiny, condensed orb of white fire in her hand, extended her arm, and released the pent-up ball of heat right down the alien's gullet.

It didn't even manage to scream as the fire tore through it. Half of it turned to ash almost at once, and the other half nearly exploded. The ground all around it ignited from the residual heat alone and began to cook whatever remained. Whatever was left collapsed in on itself, crumbling into brittle pieces of burned meat.

"Signal gone!" Felix cheered. "You did it! It's dead!"

Anya fell back onto the ground, uncaring that Earl's frozen blood was all around her, indifferent to the nearness of his headless corpse.

"Thank fuck," she said and stared up at the dark gray sky above her.

One down.

17,874 to go.

9

Anya forced herself up to her feet after a few more moments spent sprawled out on the ground. She gave a last look at Earl's body and frowned, then looked behind her at the ruined bodies of the police officers scattered across the lawn.

"God dammit," she muttered.

She had tried.

She knew she hadn't made every decision perfectly, and already her head was spinning with could-haves and should-haves and might-have-beens.

"Anya," Felix said in a gentle voice beside her, "I've gotten a number of updates about the archive and the aliens."

"Yeah. Yeah, just give me a second."

She needed to get out of here. Not just because the sight of several brutally murdered people was making her sick, but because more sirens were drawing closer. She wasn't on the verge of collapsing anymore, but she was still weak. She didn't have the energy or the patience to deal with authorities questioning her or blaming her or anything else.

"Are there any other aliens nearby?" Anya asked Felix as she began jogging back toward the Flatbush entrance to Prospect Park.

"No. I think the nearest one is up in New Hampshire, based on their initial points of entry," the AI replied and vanished as Anya neared a crowd of people by the park's exit. Anya just grunted as she left the park and emerged onto the street.

A pair of vacant police cruisers had been driven right up to the entrance of the park, their red-and-blue lights still flashing. A small crowd had gathered around the edges of the cars and were trying to peer into the park. Several of the bystanders stared at Anya as she exited and a few held their phones up to take a picture or video.

Anya ignored them and hurried away from the entrance as she did her best to blend in with the rest of the crowd.

"Have you seen Master?" a cheery voice asked her and Anya nearly jumped. Ellie the android stood on the sidewalk not far from the gathering of people. She stood next to a gleaming black Rolls Royce that had been parked along the edge of the street.

"Uh, y-yeah," Anya said.

"Will he be coming out soon?"

"No, Ellie. He's not coming back."

"Okay. Until he does, would you like me to drive you somewhere?"

"Yeah, actually, that would be great," Anya said and Ellie opened the rear passenger door for her. Anya got inside the car and almost groaned at how comfortable and luxurious it was. Ellie slid in behind the steering wheel, pulled away from the curb, and merged with the flow of traffic.

"Where to?" Ellie asked. "I have full knowledge of every address within the continental United States and Canada, as well as traffic statistics and data for finding the optimal route. However, until I am reunited with Earl, I will not be leaving the greater New York City area."

"Perfect," Anya said and then reached for her phone to see if she had any signal yet. She cursed to herself as soon as she took it out of her pocket. While her clothing was fireproof, it did not prevent heat from moving through it. The cash Tori had given her was nothing but ash, and Anya's phone had been reduced to a warped and melted rectangle of plastic and circuits.

"Just drive up there to that burger place," Anya said and pointed ahead at a fast-food joint at the corner of the next block. Ellie drove into the small parking lot and gave Anya a salute when she told the android to stay put.

New York had long since gotten rid of its abundance of pay-phones, and Anya couldn't think of anywhere else nearby that might have a landline. She practically burst into the restaurant and banged her head on the door frame.

"Ow," Anya said and approached the counter and the short, uniformed man with a name tag that said "Zeke," at the cash register.

"Holy shit, lady. Are you okay?" Zeke asked.

"Yeah it's fine, happens all the time," she said as she rubbed her head.

"No I mean..." Zeke trailed off and gestured at her. That was when Anya realized what she must look like. She was covered in dried blood from herself, Earl, and at least two of the cops. She also had mud and scorch marks across her face and clothing.

"Uh, yeah, I'm fine. Look, do you have a phone I can borrow? A landline? It's an emergency," she said.

"Sure. You can use the landline if you want but signals are back now. Sort of," Zeke said as he offered her the cell phone from his pocket after unlocking it. "Is that... blood?"

"A little, thank you," Anya said as she took the phone. She took a moment to remember Tori's number, then dialed it in and hoped she was right.

"Hello?" Tori answered, her voice hesitant and trembling.

"Tori! It's me! I'm okay. Where are you?"

"Anya! Thank God. Oh shit, I've been... shit. Sorry," Tori said and took a deep breath before she continued. "I'm at my place. What the hell is going on? I heard explosions, and sirens are going off every few minutes."

"It's fine. Well, no, it's all pretty fucked but I'm on my way to you. Just stay put, all right?"

"Yeah," Tori said and Anya hung up, then deleted the call history from the man's phone before she handed it back. She let out a sigh of relief and leaned against the counter. That was when the smells of grilling meat, cheese, and fried onions hit her and she began to drool.

She had never been hungrier in her life.

"Lady? You sure you don't need an ambulance or something? No offense, but you look like shit," Zeke said.

"I just saw a bunch of people get killed and I melted an alien," Anya said. "And I'm starving but I burned all my money to ashes with my magic fire powers."

"That kinda day, huh? Well, some guy sped out of the drive-thru without getting his order. You can have that."

"Seriously?"

"Yeah, sure. I dunno what's going on out there but you look like you could use a break," he said and then handed Anya a paper bag with a few burgers and orders of fries and a couple cans of soda tucked inside.

"I owe you. Seriously," Anya said and felt like she might cry. Since she wasn't about to lose it in public over a greasy bag of take-out, she took the bag, thanked Zeke again, and hurried back out to the Rolls Royce.

Anya gave Ellie Tori's address, leaned back into the buttery leather seats, and began to stuff her face as the android drove. She was dimly aware that she was getting mayonnaise and ketchup and grilled onions and droplets of molten cheese over the upholstery, but she didn't give a damn.

"Felix," she muttered through a mouth half-full of burgers and fries, "What were those updates you mentioned?"

"Oh! Right, you received a significant amount of RAC and level-up experience for killing the alien."

Anya raised an eyebrow.

"No shit. How much?"

"You are now level 28, have unlocked the class selection menu, and have earned 200,000 RAC for the alien kill, plus 10,000 RAC per level for a total of 40,000 RAC, plus a bonus of 75,000 RAC for retrieval of an alien data stream, plus a 25,000 RAC bonus for making data additions to the Archive."

"God damn. What's all that shit mean? Alien data stream and all that."

"Upon its death, the alien released a burst of raw data it transmitted across the globe. I assume this was to the other invading aliens. It is taking me a while to decode, but what I can get from it so far includes more precise tracking data for the aliens."

"That's great! They'll be easier to find!"

"Correct! It is great! And yes, while I still am not able to track their exact location in real time, it will make it easier for me to narrow their signal down when we are within close proximity to one or more aliens.

"As for the other RAC bonus you received, that was for making data additions to the Archive. This included using Flame Dominion in conjunction with the ignition gel as an improvised explosive, as well as using the energy pack from Earl's weapon to recharge yourself," Felix said.

"I get bonus money when I do stuff the Archive hasn't seen yet?"

"Correct! It's pretty specific, though. Ignition gel has been used as a makeshift fire weapon before, but not at such close range and not with the Flame Dominion skill."

"Good to know. And the class menu?"

Felix brought up her main menu that showed her skills and stats, and the first thing Anya saw was that the padlock icon next to the "Class," section was now gone. The other thing she noticed was the flashing alert that said she had unspent points to use, and then a number of additions to her skill menu.

Her Flame Dominion, regeneration, and kinetic dispersal skills had all increased by two points; while her combat cognition had gone up by one.

"Whoa, hang on. My skills went up again? I thought I used up all my points," Anya said.

"Natural skill progression through applied use," Felix said. "If you've taken a base skill from the Archive and used it in an active situation, it will gradually go up. Though this gets more difficult as you raise the level."

"Active situation? So I guess I can't just stand in an empty lot and shoot fireballs at the ground all day and go up a bunch of levels."

"Correct!"

"So much for grinding skills."

"Regarding your earlier question, the class menu is now accessible to you. Classes all have stat and skill requirements. I would recommend waiting to allocate your recent points until you decide on which class you would like the most, in case you need to add points to a given stat or skill," Felix said.

"Thanks Felix," Anya said and sighed as she leaned back into the seat and drank one of the sodas in a single go.

"Hey Felix. What happens to Earl's stuff now that he's uh… you know?" Anya asked and looked at Ellie. The android seemed unaware of anything but the road in front of her.

"It's yours. You've started using it, and now that the original owner is no longer present to claim it, the Archive recognizes it as your own."

"Seriously?" Anya's eyebrows shot up, then she winced and smacked her head. "Fuck! I left all his guns and pocket dimension in the park. God, the cops are gonna have a field day with that shit."

She considered ordering Ellie to turn back around, but she suspected the park had become a hub of activity by now. Emergency services would likely be on the scene, plus more cops.

"You still couldn't access Earl's pocket dimension or fire his weapons since they were all tied to his life signs. The Archive can't change that once the items have been ordered. Same goes for any programming he gave to the android, such as not leaving New York without him."

"Correct. I can't leave the city without Master," Ellie said.

"We got it, Ellie, thank you," Anya said, then turned to Felix and whispered, "So what do I do? The Rolls is kinda cool, but it's just a regular car. And I really don't want somebody else's walking, talking sex toy around. By the way, is Ellie like you? Y'know is she…?"

"Sapient?" Felix asked. "No. According to that model's description in the RAC store, it's an all-purpose automaton with some complicated but limited programming. It's not free-thinking. As for what to do, you can keep it, or you can sell it back to the RAC store at a reduced cost depending on the integrity of the item."

"No shit?"

"Absolutely zero shit!"

"Ellie, do you have any laser guns or other weapons on you?" Anya asked.

"I do. Master insisted I carry a plasma pistol and collapsible sonic saber on my person at all times in case I needed to defend him," Ellie replied.

"Are there any fancy gadgets in the Rolls?"

"A few rifles in the trunk, as well as three spare armored dress suits."

"Jesus, Earl. You should've kept your robot bodyguard with you. Might've saved your ass."

"I estimate there's a sum total of 115,000 RAC or more worth of goods given everything here, after the deduction the store will take for used items. Everything appears to be in solid shape!" Felix said.

"That ain't nothing," Anya replied as she finished the last of the food and cleaned herself up with some napkins Zeke had included in the take-out bag. Ellie brought the Rolls to a stop just outside Tori's building a moment later.

Anya got out, then paused as she looked at the Rolls and Ellie inside. It would be good to have transportation of her own, but the RAC could buy her something even better. Plus, she wasn't sure where to put the car for the night, and if it got damaged, its value could drop.

"You sure Ellie won't feel anything if I sell her back?" Anya asked.

"No more than a smartphone or computer would," Felix said.

"All right. Do it."

A screen appeared in front of her showing the Rolls Royce, Ellie, several advanced weapons, and a set of reinforced armored dress suits. The total came out to 117,000 RAC.

"Hey, I was close!" Felix said and Anya hit the "Confirm?" button on her menu. The Rolls Royce glowed for a moment, then vanished in a sudden rush of air and a loud sucking sound followed by an almost comical pop.

"You now have a total of 457,249 RAC," Felix said as Anya hit the buzzer on the front of the building for Tori's apartment. The door clicked and Anya hurried in and took the elevator up to Tori's floor. Tori was already at the door when she arrived and rushed out into the hall, her eyes wide.

"Oh my God!" Tori exclaimed as she saw her.

"It looks bad, but I'm fine," Anya said as she followed Tori into her apartment, and this time she remembered to duck under the door frame.

Tori's apartment was somewhat bigger than Anya's, but not by much. It had a separate bedroom and a wider living room that Tori had decorated with simple, clean furniture. She had painted the walls a cheery shade of sky blue, and covered them in photos of her family as well as herself and Anya.

"What happened with the cops?" Anya asked as Tori shut, locked, and bolted her door.

"They thought I was playing a prank on them and told me they'd charge me with filing a false report," Tori said. "Which I can't blame them for, honestly. I came back here, and called them again when I heard explosions. They said they were handling it and to stay indoors."

"I guarantee you they know about it now," Anya said and explained what had happened. Earl, Jennifer and Angel, the alien, the cops, all of it.

"...and I just sold off all of Earl's stuff and got more currency out of it," Anya finished.

"And you're sure you're okay?"

"I feel like I just ran a marathon while also going twenty rounds with a pissed-off rhino. I'm exhausted, I'm still hungry, and I'm gonna have nightmares for the rest of my life about bloody puppets and people exploding. Other than that, yeah, ten-out-of-ten," Anya tried to smile and gave a weak thumbs-up. Her weak smile faltered as she remembered something else.

That voice.

"Anya? What is it?" Tori asked.

"It's... it's something with the Flame Dominion skill. I've heard a voice when I use it. Not all the time, just twice so far. The first time I thought I was hearing something, but it happened again during the fight and it was definitely not my imagination," Anya said.

"You're hearing voices?" Tori asked and quirked a brow.

"I know it sounds nuts."

"Not really, given everything else."

"It's only when I use Flame Dominion, and it's always kinda happy about it?" Anya said. She didn't know if "happy," was the right word. Encouraging? Enthusiastic?

"Is the voice telling you to 'burn them all,' or anything?" Tori asked.

"Kind of?" Anya said and shrugged. "It's only been really enthusiastic when I roasted the alien. And the very first time I got the Sun's Heart. It hasn't sounded like a psycho or anything. Just like it liked it when I went all out on that freak."

"Has Felix said anything?"

"Nope. Felix, do you have anything to add?"

"Not really. I've been looking through all of your skills and all known permutations and combinations of them that the Archive has on record, but none of it mentions hearing voices as a side-effect of Flame Dominion or any other skill you have. The closest skills that do have something like that in their description are things like Telepathy, Demon Summoning, Elemental Summoning, Necromancy, things like that," Felix said.

"Have you heard the voices? You can see and hear everything I do, right?"

"Correct! My senses are based around your own, save for the signal reception the Archive allows. And no, I haven't heard anything that you've described."

"Well, that's not good," Tori said.

"Am I going crazy?" Anya asked.

"I couldn't blame you if you were, but you don't seem crazy."

"The Archive's scan of your body and brainwaves doesn't indicate anything abnormal. You had heightened adrenaline and heart rate during your fight, but that's expected. Your brain is the same as the moment the Archive integrated with you," Felix added.

"So then a voice is really inside my head, telling me to burn stuff," Anya said with a nod. "Cool. Just... awesome."

"Hey. One thing at a time. Maybe it's another alien signal, or something else. It could be your subconscious getting louder because of your raised Intelligence or Awareness statistics or something else. But for now, you're fine, and you need to rest. But you need a serious shower first because you smell like burnt ass and alien guts," Tori said.

Anya snorted and started to hug Tori, then paused when she realized that she was still filthy.

"Oh please. C'mon," Tori said and hugged her. "You can take my bed tonight and I'll take the couch. I'll put your magic clothes in the wash and you can borrow some of my stuff to sleep in. It'll be snug, but it should fit."

"But… the aliens," Anya said.

"The nearest one is still in New Hampshire, from what I can tell," Felix said.

"And even if it wasn't, you're in no shape to fight. Those reporters and the cop you saved are already telling the authorities everything they can. We can figure something else out tomorrow. Go on, scoot," Tori said and gave Anya a gentle nudge to the bathroom.

"I owe you so much," Anya sighed.

"You don't owe me anything," Tori said, and then Anya retreated to the bathroom. She cranked up the water as hot as it would go in the shower and washed the dried blood and mud off her. The water would have scalded her a day ago, but now it was barely warm. She changed into the XXL pajamas that Tori seemed to favor, and they just managed to fit her.

"You sure you don't want me on the couch?" Anya asked as Tori put her filthy clothes in the washing machine.

"I'm sure. You wouldn't fit on it anyway," Tori replied. "By the way, I assume your magic outfit here is washing machine safe?"

"It should be. Nothing in the RAC store says it, or the enhancement runes, will be negatively affected by cleaning it," Felix said.

"It survived several explosions and some hits from that alien that would've bashed a truck in half. I'm sure it'll be fine," Anya said as she hobbled to Tori's bed.

"Let me know if you need anything," Tori said and then left Anya alone. Felix floated beside the bed, their orange light a warm comfort in the otherwise dark bedroom.

"I'll be on standby too," the AI whispered.

"Thanks Felix," Anya muttered into the pillow.

She was asleep almost at once, but dreamed of alien eyes watching her, and blood, and fire.

PART TWO
HOSTS

FROM EARTH #2

From *Brooklyn Boards*, an on-line community:

TonyBaloney: Death count from Prospect Park is up to 5: 3 cops and 2 bystanders. And a dog, maybe.

AJC1987: omg that's crazy

Bushwicked: My friend is with the coroner's office and he was there last night, and he told me it looks like somebody set off some kind of bomb or rocket, burned down a chunk of forest too. Could have set the whole park on fire.

AJC1987: Terrorists?

TonyBaloney: Dunno why they'd try and hit Prospect Park at night. Not exactly a lot going on there at night.

Mumbus_The_Chumbus: could of been a test two see if there bombs work n stuff??????

TonyBaloney: Horrible grammar aside, Mumbus could have a point.

Bushwicked: Friend overheard cops and feds talking. No signs of IED or other bomb-type shit. He saw the dead bodies too: no signs of gunshot wounds or bladed weapons, and they didn't even get singed by the explosions or any shrapnel. One of them had been torn in half or some shit.

TonyBaloney: Serious?

Bushwicked: Yeah

AJC1987: What killed them?

Bushwicked: Dunno. He just said they were real fucked up, but didn't know how they got that way. He just bagged them up once CSI or whoever took pics and stuff.

AJC1987: Crazy!!! I heard there was another maybe terrorist thing in Miami last night too. Some people killed in some kind of chemical attack or something??

TonyBaloney: I heard about that. Also news about some big explosion outside LA. Something's going on.

Mumbus_The_Chumbus: my grammer is grate

———

From *Tokyo Shimbun* (translated from Japanese):

MURDER AND EXPLOSIONS ACROSS TOKYO

Two police officers were found brutally slain in the streets of Bunkyo Ward, not far from their police box yesterday morning. Representatives of the Tokyo Metropolitan Police Department were quick to respond to any concerns for public safety and said that the matter was being thoroughly investigated.

Another attack occurred hours later at a police station not far from the site of the murders, though TMPD reports that there were no deaths. A police cruiser was destroyed and several officers were injured by what eye-witnesses claim was a "giant man in his underwear," (see attached photo), who fled the scene.

Further disturbances in Tokyo occurred yesterday evening when multiple citizens reported disturbances at Adachi City High School. Several videos were posted to the internet showing sections of the school collapsing and large explosions rocking the athletic fields. TMPD were quick to cordon the area off following the initial explosions, and the immediate area has been evacuated while investigations are ongoing.

Mayor Ito made a statement this morning following the disturbances.

"The safety of our city and our people is paramount. The TMPD is working tirelessly to investigate these incidents, and ensure the protection and peace of our home. At this time, we ask that citizens remain alert and report any suspicious activity to the police and to avoid any potentially dangerous individuals."

———

From *Jornal do Commercio* (Translated from Portuguese):
UFO SIGHTED OVER RIO OUTSKIRTS
Over 300 residents along the northern outskirts of Rio have claimed to have seen an unidentified flying object late Sunday evening.

"It looked to be about the size of a small plane, but with rockets and strange green lights," said Joao Pereira, a local market owner. "It flew across the sky very quickly as I was closing up my store. Made a really loud booming sound too."

Other residents claim it was larger or smaller, but all agree that it had rockets and green lights and a roughly elongated shape. Some pictures were taken, but all only show a blurry dark silhouette obscured by bright green smudges of light.

Several police officers also confirm they saw something, but none who were willing to go on the record or offer anything beyond reassurances that they would look into any disturbances.

———

From Oni-Chan (鬼ちゃん), an online message and image board, sub-board /PO/ (Paranormal Occurrences):

Anon-01: Are people's cell phones still fucking up? Did /PO/ confirm aliens?

Anon-02: Yes, /PO/ confirmed aliens when SETI and all world governments did not. We really did it, OP! Dumbass.

Anon-01: You know what I mean. Was there any real explanation or was it just random shit?

Anon-03: I think it was just weather patterns.

Anon-04: It was all over the world though. Dropped calls, bad connections, etc. Weather wouldn't account for that since weather is different all over the planet.

Anon-01: My phone's working fine now, at least. Home internet too.

Anon-02: Probably just incompetence on the part of telecom companies.

Anon-03: Mystery solved, OP. This thread is now for posting cute aliens.

Anon-02: geiger_rule34.jpg

Anon-03: Xeno-chan~~~~

Anon-04: This place is fucking weird

———

From the Miami Herald:

THREE KILLED IN SUSPECTED CHEMICAL ATTACK IN CORAL GABLES

Last night at some time after midnight, three people identified as Mark Gregory (37), Lupe Martinez (52), and Gavin Kincaid (21) were found at the corner of Cadima and Salzedo, dead from what Captain Delgado of the Miami PD is calling "an as of yet unknown chemical substance." The victims were found by a local resident who wished to remain anonymous.

"My dog had been barking at something around midnight, and then I heard noises from outside. Awful noises, like screams, or some kind of animal. I looked out my window and saw three people in the street, blood everywhere. It was like a nightmare," the resident said.

Police secured the area and evacuated the neighborhood, fearing that some trace chemical elements might still be present. When asked what evidence they had to suggest a chemical attack, Captain Delgado said that investigations were ongoing and he would have a statement prepared soon.

On the possibility that this could have been a terrorist attack, Delgado said, "We are looking into that."

———

From *Manish's Mumbai*, a blog (translated from Hindi):

Hey everybody, gonna take a break from the usual behind-the-scenes stuff I usually post about working in Bollywood, possibly to ruin my reputation forever as somebody who is sane and rational. This also has nothing to do with movies, sorry.

Last night I saw about thirty people get killed by a tree.

I'll upload the video later, but it's a mess and I'm trying to clean it up. But it wasn't a gang with machetes like the news is saying. It was a tree with metal vines that chased people down the street and cut them apart.

I saw it from my window. At first it was just five people, but others came out to see what the noise was, or stuck their heads out their window, or turned their lights on in their apartments, and the tree killed them. It was late and I had my lights off, so I don't think the tree saw me, which is probably why I'm still alive.

It was a big tree too, a few stories tall, and it reached into the lit windows and I heard more screaming.

I'll post the video later. I swear I'm not crazy. I'm gonna see if any survivors in my neighborhood saw anything.

————

From *Voices From Suwon*, an internet chat room (translated from Korean):

BigHONG: I saw a real superhero last night

SeoulU: like Ironman? o _ o

BigHONG: They looked more like Superman or other Golden Age American heroes.

Sweetstory0001: Golden Age?

SeoulU: It's a time period during which a certain type of hero was made in comic books, I think. Maybe Superman is the most famous example.

Sweetstory0001: Was it cosplay? Is there a con in Suwon?

BigHONG: No, he was actually flying. He stopped outside my 15th floor apartment and saluted me before flying away

Sweetstory0001: ~_~

SeoulU: ㅋ_ㅋ

Moderator: This isn't the room for sharing fanfiction. Please keep discussions about factual events in Suwon.

BigHONG: But it really happened and I'm freaking out ㅠㅠ

-THIS THREAD CLOSED BY THE MODERATOR-

10

Anya woke to the sound of the TV outside Tori's room, as well as the muffled noise of morning traffic outside. She yawned, stretched, and blinked.

Based on how she had felt last night, she expected to be sore at the very least. But she felt fine. Better than fine. She didn't think she had ever felt so alert and refreshed.

Anya checked the clock beside Tori's bed. It wasn't even 8:00 AM. She never woke up before nine if she could help it, and when she did, she still wanted to catch another hour or two of sleep.

Anya stood and stretched again, testing the movement of her arms and legs, and especially her neck.

No soreness, no stiffness, just delightful and easy flexibility. She'd had several of her ribs snapped like twigs, her arm and leg broken, lung punctured, neck gouged open and broken, spinal cord presumably severed, God only knew what else she hadn't been fully aware of.

And now she was just… fine.

Her Sun's Heart glowed within her, strong and steady, beating a soothing rhythm against her ribcage and warming her from the inside out. It was odd to think that something so comforting could have unleashed the raw destructive force it had last night.

She squinted down at her sternum.

The voice had come from there, she was sure of it.

"Hello?" Anya asked.

"Hello, Anya!" Felix cheered as they floated through the bedroom door. Felix's rosebud-shaped head blossomed open as they grinned at Anya and waved a stubby arm in greeting. "You're awake! Did you want to pick a class? Buy some stuff from the RAC store? Look for aliens?"

"Actually, I kinda just want to eat a buffet out of business," Anya said and clutched at her stomach.

"Tori already got some stuff for you," Felix said as Anya came out into the living room. Tori was dressed in jeans and a sweater, clutching a mug of coffee beneath her chin while she stared at the TV. Her vacant stare broke as she saw Anya and she shot up from the sofa and hugged her.

"Anya! Thank God!" Tori said.

"Whoa, hey. Good to see you too. What's up?"

"You've been asleep for two days!" Tori said and Anya shook her head.

"What? No. No way."

"It's true. It's currently Wednesday morning," Felix said.

"No shit," Anya said and ran a hand through her hair. "Never done that before."

"Probably the relatively low-level of your Sun's Heart needing to recover from all the use you gave it, combined with your regeneration working overtime."

"That kinda makes sense. I'd probably have died at least three times if I didn't have it."

"What?" Tori asked and her eyes widened.

"I maybe broke my neck and lost a shitload of blood and punctured a lung," Anya waved it away as if she'd only scraped her knee. Tori gaped at her and shook her head.

"But I'm fine now! See?" Anya hit herself in the chest and smiled. Tori gave her a quiet glare and sat back down on the sofa.

"You're nuts," she said.

"Maybe. Mostly I'm just starving. My stomach feels like it's going to collapse."

"I got breakfast," Tori said and pointed at her kitchen counter. A bright pink cardboard box sat open, revealing a baker's dozen (minus one) of donuts, alongside a pair of styrofoam boxes that each smelled like they contained some form of greasy meat product.

"You're a damn saint," Anya said as she descended on the styrofoam boxes. Each contained a breakfast sandwich of sausage, egg, bacon, and cheese beside a small hill of crispy home fries. Anya groaned and made herself a cup of coffee and took the food to the couch beside Tori and began to eat.

"I was about to call the hospital if you didn't wake up soon. Thankfully you snore like a chainsaw, and Felix kept telling me your vitals were fine. I recorded a few news reports on what happened in the park while you were out," Tori said and pointed at the TV. "Prospect Park wasn't the only part of the country that had some fireworks. A couple places in New Hampshire reported large-scale explosions. There was some kind of massacre on a beach in Chicago last night. The Feds said there was a gas attack or something in Miami. A massive landslide outside Los Angeles, and a skyscraper getting broken in half 'randomly' and falling over in the middle of the night in Dallas.

"And that's just America," Tori added and changed over to the BBC. The reporter there was interviewing people about a terrorist bombing outside London. She then showed Anya her phone, which Anya was pleasantly surprised to see had full bars. The news feed displayed stories of unheard of natural disasters, violent attacks of unknown origin, and strange sightings of unexplainable phenomena from all over the globe.

"Jesus Christ," Anya said as she looked between Tori's phone and the TV, which Tori had turned to what she must have recorded the morning after the attack: a broadcast from Channel 08 News.

"Hey! That's the one Jennifer and Angel were with!" Anya said, although the current reporter was an older man with short, silver hair.

"Witnesses said they heard several explosions and saw part of the park catching on fire before police arrived. We don't have any details yet from the NYPD, but they have confirmed that there were both civilian and officer casualties last night," the reporter said. The camera cut to a man with short black hair and a pressed black suit.

"Christian Riley, FBI," appeared beneath the man as he spoke.

"We are asking anybody who was inside or in close vicinity of Prospect Park around the time of the disturbance to please contact the New York office immediately with any information they may have. We are not prepared to comment on the events of last night in connection with any of the other disturbances across the country that are being investigated by other offices, but will be looking into any and every possibility," the agent said with a trace of a Bostonian accent. As he spoke, a number appeared below his name and Tori took a picture of it.

"Well, the government sure as shit knows about this now," Anya said.

"No kidding," Tori said. "So what do we do? You could probably walk right up to the feds in Federal Plaza and they'd have to believe you, right?"

"Yeah, they probably would. Hey Felix? Did you finish decoding that alien data or whatever it was last night?"

"As best I could, yeah! There's still some parts I don't understand, but I decoded most of the location information," Felix said and displayed a large map of the world that appeared beside the TV. It showed thousands of red dots peppered across the planet, with a clock in the upper-right corner that showed 8:37:09 PM EST from Monday night. All of the red dots were very near the larger, opaque circles that indicated the positions of archive hosts.

If there were more hosts in an area, there were more aliens. Anya swallowed as she saw that some hosts had had as many as five aliens land near them. She and Earl had only had to face one.

"These dots are all the exact locations of the aliens when they made planetfall Monday night. I have their precise movements recorded up until the moment Anya killed the alien in Prospect Park," Felix explained. The clock in the corner of the screen sped up to show the alien dots moving toward the host circles. The fight with the alien had only taken Anya about thirty minutes.

It had seemed like an eternity.

Anya winced inwardly as she saw Earl's signal vanish when the two of them had reached the alien around 8:48 PM. When the puppet alien had died a half-hour later, all the points of precise alien locations immediately expanded into much larger circles.

"That marks the end of the alien's data stream. Following its death, I've had to rely on the Archive's signal casting-and-receiving ability to locate the enemy. Having gotten a sample from the puppet alien I've been able to adjust how I locate the signals to be marginally more precise, but not by much," Felix said as the map continued to show what happened after Anya had killed the alien.

A lot of the circles representing the host locations started blinking out of existence.

Hundreds.

Then thousands.

"Oh my God," Tori breathed.

"Felix? How many host signals have vanished as of right now?" Anya asked. The clock on the map sped up until it reached the current time.

"4,405 host signals have vanished in roughly the last thirty-six hours," the AI said.

"That's... shit how many left is that?"

"8,649 hosts remain."

"That's it? Those alien fuckers took out a third of the hosts in a day and a half?"

"It sure looks that way, yeah! This is pretty terrible!"

"Felix, how many aliens were killed? Can you tell?" Tori asked.

"Hmm. It's a little harder to say. A lot of the aliens were grouped together and it's more difficult to separate individual signals. A conservative guess would be that 3,250 aliens were killed. As of right now, I'm detecting approximately 14,625 alien signals."

"That's better than I thought, actually. Still, not great," Anya said. At the rate they were going, the hosts would be dead before the aliens. This wasn't even including however many normal people the aliens had killed. If her fight in the park last night was any indication, civilian deaths would be high.

"Felix, you said the Archive casts and receives signals right? Can you turn our signal off?" Anya asked. "That's how the aliens are tracking me, right?"

"I can't say with absolute certainty. They may have other methods of tracking, but the Archive's signal seems like the safest bet. And no, I don't have access to that function. I think even if I did, you would then be cut off from the Archive which would mean no RAC store access, no skill updates, no nothing. There's a warning in here that Archive use is tied to host life-signs, so it may even injure or kill you," Felix replied.

"Fucking spectacular," Anya grumbled. "All right. I'm going to call the feds. I can at least let them see Felix's map and give them the numbers. How many aliens are in America, Felix?" Anya asked.

"270. Approximately."

"Which country has the highest concentration of them?"

"India, with about 745. Give or take a few based on the signals overlapping. The alien signals seem to be moving outward though and spreading into other nearby countries with fewer aliens."

"We should probably find other hosts too. I get the feeling going solo isn't the best idea," Tori added and Anya sighed but nodded.

"Just hope they're not as stupid as Earl," she said.

"I would recommend selecting your class and choosing some items from the RAC store before you get into another fight or anything else potentially dangerous," Felix said.

"I was planning on that. What are my class options?" Anya asked.

"With your current stats and skills, you have access to about 650,809 classes. Depending on how you allocate your unspent stat and skill points, that number goes up to 885,231."

Anya worked with Felix as Tori made more coffee and they discussed her options. Damage output was important, but so was survivability.

"I need mobility, too. That wind cloak you found for me was handy, but I need something to help me get around more, and faster. And maybe something to keep an alien from jumping all over the place," Anya said as she recalled how nimble the puppet alien was.

"That would be a new skill, right? Do classes give you new skills too? You've only got 4 skill points to use," Tori said.

"Classes do not impart new skills. However, classes give significant bonuses to existing skills, anywhere from five to fifteen points, as well as several extra points allocated for use at the host's discretion. Anya could take a new skill and put a few points in it, and then her class could boost it to a much higher level," Felix replied as various menu screens opened and closed around the AI, hundreds of possible classes appearing or disappearing as they sorted through Anya's criteria.

Eventually Felix and Anya settled on one class: Phoenix Monk.

"The Phoenix Monk was a warrior-caste of a now extinct race. They were renowned for their prowess in hand-to-hand combat and their command of multiple schools of fire manipulation techniques. All monks were imbued with the blessing of an 'Eternal Ember,' which would enhance their abilities and heal their wounds in battle," Felix read as the menu showed a picture of a bipedal alien that looked like a cross between a human, an iguana, and a parrot.

"The minimum requirements state you must have some form of unarmed combat skill, a fire-based combat skill, and a self-healing skill of some kind to qualify for this class. The only thing you're missing is the unarmed combat skill," Felix said and then displayed the basic upgrades the class would grant Anya.

Phoenix Monk

Statistic Bonuses

+10 Fortitude

+7 Strength

+8 Dexterity

Skill Bonuses

+10 Skill Points (Host Choice)

+10 Fire-Based Skill (Natural or magic-based skills only)

+10 Unarmed Melee Combat Skill

+10 Personal Healing Skill (Natural or magic-based skill only)

+5 Combat Strategy Skill

+5 Personal Defensive Skill (Natural or magic-based skill only)

. . .

STORE BONUSES

   +1 Free Fire-Based Artifact or Weapon Upgrade
   +1 Free Light Armor or Clothing Upgrade

"Wow, holy shit. That's quite a fucking bump," Anya said as she looked over the bonuses.

"All of your existing skills will get a bonus, as well as all of your most important stats. The only thing this class does not support is a mobility skill or a skill that would help you lock down an enemy. However, I had an idea for that," Felix said and brought up another screen that displayed a skill called "Gravity Dominion."

"This would allow you limited control over gravitational forces. You could use it to move yourself around in ways that would otherwise be impossible, as well as create fields of enhanced gravity around enemies to slow or even halt their movement entirely," Felix said. "It can also be used to repel or divert incoming attacks from close-range or long-distance."

"Wait. Could I fly with this?" Anya asked.

"You could!"

"Fucking sold," she grinned and then looked at the skill. "Felix, how many of these Dominion things are there? I've got Flame Dominion, and now this gravity one."

"Flame, Air, Water, Earth, Space, Gravity, Light, Shadow and REDACTED Dominions exist within the archive. Huh. Dunno what that last one was. No information available," Felix said and frowned. "You may not take the opposite Dominion of one you already possess, and apparently you're limited to a maximum of three. Beyond that would result in what the Archive refers to as 'critical overload of artifact energy.' The artifact you get with Gravity Dominion is called 'Singularity's Grasp,' costs the same as your Sun's Heart, and requires a minimum skill level of five."

"Wonder what that last one is," Anya said and squinted at a list of the Dominions Felix had brought up.

"You'll need to pick an unarmed combat skill to unlock the Phoenix Monk class, remember," Felix said and another screen appeared with a list of hand-to-hand skills. Anya flipped through it, asking Felix about the various skills and what they did before she settled on one called "Xhama Thul."

Felix read the description as it appeared: "A brutal unarmed combat style that focuses on pinpointing enemy weak points and exploiting them through hard strikes and grappling moves and usually dismemberment. Developed by a star-faring race of violence-enthusiasts who specifically designed the skill to do battle with various alien lifeforms."

"All this stuff, the skills, the stats, all of it, it's probably going to knock Anya on her butt, right?" Tori said. Anya winced. This was a tremendous amount of points she was going to be gaining all at once and she shuddered at the thought of the pain it would bring.

"Yeah, it's gonna do some pretty heavy rewiring of everything. Sorry, Anya, but it's really gonna feel bad," Felix said.

"Let's just do it," she said. She had to actually take the "Xhama Thul," skill first before she could take the class. She put two points into the combat skill, then winced as the menu made its adjustments. Two points wasn't much, but she was suddenly aware of the basics of what to look for in an enemy: anywhere it might have a joint or pivot point in its anatomy, and the best way to dig her fingers or knuckles in there to just cause pain or maybe start to dislocate a limb.

She glanced at Tori and a flood of information regarding her weak points and how to absolutely crush her surged into her mind and Anya winced. She shook the thoughts away and made a face.

"Wow. These Xhama Thul guys really were violent," Anya said, then confirmed her class, as well as taking the Gravity Dominion skill, and where she wanted her free points to go.

She went ahead and applied the free class upgrades to her Sun's Heart and battle regalia. The former gave her a 15% boost to Flame Dominion due to the upgrade from basic to superior quality, and the latter she retrieved from Tori's drying machine along with her cloak. She was pleased but not surprised to see that the clothes were fine, and all the enchantments were still in place.

She took a few extra minutes to upgrade each of her runes and the Mantle of the Gale from basic quality to superior, and added an additional rune to the mantle: the Rune of the Brute, which would give bonuses to her strength and Xhama Thul. She put all of it on and then looked at the confirmation button on her screen as though it were about to bite her.

"You should lie down," Tori said and Anya stretched out on the couch, her legs dangling over the side.

"Okay, Felix. Hit it," she said before she could lose her nerve. The AI confirmed her selections, and Anya held her breath.

A spike drove itself through the top of Anya's skull and shot down along her spine. She tried to scream but the enormity of the pain had literally taken her breath away. Her hands flexed, fingers curled inward, farther, farther, until they felt as if they were breaking and collapsing in on themselves. Darkness crept along the edges of her vision and Tori, Felix, and the apartment fell away from her.

Anya woke up on the floor, her face smooshed against the soft purple rug that adorned the living room.

"—ya? Anya!" Tori asked beside her and shook her shoulder.

"I'm alive," Anya groaned as she blinked and sat up. There hadn't been any effects from updating her stats and skills before, but this time she was very dizzy. Her thoughts were a storm of new information and ideas. Too much at once. She gripped the sides of her head with hands that were thankfully not crushed and took several deep breaths.

"Felix? Is something wrong with her?" Tori asked.

"No, her vital signs are normal. She's just adjusting to all the new skill data she learned," Felix replied.

"I'm okay. I just need a sec. It's a lot," Anya panted. It was another several moments before she felt like she could stand, and when she did, she almost fell over again, but kept her balance thanks to Tori gripping her arm.

Another few seconds and the dizzy spell passed and she felt normal.

Except normal wasn't the word for it.

Anya looked at her hands and decided that if she felt like it, she could absolutely bitch-slap an armored truck and send it end-over-end. She bounced on the balls of her feet and also decided that if she wanted to, she could just hop over a few buildings, or sprint all the way to DC in an hour or two.

"Wow," she said.

"Good wow?" Tori asked.

"Amazing wow."

"Yay!" Felix cheered and displayed her updated main menu screen.

ANYA NOWICKI: LEVEL 28 PHOENIX MONK
  Statistics

- Awareness-10
- Dexterity-18 (+8 from gear)
- Fortitude-30 (+6 from gear)
- Intelligence-10
- Strength-18 (+4 from gear)
- Willpower-10

Skills

- Flame Dominion-28 (+8 from gear)(+5 from Artifact)
- Kinetic Dispersal-15 (+4 from gear)
- Combat Cognition-14
- Regeneration-24 (+4 from gear)
- Xhama Thul-12 (+4 from gear)
- Gravity Dominion-12

"Yeah that'll do for now," Anya said. She had briefly considered keeping some spare stat and skill points in reserve like last time, but decided against it. The four points she had gained from leveling up against the puppet alien wouldn't make a huge difference if she used them to get another skill. Better to put them where they would make her existing strengths even stronger.

Anya waved her hand at her coffee cup resting on Tori's table. The ceramic mug twitched, then floated up into the air. Anya made the mug rotate, but kept the coffee from spilling out onto the floor.

"That's something," Tori said as she stared at the mug, then let out a startled yelp as she too began to float off the floor along with Anya and several donuts. Anya laughed and so did Tori after she got over the initial surprise.

"Now we can float around just like you, Felix," Anya said.

"It's pretty fun!" The AI said. Anya set herself, Tori, and everything else back down as gently as she could.

"Wow," Tori said and couldn't stop a giggle from escaping.

Unlike the Sun's Heart, the Singularity's Grasp artifact did not make its presence known quite as much. Anya was more aware of the pull of gravity at her feet, and a certain latent force swirling invisibly around her hands, but that was all.

The upgrade to her Sun's Heart did not hurt, thankfully, and the artifact in her chest blazed even brighter. Her menu informed her that the Sun's Heart had been upgraded from "Basic," classification to "Superior." Tori pointed at Anya's face and smiled.

"Your eyes are glowing a bit," she said.

"Huh? Really?" Anya checked her reflection in a nearby mirror. Her eyes had taken on a subtle but definite yellow glow. It would probably be much more noticeable at night.

"Huh. There's nothing in the Archive that mentions that as a side-effect," Felix said. "You can change it in the status menu for a small amount of RAC."

"It's okay. Kinda neat, actually. Maybe I'll do something with my hair later," Anya muttered. "Tori? You got that number that was on the TV? The one for the feds?"

"Yup," Tori said and handed Anya her phone. Anya took a breath, then dialed the number and prepared to tell the federal government of America that it had been invaded by aliens.

11

The Federal Bureau of Investigation put her on hold for almost an hour.

"Y'know, I'm sure government offices are busy, especially in light of... everything, but this seems like it would be a priority," Anya said as static-laced smooth jazz played out of the speaker phone. She glared at it.

"At least we have reception again. What was the deal with that anyway? All the phone signals just came back around 9:00 Monday night," Tori said.

Anya frowned. That was around the time she had been fighting the alien. Did the aliens have anything to do with the bad cell reception at all? Had they stopped? If they had, why hadn't those Engineers tried to contact Anya again?

"Thank you for holding, how may I direct your call?" a bored woman asked.

"Oh for—" Anya started to swear. This was the second time somebody had asked her this. Tax dollars at work. "I'm calling for Agent Christian Riley. I have information about the attack on Prospect Park on Monday night. I was there. Please don't put me on—"

"Hold please," the woman said and the smooth jazz made its return.

"God dammit!" Anya growled and small flames appeared at the tips of her ears. However before Tori could tell her to take it easy, the line clicked again and a man with a faint Bostonian accent answered.

"Agent Christian Riley here. Go ahead," the man said. He sounded tired and irritated. Anya was a little surprised an agent was answering phones. She had half-expected to be given to an intern or agent-in-training or something.

"Hello?" Riley asked.

"Yes! Hi! Hello. Sorry," Anya sputtered.

Tori gave her an awkward smile, a thumbs up, and mouthed, "You got this."

Felix also gave her a thumbs up.

Anya took a deep breath and said, "Let me get right to it: I was in the park Monday night. I'm the one who set it on fire. Kind of. It was to fight an alien. Three cops, two civilians, and a dog were all killed not too far from the Flatbush entrance to the park. You, or the cops, or whoever covered the scene should have found a headless man in an expensive suit, some kind of chrome rifle, and a charred lump of hair and meat with a lot of bone chunks or spikes. Plus the cops who were, uh, basically just kind of exploded."

The voice on the other end of the line was silent for a beat, then asked, "And the guy with the dog? How did he die?"

"I don't know. I didn't see that one, just sort of heard it. It was off in the trees somewhere. There were also a couple of people from Channel 08: Jennifer Chang and Angel Ramierez. They should have video of the alien. There was a cop from the 71st Precinct that I sent to the hospital nearby. He had a shiny belt on, probably fell out of the sky near the hospital with a wounded leg and side."

"What kind of wounds?" Riley asked. Anya knew that the man knew exactly what kinds of wounds. His tone did not suggest curiosity, but verification.

"Burns. But they didn't start out that way. The alien wounded him and he was bleeding out and I... I tried to cauterize the wounds shut. I didn't know what else to do," Anya said, and the panic from Monday night came back to her. The cops dead, Earl dead, the alien crawling toward her…

Tori and Felix had come closer to her, both of them on (or in Felix's case, floating above) the couch next to Anya. Tori nodded at her and Felix gave her a grin, which Anya returned after taking another steadying breath. The panic became little else but background noise before it faded entirely.

"You saved that kid's life," Riley said, his voice soft. "He said you were all banged up to hell, put some kinda gizmo on him and sent him flying to the hospital. What was that thing?"

"Emergency Relocation Harness. I bought it from some other aliens."

"Other aliens?"

"Yeah there's… look I can prove there are aliens. You just—"

"I've got enough proof. Proof ain't the problem. We know."

"You know? Since when? Has the government always known?"

Riley laughed. "Hell no. Sounds like you knew before we did. I thought it was bullshit at first but after almost two days of looking at this shit, I ain't stupid. Security footage from Brooklyn Methodist has that young cop floating out of the sky in a bubble. His bodycam showed even weirder shit. And nobody, nobody, except maybe myself, my boss, and his boss, have all the info that you just gave me. The reporters had a bit, the cops had a bit. You had it all. Well, all the stuff that I've got on file in front of me. So you're the mystery lady throwing fire around in the bodycam footage, huh?"

"Yeah. Yeah that's me," Anya replied.

"Come down to Federal Plaza. We need to talk."

Anya's stomach knotted.

"No. I want to help, but that… look I didn't want any of this to happen, okay? I didn't kill those cops. And I know setting the park on fire was technically arson but it was for a really good reason and—"

Anya paused to take another breath.

"You saw the bodycam footage?" she asked.

"Yeah."

"Then you saw the cops shoot me as soon as they showed up. I mean, I get why they did it: tall lady with flaming fists yelling at them to leave. Still not fun getting shot at."

"Yeah. Can't say I blame you for being a bit twitchy about coming down to a federal building full of itchy trigger fingers. By the way, you all right? Even with kevlar, taking a slug hurts."

"I'm fine."

"Hmm. Okay. How about we have a coffee then? I haven't had anything to eat since last night. You name the place."

Anya blinked at the phone in surprise. She supposed it could still be some kind of set-up, though if she needed to make a break for it, it'd be a lot easier to do outside of a government building filled with feds.

"Okay. Mal's Deluxe Diner in Brooklyn," Anya said.

"Brooklyn? Done. Take me about half an hour if traffic isn't up its own ass," Riley said and Anya could hear him rustling around on the other end. Riley gave her his personal cell number if she wanted to call him back, then hung up.

"He seemed kinda nice?" Tori said and shrugged.

"Yeah. Didn't expect to get asked for coffee. More like get in here now or we'll throw you in Gitmo," Anya replied.

"Are government officials usually not nice?" Felix asked.

"Depends. But usually the less you have to deal with the cops, the feds, or especially the IRS, the better," Anya said.

"Yeah the IRS is nothing you want any part of," Tori nodded.

"All right. I'm going to Mal's. You should probably wait here."

"And if we need to get in touch? Your phone is torched and you don't have any money."

"Shit. Yeah. Hey Felix, can I get cash from the RAC store? I know it's kind of a waste, but I'm broke."

"You could, and a stack of United States dollars is pretty inexpensive since the Archive considers it to be just paper. However, since your country uses serial numbers on the currency, it would be counterfeit. You could get gold or silver or something instead," Felix replied.

"No. I don't want to give people fake money. Gold and stuff would be a pain in the ass. Shit."

"I spent the last of my cash on breakfast," Tori shrugged.

"I've taken enough of your money the last few days. I'll figure something out. In the meantime, can you get me any kind of heatproof communication device Tori and I can use?"

"Sure!" Felix said and brought up a screen that showed something like a matte black coaster the size of Anya's palm. The menu labeled it as a "Hazardous Environment Communication Disc," and a pair of them were only 2,500 RAC.

"These have an effective range of up to 125 miles or so, and should be able to withstand your flame attacks. I can get you an additional insulated pouch that will also protect it and anything else inside for 100 RAC. The discs are usually attached to exoskeletons used by scientists on other worlds when entering unstable or volatile regions, but you can use them similarly to walkie-talkies."

"There were a few other things I wanted to buy. Might as well do it before I head out," Anya said.

"Like what?" Tori asked.

"During my fight with the puppet I ran out of juice. I was able to recharge thanks to a couple of improvised heat sources, but it wasn't ideal. Felix, is there anything in the RAC store that's small, portable, affordable, and contains a huge amount of heat?"

"Yes! I have just the thing!" Felix said and brought up a screen. It displayed a luminescent yellow-orange crystal about the size of Anya's thumb.

"Star's breath," Anya said as she read the item's name. "Artificial crystalline substance used to contain large amounts of heat and used for thermal batteries in a variety of devices. Not cheap though."

The star's breath was 10,500 RAC, but it could also be a literal lifesaver. Plus, Anya had RAC to spare for the moment. She added one of the crystals to her cart of items, along with two more reinforced glass containers of the ignition gel, which would be small enough to fit in the pouch.

"You should get another healing item or something," Tori said. "Felix, what's the most potent healing item?"

"That would be rejuvenation foam. It is guaranteed to bring a medically deceased person back to life within seventy-five seconds of death and regrow any and all missing body parts, including the head and brain, to full functionality. The dispenser takes a scan of the user down to their genetic code and uses it as a kind of snapshot to work off of. It's 350,000 RAC," Felix said.

"Okay, that's a bit pricey," Tori said.

"What about a stronger version of the potion I bought before? 10k or less," Anya said.

"Here we go!" Felix said and brought up another screen. A glass vial full of a viscous reddish fluid appeared on the menu. It was labeled as "Alchemical Tincture of Restoration," and was 8,425 RAC per dose, plus fifty RAC per reinforced glass vial to store them in, which Felix added to the side.

"Apply to any major wound or ingest orally in case of internal damage only or multiple smaller injuries," Tori said as she skimmed the item description.

"What is this stuff? Ruby sage, blessed powdered cinnabar, ak… akontolthweek? What the fuck is that?" Anya asked as she squinted at the ingredients.

"A rare type of medicinal herb found on the fourth planet of the Geysalla system," Felix replied.

"So alien plants and shit?"

"Yes. Not literal shit, but yes: this is a solution of plants and some minerals and enhanced with what you might best understand as magic," Felix said.

"Does it work? It'll heal me in a pinch?"

"Absolutely! It won't regrow your head or anything but it will patch up any other damage, purge toxins, and more. At the very least it will turbo charge your existing regeneration abilities."

"All right. Sold. Get me two," Anya said and placed the items in her cart, then looked at Tori. "One's for you."

"Me?" she asked.

"If I'm around you at all, there's a possible danger there. So you get one too in case shit really hits the fan."

"Works for me. This will work on normal humans, right Felix?"

"Yup! Ready to complete your purchases?" Felix asked.

"All this stuff: the walkie-talkie, the ignition gel, the healing potion, the star's breath, will it fit in that fireproof pouch?"

"It should, yes. I can also apply a materials upgrade to increase its size, durability, and heat protection for 1,380 RAC."

"Do it," Anya said as everything appeared in the air over Tori's bed and landed with a soft thud. The pouch reminded Anya of an oversized coin purse, except it was made of slightly reflective gold material. The communications discs had a single button in the center. Anya pressed it, and the other disc in her hand beeped. "Testing?"

"Testing?" Anya's voice emitted from the second disc a split second later as Tori took it from her along with the healing potion. Anya put everything else into the pouch and attached it to the belt of her regalia. After all her upgrades and new purchases, she still had 183,619 RAC left.

"Guess you're set. Good luck with the feds!" Tori said as she took the second disc and Anya pocketed hers in the pouch.

"Here's hoping it works out," Anya replied and crossed her fingers as she left the apartment.

———

MAL's Deluxe Diner was a cozy little place a couple blocks away from Anya's apartment. She and Tori had spent more than one Saturday there recovering from a Friday night outing over plates of breakfast food. It still had the original decor from the seventies: lots of dark wood paneling, orange leather booths, and amber carnival glass lamps hanging from the ceiling. The aromas of bacon, pancakes, syrup, coffee, and more delicious things had permanently infused the place over the decades.

It was comforting when nothing else at the moment was.

Anya sat in a booth by the window, scanning every car that passed by. She was familiar enough with the place to know that there was the main exit and entrance in front, an emergency exit next to the bathrooms near the back, and another exit that led into an alley through the kitchen.

Anya had ordered a coffee, orange juice, toast, pancakes, and two of the breakfast skillets. She didn't have any cash, but figured she could either get Riley to pay, or come back with money later if she had to bail.

Shit, I still gotta pay the people for their door at that coffee shop in Jersey, Anya thought as she ate her breakfast.

She paused with her fork full of eggs and peppers and sausage halfway to her mouth as she caught sight of a black sedan pulling up to the curb. Agent Riley stepped out, alone. He was either very trusting or he had people waiting nearby. Anya figured the latter. Riley spotted her as soon as he entered.

She was pretty hard to miss.

"Morning," Riley said as he slid into the seat across from Anya. He raised his eyes a little at the array of food in front of Anya as he sat down.

"Hey."

"Christian Riley, but just Riley is fine."

The agent extended his hand across the table. Anya didn't hesitate to grip it and shake.

"Anya."

"Coffee and the egg white omelet please, with onions and mushrooms," Riley said to the waitress as she came by.

"I don't have any cash, by the way. It all got incinerated during the fight," Anya said and Riley waved a hand.

"Uncle Sam's picking up the tab. I'd order more, but just looking at all that shit in front of you has probably spiked my cholesterol for a month. The cop and those reporters said you were tall, but they kinda undersold it. What are you, seven-feet and change?"

"I haven't actually measured myself since this all happened. I keep hitting my head on door frames though."

"You weren't always this tall?"

"Nope. So did you actually come alone or is somebody looking at me through a rifle scope right now?"

"I got a partner waiting in the car just up the street. That's it," Riley said and thanked the waitress as she brought him his food and coffee. "So. Aliens, huh?"

"Aliens," Anya nodded. "Felix, can you appear on the seat next to Agent Riley? Don't wanna freak the other diners out."

"Can do!" Felix said and appeared next to Riley on the inside of the booth. To the agent's credit, he only jumped a little as the glowing orange hologram blinked into existence right next to him.

"Christ!" Riley hissed, then crossed himself, then looked between Anya and Felix. "Is this thing an alien?"

"No. That's the AI helper for the Archive of Universal Knowledge or whatever the aliens sent," Anya replied.

"Accumulated Universal Knowledge Archive Project," Felix corrected and Anya just grunted around a mouthful of pancakes. From there, Anya began to explain what had happened over the last several days, with Felix occasionally interjecting to clarify or confirm. Anya gave Riley a brief display of her powers by making the salt and pepper shakers float around and summoning a tiny ember of flame to circle around his coffee mug.

Finally, she had Felix display the map of Earth with all the locations of the enemy aliens when they had landed last night. Riley took several pictures of the map, mostly focusing on America, and asking Felix to zoom in on certain locations.

When she had finished talking, Riley ran a hand through his hair and puffed out his cheeks.

"It's a lot," Anya said.

"That it is," Riley agreed.

"So what now?"

"Now? Well I'm gonna need at least five minutes to enjoy this surprisingly good coffee while I mull this over. Then I'm gonna have to start making calls, and then this will be out of my hands. President's gonna be notified, of course. Joint Chiefs of Staff too, obviously, along with every Governor of every state, Pentagon officials, Military brass, the NSA, NASA probably, all of which is above my paygrade. Until I started looking at all the camera footage last night, we figured this was a terrorist thing, likely connected to all the other crazy shit happening across the country."

Riley took a deep breath and stared into his coffee.

"I would like you to come in with me," Riley said. Anya squinted at him. "I am keenly aware that I cannot force you to do this, based on what I understand of your abilities. I can only say that I think it would be a good idea."

"Look, Agent Riley: you seem all right. You're a helluva lot nicer than I was expecting. I want to help. I do not want people to die. But I also don't want to become something the FBI, or the army, or whoever, thinks they can just order around like a drone. I'm not getting drafted into service."

"That is not my call," Riley said and put his hands up. "For whatever it's worth, I agree with you. And I'm glad that if somebody had to get superpowers during an alien invasion, it's somebody like you who seems to have some sense to them and is willing to help get some dumb-ass reporters and a wounded cop outta harm's way. But this is bigger than whatever you might want, or me, or whoever. I don't know what the brass is gonna ask, or demand of you. I just hope that when they do, you remember that."

Anya bit her lip.

She started to retort when the communication disc in her pocket beeped and Tori's muffled voice emerged.

"Anya? Anya?" she asked.

"Hey, I'm here," she replied.

"What is that?" Riley asked as he saw the disc. "Some kinda alien walkie-talkie?"

"That's it exactly! You're pretty sharp, Mr. Riley," Felix said, and the older man smirked.

"I went out to get some cash from the ATM down the street and I came back and there's a lot of guys in tactical gear in and around my building," Tori said. "Holy shit! They just set off a smoke bomb in my apartment or something!"

"What the fuck?" Anya asked and then glared at Riley. He frowned and shook his head.

"Not me. My boss probably traced the phone records to whoever your friend is there," he said.

That was when a loud bang came from the kitchen, followed by shouting. The swinging door to the back of the restaurant opened and a line of men in black tactical gear wielding small submachine guns emerged. A heavily armored black van came to a screech in front of the diner, and more men in tactical gear stormed out, guns trained on the diner. Anya had passively sensed a number of heat sources, but it was Brooklyn. People were everywhere.

"God dammit," Riley swore.

"Hands in the air! On the ground!" one of the men shouted at Anya as the others spread out around him. All of them had their guns trained on Anya's face, and she sensed the heat signatures of the other men taking up positions behind parked cars. The diners in the restaurant screamed in alarm and ducked behind their tables while the staff hid under the counter.

"Stand down!" Riley snapped. "I have this under control, she isn't a threat!"

"Anya?" Tori asked from the communicator.

"I'm leaving," Anya said and stood up, towering over the men pointing their guns at her.

"Down! Now!" one screamed and clicked the safety off his weapon.

"Do not fire that in here!" Riley demanded.

Anya slammed the men closest to her down to the floor of the restaurant with a heavy wave of gravity. They had time to grunt before they hit the floor, and they wheezed as the invisible force pushed them against the tile.

"This did not go well," Anya said to Riley and then walked toward the exit.

"Bye Mr. Riley!" Felix said as they vanished.

Anya ignored the armed officers or agents or whoever they were as they shouted commands at her when she stepped outside. Instead she shot herself into the air, and away.

12

nya told Tori to stay where she was and be ready for a pick-up. It was quite literal as Anya dropped down from the sky, grabbed her friend around her waist, and then took off again before anybody could react. Tori let out a whooping shout halfway between excitement and terror as they flew over Brooklyn and landed on a rooftop several miles away.

Tori shivered in the wind, and Anya conjured a large flame between them which the former edged closer to with a sigh of relief as the latter relayed what had gone down in Mal's Deluxe Diner.

"So. Assaulted some federal agents with gravity magic, huh? Just a few light felonies to start the day?" Tori said.

"I was worried they would try and shoot me and hit other people. Plus I didn't want to get shot. My armor and cloak probably wouldn't even let the bullets get to me but it still stings!" Anya said and Tori laughed. "What? What's funny?"

"Bullets sting, she says," and Tori laughed again. "Like they're bees or thorns or something."

"Well, they might as well be now."

"How long have you been bullet-proof? Has it even been forty-eight hours?"

"About. I think. I also don't know if I'm actually bullet-proof yet. Just the armor and cloak did a good job when I got shot the other night, plus the kinetic dispersal skill."

Anya sighed and looked at the little fire between her and Tori.

"Did I fuck up?" she asked.

"Hell no. Even if Riley was being straight with you, those guys raiding my place and trying to smoke me out, sticking guns in your face and maybe putting innocent diners at risk, it was completely over-the-line. I would've left too," Tori replied. "But..."

"But?"

"You're gonna have to deal with them sooner or later. If not them then somebody else. Fly to Canada or Brazil or wherever. Ours isn't the only government that knows about this now. Can't be. And even with all the hosts that died last night, there's still thousands of them. Thousands of people with superpowers and access to alien technology and literal magic. That last one is still kind of messing with me, but I'm trying not to think about it too much.

"No government could just let people like that run wild. And even if all the other hosts miraculously joined together in a big happy family, however many thousand are left is a drop in the bucket compared to all of humanity. You can fly and summon fire, but you can't arrange an evacuation of a city, or coordinate existing emergency services without some kind of governmental cooperation," Tori said.

"Yeah," Anya sighed.

"You've done a good job so far, as good as could be expected from anybody in your situation, I think, but you can't do it all alone."

Anya nodded, then tapped her chest. Her menu came up and Felix floated into view.

"Felix, can you show me the nearest hosts?"

"Sure can!" Felix said and expanded Anya's menu to display the whole of the East Coast and much of the Midwest. There were a few large circles near Florida, a couple up in Canada, a couple more near Chicago. All of their circles were relatively large, which—according to Felix—meant he did not have a very precise lock on their location or they were moving around a lot.

The exception to this was a single speck down in Virginia, almost in the center of Norfolk. Anya zoomed in and saw that while its location wasn't precise, the circle that indicated the host's possible area was significantly smaller than any other on the map. It was also the closest.

"What's up with this one?" Anya asked and pointed at the speck of light.

"That host has apparently not moved around much since they got the menu," Felix said. "Looks like they've stayed within a half-mile or less radius of where they were whenever they got it. I can't narrow it down further than that until we're actually close to them."

"Can you show me where the enemy aliens are?" Anya asked and then tried to recall the name the Engineer had given them. "The nossi... nosey... the knowledge eaters."

"Gnosiphages," Felix said and overlaid the approximate positions of the hostile invaders across the map. One was somewhere up in New Hampshire, close to the borders of Maine, Vermont, and Canada. There was another near Chicago, and three in Florida.

And there was another one somewhere in Virginia, the outer edge of its possible location a few miles away from the lone host in Norfolk.

"Uh-oh," Tori said.

"Yeah. Why isn't this guy moving? They're a sitting duck," Anya said.

"It's possible they haven't activated their Archive yet and don't know about what's happening," Felix said and Anya raised her eyebrows at the AI in surprise. "The Archive has to be manually activated first, either by the host themselves or somebody else. Until that initial activation, nothing will happen."

"So this person, maybe thousands of people, could have no idea they got hit with alien technology? It literally knocked me on my ass when it crashed through my window. How would somebody not know?"

Felix shrugged. "Maybe the integration process wasn't as violent for them, or they were asleep, or they thought it was something else. Remember: the Archives were not originally intended for Earth, and were not functioning properly on arrival. This host's integration process could have varied wildly from yours."

"I'm gonna punch these Engineer guys in the gut if I ever see them," Anya grumbled. "All right. I'll deal with Riley and the government and their bullshit later, but you're right, Tori: I can't do any of this alone. I mean, you've been a huge help but…"

"I know what you mean," Tori nodded. "More people with magic and laser guns would definitely be a big help."

"If I get ambushed by an alien, I might not be able to beat it, and when I contact the feds again, I don't want them trying to strongarm me into anything. I'm gonna go pick this guy in Norfolk up and let them know what's going on before that alien gets there. Hopefully."

"About that," Felix said and rewound the time for the map that showed the host and gnosiphage positions. While the circles showing the host positions moved around somewhat, the alien circles were almost entirely still. "None of the aliens in North or South America have been active for hours. I'm not sure why, but it's worth pointing out."

"Huh. Weird," Anya said.

"You said they're mimics and shapeshifters, right? Maybe they're trying to be stealthy, not move around during the day," Tori said and pointed at the clock in the menu's corner. "Look, they stop moving around five or six in the morning."

Felix widened the map to show the whole of the planet, and any alien signals on the opposite side of the globe showed movement.

"Wow. Good catch," Anya said and Tori grinned.

"So are you just gonna fly down to Virginia with your new gravity powers?" she asked.

"I could. It'd use up energy, and I dunno if I'd want to carry the guy out of there if I had to. Felix, I don't suppose I can afford a spaceship or any other really cool rides?" Anya asked.

"The cheapest vehicle suitable for humans and capable of reaching space would be the Vostok 3KA along with the Vostok 8k72k launch vehicles. It's only 25,000 RAC," Felix said.

"Isn't that the one the Russians used to go into space back in the sixties?" Tori asked and Felix nodded.

"The RAC store classifies it as outdated technology by Earth standards and incapable of combat, so it's not too expensive."

"Also impossible for me to fly without a whole launch crew and probably years of training, or skill points, which I don't have," Anya sighed. "I need something small, but that can hold a few people. It's gotta be fast, and have some kind of idiot-proof autopilot."

"Combat capabilities?" Felix asked.

"Skip for now. That'll drive up the price and I just need it to get around. I'll fight on my own if I have to."

"Here we go!" Felix said and brought up several options. The nicest ones would have cost all of Anya's RAC, but she had a few other purchases in mind. She eventually pointed at something that looked like a stealth jet and a sports car had a baby. It had a long, sleek nose that widened out into a pair of manta-like fins along the sides and then tapered back to a sharp point at the rear. The main body was little more than a sleek mound that rose up in the rear-center of the vehicle, and had a narrow wrap-around window along the front and sides. The whole thing was matte black and Anya whistled when she saw it.

"Holy shit that thing looks rad as hell," she said.

"The ST-818, colloquially known as something that translates to the 'Shadow Ray' is a stealth vessel designed for rapid planetary movement, reconnaissance, and insertion and evacuation of small teams of scouting and special forces units. It was developed by the Luorian Galactic Union 207 years ago, and saw extensive use for several decades across multiple systems before being retired," Felix said.

"It flies via anti-gravity discs and a magnetic pulse system rendering it invisible to heat-tracking systems, as well as optic and radar cloaking devices. It has a top speed of Mach-2, and an average battery life of fifteen hours when running at maximum power. The solar cells need approximately two hours to fully recharge. It will cost extra, but there is also an autopilot module that can be installed that will provide take-off, landing, and flight capabilities."

"How much is it with the module?" Anya asked.

"180,000 RAC."

"That seems cheap for a supersonic alien stealth jet. I think the regalia and all its upgrades were more expensive."

"While it's incredibly advanced for Earth technology, it's over a century out-of-date compared to similar vehicles, and it has absolutely zero combat capabilities. There are add-ons, such as a pair of small railguns, an enhanced forcefield, anti-matter bombs, and more, but those would drive the price up to well over a million."

"Yeah, pass. I'll only have 3,619 RAC left after buying the basic model. Will the Shadow Ray fit on the roof here if I buy it?"

"Yup! Confirm purchase?" Felix asked and Anya glanced at Tori who nodded, a huge smile spreading across her face. Anya felt a similar grin as she gave Felix the go ahead, and then both women stood aside as a flash of light and a huge rush of air swept across the rooftop.

The Shadow Ray materialized in front of them and Anya and Tori both gawked at it. It was bigger than the picture made it look, stretching almost the whole length of the roof. It hovered a few inches off the surface of the building, silent and still.

"Damn," Anya said and whistled as she slid her hand along the sleek surface. She expected it to feel metallic, but the vessel almost felt like it was made of glass. "Where's the door?"

"In the back. When you enter, the autopilot module will need to register you as the primary user," Felix said. "It could register Tori, too, if you want."

"Good idea," Anya said as she approached the rear. She didn't see a door, but when she pressed against it, there was a hiss and creases appeared along the flawless surface of the Ray. There was a hiss and a soft hum as the back opened to reveal a dark gray interior of brushed metal. Four padded seats lined each side of the cabin, and a pilot's seat sat in the front center in the middle of a wide cockpit.

The cockpit itself was nothing but a curved control panel covered in a single flat screen in the center, and then smaller screens on either side. No throttle, switches, knobs, or dials visible. The pilot's seat rotated to face the rear entrance as Anya hunched to step inside. She was relieved that she fit inside the high-backed, cushioned chair, and couldn't help but giggle as the chair automatically rotated forward again once she had settled into it.

"So cool," she whispered.

"Welcome to the ST-818 Autopilot Guidance system. When prompted, please present your hand and eye to the appropriate scanner," a neutral, robotic voice said.

"It speaks English?" Tori asked as she sat in one of the empty seats behind Anya.

"The module has been modified to be suitable for Earth. It has maps of the entire planet, including all publicly known addresses. Sort of like how Ellie the android was programmed," Felix said. "It's also designed for humanoid lifeforms. There are many vehicles in the RAC store that accommodate non-humanoid forms, but I dismissed those. You can still find them if you want, but I thought something more suited to humans would be best."

"You figured right. Thank you, Felix," Anya said and the AI beamed.

Two metallic discs rose up from the floor on either side of Anya, each one hovering silently beside her.

"Please place your hands palm-down on the guidance discs, and look directly into the main display screen," the robotic voice said. Anya did as it asked and a light flashed out once from a glowing flat screen in front of her.

"Primary pilot registered, biometrics assigned. Please register secondary and tertiary pilots if needed," the voice said. Anya got out of the seat and waved Tori forward. The process was repeated, and Anya took the pilot's seat again when it was done.

"So what now?" Anya asked.

"Please either state a specific destination, or select it using the map screen. When ready, please say 'take-off,' and flight will commence. To activate stealth features, please say 'activate stealth,' and 'deactivate stealth,' to return to normal operations. Unless otherwise stated, this vessel will operate at a standard cruising speed of Mach 1.5 to conserve energy," the robotic voice directed.

"Okay," Anya said and Felix brought up her map that showed the host's location in Norfolk.

"The nearest address is 3500 Granby Street, Norfolk, Virginia," Felix said. Anya repeated the address for the Ray's computer.

"Destination confirmed. Ready for take-off," the autopilot said. Anya looked back at Tori, who was already buckled and practically bouncing in her seat.

"Are you sure you want to come?" Anya asked. "It could be dangerous."

"Anya, all of this is dangerous. My apartment got smoked out by the feds, and there's killer aliens everywhere. I'm not about to go take a run at one of these gnosiphage things, but if you think I'm missing out on flying in an extraterrestrial stealth plane, I don't know if we can be friends anymore. Plus, somebody has to back you up for the time being. Or at least pay for all the food you need to inhale now."

Anya smiled at her and said, "Thank you, Tori. Really. Okay, Shadow Ray, activate stealth and take-off!"

"Confirmed. Time to destination is approximately ten minutes," the autopilot said. Anya and Tori both let out a whoop as the vessel lifted into the air, rotated itself south, and then sped off toward the horizon.

13

Both Tori and Anya had tried to make sense of the many readouts and displays as the Ray flew itself toward Virginia. The readings were all in English, which helped, but not very much. From what Anya was able to gather, the hovering metal discs on either side of the chair controlled the direction and speed of the craft. All of the screens along the cockpit's control panel were touch activated, but so far, Anya had only figured out how to use the Ray's map: zooming in and out was almost exactly like doing the same thing on her phone.

The other screens displayed power reserves, system functionality, and other important data that Anya had absolutely no clue about. She tried asking the autopilot about what she saw, but it only informed her that it was not a licensed instructor and could only pilot, not teach. It wasn't an AI like Felix, so it just kept repeating the same stock phrases over and over.

Barely any time had passed at all when the autopilot informed them they had arrived at their destination.

3500 Granby Street in Norfolk, Virginia was not a house, which is what Anya had expected. Maybe an apartment complex, or a hotel, or an office building.

It was a zoo.

The Virginia Zoo spread across a large plot of green land beside the Lafayette River, its animal exhibits surrounded by lush trees and woven between by carefully manicured pathways. It looked like a perfectly nice place to spend an afternoon from the air as Anya hovered overhead, and would hopefully stay that way.

The large opaque circle on Anya's map that showed the approximate position of the gnosiphage alien somewhere within its miles-long circumference had not moved an inch during the flight from Brooklyn. The much smaller circle within the confines of the zoo hadn't moved much either, maybe a few yards in any direction.

Anya prayed the gnosiphage would stay where it was, and not turn the zoo into a bloodbath.

The Shadow Ray's autopilot landed inside the zoo's grounds at Anya's direction, nestled between some trees off one of the smaller pathways. The Ray was silent as it descended, and almost entirely invisible to the naked eye, if the optical camouflage was working properly. None of the people enjoying the sunny afternoon even glanced up as the stealth craft settled within a patch of grass that was just large enough to accommodate it.

"What're the odds this guy—or gal, or whoever—hasn't even turned their archive on yet?" Tori asked.

"I'd say pretty high if they haven't moved much this whole time," Anya replied as she rotated around in the cockpit seat and exited the Shadow Ray out the back alongside Tori. The Ray still had its stealth on, and at this close range Anya could easily make out its shape hovering above the grass. However, she also knew to look for it. It was much harder to see after she and Tori stepped out, closed the hatch behind them, and had gotten a few yards away. It resembled a kind of static heat shimmer floating above the ground; easily ignored unless somebody happened to walk right into it. Anya made careful note of where she had parked the vessel (especially since it did not emit a heat signature), and then strode out onto the pathway.

"I'm narrowing in on the signal," Felix said in Anya's ear. "It's about 1,500 feet in front of you."

"That would put the guy in the Asian animals area," Anya said as she plucked a folded map up from an information stand. The Asian animals portion of the zoo had been dubbed "Africa-Okavango Delta," which consisted of a few squat buildings gathered around an open grassy area with a man-made river inside of it. Giraffes, zebras, and antelope had grouped together along the river and wandered across the open fields. Smaller enclosed exhibits featured lions, a rhino, and more, which Felix directed Anya around as she went further into the park.

"If this guy's a nut, haul your ass back to the Ray. Get it somewhere far away and I'll catch up when I can," Anya whispered over her shoulder.

"All right. Any idea who it is yet?" Tori asked.

"Felix?"

"Ummm, still about 200-300 feet ahead," the AI replied.

"If I had to guess I'd say a zoo worker. Felix said earlier the signal was a few hundred yards wide when we were in Brooklyn, and I noticed some houses across the street. If they live close to work and don't have a social life, it'd explain why they didn't move much," Anya said and Tori nodded her agreement, but her eyebrows drew together and she chewed on her lip as she thought.

"What's up? You've got your thinking face on," Anya said. Tori blinked and looked up, then shook her head.

"Nothing. Just… wondering about some things."

"Anya! Fifty feet! Straight ahead!" Felix said and Anya waved Tori forward as she tried to look everywhere in front of her at once.

They had come to the Giant Pangolin exhibit, where a number of creatures that looked like huge armadillos covered in heavy scale armor and with gigantic foreclaws waddled around a sandy enclosure. They were all weirdly adorable, walking on their hind legs and using their long, wide tails for balance while they clutched their forelimbs against their chests in a shy, uncertain manner. Others had curled themselves up into defensive balls in the corners the exhibit. Another scratched at the ground with its massive claws and licked in the dust with a tongue longer than Anya's arm.

There was a single man inside the enclosure who the pangolins ignored. He looked to be in his mid-forties, with a black-and-gray beard and a fair amount of weight in his middle. He wore glasses and a khaki safari uniform with a name tag that identified him as "William." William pointed at children at the edge of the enclosure as they raised their hands to ask questions, which he seemed delighted to answer.

"That him?" Tori asked. "He looks like a nice enough guy."

"Anya, can you get closer?" Felix asked and Anya complied and got as close to the edge of the pangolin exhibit as she could. She got a lot of stares, some of them a bit hostile, and she realized that outside of New York, her attire and size were no longer so quickly dismissed as just one more oddity among millions.

"Hello," Anya said and smiled at a young girl who was staring up at her, mouth agape. The child's mother snatched her up and hurried away with her, but Anya only smiled and waved at the little girl as she stared at her over her mother's shoulder.

"That our guy? Or somebody in the crowd?" Anya whispered.

"No, not in the crowd, and not that guy," Felix said. "To his immediate left, your right."

Anya glanced down.

On the ground of the enclosure.

At a pangolin.

"You've gotta be fucking kidding," Anya said.

———

SHE AND TORI munched on some hot dogs they had gotten from a café just outside the African section of the park. They stood a short distance from the café, enjoying the sun and keeping an eye on the distant animal exhibits.

"And you're sure?" Anya asked. She was on her third hot dog while Tori was only halfway through her first. She was really going to have to find a way to pay her friend back for all the food.

"I'm sure," Felix replied. He had materialized in a bush behind both women so Tori could hear as well. "We were close enough that I could zero-in on the signal precisely. It was definitely the pangolin."

"Well, that would explain why they haven't activated their menu," Tori said.

"Yeah. Fuck. I was really hoping it would be somebody who could help. What the hell, Felix? I thought the Archives were for humans only?"

"So did I! I suspect the Engineers did too. But they had to reprogram them to integrate for an entirely different species on the fly and at short notice. Maybe they made some mistakes. Maybe it targeted the nearest mammal in a certain area, or had some other criteria."

"Will the Archive even work in something that isn't human?" Tori asked.

"It's sending out a signal, which means it has basic functionality. If it's fully activated it may make additional adjustments to the pangolin. There's data in here about fail-safe systems in case of what it calls 'improper or unintended integration,' but I don't have access to it since Anya's menu didn't need it and it got deleted once integration was successful."

"If we leave it alone, then no problem, right? It'll just keep scraping around in the dirt and eating ants," Tori said.

"Yeah, but there's an alien somewhere a few dozen miles away. Nothing to stop it from coming here and killing anybody who happens to be around when it arrives. Plus, Felix said all the Archive needs to activate is for somebody to touch it. If that pangolin goes to a vet or whatever, they could activate it by accident and who knows what could happen?" Anya asked.

"Yeah. Damn."

"By the way, Felix, I take it the gnosiphage still hasn't moved?"

"Nope! No movement!" Felix replied.

"At least there's that," Tori said.

"Fuck it. I've already committed a few felonies in the last couple days. Guess I'll add kidnapping animals from a zoo to the list," Anya said as she finished her hot dog.

"Whoa! Just like that? You don't wanna maybe talk to the zoo staff or anything first?"

"What's the point? They won't believe us at first, we'll have to show them my powers, they'll freak out, we'll waste time calming them down, blah blah blah," Anya waved her hand. "So instead, you go get the Shadow Ray prepped, I grab the pangolin and fly over to you."

"And you think that won't freak people out?"

"Oh, it will. It'll just be faster. Besides, I don't think that all of this stuff is gonna stay hidden for much longer. Right now people just think its terrorists or natural disasters or something, but that won't hold for long. I don't want to put people in danger, but I also don't want to tip-toe around this shit anymore."

Tori put her hands up. "All right. I'll go get the Ray."

"Thanks Tori. Hey, before I forget, has Riley tried to call you back on your phone yet?"

"I put it in airplane mode and shut it off once the feds broke into my apartment. I'm not sure if that'll stop them from tracking it, but I wanted to be sure. Plus, now that we got a supersonic alien stealth vehicle, seems like them catching me is less of an issue."

"Mm. After this I should probably call Riley. Shit."

"One thing at a time. Pangolin first," Tori said and then waved as she jogged off back toward the Shadow Ray while Anya returned to the pangolin enclosure.

William the caretaker had gone, and the big crowd had left, but there were still a number of visitors around taking pictures and cooing over the pangolins.

"Which one?" Anya asked as she studied the creatures. While she had no doubt she could pick them up, she was worried about how feasible it would be. The animals were big, about the size of a large dog, not including their long tails. She didn't want to hurt the poor thing, but she also didn't want to make more of a scene than she had to.

"About 20 feet in front of you, to your right," Felix said and Anya nodded as she saw it. The host pangolin was trundling around against the far wall of the enclosure, leaning up against it and sniffing at the air.

Anya reduced the gravity around herself and jumped effortlessly up and over the enclosure's wall. She went up a good twenty feet, overshooting it a bit, and came to a gentle landing near the pangolin.

A few people gasped behind her and one or two screamed in sudden surprise.

"What the hell?" one said.

"Did she just float?" another asked.

"Cooooool," a kid said and somebody else clapped. Anya resisted the urge to bow and approached the pangolin.

"Hey, little guy. Just c'mere for a sec," she said as she knelt down. The pangolin turned to face her, curious. When she reached for it, it drew away and then curled itself into a ball.

"That'll work," Anya said and then lightened the gravity around the pangolin to make it easier to hold. Even with her increased size and strength and the reduced gravity, it wasn't easy. The pangolin wasn't too heavy, the lessened gravity helped with that, but it was awkward as hell to hold the creature against her and make sure it didn't wiggle away. Its armored scales definitely would have jabbed her and likely shredded any normal clothes, but her enhanced cloak and regalia held up fine.

"Hey! Hey, what're you doing? Get out of there!" somebody in the crowd shouted. "Security!"

"Uh, nothing to see here, folks," Anya said, and then floated herself up and away over the treetops. More collective gasping and shouts followed her as she flew away, trying to keep her speed down to not unnerve the pangolin more than she already had. It was emitting some kind of raspy, coughing, huffing sound in alarm and started to squirm in her grip.

"I know buddy, I'm sorry about this," Anya winced. She set down among the trees where the Shadow Ray waited. There was a moment where Anya panicked, unable to see the vehicle, before her eyes adjusted to the shade beneath the trees and she made out its pseudo-invisible, shimmering form. The rear hatch opened and Tori emerged, waving her in.

"C'mon!" Tori said and slid into the cockpit seat as Anya hunched inside and set the pangolin down as gently as she could and closed the hatch. "Where to?"

"Anywhere with an empty field and at least 50 miles away from that alien!" Anya said. Tori fiddled with the map for a few moments, talking with the autopilot as she did, and then the Shadow Ray bolted toward its destination.

Anya left the pangolin on the floor where it was as she took a seat. The animal remained curled up in a ball with its claws clutching its tail. It huffed now and then, but did nothing else.

"Five minutes to, uh, some farm fields someplace in Delaware," Tori said.

"That'll do," Anya sighed.

"Why a field?"

"Because I need to find out for sure if this guy's Archive works or not. If it doesn't, then fine, I guess. Maybe we can spare an hour or two to drop him off in Africa with other pangolins, away from people. If the aliens want to kill him that much then, shit, I dunno. But if its system works just like mine, then I don't want this guy near people. If it decides to go on a rampage, or blow itself up, or whatever, best to be out in the middle of nowhere."

"Do you even know where to press? Or tap? Or whatever to turn it on?"

"Nope. Felix, can you tell where the Archive connected with him? God, please don't let it be on its asshole or something."

"I can try to narrow it down," Felix said as they appeared over the pangolin and began floating around it. After a few moments, he pointed at the creature's back end.

"Oh come on! Seriously?" Anya asked.

"Not its asshole, but probably on the outer rear leg somewhere. Not sure which leg though, I can't narrow it down any further," Felix said.

"I'll figure it out when we're not flying around at Mach speed."

It didn't take them much longer to reach a wide, empty series of fields somewhere in Delaware. The Archive's map showed them several miles northwest of Georgetown, but well enough away from any casual passersby or crowds.

"C'mon little guy," Anya said as she lightened gravity around the pangolin once more and carried him outside. The field they had landed in looked like it might be for corn. It was one of maybe a dozen on either side of a narrow, cracked road. Some abandoned buildings of concrete and corrugated metal dotted the edges of the fields, and beyond them were dense walls of leafless trees.

Tori came out of the Shadow Ray after Anya, but kept her distance from her and the pangolin. The pangolin huffed and squirmed when Anya set it down in the cold dirt of the field. It emitted something like a squeal when she tried to tug one of its rear legs down as gently as she could.

"Sorry! I'm sorry!" Anya winced and stepped back. The pangolin curled back up into a ball like before, clutching its tail with its fore-claws. If that was how it usually laid down, she could see why it hadn't touched its rear legs yet: its huge tail covered them almost entirely.

"You need help?" Tori asked.

"No, I just gotta do this. I'm sorry buddy but I promise I'm not trying to hurt you," Anya said and once more tried to force the pangolin's tail down without injuring it. The animal was stronger than it looked, but Anya's patience was rewarded: she finally managed to grab its hind leg and pull it away from its body as gently as she could.

Anya pressed on its legs in several random places, and was about to resign herself to having to try the other leg when the pangolin squealed again after she poked it near where its leg connected to its hip. Anya backed away, worried she had finally hurt it somehow.

The pangolin uncurled itself, its entire body stiffening, limbs and tail extending, and it shook as if it were having some kind of seizure.

"What the hell?" she muttered. "Felix?"

"I don't know! I don't have any data on this," the AI replied.

"Anya? Felix? Is everything okay?" Tori called out and took a step forward.

"Stay there! Something's going on—whoa!" Anya cried and leaped away from the pangolin. Its head grew several sizes, and then its body grew in proportion. It had been the size of a larger-than-average dog. Now it was almost double that.

"What the actual fuck?" Anya had ignited her fists without even realizing it. Her new fighting skill, Xhama Thul, kicked in. It told her the pangolin's underside was most vulnerable but also that it had poor balance without its tail. Getting behind it and twisting its tail to the side would topple the armored critter. Its belly would be exposed to her attacks and she could keep away from its claws.

Anya was still pretty preoccupied with wondering what the hell was going on with the pangolin, but couldn't help but nod in appreciation at what Xhama Thul was telling her. The pangolin's body relaxed, and its long tongue slipped out of its mouth and flopped into the dirt.

"Anya?" Tori asked, a slight tremble in her voice.

"It's okay, Tori," Anya replied as she extinguished the fire around her hands and stepped away. "I think it might be dead."

The pangolin blinked, pulled its tongue back into its mouth, and then looked up at Anya with bright, curious eyes. It cocked its elongated head to the side as it looked at her, then stumbled to its feet.

Anya went on guard again at once, fists clenched.

The pangolin looked at her, then down at itself. It looked at the sky, the dirt, its claws, then back at Anya. It took a step toward her and Anya tensed. It didn't appear hostile, it was full of openings to attack, and its shuffling steps were slow and awkward.

The animal stood in front of Anya and stared up at her.

It spread its arms.

And it hugged her.

"What the fuck?" Anya whispered.

Then the pangolin spoke.

"You save me. Thank thank. Have ant?"

14

nya had to cling to the pangolin so she didn't fall back on her ass. The animal had spoken to her. In English. As he looked up at Anya with obvious adoration in his eyes, his mouth opened a little in what might have been an attempt at a smile.

"Uh," Anya said. "Yeah. Hi."

"Yeah, hi," the pangolin repeated. "Thank thank."

"Ooookkaaaaay. This is not what I was expecting."

"Make big think, go away small land. Thank thank."

"Awww!" Felix said.

"That's so adorable!" Tori said and clutched her hands together beneath her chin. "He likes you!"

"Thank God for that I guess," Anya said. She reached down and gently touched the top of the pangolin's armored head. It stretched up and pressed its head into her palm. "You're not gonna go crazy or anything?"

"Crazy or anything?" the pangolin repeated. "Crazy. Crazy."

"Crazy bad," Anya said. The pangolin stepped away from her, its eyes wide, then curled up into a ball again.

"Bad!" it cried.

"No no! Not you or, uh, shit. Felix, how can I get this thing to have its AI to come out?"

"Once primary activation has occurred, the only person who can activate or interact with the Archive is the initial host," Felix said.

"Of course. Shit. Okay, uh, pangolin? Hello? Friend?" Anya asked and squatted down beside the pangolin. He lowered his tail just enough to peer at her.

"Friend?" he asked.

"Yes. Friend. Can you touch here?" Anya asked and pointed to where she had first activated the menu on the animal.

"Touch?"

"Yeah, buddy. Touch. Like this," Anya said and poked herself.

"Touch. Touch," the pangolin muttered as he unrolled, stood, and cocked his head to the side as he watched Anya. Then he extended his long tongue and licked her hand.

"No, that's lick."

"Lick."

"No, touch," Anya said and poked herself again. The pangolin blinked and looked at its long claws. It poked itself and Anya and Tori and Felix cheered. The pangolin, not understanding but quite happy they were happy, also cheered and began poking itself all over.

Eventually, it found its Archive activation spot, and the Archive's main menu screen appeared in the air. It glowed a bright, cheery yellow, and appeared to have the same basic layout, except none of it was in English. It was in some sort of crude pictograms that squiggled and moved and rolled. The pangolin cocked its head to the other side as it studied the archive screen.

Thankfully, the glowing button in the corner that indicated "HELP," was in the same position as it had been for Anya. She pointed at it and smiled at the pangolin.

"Touch here," Anya said.

"Touch heeeeeere," the pangolin said and drew out the word, as if trying out how it felt on his enormous tongue. He reached out and poked the glowing "HELP," button with a claw, and then squealed in horror as the archive AI appeared before him.

Unlike Felix or Bobo, this AI did not look like a human baby, it resembled a chubby, infant pangolin, except its head was a buttercup flower and glowed a sunshiny yellow. The AI saw Anya, squealed, and floated behind the pangolin.

"Great, they're both chickens," Anya grumbled.

"I can't really blame them. I seem to recall you were pretty freaked out by all this too," Tori said as she stood next to Anya and looked down at the cowering pangolin and his AI.

"Hey, AI guy. I need you to help us with this situation we got here," Anya said and waved a hand at the AI. "Kind of an end-of-the-world type thing going on."

"The AI probably won't understand you much better than the pangolin," Felix said. Anya recalled how very literal and not-forth-coming Felix had been the first day she'd had them. They had learned lightning fast, and mostly understood her metaphors and idioms now, but it had still taken them some time.

"The AI has the same language barriers as the host," Felix continued. "For example, you don't speak Norwegian, so neither can I. The AI is at the same English level as the Pangolin."

"How'd he even know to pick English though?" Anya asked. "And why the hell did he get so much bigger?"

"Prior to integration, the Archives scan the planet they land on and the area of the host they merge with so the helper AI can communicate effectively, but not beyond the bounds of what the host is capable of. It picked up on all the English around the zoo but not whatever pangolins use to communicate, so it had to compensate by giving him a base level of English. If I had to guess, I'd say that's what the fail-safe system does: gets a host up to basic understanding and capability. As for why he's bigger, I guess it also had to increase his brain size, which meant making the skull bigger, which meant growing the rest of the body to support it."

"As good a guess as any," Anya said. The pangolin uncurled from its ball just enough to look at Anya with one eye. She smiled and waved at it. The yellow pangolin AI waved as well. "Does the AI still know what to do?"

"I don't know. This is new territory for me, and the Archive too, I'd guess," Felix said.

Anya pointed at the menu screen, then the AI.

"You, help him talk, yes? Talk good?" she asked.

"Me talk good, ook ook," Tori said in a gruff, caveman voice.

"You wanna try this? Try communicating with a newly sapient animal and his helper AI?" Anya asked and raised an eyebrow.

"You're doing great. Like Jane Goodall but for pangolins," Tori laughed.

To Anya's surprise, the AI floated next to the pangolin's ear and began whispering and pointing at the screen. Whatever it was saying, the pangolin seemed to understand, and it poked at its menu with its claw several times. The menu blinked, and the pangolin tipped over again with all the grace of a felled tree.

Anya realized she was seeing the pangolin upgrade itself. This was what she probably looked like when the pain hit her.

The pangolin relaxed after a second, and his screen reappeared.

It was in English, this time.

PANGOLIN: LEVEL 11 PANGOLIN
Statistics

- Awareness-4
- Dexterity-2
- Fortitude-5
- Intelligence-2
- Strength-2
- Willpower-3

Skills

- English-3

"Can you understand better now?" Anya asked the pangolin.

"Understand you. Am… confused? Scary. Big think, happens fast-fast. Have new…thoughts. Speak is bad. Sorry?" he replied.

"No, little guy, you don't need to be sorry," Anya said. He wasn't exactly little, but his voice was so soft, almost childlike. "It was an easy life, I bet. Just dig around and eat ants. I'm sorry for making things so complicated for you.

"Complicated," the pangolin repeated, then looked up at Anya and smiled. "Ants!"

He turned away from Anya, Tori, and Felix, and began to dig in the dirt of the field. His tongue flicked out as it dug, darting out to the ground and then zipping back up again. The pangolin hadn't bothered to close his menu, and Anya focused on his level.

"He's 11 years old?" Anya asked.

"I suppose so. Normally the Archive is absolutely prohibited from entering any creature that would qualify as a child for the host race. However, while the pangolin is only the age of a human child, it may be at physical maturity for its species," Felix said.

"I guess it's good to know that these Engineer guys aren't targeting kids," Tori said.

"Yeah, they're not evil, just really fucking incompetent," Anya rolled her eyes.

"Please tell me we're keeping him," Tori said and looked up at Anya, her eyes sparkling.

"He's not a pet!"

"No, but he's so cute. And lonely. And he seems to like you."

"I wasn't planning on just ditching him in the field but... shit! Where would I even keep him? He's gotta be, what? 200 pounds now? At least? How many ants you got lying around your apartment?"

"If your argument for not keeping that sweet little cinnamon roll over there is because he might need a lot of food and he's very big, you oughta check out a mirror and my food bill for the last few days," Tori said with a barely-concealed smirk and a poke to Anya's stomach.

"Fine, we'll keep him. But we really need to get our food situation sorted. I'm already hungry again."

"You're gonna replace all that muscle with fat if you keep eating junk like you've been doing."

"Actually, between Anya's fortitude statistic, her regeneration skill, and her Sun's Heart, she pretty much burns everything up. Her metabolism is through the roof," Felix said.

"Pizza and ice cream every day, here I come," Anya said with a grin.

"God, you suck," Tori sulked.

"Uh, Anya?" Felix said.

"Yeah?" she replied, not liking the slight quaver that had entered the AI's voice.

"All of the gnosiphages have disappeared."

"What? Like, they all died?"

"No, I don't think so. When the alien died in the park last night, its signal flared and then faded. All the aliens on the map just kinda... blinked out. Some of them may have been killed by hosts, but there were a lot of aliens miles away from anybody, like the one in Virginia, and they just vanished."

"Shit," Anya said.

"Yeah. Bad enough when we had a basic idea where they were," Tori said.

"Scary?" the pangolin asked. "Bad?"

"It'll be all right little guy," Anya said. "It's just one more reason to find other hosts and connect up, stick together, watch our backs. And stay away from crowded places. Felix, where are the next closest hosts?"

"The area in and around Chicago," the AI said and Anya grimaced.

"So much for staying away from crowded places," Tori sighed.

"Yeah. Tori, can I borrow your phone? I should call Riley and let him know what's up," Anya said.

"So you're gonna give the feds another shot?" she asked and Anya nodded.

"It sucks, but yes. I'm still not gonna bow down to them or anything, but if I can help, I will. I just really want to be with other human hosts when I do it, especially now. Uh, no offense, little guy," Anya said and smiled at the pangolin.

"Off fence? Fence off?" he asked and cocked his head to one side and then the other, the tiny nubs of his ears on the sides of his head flicked forward and then back as he considered the words.

"We'll work on it," Anya said as Tori handed her the phone and she checked the screen. "Oh yeah. Riley has definitely been calling. Thirty-eight missed calls."

Anya tapped the agent's number and barely had to wait for the first ring before the call was picked up.

"Hello? Anya?" Riley asked.

"Agent Riley."

"Look, I've spoken with my boss and that bullshit at the diner and with your friend's place was not our call. My now former gung-ho manager thought he'd send the troops charging in like the fucking cavalry without clearing it. He's currently on administrative leave. We've spoken with the President himself and he's agreed to pull back for now," Riley said in a rush.

"Good. I'm glad. Because it was really fucking stupid."

"No shit. If you wanna look at filing an official complaint with the Bureau, we can facilitate that," Riley said and Anya snorted.

"Tempting but I think we have bigger problems. Look, my little AI friend just informed me that all those alien gnosiphage signals disappeared. Felix, can you bring up the map?"

Felix nodded and brought up the map, and Anya switched over to a video call with Riley. The agent had propped his phone up on a table in some kind of conference room with a number of very important, older people in expensive suits. A spike of panic hit Anya as she recognized some of those people from the news: two senators, the Secretary of Defense, and the Speaker of the House. There was a rather severe looking woman in her sixties sitting at the head of the table, her gray hair pulled back in a knot so tight it made her scalp look as if it were made of brushed metal. Her skin was a dark brown, and the few wrinkles she did have looked less like sagging skin and more like grooves carved in ironwood. Glasses perched on the end of a dainty nose, and her eyes stared, unblinking, at the camera on Riley's end.

Anya didn't know the woman or the other people at the table by sight, but assumed they were at least as important. She took a breath and flipped the camera phone around to show the map.

"Felix, rewind the map to a few minutes ago, right before you lost the signals," Anya said and Felix complied. "This is the last general location we had of the aliens. We don't think they died, just that their signals are gone."

"Show us the AI," the black woman at the head of the table said. Her voice was stern, crisp. It was a voice that was used to being listened to, and followed.

"Who are you?" Anya asked.

"This is the Director of the FBI, Suzanne MacDougal," Riley said. "We'd all like to see the little orange fella, if you wouldn't mind, Anya."

She grunted but nodded.

"Say hello Felix," Anya said as she panned the camera over to the AI. They waved.

"Hello!"

"What in God's name is that?" one of the other people at the table asked. The pangolin had waddled into the frame and was digging in the dirt.

"That is a giant ground pangolin from Africa. Well, he's technically from the Virginia Zoo. We sort of stole him," Anya said.

"You did what?" another person asked. That one Anya recognized as one of the senators from New York.

"The pangolin also received the same sort of thing that I did. Leaving him in the zoo would have been dangerous, so we took him with us," Anya explained. "Also he can talk now. Say hello, little buddy."

The pangolin looked up from where it was licking the dirt.

"Hello? Hello!" he said and stood up high on his hind legs.

"Good lord," the Senator said.

"Is that some kind of vehicle in the back?" MacDougal asked.

"Yeah. We needed to get around so we bought an alien stealth plane off the store the Archive provided," Anya said. She decided it was best to be upfront about everything. If she wanted the feds to be straight with her, she didn't want to be the one to come off as a liar or a sneak.

The conference room filled with muttering behind hands as the men and women around the table leaned in toward each other. Anya could only imagine some of them practically wetting themselves at the idea of an extraterrestrial stealth craft.

"Can you understand why the government might be… uncomfortable with the sort of technology and power you've displayed being in the hands of a civilian?" MacDougal asked.

"I can. Can you understand why I would be… uncomfortable coming in to work with people who pointed guns in my face a couple hours ago?"

"The people responsible have been reprimanded," MacDougal said.

"Which is why we're talking now," Anya replied. Off-camera, Tori winced a little and put her hands up in a silent gesture to take it easy. Anya rolled her eyes and added, "Look, I get it. This is all very strange and unsettling, to put it lightly. But if you—"

"Anya!" Felix said and waved his tiny arms at her as he floated in front of the map which zoomed in on Anya's current location, as well as the alien signal that had appeared moving toward them at speed.

It was almost on top of her.

"Oh shit," Anya said.

"What is it? What's going on?" Riley asked.

"Bad alien!" Anya snapped. Tori bolted into the Shadow Ray and Anya snatched the pangolin up and shoved it inside even as it squealed.

"Behind you!" Felix said just as Anya heard a loud whistling sound. She glanced behind her as a dark shape fell out of the sky and landed a hundred feet away from her in the field.

It was tall, taller than her, and covered in gleaming black scales and plates of organic black armor. It had the basic shape of an enormous snake, a cobra, but the hood at its top reminded Anya more of something an ancient pharaoh might have. Its face was more human than serpentine, with skeletal sharpness. The sides of its face extended out and curved around into sharp horns, and its three narrow eyes—two where they would normally be and a third in its forehead—glowed a cold, ethereal blue. More of the blue light spilled from gaps between its armor and scales and from deep within a mouth lined with narrow fangs.

Four arms, each of them ending in clawed hands that grasped at the air, extended from its upper torso, while its serpentine lower-half lashed in the dirt of the field. It pointed one of its long, brutal claws at Anya.

And it spoke.

"Thief," it said in a deep, growling voice. Anya's eyes widened.

The puppet in Brooklyn had talked, but it had been nonsense. Just the babbling of a broken toy, or a machine with a set number of catch-phrases. When this thing spoke, Anya felt the intent behind the single word.

"Jesus," somebody on the phone whispered. Anya had been pointing the phone at the alien without realizing it. Her shock at seeing and hearing the alien broke, and she chucked the phone into the Shadow Ray and slammed the door shut.

"Get out of here!" she yelled at Tori, and then ran away from the stealth craft. "Hey! Asshole!"

The Shadow Ray lifted into the air and began to take off. The alien glanced at her with its blue eyes, then lunged for the Ray.

"Nope!" Anya shouted and dove for the creature as it flew upward. She reached for it with a pull of intense gravity. Invisible claws of force extended from her hands, surrounded the snake, and yanked hard on its tail. The pharaonic cobra plunged back to the ground with a snarl and whirled to face Anya as she landed a short distance away from it. The Ray lifted above the distant treeline, and shot off.

The gnosiphage glared at Anya, all three of its glowing eyes wide with malice and obvious killing intent. She had its full attention.

"Well... fuck," Anya said, and raised her fists.

15

ombat cognition fed Anya information in a rush even as she ignited her fists and dropped into a low, defensive stance.

1) This was likely the alien that had been a few dozen miles away from the Virginia Zoo.

2) It had caught up to them very quickly, which meant it was somewhere in the neighborhood of being as fast as the Shadow Ray.

3) That meant running from it would be difficult. Plus if she were in the Shadow Ray, she would be putting Tori and the pangolin in danger. If it wasn't the alien near the zoo, then it meant it had come from even further away and was even faster than the stealth craft and running wasn't an option at all.

Xhama Thul was telling her to look for weak spaces between its plates of armor, to avoid the powerful-looking tail, and to try to use its arms as fulcrums and hyper-extend them or break them if possible, then go for the eyes or throat via the mouth.

It was also mingling with her dominions, coming up with combinations of gravity and fire and grappling techniques in a flood of potential attacks that almost overwhelmed Anya.

And all of it in a matter of rapid heartbeats.

Anya sprang forward, her gravity skill keeping her light on her feet and ready to dart back in a second. The serpentine alien hissed and darted to the side, all four of its arms up. It swiped at her and she dodged its claws enough to save her throat from getting slashed, but not enough to avoid her bicep getting a cut.

She backed away and glanced down as the cut sealed itself almost at once. The alien noticed this too and narrowed its eyes at her.

Then, it went eerily still, and its arms and tail stiffened for an instant.

Anya had a moment of deja vu, then realized why.

The pangolin had looked the same way when it had activated its menu and gotten its skill with English.

The alien had just updated itself.

The gnosiphage's throat bulged, and then it opened its mouth and vomited something viscous and green at Anya in a wide spray. She dodged again, but the spray had rocketed out of the alien's throat and a few strands of the gunk landed on Anya's thigh. There was a hiss, and she cried out as the acidic, foul-smelling goop ate the enchanted fabric of the pants and touched Anya's flesh.

She screamed in surprise and pain as the liquid ate at her skin, exposing raw flesh and muscle beneath. Regeneration tried to heal it, but the acid stuck to her like rubber cement, and it kept eating, forcing her regeneration to work overtime until the gunk had been neutralized.

Anya stared at the alien in dawning horror.

It had seen her regenerate and updated itself to counter her skill.

That's why it was probably so fast, too. It had sensed her flying away in the Shadow Ray and probably updated itself to match her speed.

"You motherfucker," Anya whispered.

She had to kill it, fast.

Anya feinted to one side, and the alien took the bait. It vomited another spray of acid but Anya reversed direction and charged at it from the other side. She had expended too much energy on missed and inefficient attacks during her fight with the puppet alien. She would get in close, stay close, and out of the way of the serpent's acidic mouth.

The gnosiphage hissed and tried to dart back, but Anya slammed it down again with a surge of gravity ten times stronger than Earth's standard. It slammed into the dirt and a sudden crater appeared around it from the swell of g-force. She focused the gravity on the creature's hands and tail, keeping them pinned just long enough to slam her gravity-weighted fist into its eye and ignite a burst of heat that flared white-hot. The alien screamed and writhed beneath the attack and the crushing pressure around it.

It rolled over, its throat swelling, and Anya grabbed a bottle of ignition gel from her belt, and threw it into its mouth as she lit it. It exploded and covered the serpent's maw and the front of its chest with sticky, licking flames. The alien vomited out fire and acid as Anya leaped away and slid to a stop.

The alien puked fire and gunk onto the dirt even as it lashed wildly at her with its tail. She rolled and flew, always keeping just out of its reach. Whenever she would try to fly farther away, it rushed her even as it continued spewing out flaming bits of gel and what Anya hoped were its internal organs, or at least whatever it was using to spit acid.

It raised its claws again and Anya saw that they were now coated with a familiar green-tinted fluid, and she cried out as the claws swiped at her. She raised her forearms up just in time to save her face and chest, but was knocked back end-over-end across the field.

The armored forearm guards of her regalia took the worst of the hit, their enchanted metal hissing from the acidic claws, but both of Anya's arm bones had been shattered. The hit had radiated up to her shoulders and all the way through her. The puppet alien had hit like a truck, but this thing hit like a goddamn tank.

Anya's arms hung at her sides, useless for the moment.

It had changed where the acid came out of its body when she'd wounded its throat.

"This is bad," Anya said. Her breathing had become heavier, but she wasn't tired just yet. Her arms popped and cracked as they repaired themselves and she grunted as she rolled her shoulders.

She grabbed her second, and last bottle of gel from her belt and readied it in her hand.

The alien hacked up the last of the flaming gel, then stiffened again.

Its scales became shinier, almost glassy looking. Anya didn't know what that meant, but she was sure it wasn't anything good. She leaped into the air, trying to get behind the alien, and focused an immense amount of heat and gravity around her extended foot.

The alien slithered to the side but Anya yanked it back again, and smashed another bottle against its side.

The gel slid off the shiny new carapace, like rainwater off wax.

"Oh shit," Anya said, and the serpent's tail hit her full in the side. She had a split second to reduce the force of the impact with a gravitational buffer, but the blow still sent her soaring through the air and across the field. The air itself boomed from the force of the impact, a shock wave emitting from the point where it had struck her, and Anya coughed up blood as the whole side of her body radiated pain.

She skidded across the field, tumbling and rolling at a speed that by itself would have killed a normal human, but barely registered with her. Most of her attention was on the pain in her side and keeping track of the pharaonic cobra. It was already slithering after her, coming at her like an armored bullet train from Hell.

Anya halted her tumbling by slamming herself down into the ground, then reducing the gravity around the gnosiphage. Its forward momentum sent it floating up and away, well past Anya, and high into the sky. It writhed helplessly in the air, and Anya thought about sending it further away, but the further it got from her, the harder it was to exert any sort of control over its personal gravity.

Anya clutched her fist together and sent the cobra slamming down into the Earth, hard and fast enough to send up a towering pillar of dirt and dust. She clutched at her side as it healed, wincing as ribs snapped back together, and organs put themselves back in their proper place.

"Anya, this thing is different," Felix said beside her.

"Yeah, no shit," she replied.

"No, I mean it has a different type of signal than the other aliens. I couldn't tell earlier because we were so far away, but now I can tell that it's not the same. The one last night was just emitting a single stream of data. This one's emitting something like a whole network," Felix said.

"So it's a bunch of aliens crammed into one?"

"Maybe? I'm trying to decode what it's putting out, but it's more complex than the puppet last night. There's something else too."

"Spit it out."

"I can't access the Archive."

"What the hell does that mean?"

"You have access to all the skills you've already taken, but I can't see anything in the Archive itself which means no updating skills and no buying anything from the RAC store."

"Uh oh," Anya said. She only had one of the star's breath crystals and she was just starting to get winded. If the fight dragged on too long, she'd be out of luck.

"Well, thanks for the update, I guess. One more reason to put this fucker down ASAP," Anya said and spat. The gnosiphage emerged from the dust cloud and eyed her from across the field. Anya spread her arms wide.

"Right here!" she said. The alien kept its distance.

It stiffened again.

"God dammit," Anya said. "Now wh—"

Black spikes emerged from the alien's back and shot into the air, at least three or four dozen. The tips of them glistened with green fluid, and all of them arched up, and then shot straight at Anya.

"Shit!" she said, and created a kind of gravitational repulsion field around her. Most of the spikes went zipping away, pushed or pulled by the opposing gravitational force, but a few still got through. Anya dodged most of these, but a few still managed to scratch her and eat at her skin.

One of them punctured her shoulder and she hollered as it injected more acid into her. Anya yanked the spike out and doubled over as her veins were devoured by the chemical burn. She vomited from the agony of it, her eyes tearing up.

Her vision was blurry, but she just saw a dark shape from the corner of her eye and flipped over backwards as the tail swept under her. The tail glistened with more spikes, and Anya forced herself to ignore the pain long enough to turn her flip into a spinning kick, her foot once more carrying a well of gravity and burning hotter than the sun.

She connected with the snake's hissing mouth, and even through the cloud of pain from the acid still chewing her insides, Anya grinned savagely as she felt its jaw, and the whole side of its face crack and sizzle from the burning impact.

It cried out and writhed away from her again, clutching at its face.

"Haven't countered the heat yet, have you, asshole?" Anya asked. "Gotta say I'm curious as to why."

"Thiiiieeeef," it hissed at her again from its ruined jaw. "Ouuur-rrrssssssss."

"Fuck you."

Anya propelled herself forward even as the snake tried to put more distance between them. She wasn't about to let it get away and launch more of those spines at her. She could see it growing more of them from its back, but it wasn't firing them yet.

Anya ducked under a pair of claws, then seized the wrists of them both in one hand, then brought her knee up behind the elbows even as she yanked the wrist backward with all of her strength and intensified gravity.

The snake roared as she broke, then snapped two of its arms off at the elbows, then shoved them both—claws first—into its gaping mouth. It twisted around and tried to get her with its tail again, but she shoved it away hard, then sprang forward and got under the side that now lacked arms. She forced her fingers under one of its larger armored plates and pulled.

Blue light spilled out of the gap, and Anya shoved her fist inside and ignited it.

Flames spewed from the alien's side, out from between other gaps, and its mouth.

More! More fire, little one! A now-familiar deep voice echoed inside Anya's ear, or maybe her mind. Anya didn't question it. She laughed as her Sun's Heart swelled and she lit up the whole field like a miniature nova.

A column of fire and light ten stories high shot up from the center of the field, Anya and the serpentine gnosiphage at its center. Anya could no longer see the alien through the flames, and so she didn't see one of those black spines emerge from its chest, and fire into her own.

The pillar of flame and light vanished at once, and Anya fell away.

Anya looked down as she took a stumbling step backward.

The spike had pierced her chest just left of center, through both her regular and Sun's Heart.

"Ugh," Anya said and fell to one knee. The gnosiphage screamed and thrashed in a mad vortex of tail and limbs as smoke billowed out of it. Its carapace glowed from the residual heat that still clung to it and its efforts to cool itself with the chilly dirt of the field were having little effect. It fired more spikes, but without any aim or direction, just lashing out at anything around it.

Anya was cold. The only burn came from the deadly acid pumping through her. She had enough presence of mind to yank the spike out of her chest and throw it away, and keep some of the other errant spikes away from her by pushing them away with her repulsion field, but she was fading. Her vision darkened at the edges as she fumbled in her pouch for the star's breath crystal.

She tried to pull heat from it, but even that ability was weakened. Her Sun's Heart was too damaged to work properly. Regeneration struggled to repair the damage, as the glowing heart was also its primary source of energy, and the acid was working through her faster than it could heal.

Anya scrabbled for the spare healing potion Tori had advised her to buy. Her vision darkened and her fingers became clumsy as the acid worked itself through her. She fumbled her way into the fireproof pouch on her belt and withdrew the small vial of red fluid.

"Pour it directly onto your wound!" Felix said and pointed at Anya's chest. She tore the stopper off the vial with her teeth, and dumped its contents over the acidic puncture above her hearts. She arched her back and screamed as the potion went to work. It burned worse than the acid, but only for a moment.

Anya's hearts both pumped, then surged like living engines as they began to heal. It was the inverse of the acid: the more her hearts healed, the faster they pumped clean blood through her, the faster her regeneration sped up.

She gripped the star's breath crystal in her hand and soaked up every last ounce of heat within it. Her Sun's Heart drank it greedily, replenishing her, boosting her natural and supernatural healing abilities and bringing her back up to her feet.

She had survived.

Barely.

But now she was out of potions, star's breath, and her RAC store was locked off.

The alien still writhed on the ground, but its armor had cooled significantly. It had melted in places, sloughed off its body in others. One of the horns on the side of its face had been broken off, and a huge section of its tail was just gone.

Anya could barely stand—even with most of her energy restored her muscles still threatened to give out at any moment—and the alien was coming around. It sensed her moving, and roared at her from its broken mouth. It shook itself and reared up across from her.

It looked worse than she felt: minus half its arms, most of its mouth, and large portions of its upper and lower torso. But it also had murder in its glowing teal eyes, all three of which were locked onto Anya.

She braced herself for whatever it was about to throw at her.

Something whooshed behind Anya and then a black streak sped past her and slammed into the alien.

The Shadow Ray.

The stealth aircraft rammed the alien head-on with a deafening boom of impact and sent it flying across the field. The craft itself spun to the side and then came to an abrupt halt a few yards above the field before landing and the back hatch swung open.

"Tori! No!" Anya cried, then stopped when half a dozen men in combat fatigues carrying rifles jumped out. They glanced at Anya and one of them, a short man with dark skin and a gleaming bald head, looked aside at where the alien was picking itself up.

"There! Fire!" the man shouted.

The men in fatigues opened fire. One of them had some kind of rocket launcher and stood away from the others as he took aim and fired the weapon. Their bullets and the single rocket all slammed into the alien and pushed it back. Most of the bullets pinged off the serpent's armor plates with bright flashes of sparks, but many of them found their way into the large gaps Anya had created. The rocket actually tore one of the holes in its side open further and blew its already exposed innards apart even more.

The alien roared, then curled what remained of its tail beneath it, launched itself into the air, and away. In seconds it was just a black dot in the sky heading out to the Atlantic, and then it was gone.

"Anya!" Tori yelled from the Shadow Ray as she emerged and ran toward her.

"You fucking idiot," Anya said and hugged her friend. "The fuck were you thinking?"

"That you were gonna die!" Tori said, on the verge of tears, and punched her arm. She winced and shook her hand and Anya chuckled, then wheezed.

"Go check where it took off," the bald man told one of the other men in fatigues as he approached Anya. "You, contact the Colonel and tell him what direction that thing flew off in. They should have the drones ready by now."

"Who are these guys?" Anya asked as she leaned against Tori.

"Air Force. I told Riley what was happening and that lady, MacDougal, she said there was an Air Force base nearby and had somebody else call them and tell them you needed back-up. It took us maybe two minutes to get there and a little while to get some guys and come back. Holy shit, what happened to you?"

"Acid," Anya coughed. She was getting better by the second, but her limbs were heavy, and every muscle ached and protested her movements.

"Sergeant Dransfield, USAF," the man said. He was sturdy looking, somewhere in his mid-forties. "I take it you're Anya?"

"Yeah. Thanks," she said.

"Not entirely sure what's going on, but you're supposed to come back to base with me."

Anya started to protest when Tori put her hand on her shoulder and whispered so only she could hear. "Anya, you can barely stand. Just give these guys a few minutes. We can take off later if we have to."

"Yeah. All right," Anya said and managed to walk herself into the Shadow Ray. Tori took the pilot's seat and Anya settled herself into the passenger seat just behind her. The other airmen piled in, just managing to fit inside. Anya blinked as Tori took off and she looked around the cabin.

"Where's the pangolin?" Anya asked.

"Had to leave him at the base. He's fine. I told them if anybody hurt him or did anything weird to him, you'd be upset," Tori said.

"The Colonel is letting him wander around a secluded area of the field with an armed escort," Dransfield said. Anya nodded as she leaned back into the chair.

"Is the Ray all right? How'd you get it to crash into the alien?" Anya asked.

"It has some kind of temporary kinetic shielding in case of impact. I had to tell the autopilot to override safety collision features and had it hit that snake thing. The stealth function is a bit damaged, and the kinetic shields used up almost all of the battery. We've got enough to get to the base and then it's going to need to recharge. And no stealth until we can buy a repair from your menu—if that's a thing—or we find some kind of alien mechanic."

"Gotcha. How long to the base?"

"Two minutes, tops."

Anya sighed and closed her eyes.

"Hey Mister Sergeant," Anya said, "when we get to your base, can you show me where the mess hall is?"

"If the Colonel approves it," he said. Anya grunted, then allowed herself an all too brief respite while the Shadow Ray sped over Delaware.

16

D over Air Force Base was pretty much what Anya expected: a lot of utilitarian buildings and runways, the former mostly crammed to one side to make room for the latter. A lot of big planes, for heavy cargo most likely, were all parked near a series of curved hangars, with a couple taxiing onto the nearest runway for take-off. Smaller craft, including a few fighter jets and some helicopters, were positioned around the base, all organized together in neat rows.

Tori had landed the Shadow Ray where Sergeant Dransfield instructed: just to the side of one of the larger hangars, where some temporary walls of canvas and metal pipes had been erected to conceal the Ray from sight. When they exited, Anya was relieved to see the pangolin waiting for her alongside an elderly gentleman in combat fatigues similar to Dransfield and the airmen. While Anya didn't know much about military ranks and what insignia meant what, she figured the eagle on the old man's shoulder straps was pretty important. The name patch on his chest identified him as Perkins.

"Colonel Perkins," Dransfield said and saluted. "Our guest was wondering if she could have access to the mess hall."

"I think that can be arranged. Get your men sorted, and report to my office in twenty," the Colonel said, and Dransfield and the airmen hurried away.

"Hello!" the pangolin said and waddled toward Anya and Tori.

"Hey, little guy," Anya said and patted his head as he hugged her leg. She was going to have to think of a name for him.

"Welcome to Dover Air Force Base, miss," Perkins said and then waved a hand towards the base. "Mess hall's this way. Hope you don't mind having a chat while you eat."

"I think I can manage that," Anya said as she followed the Colonel away from the Shadow Ray. She was loath to leave it behind, but Tori had secured it before they left, and the autopilot had confirmed it was "immobile." She knew nobody but either of them could fly the thing, but thought they could try towing it.

If that happened, she would deal with it.

She glanced to the side as they crossed the tarmac between hangars and a group of airmen walked along with them, but at a distance. Each one had a rifle, but they didn't appear too jumpy, just curious. One of them was actually smiling at the pangolin.

"You need a medic or anything?" the Colonel asked as he looked Anya over. Anya glanced down at herself and winced. While she was still entirely clothed, there was a sizable tear in one of her pant legs, and the center of her top had a melted hole in it. She was also covered in her own blood and flecks of alien gore. She made sure her Mantle of the Gale covered most of her, which it did, and shook her head at Perkins.

"No, I'm doing better. Just food. A lot of it."

"We have that. Airmen are a hungry bunch," he said and smiled. It was a little tight, a little forced, but Anya had to give the man credit: he seemed pretty calm for having just sent a group of men to shoot at an alien, having a UFO in his base, and leading a talking pangolin to the dining area.

"Thank you," Anya said. "For sending your men, I mean."

"It was an order from General Atkins, come down from President Hanover."

Anya just nodded. She didn't know who Atkins was, apart from a General in the Air Force, but she sure as hell knew about Hanover. She hadn't voted for him in the last election, but that was because she had been doing a double shift. Honestly neither candidate had seemed all that great, so she didn't really care, but still.

The President.

"I don't know everything that's going on, but I generally do not send my airmen out in foreign aircraft at a moment's notice to engage with an enemy we don't know anything about. Especially not on such short notice. But chain-of-command says jump, I don't even ask how high. I get to jumping."

"Well, I appreciate it," Anya said as they entered a large building that eventually opened up into a cafeteria. It was deserted save for the many round tables and chairs in neat rows. The kitchens against the back wall behind a serving counter were empty as well, but there were trays of food available. Most of their armed escort remained outside, but four of the airmen followed them in and stationed themselves at the primary exits of the cafeteria.

Perkins sat at one of the tables and waved at the serving counter.

"Help yourself. I'll be here when you're ready," he said, and then motioned at one of the airmen who ran over, whispered something to him, snapped to attention, then ran off.

Anya helped herself to several trays worth of food: foot-long roast beef sandwiches, meatloaf, pizza, mashed potatoes, and, after some consideration, a giant metal bowl full of fresh fruit. She had to make several trips back and forth, and by the time she was done, most of the table was covered in trays of food, along with bottles of coke and water.

"You certainly have an appetite," Perkins said and arched a gray eyebrow. Tori had taken half of one of the roast beef sandwiches and a salad for herself. The pangolin stood at the end of the table, his nose twitching at the food curiously.

"Side effect of magic powers," Anya said as she began to devour her meal. Perkins seemed content to let her eat in peace until the airman from before returned carrying a laptop computer, which he handed to the colonel. He thanked the young man, who resumed his post by the door, and opened the laptop.

Anya almost choked on her food when she saw the same conference room from the earlier call with Riley. Riley was there, along with MacDougal and a few others from before. There was another window on the screen that also showed the Oval Office and President Hanover.

"Good afternoon, Mr. President," Perkins said.

"Colonel," Hanover said and nodded. "This must be Miss Anya. And an... armadillo?"

"Pangolin," Anya said and thumped her chest as she swallowed.

"Hello! Pangolin, here. Me, pangolin," the pangolin said, then waddled away to inspect a random spot on the floor.

"Okay," Hanover said, then leaned to the side to somebody off-camera and asked, "We're sure this isn't bullshit?"

There was a whispered response and the President shook his head.

"All right. Colonel, can you confirm what my people are telling me? Aliens?" Hanover asked.

"There is a hovering aircraft of unknown origin currently floating next to one of my hangars, sir. You saw the talking pangolin as well as I did. And the brief conversation I had with Sergeant Dransfield confirms that he and his men did engage with a non-human creature that flew away at high speeds. I think it's safe to say that something unusual is going on, yes," Perkins said.

"I gotta tell you, not good. All this shit going on, makes my administration look mighty incapable. Next year's an election year too."

"Plus, you know. All the people being murdered by killer aliens," Anya said. Hanover just nodded as if it were an afterthought and then squinted at her. MacDougal cleared her throat.

"And this fire stuff you do? What about that?" Hanover asked.

Perkins looked at Anya and raised his eyebrows. Anya held her hand up in front of the camera and ignited it. Perkins jumped back, but steadied himself at once, and raised a hand even as the airmen at the doors reached for their rifles.

"Stand down. We're good, here," Perkins said.

"I've seen it in-person, sir. And the Artificial Intelligence," Riley said. "It's not a trick."

"Felix, c'mon out," Anya said as she extinguished her hand, and Felix appeared beside her.

"Good afternoon! Nice to meet you!" they said.

"I'll be damned," Hanover said.

"Field offices for the Bureau in California, Texas, and Montana have also made contact with these host people," MacDougal said. "None of them have come to any in-person meetings, but they've all given information similar to what Anya has provided. By the way, just so all our cards are on the table, am I to assume that you are Anya Nowicki?"

Anya didn't see any point in hiding it, so she nodded.

"Yeah. Found me after you busted down Tori's apartment?" she asked.

"It's our job to investigate, yes. Your driver's license from South Carolina has your height listed at five-foot-two. Agent Riley says you're somewhere between seven and eight feet tall," MacDougal said.

"Side effect of making my basic statistics increase," Anya said.

"Same reason that over-sized armadillo can talk?" Hanover asked.

"Pangolin. And sort of. His Archive had to make his brain and body bigger as some kind of fail-safe so it could work properly. Also gave him some English."

"Maybe it's better if you just start from the beginning," Hanover said. Anya began to explain, again, everything that had happened since Friday night. Tori took over occasionally as Anya ate, with Riley and MacDougal confirming what they had from police reports and their own information from across the country.

While Anya was aware that time was passing, time that the aliens had to hunt her or other hosts, she also knew she wasn't much good in a fight now. Her Sun's Heart felt good again, but not great. The usual sensation of having a dynamo in her chest now merely felt like a slowly growing bonfire, getting stronger by the second.

And the voice had spoken to her again.

"You haven't had any contact with these Engineer people since Monday morning?" Hanover asked, pulling Anya's attention back to the screen. Anya belched, then covered her mouth. Tori covered her mouth as she laughed and Anya cleared her throat.

"Sorry. No, nothing since then. Right, Felix?" she asked.

"Correct! I've been trying to follow their line of communication back, but my range doesn't extend beyond a few thousand miles past Earth's atmosphere. That's also reducing, by the way. It's subtle, but

I'm finding it more and more difficult to track the other hosts as well," Felix said.

"Shit. That's not good," Anya said.

"You malfunctioning or something?" Hanover asked.

"Nope! Based on what I've seen regarding my ability to receive signals from hosts, the Engineers, and the gnosiphages themselves, I suspect they are responsible for communication and signal disruption. They're probably getting better at it as time goes on, which is why their signals all vanished earlier."

"Can you make your signal vanish?" MacDougal asked.

"No, unfortunately. The Archive is set to be an open line of communication with the Engineers at all times by default. I cannot make changes to the functionality of the Archive itself, only access data within it to a limited extent."

"So they're blocking your signal to the Engineers, but not enough to make you impossible to find," Perkins said and Felix nodded.

"The next nearest hosts are somewhere around Chicago?" MacDougal asked and Felix gave her a thumbs up.

"That's correct!"

"Perhaps it would be best to establish contact with them before the signal erodes entirely," MacDougal said.

"Mm. I'd like to know who all these hosts are, start some kind of list," Hanover said. Anya and Tori exchanged a look and Riley cleared his throat.

"I'm sure they could use some support, if Ms. Nowicki's experience is anything to go by," Riley said.

"Uh-huh," Hanover said and waved to somebody off-camera for something.

"I was planning on finding them as soon as I could," Anya said.

"You'll take some people with you, direct them to where these other host folks can be found," Hanover said. "I'd like you to remain on base, answer some more questions. Can you use your menu thingy to buy stuff for us? Be a helluva win to get some alien gadgets for the R&D fellas."

"Yeah, I'm not doing that."

"Excuse me?"

"I'm not giving you access to a store full of extraterrestrial weapons for you to poke and prod at. Period."

"And I suppose you think you're the only one who should have access?" Hanover asked as an edge crept into his voice.

"No! I don't think anybody should have this shit! Whoever these Engineers are, they're absolutely out of their fucking minds for randomly distributing the Archive on an unsuspecting, unprepared population. But since there happen to be several thousand homicidal monsters from another galaxy trying to kill me, I'll use what I can until things calm down."

A silence stretched out between Anya and the people on the screen. Tori looked at her with obvious concern, and the airmen standing by the doors began to fidget.

Hanover glared at her, opened his mouth, and MacDougal jumped into the silence before the President could speak.

"Based on the reports and video I have from Agent Riley, I think Ms. Nowicki is needed in-person to find the other hosts. Having her off-site could cause delays. However, I think it's wise of the President to involve our own people," she said. "Agent Riley would like to join Ms. Nowicki, I'm sure."

"Oh. Uh, yes, ma'am," Riley said.

"As for the alien store you have access to, I think it would be beneficial to everyone if we had some more information about it. There are other avenues than guns and bombs we can pursue. Think about it sir: you could be the President who helped discover a cure for cancer, or oversaw the invention of flying cars. Who knows what else?" MacDougal asked, and Anya didn't miss the gleam that came over the President's eyes. "A shame to rush ahead before we know more."

"Y'know I do like the sound of that," he said. "But one person having all of that at her beck-and-call…"

"Several thousand people. Two of whom are in Chicago right now and need to be found. Maybe they would be more accommodating? And having access to more hosts would mean more resources down the line," MacDougal asked. Anya had to admit, the woman was smooth.

"Right, right. Time waits for no man. Gotta show these folks we're team players first. So, I'll hand this over to the Bureau, then?" Hanover asked.

"The purview of the FBI does include investigating attacks involving weapons of mass destruction within our borders, and I would say these aliens qualify," MacDougal replied with a gentle nod.

"I'll leave it to you for now. Rather not waste time with inter-departmental dick-waving. Don't disappoint me, MacDougal. Colonel, see that Ms. Nowicki there is good to go. And find those other alien folks or whatever they are!" Hanover said, then waved a hand and the line disconnected.

"Good day, everybody," MacDougal said. "We'll be in touch, Ms. Nowicki."

The call ended and Colonel Perkins closed the laptop.

"Well, until I hear otherwise, you're free to finish your meal, wait for Agent Riley to arrive, and then take off for Chicago, unless I hear otherwise," Perkins said. "Now if you'll excuse me, my sergeant needs to fill me in on what happened out there in a more official capacity. If you need anything else, within reason, any of the airmen here can help you or contact me."

"Thank you, Colonel," Anya said as the Colonel stood up from the table and left. The airmen remained behind to keep an eye on her while she ate. Anya was on her fourth tray of food, finally starting to feel full, when Tori nudged her and showed her a series of messages on her phone.

RILEY: MacDougal wants to talk, privately.

RILEY: Sooner would be better than later.

RILEY: Just trust me on this one.

Anya sighed, but nodded and discreetly took Tori's phone and pocketed it before she stood up and looked at the nearest airman. He couldn't have been much older than nineteen, and his eyes widened a little as he stared at her.

"Hey, I gotta use the bathroom," Anya said.

"The bathroom?" he asked.

"Yeah, man. I just ate five pizzas."

"Right! Yeah, sorry. Just over there, ma'am," the young man said and pointed at a hallway at one end of the mess hall. Anya thanked him and made her way to the women's bathroom and entered a stall before she took out Tori's phone and dialed Riley.

The call was answered at once and MacDougal's face appeared. She squinted at Anya.

"Are you in the toilet?" she asked.

"You said you wanted private, and Riley said not to keep you waiting. This was the closest option," Anya said.

"Mm. I hope you understand what happened back there?"

"Maybe just clear it up for me so we're on the same page."

"I kept the President from pressuring you into using your menu to acquire alien weaponry, which I have no doubt you would have continued to refuse, and escalate the situation into something inconvenient for everybody. Same page?"

"Yeah, that sounds about right."

"Good. We can both make each other's lives significantly more convenient, Ms. Nowicki. We can also do the opposite. I have no doubt that you can do as you please, but from what I've gathered from Riley and those body cams from the NYPD, you want to help people."

"Pretty much."

"Good. So do I. Hanover is only willing to help to the extent that it makes him look good and puts money in the pockets of his campaign donors. I can handle Hanover so long as you're willing to work with me. Deal?"

"Sounds fair," Anya agreed. "Just don't expect me to surrender myself to the government and we should be okay."

"I'll keep that in mind. When are you departing for Chicago?" MacDougal asked and Anya looked down at herself.

"I'm functional, but I'm no good in a fight. I hate to, but I need rest. A couple hours, at least. Then I can go."

"You look banged up. I'll send Riley down to Dover and you can take him with you from there."

Anya winced a little and MacDougal raised her eyebrows at her.

"I'm not saying I won't but I'm worried about his safety. The guys the colonel sent to fight the alien were a big help, but that alien was already seriously wounded. If they had been there from the start, they'd probably be dead. Did you see what that little puppet did to the cops?"

MacDougal thought for a moment and sighed. "I did. Riley is going with you, but he should stay with that flying car or whatever it is you have. He can help protect your friend if she's going too. And that pangolin thing."

Anya couldn't take her friend and the pangolin around with her forever, but for now it was better to keep the pangolin moving, harder to pin down by the aliens. As for Tori... well, Anya was pretty sure her friend wanted to come but wasn't certain if she would insist on it. She could think about it after she rested.

"Fine. Not my fault if an alien smushes him though," Anya said.

"Happy to do my best to avoid that," Riley said from off-camera.

"Tori can come pick Riley up. It'll be faster," Anya said.

"That'll be fine. Have her call again when she's ready. Good day, Ms. Nowicki," MacDougal said and hung up before Anya could respond. She rolled her eyes and sighed.

"Fucking government," she said. She left the bathroom to go tell Tori the deal, and then find a shower and a bed and try to sleep while she could.

FROM EARTH #3

From *Rutherford International News Network:*
POSSIBLE NUCLEAR ATTACK OUTSIDE OF BENGALURU

It has been confirmed that a weapon of mass destruction, possibly nuclear, is responsible for the massive explosion just outside Bengaluru. Death toll estimates range from 10,000 up to over 175,000 or more in the wake of the attack, with many more expected due to injury and possible nuclear fallout if a nuclear weapon was responsible.

Several members of the local and national government could not be reached for comment, and it is unknown if they were victims of the attack, or are merely being sequestered for safety until more information comes to light. Much of Europe and Asia has already responded with emergency services and medical aid, and evacuation procedures are in effect for areas around Bengaluru and the surrounding areas regarding the possibility of fallout.

All NPT-designated nuclear weapon states across the globe have denied any knowledge or involvement in the attack. Other states possessing or suspected to possess nuclear weapons have likewise denied the attack.

———

From *Helsingin Sanomat* (Translated from Finnish):

36 CANCER PATIENTS AND MULTIPLE OTHER CASES CURED OVERNIGHT IN HELSINKI

36 patients in the cancer ward of Helsinki University Hospital went to sleep Sunday night with uncertain futures. On Tuesday morning, they awoke with their cancer gone, as if it had never been. Daily check-ups confirmed the absence of any and all cancerous growths, even in several stage-4 patients.

"It is a miracle," Eida Koskinen, 54, said after her third examination to confirm the absence of her stage-4 lung cancer. "Yesterday I could not breathe without pain, now, it's like I have the lungs of a teenager."

"It wasn't just those in the cancer ward," said Dr. Harkonen, director of HUS. "It was everybody with a terminal or incurable disease. HIV, Leukemia, AIDS, just gone. In one night. We're keeping all 106 cases here for observation and some testing, but the exams show that they're all perfectly, impossibly healthy."

When asked how or why this could have happened, Dr. Harkonen said he did not have any comment.

A nurse spoke under the condition of anonymity.

"There's some footage on the security tapes of a tall man in a long coat coming in last night around one in the morning. I spoke to him, but it was strange. I don't remember anything specific about him. He went to every room for a few seconds, then left. He gave several small boxes to the different nurse stations. They were all full of different vials, pills, and such, and a note to test them or call several of the top pharmaceutical companies around Europe for confirmation that they were cures."

When asked what the medicine was a cure for, the nurse replied, "Everything."

Multiple members of the HUS staff shared similar stories, also under the condition of remaining anonymous.

"No comment," Dr. Harkonen said again when asked about any strange visitors to the hospital.

UPDATE: Multiple hospitals and hospices in Finland, Norway,

Sweden, and Denmark have all reported similar occurrences within the last two days, including that of a "tall man in a coat with boxes full of medicine," that could not be identified, as well as any terminal or seriously ill or injured patients having their ailments cured.

UPDATE: A similar story is circulating in Thailand, though eyewitnesses report a woman and not a man delivering packages full of medicine and stopping in patient rooms.

————

From The Daily Telegraph:
THE ORCA-MAN OF COTTESLOE BEACH
Several photos and video of a large creature emerging from the waves of Cottesloe Beach have appeared online. Many posters have dubbed the creature "Orca-Man." Videos show a towering humanoid figure with a broad head, a fin, a long tail, and black-and-white skin stepping out of the waves at night alongside two much shorter men carrying surfboards.

At first dismissed as a hoax for being dark and too blurry, additional pictures and video have surfaced over the last several days of what one blogger called "a bipedal whale-like monster, or guy in a really great costume." Daytime video clearly shows a tall humanoid figure with a tail, a fin, two legs and arms, and a very orca-like countenance running into the ocean. Further video shows a full-sized orca whale swimming away from the shore, and still other videos show the Orca-Man exiting the water hours later.

"It's clearly all just a hoax or a game," local Officer Angus Taylor said. "Somebody with a nice costume or too much time in a video editor making waves, no pun intended."

Others say it's genuine. Frank Lee, of Peppermint Grove, says he saw the Orca-Man walk onto the beach, and even spoke to him.

"If that's a costume it's the best costume I've ever seen. It looked too real though, way too real. And he spoke to me! He said he'd come for fishing after his friends told him they couldn't afford to feed him any more and he smoked all of their weed. I'll tell you one thing, he's definitely an Aussie. Called me a [expletive] and then drank all my beer."

———

From *Oni-Chan* (鬼ちゃん), an on-line message and image board, sub-board /B/ (Bots & Mecha):

Anon-01: mecha-in-rio.webm

Anon-02: What movie is this?

Anon-03: Not a movie. Real. Sauce: www.rinn.com/brazil

Anon-02: No fucking way.

Anon-01: I couldn't believe it either, but I speak Portuguese and all the local news, all the forums, all the blogs, all the social media, it's all about this thing. Shitload of pics and video. No way it's fake.

Anon-04: It's on the news now. I must've missed it with all the shit happening in India.

Anon-05: Scary that somebody has nukes or something and just decided to erase part of a major city.

Anon-06: Fucking terrorists or some rogue government assholes somewhere.

Anon-01: Excuse me. GIANT. ROBOT.

Anon-03: It looks like it has missile pods on the side or something. And a sword? Badass.

Anon-02: Did it blow up the city?

Anon-01: Nope. There was some kinda terrorist attack in Rio, lots of explosions, then this thing showed up and cleaned up the mess and flew off. Saved a whole bus full of people by picking it up and moving it.

Anon-02: Anybody else think all this stuff happening over the last few days has been kinda weird?

Anon-07: "Kinda." It's the fucking apocalypse you brainlet

17

Anya was given a female escort and directed to the showers, then an empty dorm room with a pair of beds, wardrobes, and desks. The pangolin had followed her with his own escort, but was currently outside, cheerily ripping up the grass and gorging himself on ants.

"Felix, wake me up in two hours. I don't want to lose another couple of days napping," Anya said as she collapsed onto the bed.

She was asleep before she heard the AI respond.

———

Anya was somewhere warm.

She was also floating.

It felt like being fully submerged in water that was just the perfect temperature.

Soothing.

Peaceful.

Then somebody ruined it by speaking.

"Hey there, little ember," a voice said, now very familiar to Anya as the one that had been inside her head.

She was hesitant to open her eyes, afraid she would wake and leave this cocoon of pleasant, toasty tranquility.

"You've got a gift for it, y'know? A real natural," the voice said and Anya snapped her eyes open.

She did not awaken to the plain military dorm room she had fallen asleep in, but a limitless expanse of sunset. It was a never-ending field of ocher light punctuated by gently undulating cascades of color: tangerine, rose, and coral. An aurora borealis of fiery hues without end.

The only other thing that Anya could see was a small bird, like a sparrow but made of pale yellow light. It stood on the empty air in front of Anya and fluttered its wings.

"Go away," Anya said and closed her eyes again.

There was a chuckle, full of genuine amusement and cheer. Anya vaguely recalled her father laughing like that when she had done something silly, or brash, or especially if she did something her mother had found "inappropriate for nice young girls."

A lot of the things Anya had done had fallen into that last category, according to her mother.

Nathan, her youngest brother, had also received a lot of scoldings about what was "appropriate," for young men. Their mother's admonishments had gotten to him more than they had Anya.

Anya pushed the thoughts back and turned away from the bird.

"You call me into your heart and then tell me to go away? Not very nice of you, is it?" the voice asked. Anya cracked an eye open and saw that the little yellow bird now stood on top of her foot.

"So you're the Flame Dominion, or something?" Anya asked.

"Sort of. I'm what you might think of if you thought of the Flame Dominion as a thing you could talk to."

"Wow, that clears everything right up. Solid explanation there, pal," Anya said and sighed. "God, I just want to sleep!"

"You're definitely sleeping, little ember. And you'll rest well here, even on the edges of the Dominion. The fire soothes as well as sears. It's why we're chatting in the first place. You like both, don't you?"

"Like both of what?"

"You like your friend. You like to soothe. You like to be the safe place to be beside. But you also like to burn. You like to devour and devastate. Y'know, blow shit up real good. Not a lot of folks that enter the Dominion of the First Fire like both. They usually just want fireballs and never really think much about having a fireplace."

"I literally took this power to kill aliens."

"You did. You've been doing pretty well so far. I love that you've gone for the up-close-and-personal route. You've no idea how sick I am of some reedy little wizard or pyromancer shooting lasers or fireballs from miles away. Absolutely boring. You? Ah, when you got in that puppet thing's face and breathed fire right into its gullet? Just outstanding work, there. Ditto for fisting that giant snake in the ribs and lighting it up like the 4th of July on steroids."

"Yeah that was pretty badass," Anya agreed. "That really doesn't sound very soothing to me, though. Melting a monster alien puppet and a giant snake is pretty solidly in the 'searing' category of things."

"You also took it to protect your friend, you used it to protect people you'd known for only a few moments, and total strangers you'd never seen before. You've used it to heal that wounded cop, to warm your friend on a cold roof, and more than that, you have the— How do I put this?—the desire to do more of both: the helping and the hurting. Even if you're not physically using the flame to help people, you still want to be the one they come to."

There was a pause, and then the bird asked, "Is it because you couldn't be there for your little brother when he killed himself?"

Anya glared at the bird and swung at it. Her fist passed through it harmlessly and she tried again. Same result. Anya clenched her fists at her side instead and loomed over the bird.

"Not your fucking business. At all," she said.

"Fair enough. Sorry about that."

Anya just grunted and folded her arms.

"How do you know about that?" she asked.

"You invited me into your heart, remember? Literally and metaphorically. Haven't you noticed the connection between the fire and your emotions? You get mad, you have a flare up. You get happy, and feel warm and toasty."

"I just thought it was... I dunno. I didn't think it was like that."

"Sometimes it isn't. You're unlikely to connect with the Gravity Dominion the same way. It's probably only ever going to be a tool for you. Honestly you're not missing out on much there. Always found that one to be a bit too heavy-handed with things."

The bird chuckled again and Anya frowned at the pun.

"But, as I said, we like both, and it's obvious you do too. Soothe and sear. The inferno and the campfire. Charred enemies and toasted marshmallows."

"Real cozy imagery. If you're gonna be this chatty with me every time I try to go to sleep, I'm getting rid of this Sun's Heart thingy when I can get a respecification token," Anya said.

The bird laughed. It was more than a little surreal hearing such a deep, jovial sound come out of such a tiny animal. Or at least an animal-shaped manifestation of an otherworldly domain for the concept of fire.

"What you have inside your chest right now is as much a Sun's Heart as dog shit is a diamond," it said. Anya looked down at herself. She was glowing like the bird, but much fainter. There was a beating in her chest, as strong as ever, and magnified by the artifact the Archive had granted her.

"What do you mean?" Anya asked.

"I mean that the 'Engineers,' are little more than half-rate counterfeiters. But the toy they granted you is enough for us to talk. But only just. We'll see each other again, later."

"You're leaving? I've got kind of a lot of questions about all of this," Anya said.

"Believe me, I'd like to stick around and burn away the hours with you, but you're not ready for too much time here."

"Why not?"

"You would literally combust and then explode."

"All right. Let's avoid that."

The bird chuckled again and waved a wing at her as it fluttered away.

"Until then, burn bright, little ember. Warm your friends, and burn your foes."

And Anya awoke.

———

FELIX FLOATED ABOVE HER, and the rose-headed AI blinked its big, cartoon eyes.

"Hey, great timing! I was just about to wake you!" they said.

Anya sat up and looked down at herself. She flexed her arms, then stood and bounced on the balls of her feet.

"Wow. Nice," she said. She had never felt better. The aches, the fatigue, the lingering pain of the acid, all of it was gone.

"Feeling better?" Felix asked.

"Yeah, like, a million times better."

"Good! I have some good news for you too! While you didn't get a full level up from that fight with the snake gnosiphage, you did get some natural skill increases during the fight, and more RAC for Archive contributions!"

"Awesome! What'd I get?" Anya asked and Felix expanded the menu. Combat cognition and kinetic dispersal had risen by one point each, while Flame Dominion, regeneration, Gravity Dominion, and Xhama Thul had all increased by two. She'd also received 125,000 RAC for her Archive contributions which included some of her Xhama Thul fighting moves paired with her Dominions, and the combination of that healing potion in conjunction with the Sun's Heart and regeneration.

Anya looked down at her torn, and filthy cloak and battle regalia.

"Can I repair this stuff, or do I have to get new ones?" Anya asked.

"The RAC store can repair any item purchased from it for a fraction of the original cost. That includes the Shadow Ray," Felix replied. "The Archive can fix your regalia and cloak right now, but we'll need to be standing next to the Shadow Ray before we can fix it. Everything will cost about 56,783 RAC."

"Get me another one of those healing potions and a star's breath, too," Anya said, and then blinked as her clothing fluttered, then flashed, and was repaired and cleaned. Anya considered getting more ignition gel, but held off. It wasn't too expensive, but twice now, the aliens had countered her use of it. She might need to think of an alternative. After repairing everything (Felix set some RAC aside for when they reached the Shadow Ray) and buying the star's breath and alchemical tincture, Anya had 52,861 RAC left.

Anya took a few minutes in the bathroom to wash herself at the sink, then left the dorm room and smiled at the two female airmen stationed just outside her door. One of them widened her eyes as she saw Felix, while the other kept a respectable poker face.

"Hey. Is my friend Tori back?" Anya asked.

"Y-yes, ma'am!" the airman said.

"Could you take me to her?"

"Right this way," the airman gestured to the exit and led the way back out to the airfield and the hangars. Tori, Riley, and the pangolin were all gathered outside the makeshift canvas barriers the airmen had set up around the Shadow Ray, talking with Colonel Perkins and Sergeant Dransfield. All of them looked up as Anya and her escort arrived. Tori waved, and the pangolin waddled over to Anya and hugged her leg.

"Anya!" the pangolin said.

"Hey there! You know names, now?" Anya asked.

"We've been teaching him," Tori asked. "Hey pangolin, who am I?"

"Tori! Toooorrri," the pangolin said and pointed at her with a claw. Then it pointed at the men around her. "Riley! Riiiillleey. Perk… Perky? Perky!"

"Close enough," Colonel Perkins said with a shrug.

"Dran… dan… Danfel," the pangolin finished and pointed at the sergeant. The man smiled and nodded.

"I'm Felix!" the AI said and floated down beside the pangolin.

"Feeeellliiiicks," he said. "Felix."

"What about you? You thought of a name for yourself?" Anya asked.

"We were just discussing that," Tori said.

"Anya. Felix," the pangolin said as it scratched at the ground. His yellow buttercup-headed AI appeared beside him and examined Felix with the same inquisitiveness as the pangolin himself. "My name, pangolin?"

"That's your species." Anya said. "My species is human, Felix is an AI, like your yellow one there."

"Bright friend," the pangolin said and nodded at his yellow AI.

"Sure," Anya agreed. "But you should pick a name. You'd be the first pangolin ever to name themselves."

"First. Pangolin. Pan. First. Pan. Pan!"

"You want the first sound of 'pangolin' to be your name?" Anya asked. It made sense. The creature didn't know what a syllable was exactly, but it understood the idea of word sounds, at least.

"Pan! Pan the first," the pangolin, Pan, said and pointed at his leathery chest with its foreclaws. "Pan!"

"Then Pan it is," Anya said and knelt as she extended her hand to Pan. "Good name, Pan."

Pan licked her hand, then bumped it with his head and turned away to scratch at the ground.

"Well, one problem solved," Anya said as she stood back up and looked at the others.

"Agent Riley informs me you'll be off to Chicago to find some more folks like you," Perkins said, and Anya nodded.

"After dropping me off in New York," Tori sighed. "It's probably better for me to stay away from all the aliens and stuff since I'm not exactly good with guns or fire magic or anything."

Anya felt herself relax. Tori had saved her in the field, but it could have gone very, very badly. If the alien hadn't retreated, Tori, Anya, everybody would likely have been dead, or seriously injured at the very least.

"I'm sorry Tori," Anya said. "I'd like to have you but..."

"I know, I know. It's dangerous. Don't feel too bad for me, though. MacDougal said she'd put me up in a nice hotel while some people fix my busted up apartment."

"That's decent of them, considering they broke it up in the first place."

"We do our best," Riley said.

"If you'll excuse me, I have a truckload of reports to fill out, and a whole lot of people up the chain-of-command to update," Perkins said and walked away. Sergeant Dransfield remained behind.

"No sense in waiting around, I guess," Anya said as she moved behind the canvas barricade. As soon as she was within a few feet of the Shadow Ray, it shuddered and glowed and then returned to normal.

"What was that?" Riley asked as he followed her.

"Automated repair from the Archive," Felix said.

"Great! Now I don't feel so bad for using it as a battering ram," Tori said as she climbed inside and sat in one of the passenger chairs. Pan followed her, struggled to sit in one of the chairs, then gave up and curled himself into a ball on the floor. Anya took the pilot's seat while Riley sat across from Tori, and the hatch hissed closed behind them.

Anya told the autopilot where to go once Tori informed her of the hotel she was being put up at, and they were hovering invisibly out in front of it within minutes.

"You sure you'll be okay?" Anya asked Tori as she lowered the Ray onto the sidewalk in front of the Langham Hotel, deactivating the stealth as she did. Pedestrians leaped away from the craft, many taking their cell phones out to begin taking pictures or video.

"I'll be fine. You just worry about yourself," Tori said as she exited the Ray and waved. "Bye, Pan! Be good!"

"Bye bye!" Pan uncurled himself enough to wave a claw, then curled back up as the hatch closed and Anya reactivated the stealth and flew above the city skyline.

"This might be a good time to relay the director's request that you try to keep any overt displays of alien technology or, ah, 'magic,' away from the public whenever possible," Riley said.

"I wasn't planning on doing a show in Times Square," Anya said.

"Which we appreciate, but y'know, having this stealth car-thingy pop outta thin air in the middle of 5th Avenue ain't exactly subtle."

"I was on the sidewalk," Anya smirked. "But I'll try to keep it under-wraps for now. You don't think doing some kind of announcement on national news about the invasion is a good idea?"

"Not my place to say. Higher-ups seem to think it'd cause a panic right now, and there's other things to consider: President's gotta contact our allies, see what they know, start organizing task forces, all kinds of stuff. Better not to rile the whole friggin' country up about killer aliens and people with superpowers until we've got a plan in place."

"Assuming the aliens will cooperate with that."

"Based on what we've seen so far, they mostly seem interested in you people and not mass public destruction. Nothing's blowing up the Chrysler Building or the Golden Gate yet, anyways."

"Don't jinx it."

It was pretty low-key as far as inter-planetary invasions went. A lot more cat-and-mouse and a lot less exploding national landmarks.

"So what're your orders while you're with me?" Anya asked.

"Officially? Stay in contact with Director MacDougal, help you if I can, and alert any other hosts we meet to contact local authorities if we can't get them to come with us."

"And any unofficial orders?"

"Yeah. Make sure you don't go psycho, try to keep you happy. Pay for your absurd meal tabs. All of which I was planning on doing anyway."

"Aw, Riley. That's kinda sweet."

Riley barked out a laugh.

"Just don't get me killed and try not to piss off too many elected officials and we'll call it square."

"Deal."

"So, Chicago?"

"Well, the areas around Chicago," Anya said and tapped the navigation screen a few times. The Shadow Ray adjusted itself, then darted across the sky and toward Illinois.

18

The signals from the other hosts had eroded significantly since the start of the invasion. Worse, according to Felix, the hosts in Chicago had moved around the state of Illinois quite a bit, which had dramatically widened their possible location.

Anya and Riley had no choice but to do a back-and-forth pattern across the signal's area and hope for the best. They spent the first day flying over the southern part of the state near Mt. Vernon.

"I don't mind sleeping in your alien jet, but are you okay to keep flying?" Riley asked with a yawn a little before midnight.

Anya was a little surprised at how awake she still felt. She'd started the day by getting shot at by the feds and almost dying at the hands of the snake alien, but she didn't feel it. Whatever her being inside the Flame Dominion had done, it had done wonders for her constitution.

"I'm good. We can pull over if you need food again or to take a leak," Anya replied. They had stopped at a gas station a few hours ago to stock up on food and use the restrooms, but that had been all.

"Nah. Kinda reminds me of doing stake-outs years ago. Better, actually. I can stretch out on these seats more than I could in my shitty old car."

"How's Pan?"

"Little fella went to sleep a couple hours ago and he's been out ever since."

"You should do the same. Time isn't really on our side," Anya sighed. Riley just grunted in reply, then laid down on the Ray's long seats and was snoring within minutes.

"I have some good news," Felix whispered as Anya flew low over the city of Effingham.

"Please, enlighten me," she replied.

"The gnosiphages have really scrambled the host signals terribly. But thanks to the data I got from the puppet alien, I've just managed to work around it a little bit. Not much, but I'm narrowing it down. There's bad news too."

"Naturally."

"The hosts we're trying to find, they keep moving. I'm 93.6% certain that they're north of our current location by at least thirty miles."

"Springfield, Bloomington, Peoria, Chicago of course..." Anya rattled off major cities as she studied her map. "Can you pin their signal down the closer we get?"

"Assuming they don't move," Felix said.

"Big assumption. If they're smart they'd keep moving to avoid the aliens. What do you think? Continue eliminating areas one-by-one or head north?"

"I recommend we move north. Their signal appears to be the weakest in the southern area of the state."

"Right. Can you maybe show me some areas with the highest probability?"

"Yes!" Felix said. The large opaque circle became filled with a couple dozen smaller circles of varying intensity. Many of them were around cities, but many more were out in the middle of nowhere. Anya sighed.

"Just keep your little holographic fingers crossed," Anya said, and flew on into the night.

———

It wasn't until Friday evening, two nights later, that Felix finally spoke up.

"Signal! Stop!" Felix said. Anya brought the Shadow Ray to a halt in the airspace over downtown Chicago. They had covered Chicago yesterday to no avail, and had spent most of that morning and afternoon along the border of Wisconsin. Felix had updated the signal range to show it had tightened significantly around the Windy City during that time, and Anya, Riley, Pan, and Felix had flown back.

"Take us lower!" Felix said.

"Holy shit, you found 'em?" Riley asked.

"I fucking hope so," Anya said and complied with Felix's instructions. The Ray descended a hundred feet, two hundred, before Felix had her stop again.

"There! Up the street about 500 yards!" Felix said. Riley had stood up out of his seat to peer over the pilot's seat at the map Felix had displayed above the cockpit console. The circle on the map was centered around a squat, multi-story parking garage. It shrank as Anya flew closer, and finally solidified into two dots: a blue one and a gray one.

"Uh-oh," Felix said.

"What is it?" Anya asked.

"I don't have a precise signal but there's an alien somewhere within a 5 mile radius. I don't think it's moving."

"Keep an eye on it. Better to make contact with these other hosts quick. Can I message them? Like how Earl messaged me?" Anya asked. She considered just flying in, but didn't want to scare the other hosts off.

"Sure! Now that I've got a solid lock on their location, communication should be functional," Felix said and brought up what appeared to be a standard chat window, complete with an alpha-numeric keyboard. "It's also voice activated if you want."

"This is fine," Anya said and began typing.

ANYA: Hello! I'm Anya. You know there's a hostile alien nearby? Are you okay?

Anya leaned back in her seat and stared at the message screen. The blue dot flashed and pulsed like a loading icon and then glowing blue words appeared following a name.

SAMAIRA: We're fine, and we know about the alien. Are you here for it, or something else?

Anya paused as she read the words again. Something else? What else could she be here for?

ANYA: Looking for hosts. I killed one alien already. I don't mean you or anybody any harm. I just want to help.

The blue dot pulsed and flashed again, and Anya assumed that happened whenever a host was typing. She couldn't blame the blue host, Samaira, for being cautious. For all she knew, Anya could be harmless but foolish like Earl, or she could be some psychotic murderer.

SAMAIRA: We've killed one already too, been tracking this one across Illinois for days. Come to us. We're on the roof of a parking garage nearby. We don't want a fight, but we can defend ourselves. Bring the yellow host as well.

ANYA: I'll meet you, but bringing the yellow host is a bad idea. He's young and very scared.

The menu flashed as the blue dot filled the screen and Anya's ear beeped.

"That host is trying to call you on video," Felix said.

"Fine," Anya said and tapped the blue dot. A young, pretty Indian woman's face appeared on the screen. She looked around Anya's age, and had striking angular features and wide dark eyes behind even larger circular glasses. Her black hair was pulled back in a loose braid, and she tucked a strand of her hair behind her ear as she saw Anya.

Somebody else was behind her, peering over her shoulder. It was a man who looked to be in his sixties with short white hair and a thick mustache, heavy square glasses, and a well-creased, stern face.

Anya saw herself, picture-in-picture, up in the corner. The "camera" or whatever it was sending her image to the other host, was somewhere in the center of her menu judging by the angle.

"Evening," the old man said, his Chicago accent evident even in just those three syllables.

"H-hi," Anya stammered, surprised at suddenly being confronted like this.

"What're you playing at?" Samaira asked. Her voice was stern like a school-teacher's.

"I'm not?" Anya asked.

"You want to keep that other host hidden to do what? Launch some kind of surprise attack on us?"

"No!"

"Easy there," the old man said. "She might not be like the other one."

"Other one?" Anya asked.

"Explain why the yellow host needs to stay behind," Samaira said. Anya leaned to one side as she moved her menu. She jerked a thumb behind her at the back seat where Pan sat on the floor in front of Riley.

"Oh!" Pan said and his stubby ears twitched along with his snout. He waved a claw at the screen. "Hello! Pan here!"

"Uh," Samaira's face went from sharp and stern to slack and shocked so quickly Anya snorted and had to hold in a laugh.

"Huh," the old man behind her said and adjusted his glasses. "That some kinda badger or something?"

"No, he's a pangolin. The Archive hit him while he was in a zoo and I rescued him a couple days ago, made him super intelligent, it's a story for later. He needs to stay in my car because he's very shy and very hard to ignore, and he's only level 11. I didn't want to cause a ruckus," Anya said.

"Ruckus," Pan repeated. "Ruckus. Ruuuuckus."

"And who is that next to the pangolin?" the old man asked and pointed. Riley leaned over to be more in the frame.

"Agent Christian Riley, FBI. Here with the blessing of Director Suzanne MacDougal and President Hanover to assist in whatever way I can," Riley said.

Samaira nodded and managed a polite smile while the old man scowled.

"A fucking fed, huh? Great," he said.

"Gary, don't," Samaira sighed. "We tried it your way and we're stuck. Some official help would be good right about now, don't you think?"

The old man, Gary, waved a hand at the screen and muttered something but didn't protest further.

"Sorry for that. We're just a little hesitant," Samaira said. Her shoulders relaxed and she took her glasses off to polish them on her shirt. A cat meowed off-screen and Samaira grinned downward.

"Can't blame anybody for being too cautious lately. I take it you met some other hosts then?" Anya asked.

The old man nodded and said, "We did. But I think this would all be better talked about in-person. Especially with our other-worldly visitor so nearby. It's been motionless for hours, but that could change any minute. You can bring the fed if you have to, I guess."

"Very courteous of you sir," Riley said. Gary grunted.

"Yeah, of course," Anya said. "I'll be there in a few."

Samaira closed the window without saying anything else.

"They seem a bit jumpy," Anya said.

"If their week's been anything like yours I can't really blame them," Riley said as Anya directed the autopilot to the roof of the parking garage. She deactivated the stealth in advance so Gary and Samaira could see her approach. She glanced out the window and spotted the two standing near a big old truck, a tarp thrown over the flat-bed. There was also a white house cat with black stripes, which sat next to Samaira's leg.

Anya disembarked from the Shadow Ray first once it had landed, and her cloak flapped and billowed around her as she emerged.

Chicago lived up to the city's nickname, and a biting winter wind bellowed between the towering buildings. It was made worse by the lengthening shadows as late afternoon began to fade into twilight. Anya felt nothing but the wind itself, and suspected that if she were in summer clothes she would be fine.

Riley emerged behind her and clutched his coat around himself. Pan started to follow, but then retreated back into the cabin of the Shadow Ray.

"Cold! Cold! Bad bad!" Pan said and stayed as far away from the door as he could. Anya wasn't too surprised, but irritated she hadn't thought of it sooner. He was originally from somewhere in Africa, and had been in Virginia, a comparatively much warmer place than Chicago in winter. Pan was also still entirely naked.

"Stay inside, Pan, we'll be okay," Anya said, and Pan nodded even as he shivered and she closed the hatch.

Samaira and Gary stayed near the truck, eying Anya and Riley with obvious suspicion. The truck was a faded brown Ford F-150, and the heavy tarp stretched over the back fluttered in the wind.

Gary was the first to step forward and extended his hand. It was large, and calloused as Anya gripped it. She noticed his left hand had a wedding band on it.

"Gary…" Samaira started to say and reached out as if to stop him, but leaned back with a huff. She wore a long coat over a plain white blouse and dark blue dress. The white cat flicked an ear and turned its head to the side as it studied the newcomers.

"Gary Hendricks," the old man said as Anya shook his hand. "Heck of a grip on you, young lady."

"Sorry! Sorry, I've had to get used to a lot of stuff recently," Anya replied.

"You and the rest of the planet," Samaira said, but relaxed her posture after Anya shook Gary's hand. Gary and Riley shook next, and Anya watched as the two older men sized each other up.

"So long as you're here to help and not shovel a pile of bureaucratic bullshit all over us, we'll get along fine," Gary said.

"I try to avoid paperwork where I can, sir," Riley replied.

"Before we talk, I have to ask about the alien. It hasn't done anything? It's just been sitting around?" Anya asked. "And where is it? In one of these buildings?"

They were surrounded by the city, by cars and pedestrians. If the alien was going to make a move, it wasn't going to be nearly as easy as the last two fights. She shuddered at what the puppet or the snake could have done in a place this crowded.

"We fought it and another on Monday night. But no, this one hasn't moved all day," Gary said. "We lost sight of it very briefly when all the alien signals blinked out, which is when we tried to follow its signal around the state. It came back here, for whatever reason, after giving us the runaround for a few days."

"How?" Anya asked. "I barely detected one until it was right on top of me earlier."

"Boo?" Samaira asked, and a blue AI appeared next to her. This one had a head like a weeping willow, the long strands of the branches fell around its face like hair.

"Uh, we, we fought it earlier. So I guess I was able to lock onto the signal more easily. I'm sorry I couldn't find it sooner. Are you mad at me?" Boo asked and Samaira pinched the bridge of her nose and shook her head.

"No, Boo, it's fine. You did good," she said.

"That would explain why I still can't get a lock on it," Felix said as they appeared over Anya's shoulder. "We haven't fought it or been close enough to get the signal accurately. By the way, you shaking hands with Gary has locked his signal into your communications menu. If you'd like to stay in touch, I recommend making physical contact with all future hosts."

"Do you mind?" Anya asked as she looked at Samaira. She nodded and shook Anya's hand.

"Can't risk losing sight of our allies," Samaira said.

"Agreed. So Felix, if they could track their alien better, what about the snake thing that we fought? Can you pick it up?" Anya asked.

"Maybe if we got close again, but wherever it is now, it's too far away."

"Swell. So you two fought this one on Monday, and killed another?"

"Not alone, but yes. Two other hosts helped us fight it and a second alien not long after they landed," Samaira said.

"Another two Archive hosts? Where are they?" Anya asked, though she suspected she knew.

"Dead," Gary said and frowned. "So young. Damn shame."

"There was another host too, a fifth, but they didn't fight," Samaira added with a scowl.

"Too scared?" Anya asked. She couldn't really blame anybody for being scared, but it was still irritating.

"No, they waited," Samaira said. "We killed one of the aliens and the second one retreated after being wounded. Jessica and Tyson, the hosts, had been killed. The fifth host came out of nowhere, decloaked or something, and stole the stuff Jess and Ty had bought from the RAC store. Gary and I were talking about what to do and didn't see them until they'd practically stripped Jess and Ty. They vanished almost as soon as we noticed them and retreated out of our detection range."

"A looter," Anya said.

"Yeah. Jess and Ty had some decent stuff too. Jess was in her late thirties and Ty wasn't that much younger, both had plenty of RAC," Samaira said. "And if that cowardly jerk hadn't been hiding during the fight, they might not have died at all."

"Your AI didn't get their signal?" Anya asked.

"We did and we tried to follow him, but he was too fast. Took off for Canada somewhere and we decided we should focus on finding the other alien. But it's why I got suspicious when your pangolin didn't want to come. I didn't want another looter or something to mess with us."

"Damn. Can't blame you though. What about the aliens? Did they look like puppets?"

"Puppets? No. One was a marble statue and the other was a blue mailbox. The statue was all wiggly like pudding and the mailbox was crazy fast," Samaira replied.

"We managed to kill the statue by hitting some kind of core it was using to reform anytime it was hit. The mailbox didn't have anything like that, it was just quick. Tyson held it down for a split second, and Jess managed to shoot it with some kind of laser gun. It didn't reform after being wounded, just killed the two of them and then ran off," Gary said.

"The one I fought looked like a puppet and could regenerate, but it was kind of slow over open ground," Anya said. "And there was another, like a big demonic snake thing. It kept adapting to me as I fought it. Sort of."

"What happened after the mailbox alien ran off?" Riley asked.

"Gary and I were exhausted, but we tried to follow it. It was too fast and got away. We've been tracking it since. Our AIs picked up its signature this morning, said it matched the one from before," Samaira said.

"So why did it quit moving?"

"We figure it's been healing itself or waiting for back-up from other aliens, maybe," Gary continued. "But we haven't dared go near it or too far away from it because of where the darn thing chose to rest."

"The Water Tower Place," Samaira said and looked up the street.

"The Water Tower Place?" Anya asked. "It sounds like a city facility for water treatment or something."

"It's a shopping mall," Samaira said and Anya's fists clenched. Riley sucked in a breath and cursed.

"Yeah. Thousands of people just having a nice day shopping. If we went in, we weren't sure what would happen. We think it may have chosen the mall for that very reason: to use people as a shield if it came to it," Gary said. "We figured we would wait until the place closed and then go to it or let it come to us here."

"Except if another alien is on the way, then we're probably screwed," Samaira said. "We're just sitting ducks waiting out here, hoping it doesn't get back-up."

"We thought of trying to clear out the mall too, but didn't know how to do it without causing a panic," Gary said. "Pulling a fire alarm would require one of us to go to the Water Tower, and if we get close enough, we might set the alien off, make it lash out. If we call in a fake bomb threat, shoppers could freak out and hurt each other, or the bomb squad could anger the alien while they're looking for a bomb that doesn't exist."

"That is something I can help with. Gimme a sec," Riley said, then took out his phone and walked a short distance away from the rest of the group as he called somebody. Anya assumed it was MacDougal.

While Riley had his muffled conversation, Anya glanced down at the black-and-white cat. It looked back up at her with unnatural intensity.

"So, what's up with the cat? It's not a host is it?"

"No, she's not. She's mine. She helps. Don't you Chandrali? Yes you do," Samaira said and squatted down to scratch under the cat's chin. The cat purred and closed her eyes.

"So, were you always this tall?" Gary asked and nodded at Anya.

"No. Unintentional side-effect of boosting my Strength stat," she said. Gary smirked, which made his mustache twitch, and nodded.

"Yeah these Engineer guys, not exactly the best at conveying need-to-know shit, right?"

"You can say that again."

"If Riley can help, you gonna be okay with that, Gary?" Samaira asked as she continued to stroke her cat.

Gary frowned. "The Water Tower doesn't close until nine. That's still over three hours away. Another alien could be coming our way right now, and I hate to think of having to deal with two of those things in the heart of my city. The first time we fought these freaks we were lucky, got the two out near Montrose Beach. Not a lot of folks out there at night in the winter you know. But here? It'd be a nightmare. If Mr. Fed can whip up a solution, I'm all for it."

Riley turned to face them as they spoke and pointed at his phone.

"Yes, ma'am. Yes, they're here. Two of 'em. Yes, ma'am," Riley said and then looked at the group of hosts. "Director wants to talk to you folks. All of you."

"Fine," Anya said.

"Of course," Samaira added. Gary snorted and spat onto the roof of the garage and said nothing else. The cat meowed.

"All right. You're on, Director," Riley said and turned his phone toward the group.

"This is Director Suzanne MacDougal of the FBI. To whom am I speaking, besides Ms. Nowicki and Agent Riley," the director said.

"A couple of concerned citizens," Gary said.

"Sam and Gary," Samaira said. Gary shook his head at her.

"God dammit, Sam."

"You fought this alien before?" MacDougal asked.

"Yes, ma'am. It's extremely dangerous," Samaira said.

"How do you think it would fare against a SWAT team or similar special forces group?"

Samaira and Gary exchanged a look.

"They'd be dead in seconds," Gary said.

"Ms. Nowicki?" MacDougal asked.

"I gotta agree. The thing in Prospect Park killed three cops in under a minute. It was shot to hell by bullets and lasers, I blew it up at least a few times, set it on fire more than that, and it still almost killed me. The one I fought a couple days ago was even worse. It ate my biggest attacks, a stealth jet to the face, and a shitload of bullets and a rocket, and that only just managed to chase it off," Anya replied. There was a pause on the other end of the line.

"What did the Chicago aliens do when you first fought them?" Anya asked Samaira and Gary.

"The statue shot lightning," Samaira said. "And every time we cut or shot a piece of it off, it just returned to the main mass."

"The mailbox one was faster than most sports cars I've seen or worked on," Gary added. "Zero-to-sixty in under a second. It mostly just tried to slam into us, but once it belched some kind of toxic gas out of its mail slot. That's how it killed the other two hosts."

"If you send a bunch of SWAT guys in, they're gonna get butchered," Anya said. "If you don't believe me, ask that cop I sent to the hospital how quickly his partners died."

"Riley?" MacDougal asked. "What's your opinion?"

"Use the cops and any other conventional forces to evacuate the premises and secure the outside. Have emergency services on stand-by. Block off traffic at a two-block radius minimum. If Anya and these other folks can't handle it, have our guys clear out along with anybody else and drone-strike the fucking building. Uh, ma'am," Riley said. Anya snorted a laugh.

"Drone strike!" Samaira gaped. "It's the middle of Chicago, practically!"

"We can be quite precise," MacDougal said. "But yes, that may be a bit extreme. All right, I'll notify the mayor of Chicago and the police commissioner. This may take a little while," MacDougal said. "Do you know where in the building the alien might be?"

"No idea," Gary said.

"But you're sure it hasn't attacked civilians?"

"Nobody's come screaming out of the building yet. And yeah, I can see inside," Gary said and tapped the side of his glasses. Anya quirked an eyebrow at him but he only smirked. "No problems yet. Like we told Agent Riley, we think it's using the people as a shield. If it starts killing them it probably knows we'll come in after it."

"Very well. I'll get things moving. Thank you for your cooperation. Riley?" MacDougal asked and Riley took her off speaker phone and had a quick, monosyllabic chat with her before he hung up.

"Good to go. Whoever's managing that building right now is gonna get a call from some important folks, and they're gonna get it evacuated. Cops should be on their way in a few minutes, National Guard and EMS a little further behind. We just gotta cool our heels up here for a few," Riley said.

"So how've you been keeping an eye on the place?" Anya asked Gary. He smirked and waved her toward his truck. It looked like a standard old F-150 on the outside, but inside was another matter. The dashboard looked like something that belonged in a fighter jet. A flat screen monitor was in the center where the radio would have been, and showed a rotating view of the shopping mall.

"Did your truck come with a surveillance system?" Anya asked and smirked.

"Nah. But I always did like working with machines, even after I quit at the factory," Gary said as he threw back the tarp in the bed of his truck. Beneath it were a number of bestial robots of various shapes and sizes that all looked like they had been cobbled together from rusty engine parts and unfamiliar technological components.

"Do you need to do anything to get ready?" Samaira asked Anya. Her eyes glowed a deep blue, and so did Chandrali the cat's.

"Nope," Anya said as her smirk grew. "I'm ready to go as soon as the coast is clear."

19

t only took fifteen minutes for signs of an evacuation to show up on Gary's monitor. The camera, or whatever Gary had rigged up outside the Water Tower Place, was several stories up and aimed down at the entrance of a department store. The small trickle of incoming and outgoing shoppers changed to an organized stream, and security guards appeared outside other entrances to stop anybody else from entering.

Police cruisers appeared at every major intersection around the building and directed traffic away. Cops took up positions near the exits and helped with escorting people away from the building. A few black armored vans were more discreet in their arrivals, all within sight of Gary's cameras.

The exodus of shoppers was steady, but controlled. Nobody ran, nobody panicked, and there were no sirens or anything else to indicate an emergency. Anya still held her breath, expecting some sign of an attack within the mall at any moment. Soon somebody would come running out covered in blood, or there would be an explosion, or gunfire, or an inhuman roar, but none came.

"While we wait," Gary said, and brought up his main menu screen by tapping the inside of his left wrist. A gray-tinted menu appeared in the air, displaying all of Gary's stats and skills. "Figure it'd be best to know what we're all working with before we go into battle."

Anya looked at Gary's menu and whistled.

GARY HENDRICKS: LEVEL 32 INDUSTRIAL ROBOTICIST
Statistics

- Awareness-24
- Dexterity-8
- Fortitude-10
- Intelligence-45
- Strength-7
- Willpower-7

Skills

- Robotics-32
- Mechanical Engineering-27
- Weapons Design (Mechanical)-21
- Factory Design and Optimization-27
- Programming Language (Ny'lethic Code)-14

"You've got a factory full of robots somewhere?" Anya exclaimed.

"Eventually, I will, yeah. But right now, no. I spent almost all of my RAC on raw materials to get factory construction underway along with some basic builder drones. Thought I had a month to get the place together like they told us at first. Clearly that wasn't the case," Gary said. "I can't fight for shit directly, but if I can make it another week or two without becoming an alien's chew toy, I should be able to make them regret ever showing their weird-ass faces here. For now, I slap together what I can out of scrap and chewing gum. Sometimes literally."

"May I ask where you plan to locate this factory?" Riley asked. Gary frowned at the agent.

"Not in America. Not your business."

Riley shook his head but left it alone.

"Uh, Mr. Hendricks," Anya started to say as she pointed at his menu.

"Gary is fine, kid," he replied.

"Okay, Gary. When I got my Archive it started me at level 24, which is also my age. But your level's only 32. I don't mean to be rude but you look a little older than that."

Gary laughed.

"Nothing to be sorry about. I'm an old man, comfortably in my sixties. However, I guess these archives only allow somebody to start at level 30, and no higher. Got a couple levels for killing that alien, but that's it."

Anya nodded as Gary closed his menu, then she turned to Samaira who blinked behind her large glasses.

"Oh, right. This is me," Samaira said and brought up her blue menu screen by tapping her collar bone.

SAMAIRA UPADHYAY: LEVEL 29 AETHERIC RANGER
Statistics

- Awareness-9
- Dexterity-20
- Fortitude-23
- Intelligence- 27
- Strength-5
- Willpower-8

Skills

- Aetheric Manipulation-28
- Aetheric Channeling-28
- Aetheric Theory-18
- Archery (Oella Mandai)-17
- Combat Acrobatics -11
- Bestial Affinity (Feline)-13

"Neither of you have gear bonuses?" Anya asked.

"Like I said, I spent all my dough on getting my factory going," Gary said. "I've built a few things for myself, but nothing that gives me any boosts."

"I can put my gear on whenever I need it. Otherwise I'd be a bit... conspicuous," Samaira said and looked Anya up and down in her regalia and cloak. A hint of a smirk tugged at one corner of her mouth.

"Gotcha. And what's this aether stuff?" Anya asked and pointed at Samaira's menu.

"It's like invisible magic clay. It's usually nothing, which means you can turn it into anything," Samaira replied. "Weapons, shields, healing stuff, traps, illusions, whatever. The Oella Mandai is an alien form of Archery that paired well with the acrobatics skill. And the affinity lets me 'speak,' to Chandrali here. She's from the RAC store. Aren't you baby?"

Samaira picked the cat up and nuzzled her, which Chandrali seemed to accept with aloof grace.

"Neat. All right, my turn, I guess," Anya said and displayed her own menu for the other hosts. Gary seemed pleased with Anya's choices.

"Very direct. Smash and burn. I like it," he said. Samaira gave a quick nod, though her eyes narrowed with curiosity. Anya saw her looking up the Dominions on her own menu later as they all waited.

After another fifteen minutes, hundreds, perhaps thousands of people had exited the mall and made their way to parking areas or other shops down the street. A few still lingered near the barricades, but the security guards and police kept them back. After another few minutes, the trickle of exiting shoppers stopped and the guards locked the doors.

"Looks like we're all clear to move in," Gary said as he studied the monitor.

"I've got my invisible alien jet I can grab if you guys need a lift over there. Figured we'd go in through the roof?" Anya said.

"I can get there fine on my own. It's only a few blocks," Samaira said.

"And I'm more of a behind-the-scenes kind of guy. I'll be staying here and sending my boys in," Gary said and pushed a few buttons on his wristwatch. His robots sprang to life and showed a variety of limbs and enhancements: piston-powered legs, propellers, small jets, and all of them equipped with crude weaponry ranging from micro-missiles to what appeared to be miniature rail guns.

"Nice. These things work?" Anya asked.

Gary nodded. "Not as much as I'd like but, well, you work with what you've got. Like I said, scrap and chewing gum."

"I'll leave the Shadow Ray here with you, Pan, and Riley," Anya said.

"How're you gonna get there?" Samaira asked.

"I can fly," Anya replied as she approached the Shadow Ray and opened the hatch. Pan was licking at the floor and looked up as she entered, but shied away from the frigid evening air.

"Cold!" Pan said, and Anya raised the ambient heat around her to a toasty warm level, and the pangolin relaxed.

"Pan, I'm gonna go for a while, all right? You need to stay here with Riley. Stay with Riley," she repeated to make sure Pan understood.

"Stay. Stay with Riley," Pan repeated. "Anya come back?"

"Yes, Pan. I'll come back."

"Okay. Bye-bye, Anya!" Pan said with a wave.

"All set," Anya said as she closed the hatch behind her.

"I'll make sure the little guy stays safe," Riley said.

"Good, let's head up and out," Samaira nodded toward the far corner of the roof of the parking garage.

"Good luck ladies. Be safe. If you're in trouble, don't hesitate to let the bots take a hit for you. I can build more later," Gary said.

"Thanks Gary. See you soon," Samaira patted the old man on the arm. He smiled at her, then gave Anya another quick handshake.

"Sam's got a communicator with her that can broadcast and receive. If you speak up, I'll be able to hear you," Gary said and Anya nodded before following Samaira to the edge of the parking lot.

"That's the Water Tower Place," Samaira said and pointed at a rectangular white building of marble and concrete a few blocks up the street. "Before we go in, do you fight up-close or at range?"

"Close range. Real close," Anya said, remembering with a faint smile how pleased the glowing sparrow within the Flame Dominion had been with her.

"Perfect. I'm at range, and Gary is support. C'mon Chandrali! Ready to give Mom a lift?" Samaira asked the cat, who curled itself around her foot, then leaped away.

"You're riding your cat to the mall?" Anya asked.

Samaira smiled at her, stepped away, snapped her fingers and changed before Anya's eyes.

Samaira's plain coat, blouse, and dress were transformed into a flowing pleated skirt of oceanic blue with high, elegant boots to match. Her top changed to a sleeveless white tunic fringed with shimmering blue and gold ribbons, and long white gloves that went up past her elbows appeared on her arms. A shoulder cape of translucent indigo material fluttered behind her, pinned into place by a gleaming sapphire, and a pale gold tiara with a matching gemstone encircled her forehead. Her hair changed too, from deep black to an ethereal blue the color of midnight, and it sparkled as though it held the stars themselves. Her glasses vanished, and fully exposed eyes that glowed with inner cerulean light.

Anya had never actually had her breath taken away before that moment. She had thought it was a cliché, just some poetic license and nothing more. But as she stared at Samaira, fully aware of some blush creeping up along the sides of her neck and into her cheeks, she did forget to breathe until her body insisted on it.

Just for a moment.

The cat had changed too, though Anya barely noticed it as an afterthought.

One moment she was a typical white house cat, and the next she was a saber-toothed tiger the size of a draft horse. Her coat glistened with the prismatic sheen of fresh crystalline snow, and her massive fangs were so white they almost glowed.

"Whoa," Anya said and took a step back. Samaira mounted the enormous cat with ease and grace, almost floating as she did.

"Don't dawdle," she said, and then patted Chandrali on the side of her thick neck. The cat/tiger launched itself into the air in a flurry of white, and flew over the streets below. Anya watched, stunned, as the tiger sprinted through the air. Her paws brought up pale blue flashes of light every time she sprang forward, running across thin air. Samaira landed on the distant roof mere seconds later, and Anya saw her turn and put her hands on her hips as if impatient.

Anya arched an eyebrow, then flexed her hands and willed herself up into the air, shot down the street and the few blocks to the roof of the mall, and landed beside Samaira with the elegance of an autumn leaf touching down.

Chandrali yawned.

"Well, glad to see you can get around, at least," Samaira said as she turned toward the metal rooftop access door. "Mm, locked."

"I got it," Anya said and ripped the door off its hinges.

"I can just unlock things, you know."

"Okay, next one's yours."

Anya glanced up as she heard a sound like a tiny helicopter, and one of Gary's robots descended on them, the propeller on its "head" whirling away. It carried a number of other smaller robots in a series of claws, and there was another copter bot behind it carrying more. The two flying robots dropped their cargo on the roof, and the smaller robots sprang to life.

Each robot had the basic size and structure of medium-sized dogs but with only three legs. Boxy heads swiveled around, each equipped with a light, a small camera, and other gizmos Anya didn't recognize. Some of the robots had what Anya first thought were laser pointers welded to their heads and flanks, but then she sensed the tremendous heat coming off of them and realized they had to be on par with Earl's chrome rifle. Others had metal pipes or tubes on their backs and sides, or machetes and blades folded back behind their legs.

"Let my boys take the lead," Gary said from a communicator Samaira had attached to the side of her collar, his voice calm and clear. "They'll find it no problem."

"Has it moved at all?" Samaira asked. The squad of crude robots filed into the stairwell behind the door and hurried down into the mall, clanking as they went. Samaira followed them, and Chandrali shrunk to her cat-size in order to get in behind her. Anya brought up the rear.

"Not an inch," Gary said.

"Weird," Samaira said.

"Felix? Any idea how close it is?" Anya asked.

"One or two floors down! Just picked up the signal when you flew over," Felix said.

"Yeah, can confirm. Exactly one floor down though, not two. Sorry, I should have said earlier. Please forgive me," Samaira's AI appeared as it said in a mopey voice.

They reached the end of the maintenance stairwell and an open doorway. The robots had already unlocked it and entered a concrete employee's only hallway that led out into the mall's main atrium. Their clanking, metallic feet echoed on the hard floor ahead. It was the only sound in the mall. The robots pushed open the inner door and descended the escalator one level.

"Still nothing," Samaira said. "We'll wait here until the robots confirm where it is."

"You said it was a blue mailbox?" Anya asked and Samaira nodded.

"Should be easy enough to spot in-doors," Gary said. Chandrali returned to her massive tiger form as they waited at the top of the escalator. The robots entered a department store, and went out of sight.

"Closing in on it now," Gary said over the comm. There was a minute of silence, save for the distant clicking and tapping of the robots below.

"Gary?" Samaira asked.

"It's not here," Gary replied.

"What do you mean?" Samaira asked and pulled her menu up. Anya kept her eyes and ears open while Samaira studied her map.

"I can see the dot on my map. Is it on another floor?" Samaira asked.

"No, my AI says the same things Anya's did. It's there, or the signal is, but no blue mail boxes. House stuff like sofas and washing machines and tables and the like. No big blue mailboxes though," Gary said.

"Can they fake their signal?" Anya asked Felix.

"I don't think so," Felix replied. "But they could. I don't have a clue what their full abilities might be."

"Wait," Gary said. "I think I might—shit!"

There was a crash of metal from below, and then some kind of throbbing pulse sound. The communicator on Samaira's collar squealed and she cursed as she grabbed it and threw it away. Metal clattered and banged and smashed on the floor below them, the lights in the mall went out, and then all was still.

"Fuck!" Anya said. She summoned a baseball-sized orb of fire in the air above her head to act as a lamp. Samaira's hair actually shimmered and cast a pale clear light around them as well. Anya stared at the earpiece Samaira had thrown down and frowned. She picked it up and held it next to her ear, then her mouth.

"Gary? Gary!" Samaira said. "The line's dead."

"Felix?" Anya asked.

"Yes?" the AI replied.

"Just making sure you're still here. All the power went out. Everything electrical, maybe?" Anya guessed.

"The Archives aren't electrical," Felix said.

"Electro Magnetic Pulse, maybe? All of Gary's robots run on batteries, so I don't think a regular EMP would've knocked them out, but something like it. If the power's out, they probably are too. And it sounded like one of them got smashed good," Samaira said. "Boo? Any change with the alien?"

"K-kind of? It's still here but, um, I-I can't pin it down as well as I could before," Boo said and sniffled as she displayed the map of the area. The single red dot had changed to a much wider opaque reddish circle.

"Shit," Anya growled, then jumped when red emergency lights flicked on throughout the mall. They cast a bloody pall over the cavernous space, but Anya was grateful for the light and she extinguished her flame.

"Try to narrow down its location as best you can," Samaira said.

"Felix, you do the same, update us if anything changes," Anya added and Felix gave her a salute before they vanished along with Boo. Anya turned to Samaira. "You okay?"

"I'm fine," Samaira said and snapped her fingers. A white bow that was almost as tall as she was appeared in her hand. It curved back in elegant lines that ended in angelic wing-like flourishes. A strand of glowing blue light connected the two ends of the bow, and there was another of those gleaming, flawless blue sapphires in the center of the weapon. Despite the appearance of the bow, Anya did not see any arrows appear on Samaira anywhere.

"I'll go first, you and kitty watch my back," Anya said. Chandrali flicked her tail and flattened her ears against her broad skull.

"Got it," Samaira nodded. Anya took a breath and walked down the motionless escalator toward the darkened department store. The sounds of one of the robots being attacked had been from there, and so had the red dot.

If the alien was there, and it had the same signal as the escaped mailbox last night, it meant that the aliens could change their appearance. And EMP powers hadn't been among the things Gary and Samaira had mentioned about the previous night's battle.

It fought Gary and Samaira, and Gary probably used robots during the first fight too, Anya thought. *And today, it used an EMP—or something like it—to shut down all electronics. It effectively took down Gary's usefulness in one attack. Just like the snake adapted to me. And the puppet, sort of.*

Anya thought back on the puppet. It had grown bony plates to shoot out and rid itself of the flammable ignition gel. But it had been growing bony protrusions all night: harpoons, barbs, claws. It had come up with a makeshift solution based on abilities it already had.

The snake had been different. It had just seemed to gain whole new abilities on the fly.

Was the alien here like the puppet, or the snake? Anya swallowed and forced herself to focus as they drew nearer to the cavernous department store.

One of Gary's robots lay intact but motionless at the entrance. Tendrils of smoke wafted out of its metal body. Anya passed it with a glance, and then saw two more of the robots to her left. She ignited several tiny fireballs in the air and sent them out slowly in front of her. They cast further illumination on the empty store and the wreck of one robot. Keeping them burning far away from her cost her some energy, but they were so small that it barely mattered. Better to see what was out there.

Something powerful had smashed the robot to bits. It had to have been fast too, and very strong judging by how far the pieces of the robot were scattered. Some of the metal plating had even been embedded into the far wall.

"Spread out a little," Anya said. They were too close together. One attack could take all of them out. Samaira didn't respond verbally, but went to the right while Chandrali veered left and Anya continued up the middle.

The store wasn't ideal for a fight, but it wasn't bad. She had sight-lines all the way to the back of the store, and there were multiple pillars to use as cover, and several exits.

That all meant the alien could get away or dodge their attacks too, of course. Assuming they could find it.

The puppet had looked like a normal puppet, save for its eyes. The statue Gary had described looked normal except for the jiggling. What-ever the alien had disguised itself as, Anya hoped it had a tell, like in poker. Something that would give it away.

The snake had just looked like a monster, though. The other aliens, they were all trying to look like something else, something normal. But the snake would never blend in. It had just been a huge, terrifying alien creature.

Anya blinked and shook the thoughts away. If she was lucky, there would be time to wonder about that sort of thing later.

She passed a series of lamps and dining tables, and approached a row of refrigerators and other large home appliances. She stopped when her foot tapped something on the ground and she glanced down.

It was more plating from Gary's robot, surrounded by several other gizmos and pieces of shattered equipment. Chunks of the robot had been everywhere, but there were quite a lot here, and most of them appeared to radiate away. There was a crack in the polished tiled floor as well, more of a small impact crater.

Anya's hair stood on end.

She looked up at a tall refrigerator with side-by-side double-doors, and a water and ice dispenser set within the freezer. It was made of brushed steel, and looked just like any of the other fridges on display.

Except that it had veins.

Vascular pathways crawled along the sides of the fridge beneath its metal plating.

The alien refrigerator turned toward Anya with a scrape of metal on tile, then lunged at her.

20

"S a—" Anya started to call out as she leaped away from the fridge. It was fast, and one of its doors swung outward so quickly that it was nothing but a blur in the reddish light. The door slammed into her, and even beneath her repaired regalia, even with kinetic dispersal, Anya's bones creaked.

She flew back several yards and landed on her feet with a grunt. If an attack like that had hit her during her fight with the puppet, she had no doubt that it would have shattered every bone in her body, if not crushed her entirely.

It didn't hit quite as hard as the snake had though, and Anya grinned.

"Anya!" Samaira shouted.

The fridge lifted up, and a number of arachnid limbs emerged from beneath it and it scuttled away at high speed. Samaira gripped the string of light on her bow between her fingers, and a lance of blue energy appeared within it. She loosed the beam of energy and it shrieked across the floor of the store and detonated against the side of the fridge in an explosion that sent the other appliances and furniture nearby flying away or shattered them outright.

There was a scuff mark and a dent on the side of the fridge, and apparently its burnished steel was not merely for show. The veins beneath the metal exterior crawled up to the dent and pushed it back out with an audible popping noise.

Chandrali followed right behind the arrow and threw her substantial weight at the fridge. She raked diamond claws across the metallic skin and sparks flew, but the fridge remained unmarked. It tilted to one side, pirouetted on several of its repulsive arachnid legs, and flung the huge cat off with a flick of one of its doors. Chandrali flew across the store and hit a concrete pillar with a resounding crack of concrete and bone. The cat was on her feet in seconds, but she looked woozy, and blood leaked from her mouth.

"Chandrali!" Samaira shouted and fired an arrow at the cat. Anya had a moment of confusion as she wondered why Samaira would shoot her own cat, but then saw the arrow didn't pierce the animal. It burst on impact in a cloud of tiny lights, and all of them were absorbed into the tiger's skin. The blood vanished, and Chandrali shook herself, good as new.

"Healing. Good to know," Anya said then shouted a warning as the fridge scuttled directly at Samaira. She fired a volley of arrows lightning-quick, but all of them bounced off the unnatural metal plating of the fridge. Anya fired herself with a slingshot of opposing gravitational forces across the store, both legs extended in a double kick, as she increased the temperature around her feet until they glowed and left searing trails in the air behind her.

She collided with the side of the fridge like a cannonball, denting the metal inward and causing it to glow and soften. She punched it with an explosion of force and fire, and then it spun away, whacking her with its heavy door again. She was ready for the door attack this time, and blocked it without issue. Kinetic dispersal managed to soak up some of the impact and convert the rest into ambient heat that Anya absorbed at once.

The fridge squealed as the still-glowing side of its armored body burned it and it spun away behind a pillar.

"Little bastard can't take the heat!" Anya laughed. It had planned for Gary's robots with that electronic-frying pulse. It had prepared for

Samaira's arrows and Chandrali's claws with its armor plating. It had not planned on Anya, and fire.

The fridge rounded the pillar, opened both of its doors, and Anya and Samaira both dove aside as something whipped out. Anya had a glimpse of a writhing fleshy mass of tentacles, and then one of them lashed up and at the ceiling.

It struck one of the many overhead sprinklers in the store, and water flooded out. It hissed louder than a nest of vipers as it splashed across the heated metal fridge, and the alien vanished behind a cloud of steam as the water doused its side. Anya had been able to sense the fridge even behind the pillar because of where she had heated up its metal body. But with the water cooling it and giving way to steam, all she could sense from the growing cloud of vapor was that there was a big hot cloud of steam in the store now.

"Dammit!" Anya said and backed away, out of the spray of water and well away from the obscuring cloud of steam.

Samaira launched another volley of energy arrows into the steam cloud. Explosions boomed and the fridge was knocked out of the cloud and onto its side, but it used its powerful doors to flip itself up again. It flicked its doors open when Samaira shot at it again, and actually deflected the arrows of light away from it and back towards Samaira. Her gossamer shoulder cape snapped to life and swirled around her and blocked her own attacks as though it had a mind of its own. Chandrali stayed between Samaira and the fridge, refusing to leave her defensive position.

"Fucker," Anya snarled at the fridge as it lashed more of its tentacles out and broke more sprinklers. The store was soaked now, and water poured down from the ceiling in a deluge. Anya could still summon fire, but it would be mildly more irritating now. The real problem was making things too hot and turning all of the water to steam and granting the fridge cover.

She could lure the fridge out into the open area of the mall, but assuming it followed, it could just hit more sprinklers out there. She considered taking it outside of the mall entirely, but instantly thought of all the innocent people out there and rejected the idea.

Well, if it was just going to keep running away and taking pot shots at them, she'd have to make sure it couldn't run anymore. Xhama Thul informed her that the refrigerator's arachnid legs looked mighty vulnerable at their joints. While the mass of legs were strong together, one-by-one, they'd be pretty weak. Shame if something happened to them.

Anya charged at the fridge, going in low to grab the legs and crush them, bend them past the point of breaking, or flat out turn them to charcoal if she had to. The fridge turned to face her, doors closed, and then something moved from the ice dispenser in the door.

Whatever it was slammed into Anya's chest like a cannonball and she was brought up short. If she had been a normal human, it would've killed her outright, blasted right through her ribcage and out her back. As it was, it only surprised her and knocked her on her ass.

It was something roughly the size and shape of an avocado. And it fell inert to the ground after hitting Anya, a crack on its side. She ducked to one side as another flew past her, and then another. The things were shooting out of the ice dispenser, one after another: three, four, five, six. Anya dodged them, smacked them aside, or just tanked the hits. They didn't feel great but her regalia and her kinetic absorption dealt with them no problem.

"You okay?" Samaira shouted at Anya as she too dodged one of the avocado things. Chandrali dodged an eighth, and slapped a ninth out of the air with her diamond claws.

"Fine! Gonna try something!" Anya said and rushed at the fridge's legs again. It leaped up and over her, but Anya yanked it back down to the ground and onto its side with a gravitational pull and then a shove. She lunged for its legs, but gasped when a whip-like electrical cord appeared from behind the fridge. The metallic tines of the cord were sharp like stingers, and it jabbed Anya in the arm. The tines couldn't pierce her skin, but just making contact was enough.

Anya had just registered the cord and the tines against her skin, and then pain jolted through her body and blue light sparked around her. Her body convulsed and her jaw was forced shut as agony sent all of her muscles spasming and she was finally thrown aside in a powerful electrical blast.

For a moment she thought the blue light had been Samaira, that the woman had shot her with one of her blue arrows. The fridge turned to face Samaira, and the black electric cord rose like a snake behind it. Its sharpened prongs crackled with electricity.

Anya's regeneration was already taking care of the pain and the shock and she got to her feet. She took a step forward and stepped on something that crunched.

She spared a quick glance down and saw the remains of those avocado-shaped projectiles the fridge had shot. It had broken open, and was hollow inside. Anya squinted at the shattered projectile, then her eyes went wide.

They weren't just projectiles.

They were eggs, and they had hatched.

"Uh-oh," Anya said. "Samaira, this thing's making babies!"

"It's what?" Samaira asked and then screamed as something attacked her and Chandrali roared in response. Anya started to run toward them, but spun around instead when a rapid tap-tapping approached her from behind.

She had heard a sound like it hundreds of times in or around her apartment: the quick, scurrying, tiny tipped feet of cockroaches on tile or plaster. She didn't sense any additional heat sources around her, but the sound was enough to tell her that something was closing fast.

She spun on her armored boot and her stomach twisted in disgust at the thing that crawled out from under a fallen dining table. It was the size of a corgi, already several times larger than the egg would have allowed, and it was still growing as Anya stared. It had the slick, chitinous brownish exoskeleton of a roach, and the head of a malformed human infant. It opened its eyes to reveal black, segmented surfaces, and a mewling mouth lined with needle-sharp teeth that drooled a clear viscous fluid. It had stubby centipede legs that clattered on the wet tile floor, and the arching tail of a scorpion.

"Fucking nope," Anya said as she beheld the rapidly growing horror in front of her.

And there were at least a dozen of them in the store right now.

"Guuuuulll," the creature cooed and rushed at Anya. It was now the size of a pit bull, but it seemed to have stopped growing there. She ignited her foot and the air around it to several thousand degrees, and held the disgusting abomination in place with an invisible claw of gravity.

Her flaming kick turned the repulsive thing to so many bits of flaming mush. Whatever the things were, they were fragile. Anya brought her foot down onto the creature's flaming guts just to make sure it was dead, then leaped across the floor to go help Samaira and Chandrali.

Well, she tried.

She jumped, but something held her down and she wound up ripping a huge section of the floor off and stumbling onto her face. She glanced down to find that her foot had been glued to the floor she had just torn up. The roach-creature's guts and blood had dried to cement-like texture and acted like some kind of super-adhesive.

"Little fucker," Anya swore, then glanced up as something charged at her.

The fridge.

Anya curled up into a defensive ball, but the alien refrigerator put all of its weight and speed behind the charge. Anya flew across the store and into, then through, a cement wall.

"Ow," Anya winced and popped her neck. Still, considering that charge would have turned a normal human to paste, she was doing fine. No broken bones, even. She had barely used regeneration, and she was far from needing the star's breath crystal in her pouch, let alone the healing potion. Had she gotten that much stronger or was this alien just weak?

Samaira screamed from outside again and Anya swore. It might not be too much of an issue for her, but the same wasn't true for Samaira and her overgrown cat.

Anya kicked the remnants of floor that clung to her boot off of her, then launched herself back out through the hole in the wall. More of the fridge-spawn emerged from nearby, and vomited their super-adhesive at her. She lit them on fire as she passed overhead, the air around her body now hot enough to make the flying glue-spit sizzle and evaporate.

The refrigerator lashed at Samaira with its tentacles. She had constructed a translucent blue orb around herself, but it cracked under the blows from the fridge. Chandrali had killed several of the fridge-spawn, but the cat was also coated in the glue and her movements were stiff and awkward.

"Hey freak!" Anya shouted and dove low again. The fridge spun around, swung one of its doors wide to bash Anya, but she ducked under it, and made a wedge of gravity around her feet that lifted the fridge up enough so she could grab its spindly arachnid legs.

She ignited her palms, and used all of her strength and gravitational force to literally yank the legs out from underneath the fridge. It squealed in pain, and tried to skitter away on the few legs it had left.

"Nu-uhn," Anya said and her Sun's Heart flared in her chest. Her hands flexed, and she felt invisible claws of force around her fingers, beckoning the fridge to her. It turned from her and made to flee, but Anya lunged forward, covering half the store in a single, inhuman leap. The electrified tail of the fridge lashed out at her, but Anya snatched it, and ripped it straight off with a loud grunt of effort. The fridge attempted to scramble away again but Anya grabbed it by its sides before it could go far.

She superheated her fingers and dug them into the refrigerator's metal sides. The armored exterior softened beneath Anya's grip as if it were nothing more than wet clay. The fridge thrashed in her grasp, flinging its doors open and slamming them shut, lashing with its tentacles and scratching at her feet with its injured legs.

"Hey Mr. Alien, you ever watch pro-wrestling?" Anya asked. She dug her fingers further into the metal and made the fridge squeal in agony. She grunted and lifted it up off its wounded legs, her back arched as she flexed her arms. With a mad laugh she bent backward and suplexed the refrigerator.

The floor collapsed under both of them from the force of the impact, and Anya flipped the gravity around them so the fridge landed on its back and she landed on top of it. She slammed her fist down into the ice dispenser and broke through the fridge's protective shell. Its tentacles behind the doors writhed around her fist, pushing fruitlessly against her.

There was a roar of fire as Anya turned everything around her fist and arm into a small, localized nova, and blew the doors off the fridge.

She was blown back by the blast as well, but she didn't care. She caught one of the refrigerator's doors, and then lifted it over her head, ready and willing to beat the alien to death with its own body parts.

But it was already done.

The inside of the alien refrigerator was nothing but a charred, brittle clump of scorched tentacles that crumbled before Anya's eyes.

"You got it!" Felix cheered.

Anya sighed and threw the door to the ground with a heavy bang. It occurred to her that the door probably weighed several hundred pounds by itself, and she had just chucked it aside as if it were nothing more than a piece of plywood.

It also occurred to her that she was a little disappointed that the fight was over. She was also relieved that she wasn't beat all to hell, and that nobody had died.

But still.

It had been fun for a few minutes there.

Anya stared down at the ruined and smoking remains of the alien. The holes where she had dug her fingers into the metal smoked and glowed with fading residual heat. She had quite literally torn the thing apart and roasted it alive, and she had delighted in doing it.

A part of her worried if this was normal.

But a much larger part, and growing like a carefully tended fire, only wanted more.

21

"Hey. Little birdy. Is this you?" Anya said and looked down at her chest, where her Sun's Heart beat happily within her ribcage. She'd always been a little snippy with authority, maybe had something of a temper. But she'd never delighted in ripping anybody apart and burning them to cinders.

Granted, she had also never really done that before, at all, prior to the invasion. And she supposed the aliens weren't really the same as humans. They had come here and started murdering people first, after all.

Still, after her conversation with the glowing bird a couple days ago, she wasn't so sure this feeling of mad elation during battle was her own.

"Birdy?" Anya said again.

"Anya?" somebody said above her. Anya jumped and then looked up through the hole she had made in the floor. Samaira peered down from above, a few smears of blood on her face and clothes, but otherwise intact. Small threads of blue light emitted from the sparkling azure gem in her tiara and caressed her face, neck, and shoulders. Wherever they touched, any injuries vanished, and her clothes were cleaned.

The threads were mostly focused on Chandrali, who had returned to her house cat form and was clutched to Samaira's chest. Her white fur was more than a bit bloody, but the cat was still breathing and alert.

"Oh! Hey. You all right? And your cat?" Anya asked, aware she was blushing but hoped it wouldn't show in the dim glow of the mall's emergency lighting. Having a new acquaintance catch her talking to the front of her shirt wouldn't be among the best impressions to make.

"Yeah, thanks to you. Mostly some superficial cuts and scrapes, nothing I can't heal. You were amazing, though," Samaira said. "Chandrali and I mopped up those little ones no problem. That refrigerator was a nightmare. It wasn't anything like that during our first fight. It specifically changed itself to take me and Gary out. If you hadn't been here..."

"Nasty fuckers, aren't they?" Anya said and looked down at the dead husk of the alien. She kicked its side with a hollow bang.

"Oh! Oh! Data stream! Alien data stream!" Felix said and darted about in the air around Anya's head. "Level-ups too! And RAC! And-and-and—"

"Take a breath buddy," Anya said. "We'll deal with it when we're out of here."

"I got the data stream too. Sorry Felix got to it first. I'll try to do better next time, but I doubt it," Boo said beside Samaira. She rolled her eyes.

"My AI needs therapy," Samaira said. "So, head back to Gary?"

Anya nodded and floated herself back up through the hole in the ceiling/floor. Both women and cat returned to the roof where Samaira paused.

"Uh, Chandrali is still a bit wounded. If it's okay, could you maybe give me a lift?" she asked.

"Yeah, no problem. I can just float you guys back with me," Anya replied.

"Do I need to grab onto you or anything?"

"Not unless you want to," Anya said as a joke, then realized how it sounded and cleared her throat. "I mean, no, just don't move around too much."

Samaira looked aside as she nodded in response. Anya winced

inwardly, worried she had offended the woman, then quickly floated the two of them and the cat up off the rooftop, and over the streets of Chicago. They landed on the roof of the parking garage beside Riley moments later.

The agent was on the phone as they landed, and a look of extreme relief crossed his face as he saw them.

"They're here. Yeah they look fine. Yes ma'am. As soon as I get the details. Yes, ma'am. Bye," Riley said.

"Thank you," Samaira said to Anya as her clothing shimmered and she returned to her normal civilian clothes. Anya made a note to ask her how she did that. She liked her regalia and cloak, but she would also have liked to have some jeans and a t-shirt back.

"What happened?" Riley asked. "Gary said his robots blew up or something and then we just heard explosions and banging from all the way back here. Is it dead?"

"Oh yeah," Anya said and popped her knuckles.

"Where's Gary now?" Samaira asked.

"Turning all the cars on the floor below us into a damned droid army or something. Should probably go stop him," Riley said and rubbed his chin. All three of them went down a floor and Anya almost burst out laughing at the sight: at least a dozen cars had been disassembled and a small squad of three-legged robots made of their remains were all hurrying around the garage and bringing spare parts to Gary.

The man himself stood over a makeshift table he had made from some pipes he'd ripped off the ceiling and the hood of an SUV.

"Gary!" Samaira called. The man looked up and turned toward them, away from whatever he had been working on. He had some kind of metal gauntlets covering his hands and forearms. The fingers ended in a variety of tools: blow torches, a laser cutter, clamps, power drills, and more gadgets extended from the forearm sections of the gauntlets. Some kind of translucent shield of light had expanded from around Gary's glasses to cover his face. He tapped the side of his glasses and the shield vanished, and the gauntlets folded up and in on themselves until they had turned into a silver watch on Gary's left wrist.

"Thank God," Gary said. "You okay, Sam?"

"I'm fine. We all are. And the alien's dead," she replied.

"Good. Rotten little bastard. I was just throwing something together for backup. Didn't expect the thing to fry my bots. Should have, though. Stupid of me."

"Can't plan for everything. I probably would have just retreated if Anya hadn't been there. We would've figured something out."

Anya thought of the foul, scuttling little alien bugs that spat and bled glue. Samaira might not have been able to retreat at all if one of them had gotten her and she'd been alone. She shuddered. Just one more reason to take the aliens out quickly: if you fought one and it ran, it would just come back specifically designed to kill you.

Anya had barely survived her fight with the snake gnosiphage.

It was out there, still, maybe hunting her down right this moment with a whole new set of powers designed to counter her even more than last time.

Anya's ear beeped and she almost jumped.

"You're getting a message from Pan," Felix informed her. Anya brought up her communications window to see a video of the pangolin inside the Shadow Ray. His long snout was almost touching the camera, and his little nostrils flared as he spoke.

"Anya? I've gotta go to the bathroom. I don't think I should do it in here, though," Pan said, and Anya blinked as he spoke. He spoke in complete sentences. He even used contractions.

"Yeah, I'll be right up," Anya said and jogged back up to the roof of the garage. Riley was on the phone again and waved to get her attention. She just nodded at him as she ran past and opened the Shadow Ray.

"Thank you! Excuse me!" Pan said as he waddled as quickly as he could over to a corner of the roof. Anya blinked again, and Riley paused in his conversation as they stared after the pangolin.

He was wearing clothes. Pan had purchased a pair of baggy, dark green pants with a hole for his tail, and a loose black coat that looked something like a short-sleeved kimono from the RAC store. He wandered behind a car for privacy and took care of business. When he emerged after a few moments, Anya grinned at him.

"So, I'm assuming you figured out the RAC store? Upgraded your English skill a bit?" she asked.

"Yes! I was talking to Bee-Eff, that's for Bright Friend, and they helped me figure this out. They kept saying I need more of this English stuff to learn, and help you. And I want to help! Also they said most people who talk also wear clothes, and it would help with the cold air," Pan said.

"Yes, ma'am he's wearing clothes now," Riley muttered into his phone, then looked up at Anya. "The director wants to know what you plan on doing now. She's got some calls to get through tonight, then she's going home until first thing tomorrow morning, when she hopes you will join her in Manhattan for a meeting."

Anya sighed, but remembered what MacDougal had told her: they could both make each other's lives a lot easier, or a lot harder. There hadn't been a single casualty at the Water Tower Place tonight, in no small part due to the coordination of the FBI, the Chicago PD and EMS, the Mayor, and probably more politicians and officials and middle-managers that Anya had no idea about.

That wasn't the sort of power she could just pick up from the Archive.

At least, she didn't think so. She'd have to ask Felix about it later.

"All right. I'll be there. Just tell me where and when," she said.

"She says eight in the morning, sharp, 26 Federal Plaza. Somebody will meet you out front," Riley said.

"Done."

"Any chance of you getting the two downstairs to join us?" Riley asked, listened to MacDougal for a moment then added, "And the pangolin?"

"His name is Pan, and he'll be sticking with me, yes. The two downstairs... it's up to them. I'll ask. No promises though," Anya said with a shrug.

"That'll be fine," Riley said and hung up after another moment. "Don't suppose you could give me a lift back to Manhattan? I still got some shit to deal with."

"Yeah. Let me check with the others first," Anya said, and she,

Riley, and Pan went back downstairs. Anya filled Gary and Samaira in on the meeting with MacDougal tomorrow.

"I'm not gonna make you come with me, but Riley's been nice, MacDougal has been reasonable, and they both helped us save people tonight," Anya said. "I was pretty against getting involved with the feds at first but it's going okay, so far. Knock on wood."

"I'll go," Samaira said. "I've wanted to contact somebody but I just haven't made time to. Everything has been going so fast since it started."

"Hm," Gary grunted and looked between Riley and Anya. "I'll go to New York with you, but I'll stay out of any fed buildings for the time being. Give it a while, maybe we'll see how it goes."

"All we ask for is a fair shot, Mr. Hendricks," Riley said.

Anya's stomach growled, interrupting the moment.

"You hungry, kid?" Gary asked Anya, who just nodded. "Good. Me too. Get in your fancy space car and follow me. I know a place. You're welcome too, I guess, Agent."

Gary slid his hand over his watch and it expanded into a type of complicated keyboard that covered most of his forearm. He tapped something into it faster than Anya could follow, and all his robots began to reassemble the cars they had torn apart.

"No sense stripping people's cars apart now. I'll hit the junkyard later. Sam, you riding with me?" Gary asked, and she nodded as she followed Gary back up to the roof with Chandrali. Anya, Riley, and Pan got into the Shadow Ray and waited.

Anya expected to fly overhead as Gary drove his truck along the roads. She was only somewhat surprised when the old F-150's tires folded in and up under the truck, and then it lifted up into the air almost as smoothly as Anya's Ray. He gave them a wave to follow him and took off across the city.

"Follow that truck, autopilot," Anya said, and they flew after.

22

They all landed behind a tiny white building with red trim and a sign that read "Aaron's Drive-In/Take-Out." The parking area behind the building was mostly vacant except for a large trash bin, and had plenty of room for Anya's Ray and Gary's truck to land side-by-side.

"Just get me whatever. And the Bureau's paying again. I know what your food bill looks like and I think Uncle Sam's the only one who can afford to feed you," Riley said with a smirk as he handed Anya a credit card. "I'll hang out here with Pan and talk about... I dunno."

"Ants!" Pan cheered.

"Yeah, sure. Ants. Uh, you like red ones or black ones more?" Riley asked as Pan clapped his claws together and the others entered the restaurant. Anya inhaled the rich aromas of frying onions, potatoes, beef, butter, and other heavenly scents as soon as the doors opened.

The diner was small, with only a few circular tables surrounded by bar stools and a narrow counter facing the window for seating. The walls were white tile and fire-engine red, and a huge glowing white menu hung above the register that listed delicious foods in bold red print.

"Heya Gare," a middle-aged man said from behind the counter with a nod. "Don't usually see you out this late."

"Just showing my friends around town," Gary replied. "The usual, please, to go."

"You got it. And you two?" the man asked. Anya ordered three burgers on pretzel bread with sides of fries and cokes for herself, and a fourth set for Riley, while Samaira got fried fish tacos and onion rings. Anya paid for everything with Riley's card, and they were given thick cardboard boxes spotted with grease and lined with crackling wax paper. The smells of the food taunted Anya until they all went back outside.

The wind had died down, but Anya summoned a basketball-sized flame for the others to gather around if they were cold. Samaira's tiara appeared on her head and she pointed a finger at Anya's flame. The flame became encased in a crystalline blue orb that seemed to magnify both the heat and the light, while keeping the others from getting singed as they drew closer.

"Neat trick," Anya said.

"Why, thank you," Samaira said with a smile. Anya handed Riley his food and he took it gratefully. Pan was babbling about digging now, which Riley listened to for a while with a bemused look on his face. Eventually Pan turned to Samaira and Gary.

"What about you? New friends? Do you like ants?" Pan asked. "And digging?"

"Can't say that I do," Samaira said.

"I'm more of a beer and auto shop kinda guy," Gary replied.

"That's okay. Still friends," Pan nodded.

"Hey Felix?" Anya asked. And the AI appeared at once. "Now would be a good time to fill us in on all the crap you got after we killed the alien. Since we're all stuffing our faces."

"Right! Still decoding a few things, but I'm getting better at this! Give me a minute!" they replied.

Anya nodded and she looked over at Samaira with a grin.

"So, I take it you were a fan of those magical girl cartoons?" she asked.

"A little," Samaira said and smirked. "You a fan of pro-wrestling?"

"A little. Well, my little brother…" Anya started to say "was," but stopped herself and said, "I used to watch it sometimes when I was little."

"Any particular media franchise inspire you to build robots, Mr. Hendricks?" Riley asked.

"Gary is fine, Agent," he said.

"Then Riley is fine with me. Nobody calls me Christian except my wife and my ma."

"Well, Riley, I picked the skills I did because I always liked working at the car factory, and I figured we'd need an army if we were in a war. And seeing as how I know firsthand what can happen to humans in war, I decided it'd be better if my army was metal instead of flesh and blood. And if we win this little invasion, it'll be good to put those skills to use after the aliens are gone. Maybe start solving some of our own problems, clean energy, things like that."

Anya paused with her second burger halfway to her mouth. Gary had a point. She'd picked her powers to protect herself, Tori, and kill aliens. She hadn't given a second's thought to any long-term skill selection.

"I picked fire powers cause it sounded cool and I was scared an alien would kill me," Anya said, suddenly feeling a bit shitty about herself. Her Sun's Heart beat inside of her, suddenly warmer than usual. While what she said wasn't a lie, it didn't feel entirely accurate either. Maybe she should ask the bird about it later.

"I did basically the same thing. I mean, my aether skills have practical use outside of combat, but that's because I wanted something flexible. I'm thinking I might keep it after the invasion, though," Samaira said.

Anya frowned. What good would she be outside of a fight? Use Gravity Dominion to lift heavy things around?

Gary seemed to sense what she was thinking and smiled.

"You did what you needed to survive. If you hadn't chosen what you had, we'd probably all be dead by now," he said. "And I think that's going to be important going forward. All of us bringing something different. I think if we just try to optimize and all get the same skills, the aliens will just adapt to that and squash us. For whatever reason, they can change themselves and we can't. At least not until level 50 and one of those token thingies."

"Respecification tokens!" a new voice said.

A small flash of grayish-white light announced the arrival of Gary's AI as it appeared on his knee. Like Felix and Boo, it had a chubby, infantile body, and a head in the shape of some kind of plant. This one had a thick bulb with a pointed peak, and oblong petals stretching up and out. It had a stern, eager expression on its face and folded its tiny arms over its chest as it materialized.

"I got the enemy intel!" it said in a rough voice. "How about you take some real fighting skills and we go clean this planet up?"

"Wow," Anya said and raised her eyebrows.

"Yeah, Gizmo here is very enthusiastic about fighting," Gary said and shook his head.

"I got it too! I'm helping!" Felix said as they appeared beside Anya.

"I got it as well, but I was last. Again. Sorry," Boo moaned as they faded into existence reluctantly beside Samaira.

"It's fine, Boo," Samaira sighed. "Just show us what you got, okay?"

"O-okay," the blue AI sniffled and then it and all the other AIs projected their various colored maps in front of their hosts.

The maps showed the precise locations of the aliens and the vague positions of the hosts, like it always had. The time and date in the corner indicated that the map and positions of aliens and hosts were from Monday night, prior to Anya killing the puppet alien.

A clock in the corner fast-forwarded and the various dots moved around the map, which was all the same data Anya had gotten from the puppet. The aliens homed in on hosts and many of them went dark, with only a few of the red alien's lights vanishing. She saw her dot and Earl's converge on the red dot in Brooklyn, Earl's winked out, and then the red dot of the puppet. That was as much information as she had gotten from her first fight: all the movement from when the aliens entered the atmosphere to when she killed the puppet itself.

But now Anya had everything the fridge alien had known from Monday night until its death a short time ago. Almost a week's worth of data.

She went pale as she watched the map.

The red dots coordinated, came together when possible, and hunted down hosts with brutal efficiency and accuracy. Most of the hosts were alone, and they almost always disappeared.

"Dear God," Gary said. Anya couldn't keep track of all the hosts vanishing. Monday night and Tuesday morning were the worst, but throughout the week, the aliens had been lethally busy.

"Felix, how many?" Anya asked. "How many hosts have died in total now?"

"As of the fridge-alien's death, exactly 11,918 hosts have been killed. 7,513 of those since the last time you checked," Felix said and the petals of their rose-head drooped.

"How many were there to begin with?" Samaira asked. "Thirteen thousand and something?"

"13,054," Anya said.

"Friends are gone?" Pan asked. Anya nodded.

"Eleven thooouuusaaaand," Pan said. "How many is that?"

"Way too many," Anya said.

"How many are still here? A lot?"

"No, only 1,136 left alive," Gary said and leaned back against the side of his truck.

"Hell," Riley said. "And that's in under a week."

"It may look grim, but don't even think about running away! Retreat is the coward's way!" Gizmo said. Anya noticed some of the hosts' vague orange circles widening until they simply vanished.

"I'm not going anywhere, you idiot. Couldn't blame some folks for wanting to, though," Gary said.

"Yes you can! You should blame them non-stop!" Gizmo insisted.

"10,947 deaths were due to the enemy aliens. The other deaths appear to be accidents or probably... y'know," Boo said and made a hanging gesture with their tiny mitten hand.

"Suicide," Anya said and put her face in her hands.

"The other coward's way out!" Gizmo said.

"Stow it or I'll delete you," Gary snapped at the AI.

"It's not all bad news," Felix said. "The highest death rates happened in the first thirty hours. After that, well, see for yourself."

Felix highlighted several areas of the map where hosts joined together. In those instances, it was almost always a total victory against any nearby aliens.

"Over seventy-five percent of enemy aliens have gotten their butts handed to them!" Felix said. "Teaming up is a great strategy."

"No kidding," Samaira said.

"How many enemy aliens are left?" Gary asked.

"5,408 targets, of the original 17,875!" Gizmo said. "We may not have the numerical advantage, but we're tearing them down!"

"Assuming most of the other hosts aren't opportunistic looters like the guy last night," Samaira said.

"Or psychos," Riley added. "Still waiting for our first Earthling super-villain to show up."

"It all sounds really bad," Boo moaned.

"Stop moping," Samaira said.

"Whoa," Anya said as she looked at her map. "Check out Tokyo a few days ago."

The map had been running in a loop, showing the progression of the enemy aliens over the last week. Five aliens had converged on a single host at the edge of Tokyo. After what the clock told her was a fight that lasted several hours, all of the enemy alien signatures were gone, and the single host remained.

"Holy shit," Gary said. "One guy?"

"Or gal," Samaira said.

"Or gal," Gary acknowledged.

"This would've been around noon Chicago time," Anya said. "My friend had an idea that the aliens only move at night. I fought that snake alien in the afternoon, so I know that's not entirely true, but that one was different somehow."

"Yeah, we noticed that too. When we were chasing the fridge alien, we almost always caught up to it during the day, but usually lost it at night. Why? Are they nocturnal?" Samaira asked.

"No, I don't think so. I think since they're trying to blend in, they prefer not to move in the day, use the time to change themselves maybe, or recover from injuries, or communicate with the others. Who knows?" Anya shrugged.

"Lookit this one here in Texas," Gary pointed to a host-circle approaching a red dot just outside of Dallas. The circle narrowed to a dot as it got closer to the alien, and then the enemy alien began to move when the host was almost on top of it. The host dot vanished and the red alien dot became motionless once again.

"Glad we decided to keep our distance until the mall was clear," Samaira said with a shudder.

"Yeah no kidding. Would've been a blood bath if that refrigerator went nuts in that mall," Riley said.

"The bad aliens sleep during the day?" Pan asked.

"Kind of?" Anya replied. She wondered again about the snake gnosiphage. She had kept well away from it, but it had still pursued her.

"So maybe they change their shape and abilities during the day. I still feel like the refrigerator alien was just flat out stronger than when we fought it as the mailbox," Samaira said. "The mailbox only had a couple moves: ramming into us at high speed, and the gas attack. It had a much more versatile bag of tricks tonight."

Anya tapped her finger against her chin as she thought. The puppet had been pretty basic as well. It could regenerate, grow bone weapons and armor and limbs, and it was strong. That was it. The fridge had an electric tail attack, was incredibly fast, heavily armored, strong, and it could birth glue-spewing scorpion-roach monsters. The snake-gnosiphage had been worse than both of them.

"I have an idea!" Felix said. "I've been decoding the alien signals and they're somewhat similar to those the Archive system emits. Maybe they have similar functionality too."

"Uh-oh," Anya said and the hairs on her neck prickled.

"Oh God," Samaira added.

"What am I missing here?" Gary asked.

"I'm in the dark too," Riley said.

"Bad things?" Pan asked and started to curl into a ball.

"We level up from those fights. This one with the fridge, how many levels did we get?" Anya asked.

"You got four! Congratulations!" Felix said.

"Yeah, awesome, but the puppet gave me four as well, and I'm at a higher level now. In a game, you have to kill stronger and stronger enemies to level-up, as the distance between levels grows bigger the stronger you get. I assume the Archive system works similarly?" Anya asked and Felix nodded. "So that would imply the fridge was tougher. But when it was just a mailbox it wasn't as strong. But it killed two hosts. So…"

"So the aliens can get stronger by killing us," Gary finished. "Damn."

"I have something to add," Boo whispered and raised their tiny hand.

"Go ahead, Boo," Samaira said.

"The data streams I've decoded from the aliens clearly show that upon death, each alien transmits their data to every other living alien."

Everybody exchanged glances.

"So when an alien dies, all the knowledge and intel it gathered gets sent to everybody else?" Riley asked.

"To the other aliens, yes," Boo nodded.

"Can confirm," Gizmo said.

"Me too!" Felix added.

"So they get smarter whenever they die, and stronger whenever we die," Anya said. "Felix, can you pinpoint the aliens that have killed the most hosts?"

"I sure can!" Felix said.

Two alien signatures blinked on the map.

The first started in northern China near Beijing, then along the coast to Shanghai, then took a sharp line into the middle of the country and headed southwest toward India. The second dot started in Vancouver and made its way down to Sacramento after zig-zagging across the Pacific Northwest at an incredible rate. It eventually flew to just outside Norfolk, Virgina, then to an empty field in Delaware, and then finally out into the middle of the Atlantic, where it waited for a few hours, then to the west coast of Africa where it began tracking hosts again.

The snake gnosiphage.

The number beside each of the dots was eleven. When the snake had fought Anya, it had been at a seven. It had killed four more people since she had fought it. If Felix's estimate was right, then it had nearly doubled in power in a single evening.

Anya said a silent thank you for Tori and the airmen from Dover. She would absolutely be dead without them.

"Holy shit," Samaira said. Pan's AI let out a terrified squeak and cowered behind him. Pan himself curled into a ball. The alien in China was followed by a growing number of other aliens by the time the map data caught up with the current time. The snake gnosiphage acquired five alien tag-alongs in Africa as well. Numbers appeared beside the follower aliens, with the smallest being two and the highest being eight.

"If the fridge today got that much stronger just from killing two hosts, I can't imagine what those monsters must be like," Anya said as she stared at the blinking red dots.

Gary polished his glasses in thought while Samaira put her face in her hands. Chandrali flattened her ears and curled into Samaira's lap. Riley chewed idly at a drinking straw while he stared at the map, as if in shock. Anya looked at all the red dots, the orange circles, and how the former stalked the latter.

She felt herself spiraling down as she watched the map continue playing its loop of the last twenty-four hours. Thousands of hosts killed.

That wasn't counting any nearby people who had been unlucky enough to get drawn into the fights, like the cops in Prospect Park. How many more would die? What kind of horrible nightmares were stalking China and West Africa?

Anya looked at Gary as he looked up at the stars, at Samaira with her shoulders slumped and her face in her hands, at Riley with his distant gaze, and at Pan, curled into a ball next to her on the ground. She thought of Tori back in New York, of all the people at the Water Tower Place and the Virginia Zoo who had been in mortal danger and had no idea. She even thought of her mother and brothers in Clemson.

"Fuck 'em," Anya said.

"What?" Samaira asked as she looked up. Gary quirked an eyebrow at her and Riley finally managed to blink.

"I have a tiny sun in my chest that lets me melt or blow up

anything I want, I know alien wrestling, am strong enough to knock out an elephant, and I can fly. Samaira, you're an actual magical girl who can shoot explosive transforming arrows and you have a giant tiger with diamond claws for a pet.

"Gary, you can build a robot army in a few minutes from scrap. Riley, without you and MacDougal, hundreds or thousands of people would have been killed tonight. And Pan," Anya paused and looked at the pangolin as he uncurled a tiny fraction from his ball and stared up at her with one eye, "you are very good at eating ants."

"I like ants," Pan replied.

"We'll work on other stuff later," Anya continued. "My point is, we've killed two of these freaks so far and me and the air force and my best friend beat the shit out of a third. That fucker right there," Anya pointed at the snake's signal with its tally of murdered hosts.

"The aliens outnumbered us from the start and we've still killed more of them. There's hundreds of people like us out there, and most of the other hosts are doing what we are: teaming up. So fuck these aliens. Looking at what's been going on is intimidating as hell, but I'm not dead yet, and neither are most people. We can fight, and I'm going to."

"Yes! You can be my new host if you want!" Gizmo said and Gary rolled his eyes.

"Quiet you," Gary said with a smirk then looked at Anya. "True enough though. Well said, kid."

"Thank you for that," Samaira said. Felix grinned up at Anya and gave her a double thumbs up. Riley smirked and nodded.

"I think it's still a miracle any of us are sane with everything that's happened since Friday night," Anya said. She had a memory flash of Earl's head getting slapped off and the brief glimpse she had seen of the police officers exploding and quickly slammed those thoughts to the back of her mind.

For all her words about screwing the aliens, the thought of the puppet butchering the cops and staring at her with its hateful intelligence still made her sweat.

"I've been touch-and-go a few times," Samaira said and Gary grunted out a weak laugh.

"What now? It's night, the aliens will be moving around," Gary said.

"I've got to make my way to New York for a meeting with Director MacDougal tomorrow morning. Plus, I should drop Riley off and check on my friend."

"Can I still come with you?" Pan asked. Anya smiled at him and nodded and he clicked his claws together in a tiny clap.

"We should stick together, or at least within a reasonable distance," Gary said. "Samaira and I were talking about leaving Chicago and looking for others. Be silly to part ways after we ran into each other. I'm not setting foot in a government building, but we'll watch your back and stay close. New York's probably got some pretty good scrap yards around it I can poke through while you're having your meeting with the feds. If you need me, I can be there lickety-split."

"Yeah. No more going solo, for any of us," Samaira agreed and smiled at Anya then Pan.

"The Bureau will back you as long as MacDougal's at the helm. She's no dummy," Riley said.

Anya felt her shoulders relax. Just hearing Riley, Gary, and Samaira say that she wouldn't be alone unwound a tension she hadn't been aware of seconds before. Pan clicked his claws together again and bumped his head against Anya's side. Anya patted him on his scaly back and entered the Shadow Ray to prep for take-off.

Tomorrow would be another busy day.

23

The aliens were dead.

A light snow fell on their remains, what little was left of them. One of them had appeared as a towering lamppost, while the other had a passing resemblance to a tree. The lamppost had possessed a giant glowing eye instead of a lightbulb, and the tree had patches of coarse, needle-like hair sprouting out of its trunk, and leaves like razor-blades.

Harrison Evans knelt in the snow, shivering as he looked at the pieces of the aliens scattered around him.

"Are you all right?" a man asked. He was shorter than average, but not by much. He wore a long white trench coat with a high collar and purple lining. A hi-tech looking piece of white body armor protected his chest, and sleek white pants were tucked into boots that matched the design of the chest-piece. A helmet covered his face: the front and top of it were made of some kind of mirrored gold material while the sides were polished white. The man's voice was modulated as it came out from within the helmet, but had a very distinct French accent.

"I-I think so," Harrison asked.

"Of course he's all right. We did all the work, didn't we?" a woman said, standing not too far away. Her accent was posh and British, her skin a light tan, and her facial features sharp but pretty and distinctly Eurasian. Her hair was short and spiked and dyed a vibrant shade of cyan. She was taller than the man by a few inches, but looked larger due to a billowing black cloak over gothic armor. Cloak and armor covered her well, but could not entirely conceal a curvaceous figure beneath.

Several figures stood around the woman in defensive positions: skeletons clad in heavy plate armor and wielding huge claymores, axes, and pikes; a few wraith-like forms that consisted of little else but ornate black and purple robes, and glowing points of light for eyes within the shadows of their hoods; and bestial creatures that resembled half-rotted wolves, cougars, and eagles.

The woman and her grim entourage stood near a massive black carriage adorned with wrought-iron spikes and gold filigree. Four skeletal horses in spiked armor were lashed to the front of the carriage, their reins held by a spectral form that sat atop the carriage itself. Whenever the skeletal horses stamped their feet in the snow, pale blue fire flared around their hooves.

"Yes, but we're happy to help," the man said. "It's why we're here. What's your name?"

"H-Harrison," he replied. "Harrison Evans."

"Harrison. I'm Renn, and this is Mona," the man said and offered his hand to Harrison. It was covered by a gauntlet that matched Renn's chest armor and boots, and Harrison shook it.

"Charmed," Mona said and smiled at him. One of the skeletal warriors at her side clacked its teeth together. Mona poked the hulking undead figure in its exposed ribs. "You be nice, now."

"What level are you, Harrison?" Renn asked.

"Level 25."

"Is there a reason you didn't fight?"

"They... I don't like using them. It makes them stronger. I made a mistake and if I call them they say things. Do things."

"Can I see your menu?"

"No!" A raspy voice suddenly said from behind Harrison's back. A pair of glowing ember eyes flared from within Harrison's shadow and glared at Renn. "Mind your fucking business!"

"Oh? Who's this now?" Renn asked and cocked his head to the side.

"Harrison! We talked about this. Get this one to fuck off if you know what's good for you!" the raspy voice said. Harrison's eyes widened with fear as he looked back at his own shadow and the eyes within it. Several more pairs of eyes opened beside the first, and a whispering chorus of threats emerged.

"Break your fingers—"

"Flay you—"

"Rip your ears off—"

The voices all hissed and Harrison covered his ears and shut his eyes.

"Maybe I can talk to you then," Renn said and extended a hand, fingers splayed wide. "Let's see… whatever you are, you have a brain. Not much of one though."

Renn extended his hand further and flexed his fingers. The cascade of threats turned at once to a series of squeals and curses.

"Stop it! Stop!" the first voice said.

"Come out where I can see you," Renn said. "And if you hurt this young man I'll make this so much worse."

"All right! All right! Just fucking quit it!" the voice said, and then the speaker appeared.

It jumped up and out of Harrison's shadow and Harrison shrank away from it. It was a dwarfish figure, no more than three feet tall. The creature was built like a miniature body-builder, with thick slabs of muscle across its upper torso, its skin leathery and crimson. Its legs were goatish and covered in thick brown hair, and it had a face like a mandrill. Blunt fangs stuck up from its lower jaw, and squat horns poked up from the top of its skull. A pair of leathery wings flapped at its back in agitation, and a long forked tail whipped through the snow behind it. Three more figures like the first emerged from Harrison's shadow, all of them clutching their heads.

"Harrison? Show me your menu, please," Renn said.

"Don't you dare, you little shit!" the red-skinned creature said.

Renn lifted his hand at it, and the creature screamed as an invisible force yanked one of its arms out of its socket, then broke it at the elbow. The other creatures leaped away, snarling at Renn. Their tiny eyes glowed fiery red in their sockets.

"Can't take all of us human!" another one of the creatures said.

"Oh, I beg to differ," Renn replied. Five figures emerged from Renn's back: all of them exact copies of himself. Each one raised their hands. "No more interruptions."

The creatures looked at each other, and backed down. The one with the broken arm huffed and grunted piggishly in the snow.

"Show me your menu," Renn repeated. Harrison tapped his wrist. A pale green menu appeared in the air between himself and Renn.

HARRISON EVANS: LEVEL 25 HUMAN
  Statistics

  - Awareness-10
  - Dexterity-5
  - Fortitude-6
  - Intelligence-10
  - Strength-6
  - Willpower-10

  Skills

  - Infernal Summoning-15
  - Infernal Speech (Pandemonic)-5
  - Transdimensional Sight-5

"Infernal? Like bloody demons?" Mona asked and raised her eyebrows. The skeletal figures around her moved to guard her but she waved them down. "Actual demons?"

"Majordomo?" Renn asked and a glowing purple hologram appeared beside him. Harrison recognized it as the archive's AI system, though it looked different than his. Renn's AI had a head shaped like an orchid, its face partially hidden by the petals.

The AI spoke to Renn in rapid French. Harrison could pick out bits and pieces of it, but not much. Renn nodded as the AI spoke, then waved a hand and the purple AI vanished.

"Not demons like we usually think of them. Less spiritual agents of divine punishment from the afterlife and more chaotic inhabitants of a hell-like dimension. The Infernal Plane, according to the Archive," Renn said.

"Why the hell would you want something like them around?" Mona asked Harrison. He sniffed and shrugged.

"Figured they could kill the aliens for me, keep me safe. And it sounded cool. I didn't know they'd be like… this," Harrison said and gestured at the snorting, dwarfish figures. "I mean, you probably picked your skeletons and ghosts for the same reasons, right?"

Mona's face went still for a moment. She smiled after a beat, but it didn't reach her eyes. "Got me there. Always wanted to lead a bunch of zombies into battle."

"You haven't used all of your stat and skill points? Or taken a class?" Renn asked.

"No. I didn't want to spend too many at once when I first picked the skill. When these things showed up, they started threatening me whenever I tried to pull up my menu."

"Because you're a pissy little crybaby!" the imp with the broken arm snarled. "Not gonna listen to you! Can't make us!"

"Oh, but I think he can," Renn said.

"I know he can," one of his duplicates added.

"That's why you've kept him from enhancing himself. You know he'll shackle each and every one of you *petits diables*, no?" another duplicate asked.

The imps grumbled but did not reply.

"There must be some kind of imbalance between the skill and the stats," Renn said. "Something like a minimum requirement to keep them under control, or maybe an item…"

Harrison perked up. "The AI said I needed a thing called the Onyx Key of the First Infernal Gate to summon them. I got that. It said there was other stuff too, but I didn't want to spend all of my store currency at once, figured the key was enough to start."

Mona clicked her tongue and shook her head. "No offense, Harrison, but that sounds incredibly stupid of you. Makes sense though. I had to get a few items to keep my bone-boys in-line. Otherwise they'd just go all over the place, willy-nilly."

"Why don't we talk about this over some tea?" Renn asked. His duplicates knelt behind him and faded seamlessly back into his body until there was only one Renn left. "It's very cold out here, isn't it?"

"Harrison! If you—" the broken-armed imp started to say but did not finish. Renn flexed his hand and the creature howled, gasped, shuddered, and collapsed into the snow. Black blood leaked from its donkey-like ears, nostrils, and the corners of its eyes. It did not move or speak again.

The other imps drew together and stared wide-eyed at Renn.

Mona laughed.

"Tell the others to go away," Renn said to Harrison. Harrison blinked at him and Renn just nodded his head.

"G-go away," Harrison said. "Get back in my shadow and stay there."

The imps didn't move.

Harrison lifted his finger towards his menu.

"I think I will raise some of these skills, maybe get some really nasty ones to put you in your place. So do what I say or it's going to get ugly."

The imps exchanged glances, looked at Renn, then scrambled for Harrison's shadow and dove into it. Their glowing eyes peered out of the shadow for a moment, then blinked out.

"Nicely done," Renn said.

"We'll make a demon general or whatever out of you in no time," Mona clapped her gauntleted hands together. "Summoning's lovely when you get enough points into it."

Renn stood, then helped Harrison to his feet. Mona opened the door of the carriage to reveal a plush interior of red velvet seats and thick carpet. Her undead entourage sank into the ground or dissipated into mist when she climbed inside. Renn sat beside her and Harrison took the seat opposite.

Mona knocked on the wall behind her, where the spectral coachman sat. There was a whip of reins, and a ghostly howl from the horses, and then the carriage sped up into the dark winter night.

Mona tapped on a panel beside her, and a wooden table rose up in the center of the carriage. A silver tray with a porcelain tea set was already on the table, and the carriage filled with a sweet, floral aroma. Steam rose from the teapot's spout and wafted around the carriage.

"Where are we going?" Harrison asked as Mona poured them all tea.

Renn tapped a button on the side of his helmet, which clicked and folded back into a thin white collar around his neck and exposed his head. He didn't look much older than Harrison, maybe early-thirties at the oldest. He had short, unkempt brown hair, and pale green eyes. His face was plain but pleasant enough, and his expression was neutral, bordering on sleepy.

"West coast, near Vancouver. Mona and I have been making our way west from Europe, trying to help people like you along the way: solo hosts with aliens near them," Renn said as he took his teacup. "Thank you, Mona."

She smiled at Renn and winked at him flirtatiously.

"What did you do before the invasion?" Renn asked.

"I worked at a call center. Paid for shit. Thought getting the Archive was my big break, like the lotto," Harrison replied. "But it's just been a nightmare."

"You've had a rough start, but that's going to change. A lot of things are. For now, I think it's best that we're all on the same page. We find others like us, we find the aliens, we kill them, down to the last. After that…"

Renn paused and smiled at Mona.

"After that, I think we'll need to make some changes ourselves. It's clear that we can't just devolve back into the petty in-fighting that's been Earth's legacy up until now. We're not alone in the universe, and we won't survive if we keep at each other's throats.

"I want to help people, Harrison. Not just you and the other hosts, but everyone. For now that means dealing with the invaders. But when it's done and we win—and we will win—it will mean altering the way things have been done in favor of something new. Something better. Would you be willing to help with that, Harrison?"

Harrison looked between Renn and Mona.

"Are you talking about world domination?" Harrison asked. Renn and Mona looked at each other, then laughed.

"*Quelle folie!* Not at all! Ah, the work that sort of thing would involve! Just thinking about it makes me want to go to bed. I'm talking about a world where the idea of anybody dominating it at all is a thing of the past. With the Archives, we can and should solve all of the problems that have plagued us. Food, water, power, shelter, resources, all of it can be taken care of now. But it's a radical idea, and not one anybody could do alone, even a host for the Archive. It's why I need help. From Mona, from you, from others like us. For now, we fight. But after, maybe fighting is just another problem we never have to worry about ever again."

Harrison sipped his tea and looked at Mona.

"You're on-board with this? How long have you known each other?"

"On-board with solving all of humanity's problems and killing aliens? Sounds like a solid deal to me. And what's it been? About a week? Five days?" Mona asked.

"About that, yes," Renn said.

"You make friends quickly in a war, I suppose. And what else am I going to do? Things weren't exactly rose-fields and gumdrops for me before all of this," Mona said. The grin on her face drooped for a moment as she gazed down at her teacup. Renn put his hand on top of hers and she smiled at him.

Harrison looked between them. They acted unusually close for people who had only known each other for less than a week. War or not.

"I owe you for saving me back there, and for helping me with the imps. I'm not signing on for your peace army or whatever you're trying to do," Harrison said. "At least, not yet. I'll definitely help you kill aliens, assuming the imps stay in their place."

"That's fair. Forcing anybody into this would go against its very purpose," Renn said with a nod. "I just ask that you keep an open mind."

"I think I can do that," Harrison agreed.

Renn smiled into his teacup and glanced out the curtained window of the carriage. The night whipped by them on their way to Vancouver, and whatever changes tomorrow would bring.

PART THREE
THE ELEMENT OF
TRANSFORMATION

FROM EARTH #4

From The Chicago Tribune:

EXPLOSIONS AT THE WATER TOWER PLACE

Thousands of shoppers were calmly evacuated from the Water Tower Place downtown moments before a series of explosions knocked out the power in the building and decimated two floors of the shopping center's top-floor department store.

Authorities are insisting that it was caused by a combination of electrical and gas lines malfunctioning, but would not comment on the presence of SWAT officers or how they had the presence of mind to evacuate the building beforehand.

Several witnesses state they saw something in the air above the shopping center, but couldn't identify what it was due to the power being out.

The Water Tower Place will remain closed for repairs for the next week at least, a spokesman for the shopping center said.

———

From Rutherford International News Network:

DETONATIONS SPOTTED ACROSS POLISH COUNTRYSIDE

Several enormous explosions have been sighted outside multiple cities and towns in the countryside near Purda.

The explosions were seen as domes of light from miles away and even by commercial airliners. The explosions, which occurred over the last few days, were feared to be attacks similar to the one that occurred near Bengaluru earlier this week. Reports from local military and other government and international sources have confirmed a complete lack of nuclear fallout, as well as much smaller zones of destruction.

Photos emerging from the sights of the detonations show circular blast areas over several dozen meters in diameter and craters over five meters deep. Large swathes of forest around the craters have been demolished, but so far, there has been no reported damage to populated areas, property, or any casualties.

———

From Cape Times:

BIZARRE DISTURBANCE IN CAPE TOWN RESULTS IN MASSIVE PROPERTY DAMAGES, DOZENS INJURED

Tuesday night in Cape Town saw what can only be described as a surreal and violent disturbance: numerous videos and photos have surfaced online of what appears to be two people and a small pack of unidentified animals engaged in a battle with a garbage dumpster and a car.

An unidentified man and woman in strange clothing appeared just outside the Victoria & Alfred Waterfront at around 9:30 PM, along with a pack of animals that were described by witnesses as following the man. When asked what the animals were, descriptions varied. Video is mostly blurry, but shows 4-7 animals of different sizes and species, though what those species might be remains unclear.

Explosions and a fire commenced as the strange group began to attack a moving garbage dumpster and a car that witnesses said "ran," around the waterfront and injured several bystanders. Video from witnesses and security footage support the bizarre claims. Locals say the man, woman, and animals protected them and that the garbage dumpster and car were clearly hostile.

At this point, many speculate that this may be some kind of extreme ARG (Alternate Reality Game), or marketing ploy for a film. If that is the case, several of those injured in the attack have claimed they will be suing whoever is responsible.

––––––

From *By-the-Bay*, a Monterey-based forum:

BitGrit: Another "disturbance," in California. This one was a few miles outside the city.

KOW1994: WHAT THE FUCK IS GOING ON

ScubaKingMB: It seems like it's at least half a dozen things every day. Terrorist bomb in Brooklyn, chemical attack in Florida, gas explosion in Chicago, multiple murders in Seattle, earthquake outside LA, and now what? Another bombing outside Monterey?

PresidioPal: Dunno how much I can say, but everybody here on-base has been told to stay on alert at all times.

BitGrit: Aren't you folks at the Presidio just supposed to be students or something?

PresidioPal: We're still an active military base.

KOW1994:Is this some Area-51 shit?

HoppyXD: Oh god, not this again

KOW1994: It's not just the US! It's EVERYWHERE. Have you had your fucking head up your ass?

ModeratorAli: KOW1994, keep it civil. Everybody is nervous about what's been happening but don't make attacks.

ScubaKingMB: He's not wrong though. There's stuff like this from everywhere.

BitGrit: PresidioPal, can you tell us anything? Have they told you anything at the Presidio?

PresidioPal: Even if they had, I couldn't say. But no, I've just noticed that the higher-ups look like they're about to shit their pants at any second. My teacher had family in Bengaluru and he canceled class for the day. That like, NEVER happens.

KOW1994: You know it's some Area-51 shit QUIT LYING

ModeratorAli: Enjoy your temp ban.

———

Transcript from TalkBack: Views on the News with Brad Masterson:

BRAD: Welcome to TalkBack, where today we have noted psychologist, Dr. Kelly Houston.

KELLY: Thank you for having me, Brad.

BRAD: So, you've seen the news this past week. Everybody has seen the news. It's been one disaster, one crisis, one trauma after another. Apparently at least two-to-five terrorist attacks involving multiple people dead since Monday night, and that's just America. Then there's India and Bengaluru, explosions in Poland, and all these weird sightings people are having of monsters or UFOs or strange people. What's going on?

KELLY: Well, I have a theory, but I'm afraid it's very boring.

BRAD: Do tell.

KELLY: The terrorist attacks have so far amounted to some explosions outside of Brooklyn, a gas release in Florida, and a few other incidents. I think these are unrelated due to the varying nature of the attacks themselves and the places they occurred in: low-population areas like a park at night or an uncrowded suburb. This is assuming they're attacks at all.

BRAD: So you think these are just accidents?

KELLY: It's entirely possible they could be attacks, but less likely that it's a network of them set up by a single group.

BRAD: And everything else? The world feels like it's gone a bit crazy the last week.

KELLY: Coincidence. Occam's Razor tells us to go with the simplest solution. So either there is a network of coordinated attacks going on set up by some kind of global conspiracy, or a lot of very bad things are all just happening at once. There doesn't appear to be any rhyme or reason to these terrible events besides the fact that they're all awful. There's no common factor, no linking thread. They happen in crowded cities, in the middle of nowhere, they involve possible nuclear weapons, earthquakes, gangs with machetes, and so on. It's all too chaotic to be anything but unfortunate coincidence.

BRAD: And what about the more fantastical reports? UFOs over Brazil and that sort of thing?

KELLY: Probably mass hysteria brought on by the stress of the other events.

MALE #1: Bullshit! I saw something!

KELLY: What on Earth?

BRAD: Uh, Security? Can we—

MALE #1: I saw that thing that killed my brother! You're telling me I was just making that up?

KELLY: No! I—I—

BRAD: Security!

MALE #1: You asshole, you don't know—

MALE #2: Get him! Hold him! Hold!

KELLY: Oh my god.

BRAD: Cut it. Cut to ads! Cut t—

24

nya dropped Riley off on the roof of 26 Federal Plaza, and told him she would see him in the morning. She radioed Tori on their communication discs and filled her in on everything that had happened, and told her she would see her tomorrow, but thought it better to stay out of the city at night. She didn't want to be the victim of a surprise alien attack, but if she was, at least she could stay away from others.

Gary and Samaira had the same idea, and waited for her miles outside of New York in the middle of Fahnestock State Park, in the middle of a forest. Now that Anya had been in such close proximity to them, Felix had no problem locking onto their signals. It was a quick flight from downtown to the state park.

Gary had assembled a kind of makeshift camp while Anya had been in the city. He had set up a couple of domed tents that appeared to be made out of aluminum foil or something like it, and the remainder of his junk-bots were stationed in a wide circle around them and his truck. The bots had turned into some kind of turrets, and their heads rotated in slow, methodic circles. Samaira wandered around the perimeter of their camp with Chandrali at her side, drawing glowing blue runes on the trees and ground and rocks.

"What's all that?" Anya asked as she and Pan exited the Shadow Ray.

"Booby traps and alarms," Samaira said. The tip of her finger glowed blue as she continued to make marks in a wide circle around the camp. "If anything hostile towards us crosses them, they'll go off. If it's just a raccoon or a squirrel or a person, nothing will happen. Well, unless they really want to kill us for some reason. But nothing hostile should be out here, unless its aliens. Once they're all down and I connect them, it'll form a kind of dome over us."

"That aether stuff is really handy," Anya said, impressed. She was a little disappointed that her heat sense was mostly useless against the aliens. It would be nice to have something to detect them more easily if they decided to keep playing hide-and-seek like the refrigerator had.

Whatever the aliens were, they weren't warm blooded. She wondered if that was part of their deal as mimics: their temperature just automatically adjusted to the ambient heat or coolness in the air.

"My boys will keep an eye out as well," Gary said. "I'll sleep in my truck and you ladies can have the tents. I promise they're more comfortable than they look."

"Ants!" Pan cheered and began to dig in the ground.

"I don't mind sleeping in the Shadow Ray. It's got enough room to stretch out in," Anya said.

"I'm used to truck camping. Take the tent, kid," Gary replied and waved a hand.

"You sleep in your truck often?"

"Haven't had anywhere else to sleep for a while now," Gary said and Anya winced. He smiled at her. "It hasn't been that bad. Traveling around and doing odd jobs suits me."

Anya just nodded, unsure of what else to say. Being homeless in your sixties couldn't have been easy, or comfortable. Gary gestured at a pyramid of wood, branches and leaves he had assembled inside a circle of small stones.

"Would you mind?" he asked and Anya smiled and flicked her little finger at the pile of kindling and wood. Fire sprang to life, leaping a little higher into the air than she had intended, but she settled it down at once.

"Also handy," Samaira said and smiled at her.

"Shame I don't have any marshmallows," Gary said as he pulled a stump of a log over to the fire with a grunt. Anya contented herself with sitting cross-legged, floating a few inches above the ground. Samaira made her translucent blue shoulder cape appear out of thin air, then shook it out and it expanded. She set it down over the ground, then delicately sat, legs folded beside her. Chandrali hopped into her lap a moment later and began purring.

Pan continued to root around in the dirt at the edges of the fire, repeatedly saying "Ants, ants, ants," and "Dig, dig, dig," to himself in a simple, looping melody.

"So, feds tomorrow, then what?" Gary asked.

"Depends on what they say. If they're gonna try to draft me, I'll probably turn them down. If they just want some unofficial cooperation, then I'm on board," Anya said.

"Good for you. I got drafted in '72. Shoulda burned my damn card on the spot, but I went," Gary said.

"You were in Vietnam?"

"Technically Cambodia, but yes, the war. When I got back I swore I was done with the government. Buncha brainless bureaucrats happy as hell to just send whoever into the meat grinder. They'll do the same to you if you're not careful with 'em."

"Gary…" Samaira sighed. "It's not exactly the same."

"The war's different, but I guarantee you the governmental bullshit is the same. People arguing over who's in charge, talking about re-election or some nonsense," Gary waved his hand.

"They did help us tonight," Anya said. "And they saved me when I fought the snake."

"I know. I hope I'm wrong. I hope enough people in charge pull their heads outta their asses to actually help people for once. I'm not holding my breath though."

"Yeah," Anya said as she looked into the fire. She thought of President Hanover, so eager to get his hands on the Archive, talking about it being an election year. She sighed and lowered her head, and the fire began to dim.

"Anya?" Samaira asked.

"Sorry," Anya said and raised her head and made the fire grow again. "Fine, just worn out."

It wasn't entirely true. She was physically fine, but her brain was getting tired from thinking. Thinking about the feds, what the snake gnosiphage was up to, what to do with her powers, what to do tomorrow, how many hosts or regular people had died in the last hour. A hundred more ideas and problems and choices to make every few seconds.

"What about you, Sam? You gonna sign on?" Gary asked her.

"With the Bureau? I don't know. I'll listen to them, same as Anya. If the best way to fight the aliens is to officially join them or the army or whatever, then I guess I'll do it."

"Mm," Gary said. "Another big day tomorrow, regardless. You two should sleep."

"So should you," Anya said but Gary shook his head.

"I will, but I've got to check on my little construction project. I'll keep an eye out while I do that, take me a few hours. After that, somebody else should take a watch, just in case."

"I'll do it. I think my regeneration skill is making me need less sleep," Anya said. It was agreed that Samaira would take the last watch in the early morning, and Anya retired to her tent.

Gary was right: the tent was more comfortable than it looked. The foil-like exterior was some kind of padded insulation, not that Anya needed it. There was already a soft sleeping bag and pillow laid out, and Anya briefly poked her head out to thank Gary, who smiled and waved.

She spent a few minutes going over her Archive updates. She had gotten another four levels, bringing her up to level 32. She had also gotten some significant bonuses for hitting level 30, including 125,000 bonus RAC. She had gotten another 300,000 RAC from the fridge alien kill as well. It wasn't that much more than what she had gotten from killing the puppet, and she wondered how much stronger the fridge had been.

There was nothing to say that all the aliens arrived at the same level of strength. The hosts had varying levels, so why not the gnosiphages?

Anya also noticed that, of the three fights she had had with the aliens, this was the only one so far that did not award her any natural skill points. It was probably because she hadn't really had to push herself during the fight with the fridge. It hadn't been a total cakewalk, but it certainly hadn't been the nightmare her first two encounters had been either.

The overall boosts to her abilities weren't nearly as dramatic as when she had picked her class, but she had gotten the usual five bonus stat points and ten bonus skill points for hitting level 30, which helped.

"Hey Felix? Are there any other things like class upgrades that give me a shitload of points at once?" she asked.

"Yeah! You'll unlock a second class at level 50, which will combine with your existing class and grant you an advanced class. Lots of bonuses there. I would have mentioned it sooner, but level 50 is a while away and I know you had a lot of other things on your mind. I was planning to tell you when you got to level 40," the AI said.

"That's okay. Not much point worrying about it right now. Good to know there's something else coming, though."

Anya looked at the cost to upgrade her Sun's Heart and regalia and whistled at the cost. She currently had 477,861 RAC after the fight with the fridge alien and her contributions, plus what she had leftover from before. Upgrading the Sun's Heart artifact from superior quality to refined would cost 500,000 RAC.

When she had taken the Phoenix Monk class, the Archive had granted her a free upgrade token for it, and her regalia. Without the tokens, she would have had to either skimp on the rune enhancements or not purchased the Shadow Ray and some other things.

As it was, upgrading her regalia from refined quality to excellent only cost 111,560 RAC. Affordable by comparison to the Sun's Heart upgrade, but definitely not cheap, either.

"How come it's so much more expensive to upgrade the Sun's Heart than the other stuff?" Anya asked. "The price for the Heart doubles with each upgrade, but the regalia and the runes only go up by like, sixty-to-seventy-five percent."

"The Sun's Heart is an artifact-grade item. Very rare, very hard to make. Even at the basic quality, it's a powerful item that grants access to skills that would be otherwise impossible for somebody to use,"

Felix said. "As a result, upgrading its level of quality is more expensive. Your regalia, while based off a unique item, is ultimately just a set of very nice clothes. Magic clothes, yes, but they're much easier to replicate than artifact-grade items.

"You could save up for upgrading the Sun's Heart, but it would be a better use of your RAC to wait until level 50, when you're likely to get more free upgrade tokens. What kind of tokens you get will depend on what new class and advanced class you choose, but you could easily pick one that grants access to an upgrade for the Sun's Heart, among other things."

"Definitely good to know. Still need some upgrades though. Can't spend it if I'm dead."

Anya glanced over the improvements for upgrading her regalia and blinked as she studied the item description. For the previous qualities, superior and refined, she had been limited to either five runes of a lesser quality or three of the current quality, no mixing and matching. With the upgrade she could do both, for a total of eight runes.

"That's probably worth it," Anya said. She doubted she'd have enough money to imbue the regalia with all eight runes, but just taking the upgrade for now and saving her future RAC for getting more runes later was viable.

She also got something called the Shard of the Ever-Star, which was 85,000 RAC. It was a crystal about the size of Anya's finger that would sap a small amount of energy from her Sun's Heart as well as any ambient heat every now and then, and store it. If she needed a boost, she could drain it. Best of all the shard was reusable, so she didn't have to keep buying single-use items any more. It also held about three times as much heat energy as a single star's breath crystal.

After remembering how devastating the snake's attack on her Sun's Heart had been, she also purchased a small chestguard made of hundreds of interlocking, pale gold alloy plates the Archive identified as "Sacred Orichalcum." It was small, just large enough to cover her chest and part of her back, and pricey: 135,250 RAC . It was flexible, and thin enough to fit under her regalia.

"Extremely resistant to all damage. Blessed by spirits of protection, and layered with multiple shielding charms and capable of boosting the wearer's innate healing abilities," Felix read the description.

"What's the difference between a rune and a charm?" Anya asked.

"A rune is modular. It can be placed on or taken out of an item at anytime, and upgraded individually. Charms are innate to the item and cannot be upgraded on their own. Charms are, overall, a bit cheaper, but less flexible. They also grant small additional bonuses if they're worn in conjunction with other charms, runes, or other magical upgrades that grant similar beneficial effects," Felix said.

Anya nodded. She couldn't afford anymore big purchases, so for now, the charm would have to do. She still had 17,301 RAC available after all her purchases. Not much, but enough for any emergency consumables she might need in the future. Plus, she still had her healing potion and a star's breath crystal in her pouch.

Given how expensive everything was becoming, Anya made a mental note to curtail any future big purchases. She might upgrade her remaining runes, and buy the final Excellent rune for her regalia, but that would be it for a while. All of her purchases up until now had been essential, but she was getting worried about constantly being near broke when it came to her RAC. Hopefully with her shard of the Ever-Star and self-repairing regalia, saving the Archive's currency would be easier.

Anya put the Sacred Orichalcum chestguard on, along with the shard of the Ever-Star, which was attached to a heat-resistant metal alloy that she draped over her neck, and tucked beneath the chestguard. Anya brought up her main menu to review her purchases and all the bonuses they had given her, along with the points from her level-ups.

ANYA NOWICKI: LEVEL 32 PHOENIX MONK
  Statistics

- Awareness-10
- Dexterity-19 (+10 from gear)
- Fortitude-39 (+13 from gear)

- Intelligence-8
- Strength-20 (+5 from gear)
- Willpower-8

Skills

- Flame Dominion-35 (+16 from gear)(+5 from Artifact)
- Kinetic Dispersal-17 (+6 from gear)
- Combat Cognition-15
- Regeneration-31 (+14 from gear)
- Xhama Thul-14 (+4 from gear)
- Gravity Dominion-16 (+6 from gear)

Equipped Items & Artifacts

- Sun's Heart (Superior): Grants access to higher-level of Flame Dominion skill. (+15% efficiency when using this artifact)
- Singularity's Grasp (Basic): Grants access to higher-level of Gravity Dominion skill.
- Regalia of St. Llothec, the Ever-Burning (Excellent): Provides protection from any and all heat-based hazards, as well as kinetic damage. Also boosts the wearer's innate heat-producing abilities and endurance. 111,560 upgrade cost + 1,100 RAC per rune enhancement or upgrade (This excellent quality item has a current cap of five lesser quality runes and three equal quality runes) (+8 to Flame Dominion skill, +4 to Kinetic Dispersal skill, +3 to Fortitude statistic)
- Rune of the Shield (Superior): Provides dual enhancements to quality and defense of imbued item. (+75% to item durability parameters and +75% defensive bonus) (+2 to Kinetic Dispersal skill)
- Rune of the Shield's Embrace (Superior): Provides additional defensive covering beyond the standard coverage of imbued item. (+75% of item's defensive capabilities to any uncovered

body parts, additional +15% defensive capabilities to covered areas)

- Rune of the Maiden (Refined): Provides dual enhancements to healing and stamina of the wearer of imbued item. 15,750 RAC quality upgrade (+6 to Regeneration skill and +3 to Fortitude statistic)

- Rune of the Warrior (Refined): Provides dual enhancements to strength and agility of the wearer of the imbued item. 15,750 RAC quality upgrade (+3 to Strength and Dexterity statistics)

- Rune of the Stallion (Superior): Provides dual enhancements to speed and stamina of the wearer of the imbued item. 15,750 RAC quality upgrade (+3 to Fortitude and Dexterity statistics)

- Rune of the Mender (Excellent): Repairs damage done to imbued item, provided the item remains above 10% of total durability. Item requires at least thirty minutes to repair per 10% of damage done. 27,500 RAC

- Rune of the Comet (Excellent): Provides dual enhancements to the gravitational and heat abilities of the wearer. 64,250 RAC (+6 to Gravity and Flame Dominions)

- Mantle of the Gale (Superior): Imbues the wearer with additional speed as well as a light deflective wind-shield. + 1,100 RAC per rune enhancement or upgrade (this superior quality item has a current cap of five lesser quality runes or three equal quality runes) (+2 to Dexterity statistic)

- Rune of the Vortex (Superior): Provides dual enhancements to any wind-based abilities of the item and speed of the wearer. 9,000 RAC quality upgrade (+4 to wind-based air skills inherent to item, +2 to Dexterity statistic)

- Rune of the Greater Salamander (Superior): Imbued item is granted resistance from fire and wearer's fire-based abilities are enhanced. 12,000 RAC quality upgrade. (+100% to heat and fire resistance for item, +2 to Flame Dominion)

- Rune of the Brute (Superior): Provides dual enhancements to the power and hand-to-hand fighting ability of the wearer of the imbued item. 12,000 RAC (+2 to Strength statistic and +4 to Xhama Thul skill)

- Sacred Orichalcum Chestguard (Charmed)(Refined): Grants bonuses to protection and healing abilities of the wearer. Provides excellent defense for the covered area. 135,250 RAC (+3 to Fortitude statistic and +6 to Regeneration skill) (Bonus +1 to Fortitude statistic and +2 to Regeneration skill due to similar bonuses on worn items)

With all that sorted, Anya felt better about going to sleep. If they were ambushed, she would be as ready as she could. And she had Gary and Samaira to help if trouble showed up. For the first time since Friday night, Anya slept well.

———

ANYA AWOKE TO A SHRIEK. She literally flew out of the tent, fists and feet blazing, eyes darting everywhere for any sign of aliens.

It was dawn, the sky just starting to turn pale gray. Samaira and Chandrali (who was in her tiger form) stood by the fire, both clearly startled. Gary had bolted upright in his truck and was fumbling with his glasses as he looked around.

"What's going on?" Anya asked.

"Sorry! I'm sorry. It's okay. We're good. No aliens," Samaira said. "I was just…surprised."

Anya lowered her fists and extinguished the fire around them and her feet. She looked around for what had surprised her, but didn't have to look far.

"Whoa," she said.

"Hello! Pan here!" Pan said and waddled closer to the fire. He was flanked by a pair of vaguely humanoid shapes, each five feet tall and made of dirt, rock, and mud. They had thick, stout torsos and arms and legs to match. Their heads were little more than lumps between their shoulders, with shallow pits for eyes and wide gashes for mouths. The dirt creatures moved on their own, always close to Pan.

The appearance of the dirt creatures wasn't all: Pan had changed himself. While most of his scales were hidden beneath his black kimono-jacket thing, the ones Anya could see had been altered. They were thicker and had a metallic gleam to them. Pan's leathery skin was also not nearly so soft looking, almost like some kind of organic metal. His claws had changed too, becoming sharper, darker, almost stone-like.

He carried a thick canvas bag in one of his claws. His tongue darted down into it, then pulled out a clump of ants. Anya peered closer and grimaced as she saw the bag was absolutely squirming with a huge mass of the insects, impossible to count.

"Pan! What is this?" Anya asked as she stared at him. Pan looked at the bag, then at her.

"Bag of ants," he said. Anya couldn't help a snort of laughter from escaping her.

"I think she's asking why you look different and what these guys are," Samaira clarified and pointed at the dirt men.

"Oh! Yes! I was talking to Bee-Eff last night, that's my menu helper, and they told me there's bad things coming to hunt me. So I got scared and peed a little. Then I ate some ants. Then I dug a hole and went to sleep. Then—"

"Pan? Maybe skip ahead," Anya said.

"Okay! After I was done being scared, Bee-Eff told me I can get stronger, like Anya! I like Anya, so I thought that was a good idea, and Bee-Eff showed me how to use this thing for more than just talking English good," Pan said, turned his head, and licked the outside of his leg with his tongue. His menu appeared in the air and Anya snorted again.

PAN: LEVEL 13 GIANT GROUND PANGOLIN
  Stats

- Awareness-5
- Dexterity-5
- Fortitude-10
- Intelligence-5

- Strength-6
- Willpower-3

Skills

- English-5
- Earth Dominion-10
- Dermal Hardening-5
- Golem Summoning-6

"I'll be damned," Gary said as he emerged from his truck and studied the menu screen.

"Those... aren't half bad choices, given that he's still learning basically everything," Samaira said.

"Pan, how did you know to pick this stuff?" Anya asked. She had figured she would need to help Pan with his Archive menu and skills at some point, just something to keep him and others around him safe.

"I saw your glowy screen too! And Bee-Eff said you had the 'Flame Dominion,' which was good for fighting, but I dunno. Fire is scary. But then there was one for dirt! And it was like digging! Really, really good digging. I like digging. So I picked that, cause it's like yours, but not scary, and I like you too. And digging."

"Aw, that's so sweet," Samaira said.

"It's kinda cute," Anya agreed. "And the other ones?"

"Derm... derma... hard skin!" Pan said and pointed a claw at the Dermal Hardening skill. "If one of the bad things finds me, I don't want to get hurt, so now my skin is better. I used some of the store things? Money? I don't understand money. But I used that stuff to make my scales tougher, and the Earth Dominion gave me mountain bones!"

"Bones of the Mountain," Felix said from beside Anya.

"That's it!" Pan agreed.

"And the golems?" Gary asked.

"I like having friends, and now I can make my own. And Bee-Eff said they would work well with the Earth Dominion skill, and they could help protect me if I'm in trouble and Anya isn't there."

"Not bad, little guy. Not bad at all," Anya said and laughed. "We can help you pick out some good gear later, once you've saved up some RAC. Don't spend too much in the meantime, okay? And try not to use any of your skills when other people are around. You might hurt them."

"I'll be careful!" Pan said, then shoved his face into the bag of ants and resumed eating. Anya assumed he had simply purchased the bag and huge ball of ants from the RAC store, or found some way to use Earth Dominion to force them into the bag.

"Ah, shit, what time is it?" Anya asked.

"About 6:30," Samaira said. "I was gonna wake everybody up in another half-hour."

"Thank goodness. Plenty of time to have breakfast and get to Riley."

"Not much out here but deer and raccoons," Gary said. "So unless you feel like roasting some critters…"

"Hard pass. I'll find a 24-hour buffet or something and clean them out."

Gary laughed. "I'll join you, but you're on your own for the feds. I'll just find a junkyard and pass the time making what I can. Sam?"

"I could eat, then we can go visit Director MacDougal," she said. The three of them cleaned up the campsite, and took off for the nearest buffet that Anya could demolish.

25

"I didn't know you could get banned from a buffet," Samaira said from the passenger seat of the Shadow Ray as they soared over Manhattan.

"False advertising," Anya grumbled. "It said 'All you can eat,' right? Why is it my fault for eating then?"

"You cleaned out, like, ten of those food trays."

"Thirteen," Felix corrected.

"Thank you, Felix," Anya said.

"Does the RAC store have any kind of food pill? Something?" Samaira asked and brought up a window.

"I'm sorry I didn't think of that," Boo moaned. "I'm so thoughtless."

"I asked Felix awhile back. There's some that are about 10,000 calories, but they're not cheap. I'd probably burn through my RAC in a few days eating the things," Anya said. "There's a skill that would let me convert heat to some kind of nourishing energy, like a plant, but I feel like there's better things to spend my points on, y'know?"

"Good to keep it in mind, though. Maybe Gary can make something when his factory is up," Samaira said. "You nervous about the meeting?"

Anya shrugged. "A little. MacDougal seems all right. I think she knows not to push too hard."

Anya brought the Shadow Ray down for a landing on top of the main building of 26 Federal Plaza, where Riley was waiting. He gave her and Samaira a wave, then blinked as he saw Pan.

"You look different," Riley said, and Anya explained what had happened. "So he can do with rocks what you do with fire?"

"Kind of?" Anya shrugged her huge shoulders.

"Well, whatever. So long as he doesn't make a mess inside, I don't see it changing anything. By the way, MacDougal ordered a pretty big spread in the meeting room. Hope you're hungry," Riley said as he stepped through the rooftop access door and into a concrete stairwell.

"We actually—" Samaira started to say.

"Thank God!" Anya said and followed Riley inside.

"Do you have ants?" Pan asked and waddled after them. Samaira chuckled, then she and Chandrali followed the group down the stairs. All of them got into an elevator and took it down several levels before the doors dinged and opened on a short hallway with a polished marble floor and a reception desk at one end. A wall of opaque glass with doors on either side stretched to fill one end of the hallway, and a large version of the seal of the Federal Bureau of Investigation sat in its center.

A young woman with dark hair pulled back in a bun sat at a desk in front of the glass wall and looked up at Agent Riley as he emerged from the elevator with the others.

"Morning Ms. Newman," Riley said and nodded at her. The woman smiled at Riley, then glanced at Anya and Samaira, the latter holding Chandrali against her chest. Ms. Newman raised one eyebrow as she saw Samaira and her cat, both eyebrows as she stared up at Anya in her cloak and battle regalia, and then her mouth fell open just a little when she caught sight of Pan hiding behind Anya.

"We'll be needing three guest badges, please," Riley said, then looked at Chandrali. "The cat's just a cat, right? I mean, I know it's a tiger too, but…"

"Chandrali is not a host or anything like that. She's just a very smart cat," Samaira said.

"The director mentioned we would have some odd visitors," Newman said and scanned three plastic ID cards through a machine, then attached them to clips. She handed them to Riley while she continued to stare at the others.

Riley already had a similar card clipped to the front of his coat, and he scanned it next to one of the doors. There was a heavy clunking sound of a lock moving, and the door swung in. Anya and Samaira clipped their badges on, and Anya helped Pan with his.

"Just stay with me, don't lose those badges, and you'll be fine," Riley said and led them into the main offices.

"Thank you. Sorry for the shock," Anya said as she and the others followed Riley.

"Bye bye!" Pan said with a wave.

The office behind the glass was a long open room with computer monitors lined up side-by-side along narrow desks stretched across the main floor. Smaller cubicles and workstations sat along the edges of the room alongside rows of monitors on walls, whiteboards and other wide spaces covered in notes, photos, sections of maps, and more. The whole place buzzed with activity, hurried conversations, the drone of printers, the chatter of news stations, and more.

All of the activity came to a stop as Anya and the rest entered, and all eyes turned to face them.

"Don't you folks got work to do?" Riley asked. The crowd of agents and other office staff resumed their work, but half-heartedly. Anya was very much aware of the stares they got as Riley led them through the office and to a room in the far corner surrounded by more opaque glass. A plaque next to the door read "Conference Room A," and Riley paused with his hand on the door.

"Before we go in, you should be aware of a few things," he said. "MacDougal is still technically handling all this for now. But some of the folks in this room do not like that, and they like the idea of super-powered people running around even less. They're a bit twitchy, what with everything that's been going on around the country and rest of the world."

"I'm a bit twitchy from almost being killed several times over the last week," Anya said. Riley nodded but put a hand up to calm her.

"I get it. But you gotta try and see it from their perspective: you can literally buy alien bombs, and blow up a building by snapping your fingers. All three of you. Plus whatever the smart cat can do."

Chandrali yawned.

"My point is, they're nervous and scared, and I can't blame them too much for that. So just try not to set anybody's hair on fire if one of them gets uppity with you. MacDougal can handle them," Riley finished.

"I'll be nice," Anya said. Riley took a breath and then opened the door.

Anya was initially distracted by the sight and smell of food. MacDougal had gone all out. A pair of plastic tables had been erected in the back of the room, and were filled with pitchers of coffee, juice, and water, as well as trays of sandwiches, donuts, and other pastries. Anya controlled herself long enough to take in the rest of the conference room.

A large wooden table filled the center of the room, and was surrounded by a couple dozen chairs, most of them filled with stern-faced men and women in suits. A projector in the ceiling displayed a map of the world with thousands of dots across it, red and green, onto the far wall. Anya assumed those were the alien and host positions, respectively, that Felix had shown Riley earlier that week. The Bureau had not been idle, and several additions to the map had been made that displayed the sites of disturbances.

Suzanne MacDougal sat near the head of the table with a remote control in her hand. Anya recognized the two senators from New York, a few more senators from California, Texas, Florida, and elsewhere, and the Secretary of Defense. Several older military men were there as well: air force, navy, army, and marines, judging by their uniforms. Anya didn't have a clue who the other people were or what offices or agencies they belonged to.

"Agent Riley. Thank you," MacDougal said. "And may I introduce Anya Nowicki, Samaira Upadhyay, and the missing pangolin from the Virginia Zoo. And a cat."

"Pleased to meet you," Samaira said.

"Morning," Anya added.

"Hello! Pan here!" Pan finished.

Chandrali flicked an ear.

There was some scattered muttering around the table as Pan spoke.

"I'd seen some of the video but... I'll be damned," one of the military men said; a general in the marines if Anya had to guess from his uniform.

"Aliens? Seriously?" a senator muttered.

"It's been four days since the invading alien force arrived on Monday evening, and another two days since our guests were forcibly integrated with alien technology last Friday evening," MacDougal said. "Casualty estimates for the country are still coming in. It's somewhere in the low thousands, however."

"So the earthquake outside Los Angeles, that was aliens?" one of the senators asked.

"We can't be sure. Ms. Nowicki?" MacDougal asked and looked at Anya.

"I assume the earthquake was Monday night?" Anya asked the senator, who nodded. "Felix, can you bring up a map of California and show us the host and alien positions for that time?"

"Can do!" Felix said as they appeared in the air along with a large screen that showed southern California. Sure enough, there were four hosts not far outside Los Angeles, and three aliens. The map fast-forwarded to show the two groups meeting. Two alien signals vanished, and then all of the host signals disappeared.

The senator looked at the clock in the corner of the map screen.

"That was around the time of the quake, yes. And the reports said the epicenter of the quake was in that area. Jesus. They can just make earthquakes happen?"

"They can do just about anything," Samaira said and all eyes snapped toward her. "Uh, sorry. I didn't mean to interrupt."

"Please, Ms. Upadhyay," MacDougal said. "You're one of only three people we know of to have protected our country from these things and lived. Any insight you'd like to share is very welcome."

Anya glanced at MacDougal, who looked back at her and gave a very subtle nod.

Samaira launched into a quick but detailed overview of her alien encounters so far, and what she had learned of them from her AI. Anya ate during the brief lecture, mostly watching the faces of the senators and generals for their reactions. Her heat sense told her that several of the people in the room were nervous: a lot of warm blood pumping faster due to elevated heart-rates.

Samaira had Boo bring up her map of the world with the updated positions and casualty rates of aliens and hosts as of last night.

"So most of them are already dead?" a general asked.

"Less than a week and the alien invasion is almost over, huh?" another said.

"It's not that simple. They're getting stronger," Samaira replied.

"And some of them are different," Anya added. She laid out her encounter with the snake gnosiphage. MacDougal added to Anya's story with excerpts from a report by Colonel Perkins and Sergeant Dransfield, along with camera footage one of the airmen had gotten from the fight.

"And this does not include the possibility of any further involvement of these Engineer aliens," MacDougal said.

"And you think the FBI is equipped to handle this?" somebody asked.

"No, not as it currently stands. Which is why I've spoken with President Hanover, and he has agreed to the formation of the United States Department of Extraterrestrial Research and Defense. I will be stepping down from my position as director here, and making the move to head the new department."

There was a minor uproar among some of the people in the room. One man from the Department of Homeland Security protested, a couple of the generals said it was unnecessary, a few others openly accused MacDougal of using a global crisis to advance her own career. Then some senators retorted back at those people, who told the others they were out-of-line, and then it just devolved into people citing procedure, laws, regulations, and departmental guidelines.

"Oh, Gary would love this," Samaira muttered to Anya as the two stood to one side of the room.

"Yeah, this is what I was afraid of," Anya said.

"I wouldn't worry about it," Riley whispered beside them. "It's basically a done deal. Gotta get some more people on-board officially, but Hanover's gonna sign an executive order to form the department by the end of the week, and then try to push some legislation through Congress or something to make sure it sticks."

"And who is going to be working in this new department?" Anya asked and raised an eyebrow at Riley.

"You, if you want."

"Hard pass."

"If it's about stopping the aliens and setting up response teams to sites of attack, like we did in Chicago, I'm in," Samaira said and looked at Anya. Anya detected something like a challenge in the small woman's steady, dark gaze.

"You want to help, don't you?" Samaira asked her.

"Well, yeah, but—"

"So, help. Look at them," Samaira said and nodded her chin at the crowd of people around the table arguing. "They're scared. Imagine what's going to happen everywhere when word of this really gets out. Not some rumors on the internet, or a blurry video, but when the President gets on live TV and tells the country that aliens have landed and are killing people."

Anya looked at the small crowd of government officials as they continued to berate each other.

"It's going to help a lot of people if they know somebody is doing something. It kinda sucks that that somebody is us and we didn't get a choice in the matter, but that's how it is. One night you're studying for your master's degree between semesters, and the next night you find out you're stuck with an archive of universal knowledge and Earth is gonna be ground-zero for some interplanetary war you knew nothing about."

Samaira sighed and adjusted her glasses.

"I was really scared last night, looking at the map. Seeing how many people with the archives had died. It was awful. I kept thinking about seeing the other hosts die that night on the beach, and wondering when it's going to be me. And then you spoke up, and you made everybody feel better. That's what people are going to need to see. Not people distrusting each other or running off on their own, but being together."

Anya flinched under Samaira's gaze.

"Look," Riley said, "it'll still take a while to get everything with this new department set up. You don't have to do anything now. And maybe I can talk to MacDougal about you just being some kind of consultant, or making media appearances. But I'm with Ms. Upadhyay on this: it'd be good to just let the idea simmer."

"I'll think about it. No promises otherwise, though," Anya said.

Samaira smiled at her and Riley let out a sigh of obvious relief.

"Enough!" a loud, rough voice snapped. The room went silent and everybody turned to look at the speaker: the general from the marines. He was in his fifties or sixties, his gray hair shaved down almost to his tan scalp, and his thick eyebrows were drawn so closely together that they formed a dark iron-colored bar of hair over his eyes. He folded his arms over his chest, and the uniform strained around his biceps.

"Carrying on like this in a crisis," the man, General Tully going by the stars and nametag on his uniform, leaned forward. "If the President says he's making a new department, then we're making a new department. Director: I imagine you'll be needing some people to fill out the ranks. I happen to know many fine marines who would absolutely jump at the chance to kill some aliens and protect their countrymen."

MacDougal smiled at the man.

"Thank you, General Tully. And yes: we will need positions filled. We're scouting, of course, but your cooperation would be welcome. We're primarily looking to have people from the armed forces, NASA, the NSA, and possibly a few others. For now we'll be relying on the volunteer work of people like Ms. Nowicki and Ms. Upadhyay. And the pangolin too, I suppose," MacDougal said.

"There was one more, wasn't there?" a senator asked and flipped through a folder. "Gary? Is that all we have on him?"

"He's... busy," Samaira said and looked aside.

"He got a last name?" General Tully asked.

"Uh," Samaira said, clearly uncomfortable.

"Sam's only known him for a few days or so from what I gathered,"

Riley said. "And he got pretty cagey around me when he learned I was with the Bureau."

Anya blinked at Riley. He hadn't technically lied about knowing Gary's last name, but it was a dodge. MacDougal narrowed her eyes at him and he met her gaze. Anya wasn't sure what was going on between them, but whatever it was, MacDougal seemed satisfied. She pursed her lips and cleared her throat.

"Do we know what Mr. Gary is so busy with?" she asked.

"Building robots. His got smashed in the fight last night and he wants to be ready in case there's more aliens," Samaira said.

"Well, I'd certainly like to meet with Mr. Gary at some point. Maybe you can facilitate that, Agent Riley?"

"Yes, ma'am," Riley said.

"If our guests don't mind, I'm sure some of the senators, generals and other heads of departments would like to ask you some questions about recent developments," MacDougal added and gave a tight-lipped smile to Anya and Samaira.

Anya frowned but Samaira just smiled back.

"Of course we don't mind," Samaira said. Anya's mouth was full of food, which was probably for the best. She pulled a chair up to the table, and settled in for the barrage of questions.

26

"Six hours!" Anya said into her communication disc six hours and eight minutes later. She was on the roof with Samaira, Pan, Chandrali, and Riley.

"And you didn't blow the place up? I'm impressed," Tori said from the other end of the line.

"We're on break. I mean, honestly. Aliens running around and we're in fucking meetings."

"Well, it's daytime, so the aliens are hopefully keeping a low profile. And believe me, I hate meetings too, but these might actually be the rare kind that are worth having. I imagine starting a new federal department and organizing a response to an invading threat is something that takes some serious organization."

"Quit being rational. I wanna go fly my space car and blow things up."

"Did MacDougal or anybody give you any more trouble about wanting access to the Archive?"

"A little. Some guys from the NSA and the military, mainly. MacDougal shut them down pretty fast though. One of them outright said he wanted me to buy a space battleship for them and wouldn't listen when I told him that even if I wanted to, I couldn't afford it."

"What about the skills?" Tori asked.

"What about them?" Anya replied.

"Did any of them ask to be taught how to use the skills in the Archive?"

"They can't be taught. I mean the ordinary ones can, but not the magic ones," she said, then paused. "Right, Felix?"

"Incorrect!" Felix replied. "The Archive has only ever scanned pre-existing skills made by sapient races across the galaxy. It hasn't made anything up on its own. So for any skill, magic or otherwise, to be in the Archive, it must have first existed outside of it."

"Okay. That makes sense. But the magic stuff all comes from aliens and things like that. There was no magic here before the Archive."

"The Archive doesn't have access to all of human history, but there's enough that it does have knowledge of to suggest that wasn't always the case. Certain supernatural energies, like the aether, are present on Earth now, but below average levels. Regardless, some supernatural skills could be learned by ordinary people," Felix said.

"Some?" Tori asked.

"Anya's regeneration skill is an example of a skill that could not be learned, at least not without significant medical and genetic alterations. Currently, Earth does not have access to these, so the Archive would have to be accessed. However, a skill like the aether could be taught from scratch."

"The aether's what Samaira uses. So if she can use it here, can other people?" Anya asked.

"What about aether?" Samaira asked as she leaned around Anya's side.

Anya almost shouted. She'd failed to sense Samaira behind her, too focused on both thinking of how to grant skills to others and berating herself for not thinking of the idea sooner. Riley remained on the far side of the roof, chatting into his phone and oblivious to their conversation.

"We're talking about the skills in the Archive and if they can be taught to normal people. Uh, no offense? Is that offensive?" Tori asked.

"I know what you mean, don't worry about it," Samaira replied.

"I'm Tori, by the way."

"Samaira. Friend of Anya's?"

"Somebody has to keep an eye on her."

"Hey! I'm the one who walks your drunk ass home every Friday!" Anya protested.

Samaira and Tori both laughed.

"Go back to talking about learning magic," Anya huffed.

"It's actually something I've thought of," Samaira said. "I've been looking into how to teach aether usage to others, but it's complicated."

"Felix said the aether around Earth is kinda shitty," Anya said.

"It's not ideal. As far as I know, I'm the only one drawing on it, and there's more than enough for me to use. But imagine a lake. If it's just you taking water from the lake, you could probably make it last forever. But six or seven billion people? It'd dry up real quick."

"And other skills?" Tori asked from the phone.

"Well, the Dominions produce their own energy, but only up to the point that a given wielder of one can sustain. There's other skills kind of like that, but again, they require artifacts or other things that aren't on Earth at the moment," Felix said. "Plus, even if you did get the necessary items, it would still take a long time, just like any other skill."

"My point in starting this whole conversation was to pin down if it's even possible for normal people to learn this kind of stuff, in case MacDougal or somebody else asks. If it was impossible, then that's one less thing to fight about," Tori said.

"But it's not impossible. Just difficult and selective," Samaira replied.

An image jumped into Anya's mind, so exciting and clear that she almost squealed: Tori, in an admittedly cartoonish wizard's outfit wielding a magic wand in one hand and a thick grimoire in the other.

"What if... we let Tori try it out?" Anya asked.

"Hell yeah," Tori added.

"Try what out? The aether?" Samaira asked and Anya nodded. Samaira's brows knit together and she polished her glasses as she thought.

"The aether is actually pretty safe," Samaira continued, "especially considering the relatively small amount of it on Earth. Even if a novice failed to make a manifestation of the aether work, it would just fizzle out and revert to its dormant state. Plus, if it doesn't work, it doesn't work, and we can just tell MacDougal it's no good teaching skills to non-hosts."

"I can also vouch for Tori's character. She's not a psycho," Anya said.

"Oh, stop. You're gonna make me blush," Tori said.

"If Tori wants to learn the aether, I'd be willing to help. I'm curious about it myself, and seeing what the results of a non-host practicing it are. It's something to think about," Samaira said.

"I'll start asking Felix about beginner's aether gear we can get from the store," Anya said and the AI nodded.

"I'll ask Boo, too," Samaira added. "Though I'd maybe like to keep this under wraps for the moment. No need to spill this particular idea to MacDougal and Riley."

"I wasn't planning on blabbing," Anya replied. "Surprised you haven't brought it up yet, though."

Samaira scowled a little at that. "Just because I want to help in an official capacity doesn't mean I'm a lapdog. I'm not about to try and teach aetheric assassination skills to special ops guys unless there's no other way to stop the aliens."

"Right. Sorry. I didn't mean anything by it," Anya said. Samaira studied Anya behind her glasses, then shook her head and smiled.

"It's fine. I'm just tired. We should get downstairs," she said and made for the stairwell.

"I'll catch up!" Anya replied then spoke into the communication disc. "I should go, I guess. I'll try and swing by the hotel they put you at later, assuming I'm not dead from boredom."

"Just try not to throw any bureaucrats out a window. Though I gotta tell you, it is an absolute trial being stuck in a five-star hotel with the government picking up my room service tab," Tori said and laughed.

"You suck," Anya snorted and hung up, then braced herself for another several hours of questions and slide presentations.

———

"Look who finally made it out of the federal dungeon," Gary said later that evening. Anya, Samaira (along with Chandrali), and Pan had finally been dismissed after the sun had gone down, and they had flown out to meet Gary a few miles northeast of Manhattan.

He, his truck, and a small number of dog-sized robots were in the middle of a large scrapyard. The robots, at least a dozen of them, were crawling over and through the junk and bringing pieces of it back to Gary, who had his big multi-purpose gauntlets on and was busy welding things together when the Shadow Ray had landed.

"I feel dead," Anya moaned. "I'd rather fight aliens."

"Not me," Samaira shook her head. "I'll take a conference room with coffee over slimy aliens any day. Though it was pretty bad. Maybe a fight with a tiny alien would have been better."

"I fell asleep and pooped in the corner," Pan said.

"Hah! Good job, Pan," Gary said.

"We do not want to encourage shitting indoors," Anya said.

"So? What's the scuttlebutt?" Gary asked. "You a couple of G-men now? Or G-women, I suppose."

Anya and Samaira filled Gary in on the basics while Pan began to dig through garbage and hand random pieces to the robots.

MacDougal was forming a department with Hanover's executive order, and they wanted hosts like them to join. Samaira was in, Anya was a maybe, and Pan was with Anya. The last half of the meeting had been about immediate goals: the biggest one was finding any hosts within America's borders who were still alive and protecting them.

"You mean bringing them in," Gary said.

"I know that's the long-term goal, but I think for now MacDougal just doesn't want any more to die," Anya said.

"Of course she doesn't. Hanover doesn't either. Those are weapons in their stockpile. Can't lose your most valuable weapons," Gary said as he went back to welding.

"They asked about you," Samaira said.

"Agent Riley probably gave them my whole life in a folder," Gary replied.

"He actually clammed up when they asked for your full name. He didn't lie, but he deflected."

Gary paused.

"Well, a broken clock's right twice a day," he said.

"You should come with us next time," Samaira said.

"I'll think about it," Gary said in a tone that indicated he would absolutely not think about it. Samaira sighed and shook her head.

"For now, all they want us to do is fly around and help any hosts we find. If we see aliens, kill them if we can get them away from people. Otherwise just leave unless they change their attack patterns and start rampaging in civilian areas," Anya said. "It's all been pretty bad so far, but at least the aliens don't seem like they're interested in causing random mayhem everywhere."

"For now," Gary said and Anya nodded.

"For now."

"So you're just gonna soar around and hope you get lucky?" Gary asked.

"We're gonna use the map from the refrigerator alien we got to scout out the last known host locations. MacDougal is giving us access to reports of strange, violent incidents from around the country, having the government intel people comb through stuff that matches the profiles they're creating for alien attacks or hosts being present from local police and other agencies. We'll overlay that with the known positions on our maps and hope for the best," Anya said.

"At least they're doing something," Gary grunted.

"Wish our Archive communications stuff worked properly," Samaira said and looked at her comms window. It was still showing that their signal was blocked.

"I'm sure this probably a stupid question, but do any of your super science skills let you work on the Archive, Gary?" Anya asked.

"Pretty damn good question, actually, and one of the first ones I asked Gizmo when he popped up with the Archive. Little bastard called me a sneaky baby and said that would be cheating, and no, no such skill existed. Only the Engineers have that ability, and they're keeping it to themselves. So that means I can't directly fix whatever is wrong with the Archive comm system or the vanished host signals."

"So we gotta find a way to contact the hosts outside of the menu. Hijack a TV signal or something? Put a video on the internet?"

"I thought of that too, but after I'd picked my skills. None of the ones I have are really suitable for making complex communications equipment. It's all robots, vehicles, weapons and armor, and making a factory to make more of those.

"There might be some stuff in the RAC store that could do the job, but it's all alien stuff, and would need to be tinkered with to adapt to Earth, and that's just the same problem again: no skills for making advanced communication devices. You could put up a video on the net, but there's no guarantee anybody would see it. There's already a truckload of videos, and most of them are being called hoaxes or explained as weird but natural occurrences.

"The coding language I took is alien, and extremely advanced. It's like a symphony orchestra, while the stuff we got on Earth is like a monkey with a kazoo up its ass. Imagine trying to teach the monkey to fart out Beethoven's 5th. Even if you could tell it was supposed to be music, it would still stink."

"Charming," Samaira said and Anya laughed.

"Point being, not really something I could adapt to Earth coding languages without a lot of work and time, and the end result might not even work well. And in this metaphor, we're assuming I'm an expert at monkey musical education, which I'm not."

"So you can't do anything to help find the other hosts?" Anya asked. Gary shrugged.

"If my factory were up, I'd have access to more options. But even if I raided a warehouse full of advanced communication equipment, there'd only be so much I could do with it. I was actually thinking of raiding a few electronics stores."

"Again?" Samaira asked.

"Not a fan of stealing, but desperate times, etc," Gary said, then turned to Anya when she raised an eyebrow at him. "Scrap yards are good for metal for armor plating and a few other things I need, and most folk don't care if I paw through the junk. But some of the stuff I need is better acquired from stores. When I heard the aliens were hours away from getting here, I may have done a smash-and-grab at a few places. I can technically make what I need from all the junk here, but it's easier and faster to modify existing tech that isn't broken and rusted over."

"MacDougal gave us some cards that will charge the government's budget, now that they've set some money aside," Samaira said. "She mentioned it regarding Anya's dietary requirements."

"They compared me to the fuel budget for an F-35, which I think is a little unfair," Anya huffed. Gary chuckled.

"If they insist I won't protest too much. Rather not owe them anything though, or even have them think that I do," he added.

"It's my idea," Samaira said. "I'll tell them I insisted. Which I am, I guess."

"We should get a move on, then. Night's almost here and we should be away from people in case we get ambushed," Gary said as he began packing everything into the back of his truck. He whistled and his robots all folded themselves up and got into the flatbed as well, and they left the scrapyard behind.

27

Anya, Samaira, and Chandrali, along with Felix and Boo, sat on the nose of the Shadow Ray in the parking lot behind a deli in Topeka, Kansas a couple of days later. Both women studied their maps and were enjoying the fresh air after being inside the Shadow Ray for hours flying over the Midwest while looking for other hosts.

It was their second day of zooming around—following leads Riley supplied them from police departments and eyewitness statements that were in the vicinity of previously known host or alien locations—and so far they had had no more luck than their first day. Yesterday they had covered most of New England and turned up nothing, then returned to Gary and Pan to camp, and set out again earlier that morning.

Gary and Pan were several dozen miles away, doing their own scouting from his truck. They had all agreed that it was important to cover more ground, but always be close enough to one another for backup if they ran into trouble. Pan had requested to go with Gary, "To talk about ants more," and Gary had been happy to have the pangolin along for the ride.

The map that floated between Anya and Samaira showed a circle between Kansas and Missouri that contained at least a few thousand square miles within it. It was Felix's and Boo's best estimate for where up to three hosts might be, and matched up with a statement from a Sheriff's deputy about seeing "Something fucky," in the sky on several occasions.

Samaira sighed.

"Well, at least the numbers have stabilized," she said and looked up at the corner of the map where two numbers were displayed. Felix and Boo had each added them to the maps. While the AIs were still having a problem pinning down the general locations of the hosts and aliens, they had a much easier time estimating how many signals there were.

Felix had said there was still a margin of error of fifteen, but that was close enough to have an idea of how many hosts and aliens were still alive.

The host massacre that had occurred during the first week of the aliens' arrival had plateaued.

Finally.

The meteoric drop of hosts had halted around 1,080. As Felix and Boo continued to run their scans, the number might drop a few, then go up a few more, then drop again, but it had stayed at around 1,080 for most of yesterday and all of today.

The bad news was, the aliens' numbers weren't going down much either. Felix's best estimate for remaining aliens was around 5,210. They still outnumbered the hosts five-to-one.

"They're such creeps," Samaira said as she stared at her map.

"Who's a creep?" Anya asked, not understanding. Samaira gestured at her map.

"The aliens!"

"More like murderous fuckheads."

"I'm not much for swearing," Samaira said.

"You don't have to swear, I guess, but calling the aliens 'creeps,' is kind of underselling it," Anya said, then looked aside at Samaira. "Does it bother you that I swear?"

"No! Of course not. I just think it sounds weird when I do it."

"Weird how?"

"Like, I dunno, like I'm reading lines from a script or something. Unnatural."

"Show me. Call the aliens assholes."

"They're... they're assholes," Samaira said and her voice petered out as she fumbled over the curse. Anya laughed.

"Yeah, that was pretty weird," she said and Samaira rolled her eyes.

"See? I told you. I'm no good at swearing."

"You just need to practice."

"Do I?"

"That, or you need to use stronger language than calling the aliens creeps. C'mon. That refrigerator alien was a piece of work. A real shithead."

"This is silly."

"It'll make you feel better. I always feel better when I tell somebody that's pissing me off what a jackass they are. Or when I stub my toe or —lately—when I hit my head on a door frame."

Samaira took a breath, sat upright, and said, "The refrigerator alien was a shithead."

"Better, but you're not at a recital."

"The fridge was a shithead."

"C'mon. Put some oomph into it!"

"That fridge was a shithead and I'm glad you roasted it alive!"

Anya blinked, and then laughed again. Samaira joined her a moment later.

"You ladies feeling all right?" Gary asked from across the parking lot as he and Pan both stared at them. Anya and Samaira stared back, then resumed giggling. Gary shook his head.

"Maybe I do feel a little better," Samaira admitted.

"See? Always works."

"If only finding the other hosts were that easy."

"I guess anybody with an Archive has either figured out how to survive, or they're dead," Anya said as she studied her map. "I'm hoping whoever was around here legged it and didn't get snapped up. Maybe ran for the coast or something."

"That reminds me: I spoke with MacDougal while you were ordering," Samaira said, "She wants us to check out the East Coast tomorrow. Virgina down to Florida."

"Ugh," Anya grunted and made a face.

"What? What's wrong with the coast?"

"South Carolina," Anya replied, and when Samaira shrugged, she sighed and added, "My family lives there. I still haven't told them."

"What?" Samaira gasped, eyes widening behind her glasses.

"Yeah, I don't really have the best relationship with them. Been kinda busy. What, did you tell your family right away?"

"Well, not right away no, but after a day or two when I was sure I hadn't over-studied myself into hallucinating, yeah. I called my parents, my sisters, my brother. We had dinner and talked about it."

"How'd they take it?"

"They freaked out. Thought it was a reality TV prank at first. My little sister was into it immediately, but she's still a teenager. Everybody else took at least a couple hours to convince. Papa still isn't happy I'm out here hunting aliens, but he understands, I think. Mama is confused, but proud," Samaira smiled and Anya looked away.

It sounded nice.

Having a family that may not agree with you all the time, that could be stubborn, but they were there. They gave a shit.

Anya couldn't stop the image of her little brother springing to the forefront of her mind.

How would Nathan have reacted to the news, if he had been alive?

Anya smirked.

Her little brother would have loved it.

She would have told him how she suplexed an alien refrigerator and then blew it up, and he probably would have told her that she had to do a shooting star leg drop on the next one, and to film it. He probably would have insisted on designing an outfit for her: something loud and ostentatious and probably made from a lot of spandex and rhinestones.

Her eyes stung.

"Anya?" Samaira asked, her voice soft as she looked at her.

"It's nothing, just thinking," Anya replied and blinked as she turned away. She collected the paper and cardboard containers from their meal and deposited them in the trash can. She stood over it for a moment, took a deep breath, and then returned to the Shadow Ray.

"We should get going," she said.

"Uh, yeah. Sure," Samaira replied and climbed in with Chandrali.

Neither of them spoke as they resumed their fruitless search through the skies.

––––––––

THEY MADE camp with Gary and Pan again that night. Samaira chatted with the others around the campfire Anya had summoned, but Anya kept to herself. A couple times she caught Gary or Samaira looking at her with obvious concern, but neither of them pushed.

Pan was his usual, chatty self, quite happy to tell Anya about all the ants he had eaten, all the holes he had dug, how he summoned some golems and made them eat ants, and so on. His innocent chattering was a distraction, but a pleasant one. It gave Anya time to get away from her own thoughts, at least long enough to get to sleep.

And when she slept that night, she once again found herself floating through the fiery void of the Flame Dominion.

And the bird was back.

"Heya. Nice of you to swing by again. Been a few days," the bird said. It ruffled its feathers, which sent a cloud of sparks flying up from its back.

Anya stared at the bird, then at the void around her. It was comforting, just like last time, but she hadn't necessarily wanted to be here. She hadn't asked to be.

"I figured it was you bringing me here, or coming into my brain, or whatever this is. Not me," Anya said. She would have been irritated but it really did feel nice here. So soothing, like a day at the spa. She allowed herself to just lean back and watch the warm curtains of color around her.

"Not you necessarily, but your heart," the bird said.

"Are you speaking about my metaphorical human heart or the literal Sun's Heart?"

"Yes."

"If you're just gonna be obtuse, I'm just gonna enjoy the colors. It has been a day," Anya said and leaned back. The bird fluttered up and perched on her knee. There wasn't any weight to it, but her knee did get a bit warmer.

"You need something?" Anya asked as she looked down.

"Yeah. I need a bearer of the Sun's Heart—even your cheap-ass off-brand version—to maybe stop being such a dense dipshit and pay attention to the incarnation of cosmic-fucking-energy on her knee."

"All right, calm down," Anya said and sat forward. She wasn't really sitting—or laying, or standing—on anything solid, but she could still move her body as if she was. "By the way, I gotta ask: why do you sound like this?"

"Like what?"

"Like, you swear and you sound a lot more… casual than I would expect from an incarnation of cosmic energy. Even one that looks like a tiny little glowing sparrow."

"Because we both know that if I showed up acting and sounding like some big cosmic authority figure, you'd probably never come back here. This is what you would understand best. Besides, you've got the attention span of a rabbit on crack, so this will have to do."

"Hey!"

"All right, fine. A squirrel who's had too much candy. Better?"

"Maybe?" Anya said then leaned back again to think. If she had brought herself back here, subconsciously, then why? She'd been thinking about her little brother, Nathan, earlier. The bird had mentioned him last time she'd been here. It had also given her some answers about the Dominion itself.

"This all feels… useless," Anya said.

"Flying around in your alien jet looking for people that are probably doing their best to stay on the move and not be found? You don't say," the bird replied and laughed.

"Yeah. I'm spinning my wheels and it sucks. But I don't know what else to do."

"I think you do. Mind a little insight?"

"Please," Anya said and waved a hand at the bird.

"Fire is the element of transformation. You want to change things, whether you know it or not. How many skills are there in the Archive that would let you protect people and kill aliens? Millions? You very specifically picked the one that you would be in control of and would allow you to most directly affect your situation. You're not doing that now. You're just puttering around."

"Okay. First, I would have thought water would be the element of transformation, right?"

"Water is the element of change. It will shape itself to the situation. It's passive. Fire will reshape the situation itself, and change it into something new. If you took a hunk of ore, and put it in a container full of water, the water would flow around it and adapt to it being there. You put ore in a fire, bang, now you got metal. When you and the others set up camp, you make a fire. The empty forest or field is now a place to gather, to meet, to discuss and plan. You've got the start of a little community.

"Take Samaira—"

"Okay," Anya said, then blushed when she realized she'd said it out loud.

"Hah!" the bird squawked and pointed a wing at her as she covered her face.

"Please just ignore I said that. It's hard to keep my thoughts and my words separate in here."

"No promises. Anyway, take Samaira for example: if she were to pick a Dominion, I'd put money down that she would pick water. I'd put even more money down that she would start having talks with her Dominion just like we are now. She adapts to her situation. Her skill, the aether, it's all about adapting to the situation at hand, becoming what she needs it to be in response to what's happening. The government wants to create a new department for hosts to fight aliens? She's on-board from the word go, adapting to what's around her.

"You're about making something else happen. There's some over-lap, but every element and idea contains a portion of its opposite. Yin and Yang."

"I mean, I'm trying to find people right now, change everybody being scattered into coming together. It's not working."

"You running around looking for them is you trying to shape yourself to the situation. You should be making them come to you."

"We talked with Gary about this. The Archive comms are all fucked up and Gary can't make something to get around them."

"So? Don't you know at least two people in the news broadcasting business?"

"I—" Anya started to say and paused. Jennifer Chang and Angel Ramierez were alive and well and somewhere in Brooklyn. She'd saved their lives and they knew what was going on better than most. The feds had probably confiscated their footage, told them to keep quiet until they were ready to make an official statement.

"That would probably piss off MacDougal," Anya said.

"You're adjusting to the situation again. She's your boss now?" the bird asked and flapped its wings. It pecked Anya on her knee and she frowned at it.

"No. It's not just about me though. If I get that reporter to broadcast me saying aliens have invaded, it could cause a panic."

"Hello! People are already panicking! This sneaking around shit is only good for the aliens! Besides, you're not trying to convince the entire planet, just hosts. You don't even need to mention aliens! Hosts already know it's real. You just need a platform they have a better chance of seeing and say enough to get the basic picture across."

"If I piss the feds off, they might not be so willing to help."

"Booooo! Where's the woman that told her last boss to go fuck himself? You really think the feds are gonna let people die just because you tried to get the word out? That Hanover guy seems like he's more concerned with PR than anything else. It'd look really bad if he just pouted and refused to help because you were trying to organize. MacDougal is... a bit harder to pin down. I think she might be pissy at first, but if this works, she'll come around."

"If it works."

"Yeah. It could blow up in your face. Fire does that too. But what do you want, little ember? To sit on your ass and wait to get lucky, or try to change the situation?"

Anya bit her lip.

"I want to do something," she said. "Even if it's dangerous."

"Good! Then go do it! Also, be careful when you wake up. You've been in here a while, and there may be some side-effects when you come to."

"Like what?" Anya asked.

"I dunno," the bird replied and shrugged its tiny wings. "Hopefully no big explosions or anything."

"Wait, what?" Anya asked. The bird fluttered up, pecked Anya on the nose, and she awoke with a start.

Her tent was filled with the flickering glow of a fire, and Anya shouted in surprise as she realized her hair was ablaze. It didn't hurt, and she put it out quickly enough.

"Anya?" Samaira asked from outside. She had taken first watch that night. "What was that?"

"Nothing important," Anya said and emerged from her tent.

"You sure? I heard—whoa," Samaira said as Anya emerged. Her eyes went from Anya's face up to her hairline and Anya looked up.

"What? What is it?" she asked.

"Nice hair. It suits you," Samaira replied and smiled. Anya's hair was short, but long enough for her to pull a lock of it into view.

It was red. Not a normal shade of red like some people naturally had, but a deep, vibrant rose-red, with the occasional streak of orange.

"Huh," Anya said. "That's kinda neat."

"Used the Archive to give yourself some cosmetic upgrades?" Samaira asked. Anya considered telling her about the bird and the realm of the Flame Dominion, but decided against it for now. Tori knew, but they'd been friends for years. Anya didn't want to freak Samaira or Gary out.

"Yeah. As for the yelling, I just had a bad dream," she said.

"Can't blame you. I've had a few of those too, since this started."

"Look, I have an idea for finding people that might work better than what we've been doing, but it might make MacDougal unhappy in the short-term."

"Uh-oh."

"I still have some thinking to do, so I don't mind taking the rest of your watch."

"You sure?" Samaira asked and yawned. Chandrali was at her feet, and yawned in kind, as if encouraging her to hit the sack for the night.

"I'm sure. We'll talk about it tomorrow," Anya said. Samaira wished her goodnight with a thanks, and Anya sat by the fire until dawn, and contemplated what she could change.

28

'm still not sure about this," Samaira said later that morning.

They had all flown to Brooklyn and the Channel 08 news station, where Anya had asked to see Jennifer Chang. The reporter had come out so quickly she'd almost knocked a delivery man over, Angel Ramierez in her wake and with a handheld camcorder in his grasp.

"You wanna find people or don't you?" Gary asked. Jennifer had taken them to a small, vacant recording studio that looked like it was being used as a secondary storage unit for older video and sound equipment.

"Isn't this just a local station, though? No offense, but I doubt there's any more hosts in Brooklyn," Samaira said.

"We're just filming here. I can get the video to a friend at the RINN. They'll need a day or two to get it broadcast, but it'll be worldwide. TV and internet," Jennifer said as she attached a microphone to Anya's jacket.

Anya raised her eyebrows at the reporter. The Rutherford International News Network was one of the largest media outlets on the planet. They had a huge office and studios downtown, as well as in London, Tokyo, Beijing, and Brazil.

"Yeah, that'll do," Gary said.

"Here's the deal, though," Jennifer said and looked at Anya. "I owe you for saving us, but I'm still probably going to get in trouble for this, ditto for my buddy at RINN. Once this thing hits, I get to do a full interview with you. I know this one is gonna have to be brief, but later, I want a real sit-down with you. Your friends too, if they're willing. Any other media stuff in the future, you let me know, okay?"

"I don't see a problem with that," Anya said and shrugged. Jennifer almost squealed.

"Me too, right?" Angel asked.

"Naturally," Jennifer replied and Anya nodded.

"I'll… have to see how much this pisses MacDougal off," Samaira said.

"Maybe," Gary added.

"If I can make more friends, I'd like that," Pan said.

"Oh people are gonna love you," Jennifer said, then looked at Chandrali, who had perched on top of a box of equipment and was swishing her tail back and forth. "Is the cat one of you?"

"She's special, but no, she's not a host," Samaira said.

"I think we're good," Jennifer said as she glanced down at her own equipment, then at Angel who gave her a thumbs up. "Ready?"

Angel pointed the camera at Anya and she took a deep breath.

"Ready," she nodded, and Jennifer nodded at Angel, who turned the camera on.

"This is Jennifer Chang with Channel 08, Brooklyn news. I'm here with somebody who has been directly involved in the attack in Prospect Park last week, as well as other events that have rocked the United States and cities around the globe. What can you tell us about what's been happening?"

"The things—attacks or 'natural' disasters—that have been happening like the earthquake outside LA, the disturbance at the Water Tower Place in Chicago, and more all over the world, are not coincidences. They're coordinated attacks by a hostile force that myself and others have been trying to stop. If you're one of us—a host for the Archive—we need to come together, but finding each other is next to impossible right now. Ask your Archive 'helper,' to locate the area exactly 115.74 miles due east of where the twenty-seventh hostile combatant first appeared. We will be there for twelve hours after this is broadcast. If you're alone, we can help you. If you're not, we can coordinate.

"Uh, that's it, I guess," Anya finished.

Jennifer nodded and Angel turned the camera off.

"That's it?" Samaira asked.

"There's a chance one of the execs at RINN may not like my buddy basically hijacking their broadcast if he can't get this approved," Jennifer said. "You're sure the other hosts will know where to go?"

"Yup!" Felix said as they appeared. "All Archive AIs should have access to precise gnosiphage landing sights. While they all arrived within seconds of each other, there's enough of a gap between the precise time of touchdown that they can be numbered in order of arrival. It was the one time I had a clear signal, and Boo and Gizmo's data is the same as mine. Another AI can pinpoint the location based off the information here accurately enough."

"We thought about giving geographic coordinates, but that would mean anybody could find us," Gary said. "I'd like to avoid any government interference for the time being. Other hosts like me may want to steer clear of any big organizations."

"All right. Like I said, this may take a couple days. Do you have a phone or anything?" Jennifer asked and Anya and Samaira both gave her the numbers for the phones MacDougal had given them. "I'll call you as soon as my friend gives me the greenlight."

"Good luck," Anya said.

"See you soon!" Jennifer said as she and Angel all but dashed out of the room.

"I really hope this works," Samaira said.

"Yeah. Me too," Anya sighed.

———

ANYA HAD DECIDED to meet with Tori while they were in Manhattan. They needed to patrol more while Jennifer tried to connect with her friend, but Anya figured they could spare an hour or two.

Anya, Tori, and Samaira all met at the coffee shop in Jersey that Anya had ripped the door off of during her last visit. She hadn't really gotten a look at it during her previous visit. Its walls were lined with rough wooden planks and a variety of plants hung from the ceiling, and the whole place was filled with the aroma of roasting coffee beans, cinnamon, vanilla, and hot bread.

"Hey!" somebody shouted as Anya walked in. One of the baristas behind the counter pointed at her. The other patrons glanced up from their booths and tables to stare at the towering woman who stood hunched guiltily in the doorway. "You're that tall lady that ripped the door off last week!"

"I know. I'm sorry, I'm here to pay for it, and get some coffee, if that's okay," Anya said as she approached the counter. The barista glared at her and then went into the back room to check with the manager. After some discussion and many apologies, Anya was given a receipt for the door. She was pretty sure MacDougal and Riley would pay for it if she explained what happened, but she didn't want to depend too much on them. They were already footing the bill for her meals.

"I'll stop by the bank later and transfer the money," Anya told the barista, who just grunted. They became a bit friendlier when Anya ordered four large cups of coffee for herself, along with half the pastries and sandwiches in the curved glass display set into the counter.

Samaira ordered a single cup of tea and a scone and the two sat across from Tori, who had ordered before they arrived, at the back of the shop. Anya officially introduced Samaira and Tori, then sat next to the latter and made small talk while they waited on their order.

"So. Magic, huh?" Tori asked as Anya and Samaira sipped their drinks. Anya frowned at her cup, then pointed her finger at it and the black liquid began to literally boil. She sipped it again and nodded.

"Been talking about you being our little guinea pig with Samaira. She and Felix narrowed some items down in the RAC store and we're pretty sure it's safe," she said. Samaira opened her purse and took out a thin silver bracelet with a blue gem in the center, along with a small notebook that was barely a few dozen pages in length.

"This," Samaira said as she pointed to the bracelet, "is an aetheric focus. It will help connect you to any bits of the aether that may be around. From what I've been able to tell, the densest concentrations are in Central Park, and a bodega in Queens. I have no idea why. You can still practice in your apartment or hotel, but going to those places and just walking around or meditating should help you feel the presence of the aether more until you're used to it. I've written the address of the bodega in the notebook."

Tori took the bracelet, pinching it between her thumb and forefinger as if it were about to bite her.

"You can just put it on. It's safe," Samaira said. Tori shrugged and slipped the bracelet onto her wrist. She looked at it and then blinked and tilted her head to one side, then the other.

"Whoa," she said.

"Mm-hmm," Samaira said as she sipped her tea.

"What is it?" Anya asked.

"I dunno. It's kinda like... hearing music? But not really. There's no sound. It's just weird. Not bad."

"It feels like a current, to me," Samaira said. "Kind of like I'm standing in the ocean and I can feel the tide pushing or pulling around me. It's different for everybody."

"Cool," Tori said and grinned. "What about the notebook?"

"The notebook is some kind of aetheric primer," Anya continued. "I had Felix order it off the RAC store with the bracelet. From what Samaira told me, it's all pretty basic stuff. Mostly just getting a feel for the aether and doing a few parlor tricks. Nothing dangerous."

The aetheric charm and primer had both been very affordable: 6,750 RAC for the former and only 215 RAC for the latter. Anya had just over 10,000 RAC left to her name. Enough for another healing potion if she used her current one, but that was about it.

"There's also some blank pages in the back of the book. If you don't mind, it'd be a big help to me if you kept notes. I'd like to see how other people interpret the aether."

"Works for me," Tori said. "So if this works, and ordinary people can do magic, what then?"

Samaira frowned and bit her lip and said, "We take it from there.

Right now this is mostly just an experiment. I think it will work. Boo and Felix sounded pretty positive about it, but there's a chance it might not pan out. But if it does… then that's something else to consider. MacDougal or other people in the government will want to know."

"We don't have to tell them though, do we?" Anya asked.

"Even if we kill all the gnosiphages on Earth, I doubt that will be the end of our alien troubles," Samaira sighed. "There's probably more of them out there, somewhere. Far away, hopefully, but still. And there's the Engineers, too. Plus, the Archive is full of evidence of other alien species and organizations. All of our skills are proof of that. If Earth's defenses against extraterrestrial threats are only the current number of hosts, we're in big trouble.

"The paradigm is about to seriously shift. We can't keep all this power concentrated to just the few remaining hosts. It would be leaving the whole planet open to another attack, or worse, down the road."

"She's got a point," Tori said. "I'm happy to play guinea pig, but realistically, there's only so long you can keep the lid on the superpowers box. I'd be shocked if other hosts aren't handing out similar stuff to people they know already. Plus, didn't the feds or the cops pick up that Earl guy's laser rifle from Prospect Park already? They're totally reverse-engineering that thing right now. Guaranteed."

Anya had to agree. After all, she was about to blow the lid off of some of what had been happening along with Jennifer Chang.

"All right. We deal with the what-ifs later. We have enough on our collective plates for now," she said.

"Yeah. Enough serious talk. How's Pan doing?" Tori asked, and the three women spent the rest of the afternoon chatting about much lighter matters.

———

ANYA GOT the call from Jennifer Chang early the next day.

"Our little video is going to hit in about an hour, two tops. You should head for whatever meeting place you set up," the reporter said.

"Got it, thanks," Anya replied. She, Gary, Pan, and Samaira were once again camped out several miles away from Manhattan. Anya had the call on speaker, so they all cleaned up their campsite and were airborne within minutes.

The location Anya had selected was 115.74 miles exactly east of the city of Nuuk, Greenland. She had selected it because it was extremely remote: nothing but icy fields and mountains for miles and miles. It was also remote enough that any conventional means of transportation were basically out of luck, but any host on the run was more than likely to have some method of getting around that would be advanced enough to arrive.

It took Anya and the others a little under an hour to arrive. The area was an uneven field of pure white ice and snow, broken by clumps of black rock poking their way up from beneath. It was beautiful, in an extremely desolate sort of way.

It was also, no surprise, absolutely freezing.

The cold didn't trouble Anya at all, especially in her regalia and mantle, but Pan squealed when she exited the Shadow Ray and curled into a tight ball and insisted he would stay inside. Gary also remained inside his truck with the heater on (which was powerful enough to combat the cold), but Samaira and Chandrali didn't seem fazed by the weather. Samaira had changed into her magical attire, while Chandrali adopted her tiger shape.

"Will other people be able to handle this?" Samaira asked. Her sparkling midnight hair swept around her in the wind, making the star-like constellations glimmering within it dance and shift. The translucent blue shoulder-cape she wore curled around her in a loose, defensive shape that resisted any attempts by the wind to move it.

"Working on it," Gary said from inside the truck. "I'm reprogramming some of my defensive bots to adjust their shields for a wider range and to counter for environmental effects. They won't stop any attacks, but it should be enough to keep the worst of the cold out."

"I think I can help with that," Samaira said and made her elegant, white bow appear in her hands, then launched several glowing arrows in a wide, circular perimeter around them. They stuck up from the ground and shone with a pale blue light that spread. The temperature rose several degrees and continued to rise.

Anya could have made the whole area as balmy as a tropical beach, but it would've been a waste of energy. Gary and Samaira had things covered so she just took a seat on the nose of the Shadow Ray.

"Now we wait, I guess," she said.

———

Anya flew to Nuuk after a couple hours for the cell reception, and was unsurprised to find she had several missed calls and text messages from both Riley and Tori, as well as a single text from MacDougal.

Tori was thrilled, telling her she was all over the internet after some kind of broadcast had been interrupted. Riley was very obviously uncomfortable and advised her to come back to Federal Plaza as soon as her "stunt," was over.

MacDougal's single text was brief and to the point.

MACDOUGAL: If this works, good. If not, we'll talk when you get back.

That was it.

Anya sighed.

"Could be worse," she said. She told Tori she was glad the word had gotten out and would talk when she was back. She told Riley to calm down and that it was her idea and to not be mad at Samaira. She paused as she had MacDougal's text open and then typed her response.

ANYA: See you then.

That would do for now. She went into a nearby coffee shop and got coffee and donuts for herself, Gary, tea for Samaira, then returned to the Shadow Ray where she had left it cloaked in a nearby parking lot, near the back. Pan was inside, and he wiggled his nose at her as she took her seat in the pilot's chair.

"Good news?" Pan asked as Anya set the auto-pilot for the field where Gary and Samaira waited.

"Well, nothing bad at least," she replied.

"These other people, like us, that might be coming: will they be nice?"

"I sure hope so. They might be mean, though."

"Why?"

"Humans are... complicated, Pan. Some of them are really sweet and nice, like Tori, Samaira, and Gary. Some of them are just okay, or only mean sometimes, and some people are just... assholes."

"Assholes?" Pan asked and then tilted his head to the side and got a faraway look in his eyes. Anya had been around Pan enough that she recognized the look. His understanding of English was somewhere around a smarter-than-average child's: good for basic ideas, or conveying complex ideas in easy-to-grasp terms, but sometimes he needed a minute to process. She assumed his English skill needed a moment to translate a word he knew on a technical level, but not on a practical one.

"They're an anus?" Pan asked and Anya laughed.

"'Assholes' is a word we use to describe people who are also rude, or mean, or not nice," she elaborated. Unbidden, Anya thought of her mother.

"Assholes," Pan repeated.

"Yeah. If things go bad and some people want to try and fight or cause trouble, you run and hide. Stay with Gary if you can."

"But I wanna stay with you!"

"I may have to fight, but Gary can protect you both and you can get away. Summon some of your golem friends if you have to, but just enough to give you time to get away. All right?"

"All right. I don't like the idea of fighting," Pan said and curled into a ball.

"I know, buddy. Hopefully you won't have to, but we'll see."

They landed a few minutes later, and Samaira jogged over to the Shadow Ray just as Anya and Pan emerged. Pan seemed delighted that the area had gotten significantly warmer, and went over to play with Chandrali, who mostly ignored him.

"Hey! Did you see that?" Samaira asked and looked upwards. Anya followed her gaze and looked around.

"No. What was it?"

"Something flew overhead right before you got here. Boo said they caught a host signal for a second, but then it was gone," Samaira said.

"Hey, coffee. Nice one, kid. Thanks," Gary said and accepted the cup from Anya, along with a piece of cake the café owner had called a Kalaallit Kaagit. Anya gave Samaira her share as well.

"I didn't catch anything, no," Anya said as she continued to look around. "Felix?"

"Nothi—wait! There!" Felix said as they appeared and pointed up.

"Well, that's something all right," Gary said and sipped his coffee.

A gigantic humanoid robot, at least six-stories tall, descended out of the snowy sky and landed on the ice with a heavy thud a hundred yards away. The robot was sleek, and it gleamed in the muted sunlight that filtered through the clouds. It was mostly white and chrome, but highlighted with shades of green and gold across its chestplate and from a large samurai-like crest on its head. It knelt and then the chest swung open with a loud hiss of compressed air.

A lithe man wearing a black bodysuit adorned with sleek pieces of hi-tech green armor hopped out of a concealed cockpit. It was a fall of at least a couple stories, but he treated it as if it were no more than a couple feet. He was young, maybe around Anya's age, with dark brown skin and hair that was shaved on the sides, but styled into long braids on top and tied at the back of his head. Some kind of glowing green holographic visor covered his dark eyes, and a glowing green AI floated beside him.

Anya could see a huge grin on his face even from across the field, and he waved as he began to jog toward them.

"*E ai!*" the young man cried as he approached, then slid to a stop a few yards away. "Ah, good afternoon! Nice to meet you! Hello!"

"Hey," Anya said and grinned. "I'm Anya."

"My name is Dario. Very happy to meet you!" he said, then paused when he saw Pan peeking out from behind Anya's legs. "And who is this?"

"This is Pan," Anya said and smiled down at him. "It's okay, Pan. Dario seems nice."

"Nice?" Pan asked and then waddled out and waved.

"I try to be nice," Dario said. "Mostly do okay. You're a host too?"

"Yes!" Pan said. "Like Anya."

"Are you all American?"

"Yeah. Pan too, kind of. Don't know if he was actually born in the zoo where I found him, but I suppose," Anya replied.

"I'm from Brazil. So! Is this it?" Dario asked and looked around, hands on his hips.

"So far. We all came together, but you're the first other than us," Samaira said.

"Nice robot," Gary said and nodded at the towering figure in the distance.

"Isn't it? I built him!" Dario said with obvious pride.

"Did you? Damn fine work," Gary nodded.

"He is Golias! Very strong."

"What kinda skills you take?" Gary asked, and Dario brought up his main menu screen.

DARIO VALENTE: LEVEL 31 MOBILE COMBAT FRAME ACE
Statistics

- Awareness-26 (+10 from gear)
- Dexterity-21 (+8 from gear)
- Fortitude-8
- Intelligence-27 (+12 from gear)
- Strength-6
- Willpower-8

Skills

- Mechanical Mobile Frame Design (Defensive)-30 (+10 from gear)
- Mobile Artillery and Armaments Construction-28 (+10 from gear)
- Bio-Integrated Control Systems and Feedback (Vehicular)-28 (+15 from gear)
- Combat Piloting (Luorian Armored Aerial Response Team)-25 (+12 from gear)

"Wow, nice picks," Gary said.

"I think we have another anime fan," Anya whispered to Samaira, who chuckled and nodded.

"Glad I'm not the only one," she said.

"Golias and I have killed three aliens and helped many people in Rio. But it has been a bit lonely. There was another host from Argentina I met, but they left to go somewhere else. I started to come up through Central America, but couldn't find anybody for days. Then, today, while I'm having breakfast, boom! I see you."

Dario pointed at Anya and grinned.

"Very good idea. I considered, but wasn't sure how best to do it. I also thought if I just stood around with Golias, the aliens would catch us. This is a big, big relief."

"I'm just glad it kind of worked out," Anya said. "Even if it's just one person, that's better than what we had before. Good work making it on your own so far."

"Would you like to shake hands?" Dario asked and Anya blinked in confusion for a moment before she remembered: the AIs could permanently lock onto another host's signal if they made physical contact.

Gary was the first to extend his hand and Dario shook it with an overly-enthusiastic up-and-down motion.

"The host from Argentina, I think her name was Delfina, We shook hands too. But then she removed her signal from the communications window when she left. Said it was too dangerous for hosts to be together, a bigger target for the aliens. I disagreed but... it was her choice," Dario shook his head and sighed.

"You can remove contacts?" Anya asked and Dario nodded.

"Your AI can do it any time. But if you want the contact back, you have to have personal contact again," he said.

"Can confirm!" Felix said.

Anya was a little relieved at that, though irritated Felix hadn't told her sooner. Though she really hadn't expressed an interest in hiding from hosts to the AI: quite the opposite. She'd fully intended to make contact with as many hosts as possible, but it was nice to know she could hide from any psychos if they turned up. She, Samaira, and Pan all shook with Dario next.

"Company!" Felix said beside Anya, and she and the others all looked up.

"Whoa," Gary said.

More shapes descended from the sky.

A giant chrome egg floated down and touched the ice with a gentle thud. A black carriage covered in wrought-iron spikes and gold filigree and pulled by a team of skeletal horses burst out of a cloud as it came to a galloping stop on the ice. Something that looked like an old, cherry-red Cadillac with rockets on the underside followed behind it, and appeared to be driven by a robot and a huge figure that looked like a cross between a man and a killer whale.

A giant palanquin made of polished red wood floated down alongside a saucer-like craft and both settled near the gothic carriage. More came, all within minutes of each other: strange animals, advanced ships and flying cars, a flying carpet and other mystic means of locomotion. The field had gone from a mostly barren stretch of inhospitable ice and black rock to something that looked like an impromptu circus in minutes.

The Sun's Heart flared in Anya's chest, and she went to go greet the new arrivals.

29

Things were a bit hectic at first. Some of the figures that emerged from their rides were hesitant, while others were more like Dario: thrilled to see other hosts and eager to meet them. The empty field was filled with at least a few dozen people after several more minutes, and many of them were starting to gravitate towards Anya.

Others held back, remaining close to their vehicles or mounts, and eyed the gathering with caution. Some formed small groups of two or three and kept to the sidelines. Still others treated the whole thing like a carnival, and went from host to host to admire their rides or share their menus.

Anya remained where she was, a bit overwhelmed at the small crowd that was gathering near her. She heard a few people commenting in English that she was the one from the video. Others speaking a variety of languages glanced at her and nodded or smiled, but little else.

Anya had wanted this: hosts coming together, finding each other. But beyond that, she didn't know.

At least nobody had done anything stupid.

Yet.

"So. What now?" Gary asked.

"I guess... mingle? Give other people time to show up?" Anya said and shrugged. Gary chuckled.

"I thought you had a plan," Samaira whispered.

"I did! This was it!" Anya said and gestured at the crowd of people. Samaira pinched the bridge of her nose. "Look, at least we have options now."

"It'll be fine, kid. You did good. I like the look of that flying Cadillac. I'll go chat with those fellas," Gary said and patted Anya on the shoulder as he walked away. Pan was quick to waddle after him.

"Gary, maybe we should... dang it," Samaira said and reached out for him but he and Pan were already halfway towards the Cadillac and the huge killer-whale creature standing next to it.

"We'll stick together," Anya said to her. "C'mon, let's go see who's here."

The two women (and Chandrali) stepped forward, toward the nearest vehicle and its owner: the huge chrome egg that had been among the first to descend. Its sides were perfectly smooth, and much like Anya's Shadow Ray, it hovered silently several inches above the ground. A hatch had opened on one side to expose an interior full of scanning devices and holographic screens. A man sat in the middle of it all, and exited the craft when he saw Anya and Samaira approach.

He was tall, but still rather short compared to Anya. He was in his early thirties, and had long blond hair pulled back in a loose ponytail. Wire-framed glasses perched on a nose that had been broken at some point in the distant past, and clear blue eyes studied Anya from behind them. A scruff of darker blond beard grew along the man's jaw, and Anya couldn't help but look at him a little longer than necessary.

At first he reminded her a bit of Earl: strikingly handsome, tall, in good shape, but Earl's good looks had been artificial. He had used the Archive's status menu to alter himself and he'd looked almost like he'd had his good looks assigned by algorithm rather than nature. The man in front of Anya appeared to come by his somewhat rugged looks naturally, and was better for it.

"Good afternoon," the man said with a northern European accent.

"Heya," Anya said and shook the man's hand. "I'm Anya, this is Samaira."

"Arvo Immonen, pleased to meet you," the man said. "Thank you for your message online. I've been running around by myself non-stop since this all began."

"You and everybody else," Anya said. "Run into any aliens?"

"No, thank goodness. I'm afraid I am not very equipped to face them, which is why I rushed over here as soon as I saw your video."

"What do you mean?" Samaira asked.

"Ah, well, it is a little embarrassing. I'm a doctor, and when I learned I could take skills that healed people, that is what I did. Just a few at first, to see if it would work. I did not find out about the invasion until a day or two after I had used most of my points. I was able to take a single skill to help hide myself and avoid trouble, but not much else, I'm afraid. Here," Arvo said and brought up his menu.

ARVO IMMONEN: LEVEL 30 MENDER ADEPT
  Statistics

- Awareness-25
- Dexterity-20
- Fortitude-35
- Intelligence-10
- Strength-5
- Willpower-7

Skills

- Healing (Tactile)-25
- Body Scan-15
- Living Shadow-10
- Matter Generation (Biological)-20
- Matter Absorption (Biological)-15
- Body Manipulation (Tactile)-25

"You don't have any fighting skills? Or gear upgrades?" Anya gaped at the menu. Arvo laughed, a warm sound that made his broad chest shake.

"Not a one! Though I suspect even if I had known about the invasion from the start, I would not have picked any. I do not have the stomach for fighting," he said. "The living shadow skill lets me get out of trouble if I must. Quite handy. And this very shiny egg vehicle behind me is just as handy for running away from trouble as well. I spent my remaining store currency on the egg and more medicine and medical tech rather than gear for myself."

Samaira looked between the doctor and his menu screen.

"Wait... I've heard of you. You're from Finland?" she asked and Arvo nodded. "You're the guy who's been curing everybody!"

"What?" Anya asked.

"It was on the news: some guy appearing in hospitals around Europe and curing everything from cancer to heart disease to people with amputations from accidents or whatever," Samaira said and smiled at Arvo. "You're unbelievable. In the good way!"

Arvo smiled and his pale cheeks and ears darkened as he flushed.

"No, I just think it's what most doctors in my position would do. It's a very frustrating thing to be confronted with the incurable every day, and see how your patients can suffer. I jumped at the chance to fix that... perhaps a bit too eagerly. What about you two?"

Anya and Samaira showed him their menus and he nodded.

"Yes, I think that is much more useful for facing killer aliens," he said. "However, if either of you have any sort of injury from your fighting that you need looked at, please come see me."

"I regenerate," Anya said.

"I heal too, sort of," Samaira added.

"I think I'd like to hear about that sometime, if you wouldn't—" Arvo said but was cut off by a curse.

"Oi!" a rough, loud voice echoed across the crowd. Anya turned and saw the two largest figures, both even larger than her, standing inches apart. One of them was the killer whale creature, who was wearing a bright red floral shirt, board shorts, and flip-flops, like he had just come from a beach. The orca-man had folded his arms across his chest and spread his legs in an obviously aggressive posture. His tail lashed behind him, and smoke puffed out of his mouth and blow-hole from a comically oversized joint clamped between sharp teeth.

The other hulking figure was an equally huge man in heavy black tactical armor and a matte black helmet with a reflective visor. His posture was neutral: arms at his sides, but something about his rigidity made it obvious he was not going to be moved.

"Brody, take it easy, mate," a man next to the killer whale said in an Australian accent. He was of average height, and wearing robotic armor. Anya recognized him as the person driving the flying Cadillac she had first taken to be a robot. His very human face was now exposed, revealing tan skin and shaggy black hair.

"Nah, big 'un here pushed me. What's your fucking problem then, ya big cunt?" Brody asked, his voice also heavy with an Australian accent.

The man in black armor didn't respond. Anya would have taken him for a statue if she hadn't seen his chest rising and falling.

"Oh boy," Samaira said.

"My friends, I'm sure it was just a mistake," Arvo said as he stepped forward. "No need to be at each other's throats when there's still plenty of aliens out there."

"Hrm," the huge man in black armor grunted. He said something, but his voice was muffled inside his helmet. It sounded like Japanese. A moment later, a robotic voice translated whatever he had said into English.

"I am only here to see if you know where aliens are. I only want to kill them. I have no argument with this whale creature," the voice said.

"Well, watch where you're going then. Big as a fucking truck this one," Brody said.

"You're not exactly small yourself," the man in the robot suit said. Brody puffed on his joint, and the man in the black armor walked away after offering a slight bow.

"Well, thank goodness that wasn't a scene," Arvo said.

"Yeah, sorry about that. Brody here's a good enough fella, just not entirely used to the social niceties, y'know?" the man in the robot suit said then laughed. "Name's Cooper, by the way. I'm not actually one of you host people. Brody's the one with that Archive thing. This robot suit, Brody got it for me offa his menu store. Took me a few days to get the hang of it, but it's absolutely fan-fucking-tastic."

"You don't have the Archive?" Anya asked and Cooper shook his head.

"Nah. Ran into this big lump of blubber while I was surfing. Scared the shit outta me. Sometimes you see orcas off the coast, but not alone like him. He came up outta the water and started talking to me in this weird, broken English. Thought I'd finally smoked myself stupid."

"You don't need to smoke to be stupid, Coop," Brody said, and laughed.

"So animals can receive the Archive? And it makes them intelligent?" Arvo asked.

"There's a pangolin over there," Anya said and pointed at Pan.

"Hear that, mate? You're not the only one!" Cooper said and patted Brody on the back.

"Yeah? Damn, he's a tiny little fella, ain't he?" Brody asked and lumbered over to talk to Pan. Anya started to follow them when someone cleared their throat behind them. She turned to see four people: three men and a woman.

The woman had short, punkish cyan hair, tan skin, and sharp Eurasian features. She wore a long black cloak over plate armor; the former had some kind of mist swirling in its folds, and the latter was decorated with intricate designs and runes along its edges.

The largest man wore dark maroon leather armor and a hood that concealed his face in blackness. The second man of medium height was pale and had white hair, and wore ornate black and gold robes over a regal-looking shirt and trousers. He also had small black horns popping out of his head, and yellow eyes slitted like a cat's.

The last man was the shortest, just shy of average height, and wore a long white trenchcoat over white tactical armor. A hi-tech helmet with a reflective gold faceplate sat atop an armored neckguard, concealing his features.

"Uh, hello," Anya said. "I'm Anya."

"Pleased to meet you," the man in the gold helmet said, his modulated voice tinged with a French accent. "I'm Renn. This is Mona," he gestured at the woman, "Harrison," the man with horns, "and Kan," the man in the hood.

"A pleasure," Samaira said, though Anya thought she sounded a little tense. She couldn't blame her. There was something a little odd about the group, especially considering the company they were in. While most of the other hosts had spread out to mingle and seemed generally happy to be meeting others, these four stood a little too close together. The woman, Mona, was smiling, but it reminded Anya of the way a shark might smile at a fish. Harrison appeared neutral, and the other two had their faces hidden.

Anya's heat sense picked up a few other oddities as well. Mona was much, much colder than a normal person would be, while Harrison was much warmer. Kan's heat changed every second or so, waxing and waning in what Anya realized had to be his heartbeat. Renn seemed normal enough, heat-wise.

"We were wondering if you had any sort of plan for this gathering, or if you just wanted the hosts to meet each other?" Renn asked.

"Just meet-and-greet," Anya said. "I'm nobody's boss. Hopefully anybody who's on their own can find people to team-up with, be a little bit safer, more effective at tracking down the aliens."

"I see. Would you mind if I made an announcement?"

"Like I said, I'm not in charge. Do what you like as long as you're not gonna try and start a fight or anything."

Renn nodded at her in silent thanks, then moved with the rest of his group to the center of the gathering. He touched a button on the side of his helmet, and when he spoke, his modulated voice was much louder.

"Excuse me please," he said and raised his hands. "Excuse me."

The scattered conversations petered out to a series of murmurs, and after a few moments the field was silent but for the wind. All eyes had turned to Renn.

"Thank you. I apologize for interrupting. Can everybody speak English or otherwise have a translation device of some sort? Yes? Good. I think we should discuss a few things while we have the opportunity," he continued. "Mostly, how to save the world."

"Kill aliens," the huge man in black armor said. There was some scattered laughter at this, and Renn nodded.

"*Ça marche*. I agree. But as we've all seen so far, it's easier said than done. We have been mostly scattered, uncoordinated. If we are to win, that has to change. Anybody here who has killed an alien knows from their data streams that they have far better tracking abilities than we do, and this allows them to coordinate their attacks more effectively."

Scattered murmuring rippled through the crowd.

"Ms. Anya's plan to get so many of us in one place has already helped with that. If you didn't know, physical contact with another host will allow you to permanently follow their signal. This also allows reliable usage of the Archive's communication features, but that alone won't be enough."

"Get to the point. What are you suggesting?" a short black woman with a large curly puff of hair asked in a South African accent. She stood next to a taller man with sandy brown hair and a beard, and a small herd of strange animals surrounded the two. The biggest of the creatures was the size of a horse and resembled a cross between a cobra and a raccoon. It regarded the assembled hosts with bright yellow eyes split by vertical black pupils, and tendrils of blue electricity sparked between its twitching whiskers.

"First of all: would you please mind introducing yourself?" Renn asked. The woman huffed but nodded.

"Amahle, from Cape Town. This is Bernard," she said and gestured at the bearded man next to her who waved and smiled cheerily.

"Thank you, Ms. Amahle. As for what I'm proposing, it's simple," Renn continued, "We organize by region and what is needed. For example, Asia and North America have lost the most hosts, while Australia and South America have lost the fewest. So maybe somebody from Australia can go to Asia and fill in some gaps, and so on. After we connect with each other, communication will no longer be an issue, and if any host finds themselves in danger, a call can be sent out and nearby hosts can rush to their aid."

"Makes sense," Samaira said.

"And what if there are some, uh, less-than-helpful people here?" a thin Latina woman asked in an American accent. "Somebody set off a nuke or something near Bengaluru, somebody else set off explosions across Poland, and somebody has been murdering rich people across Europe. Oh! I'm, uh Esmeralda, by the way. From Monterey. Nice to meet everybody."

"Could be aliens though, right?" Bernard asked. "I mean, I hope it is."

"The aliens have kept their attacks localized to relatively small-scale attacks. The largest attack from an alien I'm aware of had a kill-count in the dozens. The WMD that was used near Bengaluru had a death-toll in the tens of thousands. They also wouldn't target rich people who weren't hosts," Samaira said.

"There's also some kind of media black-out going on in India. Aliens don't seem too concerned with blocking normal methods of communication, aside from some initial disruptions to cell networks when they landed," Amahle added.

"It is... a possibility. However so far the only ones specifically targeting hosts are the aliens. Obviously we are here to fight them and not our fellow humans," Renn said. "Our planet is no stranger to conflict, but whatever we fought over before must be put aside in the face of this invasion."

"Uh, excuse? Here, please?" a small voice said. It belonged to a diminutive black-haired woman with pale skin and an Easten-European accent. She had a pair of thick goggles on top of her head and ratty clothing. Everybody turned to look at her at once and she flinched under the collective gaze.

"Ah, I am Ziva. I am not doing the Bengaluru bomb. But other explosions in Poland... is me," she said and gave an awkward smile.

"Why would you do that?" Kan, the man in the red hood, asked.

"Is country in Poland! Boring! Only trees, rocks, vodka, more trees, more vodka, more rocks. I am not doing explosions at people or places. Just forest. Nobody hurt. Just fun! Also fighting the alien one time. Also fun," Ziva said and let out a short giggle. It sounded to Anya that there might be a hint of mania at the edges of that laugh.

"The news did say it was all well outside of towns. Just a bunch of trees thrown around," Mona said.

"Hmm. Well, thank you for being honest. Maybe save it just for the aliens though?" Renn asked.

"Eh. I will thinking about," Ziva said and shrugged. "Not on your team yet."

"And that brings us back to the topic at hand. You know what I'm proposing. This isn't a new nation we're forming, no contractual agreements needed. It's just a group of people watching each other's backs and trying to defend their home. If you want to join with others and stay in contact, then that's excellent. But nobody should feel forced to," Renn said. "This is just an agreement to look out for each other, and to provide assistance for any other hosts who may need it."

"And once all this is over, we can just... quit?" Dario, the mecha-pilot, asked.

"It's not indentured servitude, dear," Mona said. "It's not even a job. Just a handshake and you saying you'll help out. When the world is safe again, do what you like, or quit halfway through if you don't like it, or whatever. We're just trying to stay alive, not run your life. You can even remove contacts from your communications screen."

"Okay. I'm in then," Dario said and stepped forward. Several other people did too, then a couple dozen.

"More friends would be nice," Pan said.

"Normally I'm not a fan of groups, but yes, the benefits outweigh the risks. My only concern is who here might not be working alone," Gary said.

"Most people look like they're solo, but I see several couples and a few groups of three or more," Anya said.

"Not what I mean. I mean how many of these people are here because their government or some other organization told them to be?" Gary asked. "That Polish gal seems like a nut, but maybe it's an act. Maybe her government told her to come here, make connections, gather intel, and report to them. I'm just using her as an example, but it could be anybody."

"Oh come on," Samaira said. "That's a little paranoid don't you think?"

"Is it? You and Anya are getting pretty cozy with the feds."

"That was to help people, not become some tattle-tale for the state," Anya said. Gary held up his hands in a placating gesture.

"I know. I only mentioned it to point out that hosts contacting government people isn't so unbelievable, and that we don't know much of anything about anybody here. Some may be nice, wanting to help folks, like you. Others may not be so charitable. Something to consider," Gary said.

"If somebody is a government plant or whatever, we just remove them from the contact list, or remove everybody if we're not sure," Samaira said. "Easy as that."

"What's the best way to add people?" The Latina from Monterey, Esmeralda, asked with her hand in the air, as if she were in school.

"I'd recommend confirming individual connections with each host once you select their signal from your map. Once that's done, we can see to organizing by region and host population," Renn said. "This will also give us more time while any other hosts show up, and we can fill them in as needed."

With that, Renn switched off the loudspeaker on his helmet, and the hosts began to mingle once more, and fully connect.

30

"Are we gonna make new friends now?" Pan asked.

"That's the idea," Anya nodded. "This work for you, Gary?"

"For now. People I don't mind so much. It's the big-wigs in offices sending out orders through their secretaries that I have issue with," he said then looked up as somebody approached them.

Bernard, the bearded man with all the animals, and Amahle, the woman with the afro.

"Cool critters," Anya said as she looked at the strange creatures around Bernard, who shook her hand.

"They're elemental summons," he replied. Something like a lemur but with horns and bright red hair and smoke coming out of its nostrils approached Anya. It looked at her with glowing eyes, then leaped up into her arms. Immense heat radiated from within the creature, not too different from her Sun's Heart.

"Lolo there seems to like you," Bernard said and laughed.

"Some kind of fire elemental or something?" Anya asked.

"Got it in one."

"Bernard was a fan of those games. The ones with all the little monsters," Amahle said.

"Excuse you? Was? Still am!" he said and smiled as he petted a huge blue floating tadpole creature beside him. Amahle rolled her eyes but smiled and Bernard gently bumped her with his elbow.

"What'd you pick?" Samaira asked Amahle. "For skills, I mean."

"Energy channeling and martial arts," Amahle said as she fist-bumped everybody. "A few other things. I can hit and get hit and keep going."

They all confirmed that they had contact capability, then moved on to the next people: Cooper and Brody.

"Since I'm not actually a host, I'll have to rely on Brody's menu to stay in-touch. But we're basically joined at the hip," Cooper said. "Somebody has to keep the big dickhead outta trouble."

"No trouble. Humans are just weird," Brody said. "So complicated."

"They seem okay to me," Pan said.

"You're a very strange looking not-fish," Brody said and leaned down towards Pan. The two of them touched snouts and Pan giggled. "I guess you're all right, though."

"How many animals you think are out there?" Cooper asked. Anya shrugged.

"Honestly, the thought of a hyper-intelligent killer whale capable of walking on land and with access to unlimited superpowers would've scared the shit out of me before meeting Brody. But him and Pan… they're kinda… "

"Simple?" Cooper whispered. Anya nodded.

"Not in a bad way, just, I dunno. It's sweet. It makes sense. Why would they be evil or crazy? They're just driven by instinct for the most part. Pan seems content to make friends and eat ants and dig."

"Brody gets a bit cranky if he doesn't get to eat or swim," Cooper said.

Anya and Samaira laughed and Cooper smiled at Brody as he and Pan chatted with each other and shook hands/claws.

"Is he a shape-shifter or something?" Samaira asked. "I'm not a marine biologist but orcas don't usually have arms and legs."

"Environmental adaptation," Cooper said. "Super strength and resilience, and made his teeth some kinda crazy strong organic material too. Some other stuff but I forgot. English, obviously. He picked a few things up from me and my mate."

"I gathered," Anya smirked. She wondered if her constant cursing would influence Pan or not. They might need to have a talk about it. He seemed so cute, and him dropping F-bombs like her didn't seem like a good fit.

An elderly Thai woman approached them next and told them to call her "Yai." A magic orb on top of a gnarled wooden staff she used as a walking cane translated her Thai into English, and explained she was similar to Doctor Immonen: she had been flying around Thailand, Cambodia, and Laos since everything started, helping people as much as she could. She was a sort of nature mage, and had taken to repairing damage done to the forests by the logging industries.

Ziva, the explosion-obsessed Polish woman, got their contacts after Yai. She gave them all a quick high-five before she scurried away with a simple "Good!" shouted over her shoulder.

The man in the black body armor was next. He towered over Anya, and made Samaira and especially Pan look like toys. His exposed biceps bulged against his taught skin that had a faint grey-ish metallic sheen to it. His face was entirely hidden behind the faceless futuristic helmet he wore. He extended a hand the size of a shovel and allowed Anya and the others to touch it. When Anya added him, she saw that his name was "Jiro Yamada."

They bumped into Arvo Immonen after Jiro.

"Good to see you again. I'm glad this is all going so smoothly. Just a couple clicks and then we're all set," he said as he opened his menu."If you need anything, please don't hesitate to ask."

"I can regenerate, but it's good to know you're out there," Anya said. "Thank you for everything you've done already. I feel really, really stupid for not thinking about using the RAC store or the menu for curing cancer and stuff."

"Please. With everything that's happened? Nobody could blame you," Arvo said. "A war needs soldiers as much as it does medics."

"Wish my wife was still here," Gary said. "Could've taken care of her problem in a second."

"I'm sorry. Did she have...?" Arvo asked.

"Mesothelioma," Gary said. The doctor winced a little.

"I'm so sorry, sir."

"It is what it is. Life ain't always fair. Just glad you're out there helping people like her," Gary said and wandered away.

"He mentioned a wife to me before, but I didn't know," Samaira said.

"Damn," Anya sighed. "But he's right. You and that Yai lady are doing some of the best of all of us."

"Healing is good and all, but it's not going to stop those aliens. We need you all and your powers too. And maybe once this is all over, everybody can use those respecification tokens to get some more peace-oriented skills," Arvo said.

It was a pleasant thought: hundreds of supernatural healers erasing all disease and injury from the planet.

"You're the first regenerator I've met," Arvo said to Anya. "If you have time, and the disposition, I think observing it in action and taking a sample would help my research."

"Uh, sure!" Anya said. "Whatever you need. I mean, whatever will help!"

He smiled at her again and then walked away to meet others.

"He seems nice," Samaira said. Anya thought she heard something in the woman's voice. Nothing bad just... what was it? Some question unasked. An observation as well as an inquiry.

"Yeah, he does," Anya said.

She slowly made her way through the assembled group. There was some kind of swordsman from Barcelona who seemed exceptionally friendly, a woman with metallic angel wings, a feral-looking man surrounded by moving plants, a tall Korean man who looked like a traditional superhero right down to the form-fitting spandex and cape, and dozens more, each just as or more strange than the last.

And then there were only four people left to confirm their contacts with: Renn, Mona, Harrison, and Kan. Anya, Samaira, and Gary were all a bit pensive at first, but Pan rushed right in.

"Hello! Pan here," he said and rose up on his hind legs and extended his gleaming claws which was his version of a handshake.

"*Comme il est mignon!*" Renn said as he squatted down to Pan's level and gently took his claws between his thumb and fingers and shook. "And so much more polite than the orca. Truly, a pleasure."

"You seem nice," Pan said and then waddled over to Kan who chuckled as he shook Pan's claws. Mona seemed delighted to give him a soft pat on his head. Harrison was the only one who didn't seem interested. He tapped Pan's claws and said nothing.

"You all have been patrolling America, I take it?" Renn asked and Anya nodded. "I saw on the news recently that there was a disturbance at a mall in Chicago, along with some UFO sightings in the air around the area. Was that you too?"

"All of us," Samaira said. "Well, Pan stayed in Anya's ride, but yes."

"You saved a lot of people," Kan said. "Thank you. Many of the hosts here are mostly focused on their own survival. It's a natural reaction, but... it takes something special to think of others too in such extreme situations."

"Yeah, sure. No biggie," Anya said. "If you don't mind me saying so, you guys seem pretty prepared. Besides us, I think you're the single biggest group of hosts here. And your speech earlier was pretty convincing. You take public speaking as a skill or did you have something like this planned from the start?"

Renn laughed and pushed a button near the back of the helmet, and it collapsed and shrank down to a small white collar at the base of his neck.

He was a few years older than Anya, early thirties, tops. He had a slim face and short, mussed brownish-blond hair, and green eyes. Despite his relative youth, he had a drowsy, weary look to his face.

"No. I'm not trying to be a great leader, or any leader. I've explained this to others already but I don't want to be the boss host. Later, yes, we may need to talk about how we organize long-term, but for now, I just didn't want people to be alone. It's suicide.

"Me, Mona, Kan, Harrison: we only want to help and make the world a better place, in our own ways. We may not all be as altruistic as Yai or Dr. Immonen, but our ultimate goal is the same: save the planet and make it safer and more prosperous for her people. I'm hopeful that after realizing they aren't alone, the hosts here will act more in the interest of others and not just themselves."

"A lot easier to be concerned about others when somebody else can watch your back," Gary agreed.

"So what now? You say you don't want to be a leader but you sound like you're already thinking about what to do post-invasion, assuming we all survive. Do we nominate a host president or something?" Anya asked.

"Well—" Renn started to say before Gary held his hand up.

"Hang on. Before we do anything else, I need to know something: how many hosts do you think are here?" Gary asked. Anya and the others all turned to look at him in confusion.

"Why?" Anya said.

"Just want to confirm a few things. Gizmo?" Gary asked, and his gray AI appeared. "How many hosts exactly?"

"Thirty-seven," Gizmo said and saluted.

The others checked with their AIs and all came up with the same number.

"Uh-huh," Gary said. "But I've counted thirty-six faces in the crowd, plus my own."

"So?" Anya said. "That matches, right?"

"So, Cooper, isn't a host, remember?" Gary asked.

Anya exchanged glances with the others, then raised an eyebrow at Felix.

"He's right. You've only got thirty-five contacts in your communications window."

"Somebody's hiding," Renn said and brought his helmet back up. He looked around the assembled crowd.

"Anything?" Mona asked.

"I can confirm what Mssr. Gary said. Thirty-six faces, plus my own, but only thirty-five hosts in total. Other scans don't show anything: no heat signatures, no air disturbances, nothing. Whoever they are, they're hiding quite well," Renn said.

Anya focused on her heat sense. She picked up all the body heat around her. There wasn't anything unusual about the crowd, no subtle heat signatures that seemed out of place, other than the weirdness she'd already picked up from Mona, Kan, and Harrison.

"Felix, match each of the host signals on my map to each of the contacts, then temporarily hide them on the map. I want to see the host I haven't connected with yet," Anya said.

"You got it! Great idea!" Felix said and all the multi-colored dots on her map vanished until there was only one. It was light orange, and moving around at the edges of the group: close enough to blend in on the map with the other dots when they had been displayed, but far away and mobile enough to avoid others.

"There," Anya said and started to point but Renn shook his head.

"Don't draw attention to them. If they're nervous, they might do something foolish," he said.

"Who's this then?" A loud, rumbling voice asked. Brody stood at the edge of the group and was peering down at what appeared to be empty air. "What's the deal, mate? No need to be shy. I got some beer in the car if you want some."

"Oh dear," Renn said and started toward Brody.

"Hey! I said come out! No fuckin' around," Brody said and swiped at the air. Something invisible caused a flurry of snow to fly up and the killer whale cursed.

"You having a fit or something?" Cooper asked as a crowd began to gather around Brody. Esmeralda from Monterey was at the front of it, one hand extended into the empty air.

"You don't need to be scared," she said. "I can feel—ah!" she cried out as something hit her and knocked her down onto the ground.

"Oi! The fuck you doing?" Brody said and this time his huge black hand closed on something. The air around his fist crackled with electricity and shimmered in kaleidoscopic hues. It eventually cleared to reveal a thin man in his forties of Asian descent. He wore a long silvery cloak and hood, and sleek tactical armor.

"What the hell?" Amahle asked as she stepped forward. Her fists and eyes had begun to glow a sunny yellow. Whatever energy she was using, it wasn't heat-based, according to Anya's senses.

The man started to yell something in Chinese and then the sound of rockets echoed across the field, and dozens, maybe hundreds, of tiny green lights grew as they descended from the sky. The lights belonged to the eyes of robots that descended en masse and surrounded the group of hosts.

Most of the robots were thin, almost skeletal, with smooth heads and gleaming bodies. They each carried some kind of weapon ranging from humming energy rifles to huge missile launchers.

Several dozen of the robots were the size of a tank and landed with heavy thumps on back-jointed legs. They were covered in matte gray armor and bristled with weapons. Anya recognized miniguns and mortars, but there were other devices on the big robots that she wasn't familiar with: a glowing blue orb grasped in a thick metal claw, thin strings of metal cable that hummed and vibrated, and more esoteric weaponry.

"This is Chancellor Vastukar of the New Allied Territories. You are assaulting one of our people and will release them immediately or face reprisal," a voice boomed from each of the robots.

All of the robotic soldiers leveled their weapons at the hosts. They hummed with deadly energy.

"Well... shit," Anya said.

31

"Brought friends, huh?" Brody asked the struggling man in his grasp. The man shouted something in Chinese, then withdrew an enormous rifle from within the folds of his cloak. Before anybody could react, the man aimed the rifle up at Brody and fired a round into his chest. Brody flew backwards, smoke rising from where he had been shot, and the man with the rifle vanished in a flash of colored light.

"Brody!" Cooper shouted and ran forward.

The field erupted into chaos.

The robots shot at Cooper, and several rounds ricocheted off his robotic armor. The rest of the hosts leaped into action at once.

Domes of protective magic, forcefields, metal plating, and more defensive measures all appeared or deployed at once. The formerly quiet field rang out with the rattle of gunshots, missiles, magical and electrical energy, and dozens of other sounds as the area devolved into a warzone.

Gary pressed a button on his watch and whenever something got near him—bullets or debris—it hit an almost invisible forcefield around him. He gave Anya a wink and then ran off and vanished into the crowd before she could think to stop him.

Pan squealed in terror, curled into a ball, and then just vanished into a hole in the ground near some black rocks. Samaira's translucent shoulder cape danced around her and deflected any bullets or other projectiles that got close while she fired arrow after arrow at the assaulting robots.

Anya shouted in surprise as an explosion detonated nearby and pushed her back a few feet. Yai, the old lady, sailed through the air beside her, and Anya grabbed her and pulled her close. The old lady mumbled something in Thai, slapped Anya's hands away, then spat at the robots. Mist formed around her feet and coalesced into a cloud which Yai floated away on at speed. She waved that big staff of hers and dozens of green motes of light fell from it to the icy ground, and erupted into thick vines. The vines grabbed the nearest robots, crushing the smaller ones and tripping the larger models.

Anya jumped away from another blast and landed amidst ten of the smaller robots. All of them focused their sensors and weapons on her. Anya grinned.

Half of them held plasma weapons.

Anya clenched her fists and drew on the heat of the plasma weapons, making it expand within their casings, and then explode. The robots holding the weapons were destroyed at once, and the others were caught up in the blasts soon after. Any that survived, she pulled toward her with a swirling well of gravity and then bashed or melted them to pieces.

Part of her was worried about the other hosts. People like Dr. Immonen and a few others had said or looked like they weren't much in a fight. Part of her wanted to go find Pan and Samaira and haul them both out of there and go after Gary.

But another part of her wanted to just blow up as many of these robots as she could. It wanted to unleash the fiery storm inside her Sun's Heart and show whoever this very stupid Chancellor was that pointing a gun in her face was a terrible idea.

"You will cease your hostile activity at once," one of the huge armored robot hulks intoned in an electronic voice behind her.

"Nah," Anya said as she spun around. She launched herself at the huge walking tank and encased herself in flame and heat that ignited the air around her and turned her into a living fireball. She slammed into the huge robot, crashing into it and soaring into the air. She angled herself and the now ruined bot down to earth, and slammed it into another squad of smaller robots.

All of them were dashed to pieces in the crater she made on impact, and Anya laughed.

Am I supposed to be enjoying this this much? she thought.

Absolutely! the voice of the bird said in her mind. Anya laughed again and created a localized cyclone of fire and gravitational force. Another of the big robots was pulled away from Samaira and toward Anya, and she put her flaming red fist directly through its chest.

She wasn't the only one wreaking mayhem among the mechanical attackers. Dario had entered his huge mecha and joined the fray. The mecha withdrew a sword the length of a limousine that crackled to life with glowing yellow energy. It cut through the enemy robots like it was clearing a path through a garden, and Anya felt some minor irritation that it was taking so many of the enemy for itself.

Brody was up, a huge scorch mark in his chest, but otherwise appearing fine. He and Cooper both bounded past her, back-to-back and smashed through any robots she missed. Cooper was on defense, wielding a shield made of translucent light, while Brody punched through any robot that got close. More often than not, the whale bit through their heavy armor like nothing more than soggy-bread. He still had the huge joint stuck between his back teeth even as he attacked, though Anya noticed it had gone out. She snapped her fingers and lit it for him as he passed.

"Thank ya kindly!" Brody laughed at her and then bit a minigun in half as it tried to shoot down his throat. The gun was followed by most of the bot wielding it before Brody moved onto his next target, puffing on his joint.

Anya nodded, then gasped in pain as something ripped into her side and she was knocked to the ground. A huge robot wielding a strange weapon composed of dozens of whip-like appendages loomed over her, ready to attack again. The whips gleamed, some kind of metal, and sparks of electricity danced between them. The robot lashed at her with the strange weapon again and she rolled to the side. One of the thin whips connected with her leg. The metal strands were incredibly sharp, as it sliced a narrow furrow in her armored pants and opened the skin of her calf beneath. Bolts of electricity, at least as bad as what the alien fridge had used, connected with her skin and sent spasms through her.

Anya screamed and glared at the towering robot. Her hair became a wavering torch of incandescent fire as she deflected another whipping attack, condensed all of the electrified appendages into a tight knot with gravity, and then brought her knee up between the robot's legs. A burst of fire rose up from the point of impact and blew the automaton in half right up the middle.

"Are you injured?" a voice asked at her side. Anya yelped and almost ignited the air around her in surprise before she saw a hazy shape beside her. It cleared for a moment and the face of Arvo Immonen emerged. "I can heal you."

"I'm already fine," Anya said as she jumped to her feet, then showed him where her leg had already healed. "Has anybody died?"

"No, thank goodness. A few injuries, but I've handled those. Speaking of, I'm needed elsewhere, good luck!" Arvo might have waved at her, but it was hard to tell as his form shimmered and then became hazy, almost invisible. He was there one second and gone the next.

A current of sparkling blue energy washed past Anya and swept a squad of smaller robots away. The energy spun around them in a cyclone of cerulean hues and motes of diamond light that reduced the metallic mob to scrap in moments. Anya looked from where the energy had come from and spotted Samaira. She wove in and out of laser fire, not so much dodging as dancing.

The chaos and carnage all around Anya (no small amount of it caused by her) was only so much crude destructive force. What Samaira was doing almost didn't resemble fighting at all. Each step seemed to have rhythm, each fired arrow a flourish. Her midnight hair swirled around her like her translucent cape, accented by the swirling clouds of snow she would send up with each delicate step or slide or pirouette.

Anya knew she had probably bashed more robots than Samaira, but she also knew she hadn't looked half as good doing it.

"How're you managing?" Samaira asked as she and Chandrali landed beside her. Samaira fired off a quick volley of arrows and destroyed some nearby robots. She was unharmed, but her clothes were singed in a few places, and there was dried blood on Chandrali's side, but no wound.

Anya shook herself from her stupor and cleared her throat.

"They're not tough but they keep coming," Anya said as she melted another big robot with multi-cannons on its shoulders into slag.

"Retreat?" Samaira asked. Anya glanced around at the remaining hosts. Nobody looked seriously wounded, but several of them were sweating or had taken a knee while the hazy shape of Arvo attended them. She couldn't just leave everyone.

Besides, she was having fun.

"Hell no," Anya said as she shook her head. "I'm not gonna run from some uppity chancellor and his tin cans while other people are fighting."

"Good. Me neither," Samaira grinned and then loosed another volley of magic arrows as she rode Chandrali away. "Stay safe!"

"Not a problem," Anya said, then grunted as something slammed into her back and knocked her to the ground. She'd been hit with a shell the size of a can of coke, and it had flattened itself against her back, and broken her shoulder. Anya snarled as it popped back into place and delivered a series of flaming blows and kicks that sent the heavily-armored machine onto its back. She jumped up, then landed on its chest with both feet and a localized explosion.

"Hey!" Amahle, the woman from South Africa, shouted from nearby the newly downed robot. She punched another one of the big armored bots next to her with an almost dismissive gesture. The light that encased her fists had expanded across her body to form glowing ethereal armor. She kicked one of the smaller robots apart like it was made of foil, and sent the pieces spinning at Anya.

"Watch it!" Anya said as she swatted the chunks of metal away from her.

"Then you watch those explosions of yours. Almost took my

boyfriend's head off," Amahle replied and then jumped the length of a football field and sent out a huge shockwave among a squad of bots.

Anya's Sun's Heart was barely depleted at all, and it was hammering away inside of her, eager to unleash more, to burn brighter and hotter.

But it was clear that the fight was winding down. The robot army, in the span of perhaps a few minutes, had gone from hundreds of well-armed troops to a few dozen stragglers.

The number of hosts had dwindled significantly as well, though Anya didn't see any bodies. The hosts who were still present all looked in fine shape, if a bit tired. Brody and Cooper pummeled one of the big robots as it tried to crawl away. Mona stood at the center of her own small army of skeletal warriors and spectral shapes. Jiro from Japan ripped the minigun off one of the robots and mowed down stragglers with casual efficiency. Renn pointed his finger at several of the smaller robots and made them float high into the sky before some invisible force crushed them into tiny spheres.

Anya squinted at Renn's attack. Whatever he was using, it wasn't gravity. She would have felt the pull of any other gravitational forces thanks to her Singularity's Grasp.

"Most of the hosts ran at the first sign of a fight," Renn said, suddenly beside her, his white coat and helmet looking no less clean and polished despite the mayhem. Anya flinched at his sudden, immediate proximity. He had been several dozen yards away just a second ago, but now he was right next to her.

"Oh, sorry, I was chasing down our friend too," Renn said and pointed up. The man in the gray cloak who had been hiding floated upside down above them. Anya glanced from him, back to Renn, then across the field at where she had first seen him.

Renn was still over there, making robots and projectiles float away from him… and so was another Renn. And a third, a fourth, and fifth. All of the Renns looked identical, and all of them were making enemy robots slam into the ground or fly apart with delicate hand gestures.

"Ah," Anya said. "What is that? Self cloning? And telekinesis?"

"Something like that," Renn nodded, then looked over Anya's shoulder. Lightning blasted the last robot to bits, and the cobra-raccoon-thing that belonged to Bernard chittered and hissed at its remains. Bernard patted the creature on the back of its wide hood and it licked him with its long, forked tongue. Electricity also crackled from Bernard's eyes and the tips of his fingers for a moment before flickering out.

"Well, I suppose that will do it," Renn said and started to walk toward the remaining hosts, the cloaked man floating and struggling in the air above him. His clones, or duplicates or whatever, also walked toward Renn until all of them met and merged into one.

"Is anybody injured?" Arvo asked as he appeared at the edge of the fight.

"I got a bit singed, yeah," Bernard said and pointed at a large red welt on his arm. Amahle looked at Anya pointedly and Anya frowned.

"That was my fault," she said. "Sorry. Got a bit carried away."

"No kidding," Amahle said.

"Ah, it happens. I had trouble keeping all my babies in line," Bernard said and gestured at his small menagerie of creatures. Arvo approached him and put his hand on Bernard's arm, and the burn mark vanished at once. "Wow, thank you. That's better than ever, actually."

"My pleasure," the doctor replied.

"Anya?" Samaira asked as she emerged from the crowd. She looked the same as a few minutes ago, and better by the second. Blue sparkles floated out of the crystals on her outfit and repaired any damage done to her clothing. "You seen Pan?"

"Nah, he took off pretty quick," Anya said. "What about Gary?"

"Here," Gary's voice said from one of his junky-looking robots. It had been cut in half and lost an arm. The remaining arm waved at them, and Gary's face flickered on a screen set in its chest. "I'm fine. Made it back to my truck in one piece and sent a few drones out to fight. They got smashed by some of the other hosts, but I can't blame them. One robot probably looks pretty similar to another in a crazy fight like that. I'm actually picking up the little guy's signal right under you two, though."

That was when the earth at their feet bulged outward and Pan appeared.

"Hello! Are all the loud noises gone?" he asked.

"Looks that way," Anya said and let out a sigh.

"That was really scary."

"Scary nothing! Can we get more of these? Fuck, that was fun!" Brody bellowed as he and Cooper approached.

"Those robots were pretty pathetic," Dario's voice echoed out of the huge mecha towering above everybody.

Anya frowned. The robots had been easy to beat, but that had probably only been because there were so many hosts. Anya would have had some real trouble if she had been on her own.

Her regalia was dotted with holes, tears, and the occasional missing piece. Nothing serious, but it was a testament to the robots' weapons. She grumbled as she realized she'd have to spend some of her dwindling RAC to repair it. Again.

"Maybe compared to your big one, but they were more irritating than I'd like," Mona huffed. The edge of her cape had been scorched and torn, and her armor had been dented in a few places. Her skeletal army had shrunk as well, most of its members reduced to scattered bones and strips of ephemeral cloth and pale puddles of jelly that Anya guessed was ectoplasm.

"I'm hopeful their owner might be able to fill us in on the details," Renn said. All the hosts that remained looked up at the man in the gray cloak as he floated in grim silence overhead. "Won't you share with us, sir?"

"Asmund! Ursula!" the man shouted. A grunt echoed from the edges of the crowd and an enormous ax came spinning out of the snowy haze. Renn raised his hand and the ax froze in mid-air, inches away from his helmet. Intricate runes and swirling designs covered the ax, its edge gleamed silver, and each of the runes glowed with red light.

The man in the gray cloak fell to the ground and leaped backward with inhuman agility and speed as he withdrew his rifle again and vanished.

Renn grunted as the ax in front of him began to creep toward his helmet and its runes flared.

"Renn?" Mona asked.

"We have more company," he said, then sighed as the ax reversed its course and spun away and into the hand of its owner.

A short, stocky man stomped forward from the haze, wielding an ax in each hand. He was shirtless, his broad torso and thick arms covered in swirling black tattoos that squirmed as if they were alive. He wore thick leather pants and boots and nothing else. Long orange hair sprouted from his head and along his jaw, some it styled into intricate braids.

He wasn't alone.

A polar bear clad in black plated armor and walking on its hind legs marched beside him. The bear wielded a huge two-handed maul made of similar black metal, and a long midnight blue cape blew behind it. The bear left small impact craters wherever it stepped, and it curled its white lips to expose fangs coated in silver.

"Whoa," Samaira said. Pan squealed and hid behind Anya.

"Wait!" Arvo said and stood between the approaching figures and the rest of the hosts. He wasn't using his concealment ability, and was plain for all to see. Anya stepped forward, ready to get between him and the two other hosts if she had to.

"We don't need to fight! Nobody is dead, or injured. Please," Arvo said. Anya had to admit that it was pretty ballsy of the doctor to get between the crowd and the approaching figures. Several more robots landed behind the polar bear and the man with the axes, but they kept their weapons lowered.

"Asmund, Ursula, wait," the voice of Chancellor Vastukar emitted from the robots behind the two approaching hosts.

"Willing to talk?" Renn asked.

"Not really," the huge bear growled in a somewhat feminine voice. Anya guessed she was Ursula.

"Enough. This was not our intent," Vastukar said from a robot.

"What? Shooting us? Weird that you'd bring a fuckload of robots with guns, then," Anya snapped.

"Easy," Samaira whispered beside her.

"Our associate, Zixin, may have acted in haste. To his credit, the killer whale is rather intimidating," Vastukar said.

"Why hide?" Gary asked. "The rest of us are out in the open. Why send a spy?"

"We wanted to be sure that this was an honest gathering, and not something cooked up by one of the old-world governments to ensnare our kind."

"Like they could," Mona scoffed. "Even the lowest leveled among us could escape conventional military powers with ease."

"Not if those powers had a willing host to help them," Vastukar said. "As they did in Bengaluru."

Silence fell over the field.

"Wait, are you saying a host did that attack in India because the government told them to?" Anya asked.

"I am saying that I tried to have a meeting like this, among hosts, and the government did not care for it. How many of you are in contact with your governments now?" Vastukar asked. A few people raised their hands. After a moment, Anya and Samaira did as well.

"And they have been entirely supportive of you so far?" Vastukar asked again.

Anya didn't respond. The cops in Prospect Park had shot her almost immediately, and then the feds had raided the diner where she had met with Riley, and Tori's apartment.

But the air force had saved her life from the snake alien.

"I take it from your collective silence that it is not so," Vastukar said. "I think you'll find that if we survive the alien incursion, that our governments may begin to make demands of us, to insist on certain things. Some already are: access to the Archive store, demanding a host acquire certain skills, and so on. It will get worse. They will pit us against each other if they can.

"It is why myself and others—Asmund, Zixin, Ursula, and more—have forsaken our old lives and homes, and begun to form a new country: the New Allied Territories, in the ruins of Bengaluru. We are rebuilding it into something better, helping the people in a way the previous government could not, that no current government ever could. All hosts are welcome."

"You're going to war with a world power right now? During an invasion?" Samaira demanded.

"No war. We have already won. The old government is no more, and we have already made improvements. So it should be going forward," Vastukar said. "You are welcome to join us at any time, but do not go against us. We number more than the few people here, and we have killed many, many aliens."

"That's what we should all be doing. Not playing at kingdom-building," Renn said. "Division among our forces now could mean the end of all of us."

"And failure to plan for what comes after could mean the same," Vastukar retorted.

Renn sighed and shook his head.

"We came here to organize and protect ourselves and counter the aliens. Nothing more."

"Good. Then we have no issues," Vastukar said.

"I might have a few," Anya muttered but didn't press. The last thing she wanted was another fight.

Well, that wasn't true.

But if they fought again, there was no guarantee there wouldn't be casualties.

More beating up robots sounded pretty fun, and she was curious about how Ursula and Asmund would fare in a battle. Asmund was similar to Harrison in that his body temperature was abnormally high. She tried to locate Zixin as well, but his cloak concealed him from Anya's heat sense as surely as it did from her eyes.

"Our invitation to join the New Allied Territories remains open to all hosts, and their families. We will provide protection against the aliens and any hostile governments you may be fleeing from. However, as a show of good faith and to apologize for Zixin's unfortunate actions earlier, we will volunteer to cover India and the Middle East in the search for the invaders. Asmund, Ursula, and Zixin will also share their contact information with any who wish it."

"The hell I will," Ursula growled.

"C'mon, don't be that way," Asmund said and tucked his axes into his belt. "Zi! C'mon out!"

Zixin appeared in a shimmer of air at the rear of the crowd, muttering to himself in Chinese. Asmund grinned, though there was something a bit manic in the way his mouth stretched a little too wide and bared too many of his teeth.

"We should plan where the rest of us are going," Renn said. "I think we should be in groups no smaller than five or six, and with as many diverse skills as possible. Myself, Mona, Kan, and Harrison will take western Europe. We would like one or two more to join us, if possible."

Everybody began to separate into groups, and call out which areas they would cover. Each continent was divided into smaller regions, depending on the size. Meanwhile, Asmund, Ursula, and Zixin moved throughout the crowd, shaking hands with the assembled hosts.

"We'll take the eastern United States," Anya said to Samaira and Gary. She looked down at Pan. "You wanna stay with us or go hang out with Brody?"

"Anya," Pan said and hugged her leg. She smiled and patted his head.

"No offense to the little guy, but he's not exactly combat-ready," Gary said.

"True," Anya sighed.

"Excuse me," Arvo said from behind them, "I know I don't have any combat skills, but I would like to be of service. Europe sounds like it will be covered."

"Happy to have you," Anya said. With Arvo, they were at five hosts. However Gary was right that Pan wouldn't be of much use in a fight. The doctor could keep them healed up, but he couldn't contribute to directly killing any aliens. Gary was still of limited combat use until his factory got up and running, wherever it was. That basically left Anya and Samaira.

However, as she looked around, she saw that the few dozen hosts assembled had all been split up as evenly as they could. It was an improvement from before, but it was still only a handful of people to cover the entire planet.

"More people might come," Samaira said, as if reading her mind.

"They might," Anya nodded. She sat down on an outcropping of black stone, and waited.

It would have to do, for now.

32

A few more hosts did eventually arrive. However, there were areas other than America that needed them more, and they agreed to help out as they could. In-between arrivals, Anya studied her menu.

ANYA NOWICKI: LEVEL 32 PHOENIX MONK

Statistics

- Awareness-10
- Dexterity-19 (+10 from gear)
- Fortitude-39 (+13 from gear)
- Intelligence-8
- Strength-20 (+5 from gear)
- Willpower-8

Skills

- Flame Dominion-35 (+16 from gear)(+5 from Artifact)

- Kinetic Dispersal-17 (+6 from gear)
- Combat Cognition-15
- Regeneration-31 (+14 from gear)
- Xhama Thul-14 (+4 from gear)
- Gravity Dominion-16 (+6 from gear)

She hadn't gotten any points, RAC, or progress to level 33 during the fight with the robots. Not a single bump in any category.

"They don't want us fighting each other," Anya muttered.

"What's that?" Samaira asked as she strode over and leaned down next to Anya to study her menu. Anya cleared her throat and looked away from Samaira, at her sudden nearness, and back at her screen.

"Well before, I'd usually get something from a fight. Even with the snake gnosiphage I fought, I got 'partial credit,' I guess you could call it. I got RAC from making contributions to the Archive, that sort of thing," Anya said.

"Right, me too," Samaira nodded.

"But I didn't get anything from the fight with all those robots."

"Maybe because they weren't alive?"

"I dunno. Maybe? But the robots were made using a host's skill, so it would have been like fighting a host, right? The aether isn't alive, is it? My fire isn't. The robots were just an extension of the host's abilities. It still feels like I should have gotten something from a big fight like that. But getting absolutely nothing makes me think it's not a bug, but a feature."

Samaira squinted at Anya's menu, then at her. Her eyes widened briefly and her lips parted in quiet surprise.

"The Engineers don't want us fighting with other hosts. They blocked off any incentives for doing it," she said and Anya nodded in agreement.

"That would be my guess. No PvP allowed."

"I'm assuming that's a game thing?"

"Player vs. Player," Anya clarified. "Obviously I'm just taking a shot in the dark here. Maybe it was because the robots weren't alive. Maybe it was for another reason. It doesn't feel like it though. Just a hunch, for now."

"Good that you spotted it," Samaira said and smiled at her. Anya was somewhat aware of a rather dopey grin creeping across her face in response. She was still pretty close. Anya could just lean over a little and—

"What're you kids up to?" Gary asked as he strode over. Samaira took a step back, a little too quickly, and focused on adjusting her skirt. Anya sensed the heat rising around her cheeks and the tips of her ears.

"You two feeling all right?" Gary asked and looked between them.

"Anya may have found something," Samaira said and pointed at her menu. They both explained to Gary and he rubbed his chin.

"Maybe. Something to add to the list of questions I got for those Engineer assholes," he said. "Maybe when I get some more bots we can run some other tests."

"Maybe try sparring with each other?" Anya asked and looked at Samaira.

"That might work, but not now. If any newcomers show up, they might think we're really fighting and get scared off," she replied.

"True," Anya sighed. "Nothing to do for now but wait, then."

When it was clear several hours later that nobody else would be arriving, the few remaining hosts all bid each other farewell, and took off in their disparate vehicles.

"How fast can your egg thingy go?" Anya asked Arvo as she walked with him.

"Mach 1, I think, though it takes it several minutes to get to that speed," he replied.

"I can go a little faster, but we'll keep pace with you. Not sure how fast Gary's truck can go, especially since it's not very aerodynamic."

"Shaped forcefields, kid," Gary said and winked at her. "Probably go faster than your fancy alien jet."

"I'll take your word for it."

"Where to?" Arvo asked.

"New York. Riley and MacDougal, those are the feds I told you about, will want an update. Thankfully this all went pretty well and they won't bite my head off," Anya said.

"Screw 'em if they don't like it," Gary grunted as he got into his truck and revved the engine. Samaira got in beside him while Pan waddled into the Shadow Ray.

"I have to agree with Gary," Arvo said. "You did a good thing. I think anybody who would be against it would be more upset about losing control than anything else. It's a common thread, I'm sensing."

"What do you mean?" Anya asked.

"That Vastukar fellow. I don't agree with what he's doing, and his involvement in the bombing outside Bengaluru in whatever capacity makes me more suspicious, but he isn't wrong. World governments aren't happy with the situation. Not just the aliens invading, but individuals superseding them.

"The director at the hospital I worked at before all of this happened, he called me and said some representatives from the Finnish Security Intelligence Service came by. I guess they would be like your CIA or maybe NSA. They were not shy in demanding the director's cooperation. They told him to contact me and relay that I come in and subject myself to inquiry. I told them I would be happy to do a teleconference, but they were quite insistent it be in-person.

"I informed them I am more than willing to help, but would not be subservient. They didn't really care for that response."

Anya snorted.

"The feds in America have been kinda similar. Not as bad as it could be, but I'm wondering how long until they try and force me into something," she said.

"Hopefully everybody will remain cooperative and understanding long enough to deal with the gnosiphages," Arvo said as he stepped into his egg. "I suppose we'll speak again in New York. I've never been. Maybe you can show me around sometime?"

Anya blinked. Was he being friendly or was he asking her out on a date?

"Uh, yeah, absolutely! If things go well tonight with the feds, we can all go out and get some pizza or something," she said.

"Perfect. Even more reason to hope for a pleasant meeting with your feds," Arvo replied, then closed the door to his hovering vehicle.

"Oooookay," Anya said, still uncertain. She waved to Gary and

Samaira as they lifted off, then climbed into the Shadow Ray with Pan and followed after.

After an hour of flying, she got a stable cell signal again and the phone MacDougal had given her vibrated with missed messages. All of them were from Riley and Tori. Riley just wanted updates, and said some of the suits weren't happy with her. MacDougal was content to wait until she came back with news.

Tori just wanted to know if she was all right and if she was bringing anybody back.

ANYA: Hey. We're on our way back now. Things went mostly well. We've got a new host with us and a bunch of others have organized into groups.

TORI: That's great! Save the rest for when you're back here. Can you swing by the hotel or are you going straight to MacDougal?

ANYA: MacDougal. Riley's making it sound like some people are pissed and MacDougal's just waiting for me to show up. Would rather not antagonize them. Makes sense to update them first as well. I've let Riley know we're on our way.

TORI: Smart. See you when you're done?

ANYA: Yuuuup :)

Anya descended on the snow-swept city not long after. Manhattan gleamed in the early night and the air above it glittered with countless snowflakes. Anya directed the Ray's autopilot to the roof of 26 Federal Plaza's main building. To her surprise, Gary was there along with Samaira, and were speaking with Riley and MacDougal as she landed. Arvo landed his egg right behind her and MacDougal arched an eyebrow at the arrival of the new vehicle.

"If all you got out of the commotion you caused with that video of yours is a single host, I'm going to be disappointed," MacDougal said.

"Not quite. This is Dr. Arvo Immonen, by the way," Anya said. "Arvo, this is the previous director of the FBI and current director of some new agency I've forgotten the name of."

"The Department of Extraterrestrial Research and Defense," MacDougal said.

"Yeah. DERD," Anya said and MacDougal shot her a look.

"Good evening," Arvo replied and stepped forward.

"Evening. Does your government know that you're here?" MacDougal asked.

"No. But as a free citizen, I may do as I wish. And currently, I wish to be here," Arvo said. Anya wasn't sure if he was implying that he could just as easily wish to be elsewhere, or just stating a fact. MacDougal pursed her lips and made a "Hmm," sound.

"There are others waiting downstairs for an update, but I want you to give me the gist of what happened before we go down," she said and looked at Anya. "Ms. Upadhyay mentioned things were a bit complicated."

"Yeah, about that…"Anya said and she, Samaira, and Arvo filled the director and Riley in on what had happened in Greenland. Riley and MacDougal were silent during the explanation, though Riley's expressions shifted from surprise, to relief, to horror, to alarm, to resignation while MacDougal remained stone-faced the entire time. She might as well have been listening to somebody read the phonebook.

"How many hosts in total did you meet?" MacDougal asked and Samaira brought her menu map up.

"Forty-three," she said.

"So there's another four on the West Coast," Riley said as he looked at the map. "We should have them come in too."

"These people in India, this New Allied Territories, that's a problem," MacDougal said. She withdrew a packet of cigarettes from her coat and put one in her mouth. She patted her pockets for a lighter but Anya just pointed at the cigarette and lit it for her.

"Thank you, Ms. Nowicki," she said.

"Ma'am, weren't you supposed to be, y'know, quitting?" Riley started to ask.

"Agent Riley. I've just been told that a rogue state has formed what consists of at least four super-powered individuals who may or may not be responsible for setting off a WMD outside a major city. And one of them is a polar bear. I'm going to enjoy my indulgences while I can."

"Yes, ma'am."

"Excuse me Ms. MacDougal?" Arvo asked and stepped forward. She puffed a cloud of smoke away from Arvo and into the night and waited for him to continue. "I have a skill which can scan a person for any health irregularities. You currently have the very early stages of lung cancer."

"Christ," MacDougal said.

"I can take care of it," Arvo said and extended his hand, but stopped short of touching her when she arched a thin eyebrow at him.

"Take care of it?"

"Yes. I would need to touch your hand for a moment. Technically your skin, but the hand is the most comfortable and least invasive method."

"And you can just cure cancer?"

"Yes."

"All right," MacDougal said and extended her hand. Arvo took it, held it for a moment and closed his eyes, then released it. MacDougal regarded him, then her eyes widened and she coughed, took a deep breath, and coughed again.

"Ma'am?" Riley asked.

"I'm fine," MacDougal said as she put her cigarette out. "I'll be damned. Didn't even notice how irritating it was getting to breathe. Just like that?"

"Just like that," Arvo said and smiled at her.

"Well, this will make for an interesting addendum to my report to President Hanover."

"Do we need to meet with any more people?" Samaira asked.

"Not tonight, no. It'll take a few days to distribute the information you've given me and have meetings with the appropriate people about what to do. Hanover has been talking about getting all of you, including these hosts who are covering the western part of the States, together at the White House to meet with the Joint Chiefs and Secretaries of Defense and State."

"Hmm," Gary grunted.

"I'm aware there may be some reservations, but it's for the best. For now, just stay alert. Keep patrolling like we asked and like you've been doing. Avoid any more unauthorized broadcasts, please. At least until the President can make a public statement. This worked out better than I thought it would, but you've ruffled some feathers," MacDougal said and looked at Anya.

"Also maybe helped save some people from dying alone," she replied.

"As I said: better than I thought. That's all for now. Go relax and try not to blow anything up if you can help it. Riley? We have paperwork to tend to," MacDougal said and then stalked back inside the building.

"Yes ma'am. Be right with you," Riley said, then smiled at Anya and the others. "She's keeping it close to the vest, but she's pretty happy. Hanover, not so much. But he'll come around. You did good work, Anya. The rest of you, too. And hey, thank you, Doc. The last thing the director needs right now is a personal health crisis."

"Glad to help, Agent Riley," Arvo said as Riley waved good-bye.

"Well, you managed to not make the director of a new government agency and the President of the United States hate you," Samaira said and smiled at Anya.

"Yeah. It's the little victories, y'know?" she replied and let out a sigh of relief. The muscles in her neck, back and shoulders started to relax a bit. She'd been tense the whole time.

"What now?" Gary asked.

"I believe Anya had suggested pizza?" Arvo said.

"I could eat," Gary said.

"I know a place. We can get take-out, maybe pick up my friend, have ourselves a little picnic outside the city," Anya replied. "You guys find a safe spot, and I'll meet you there after I get the food."

"See you then!" Samaira said as she got into Gary's truck. Pan insisted on going with Anya, and was thrilled when the two got to see

Tori again when she met them on the roof of a nearby parking garage a little while later.

"Hey little buddy!" Tori said and hugged Pan.

"Hello Tori! I missed you," Pan said and hugged her leg. "We met some new friends in Greenland and assholes too."

Tori laughed. "I see you've been learning some new words from Anya."

"Technically he already knew it, I just had to teach him the proper context," Anya replied, then explained what had happened in Greenland while they flew to Brooklyn, parked on top of her building, and then went into her apartment.

"This is your home?" Pan asked as he waddled inside. "It smells like you! I like it."

"Thanks, I think," Anya said, then looked at Tori. "You're all caught up. MacDougal's doing her thing and we're gonna resume patrolling tomorrow morning."

"Sounds like things are really kicking off," Tori said as she put in an order for a dozen pizzas from their favorite place.

"Yeah," Anya sighed. "Thankfully Gary and Samaira are turning out to be pretty solid."

"Gary lets me talk to him about ants and digging," Pan said. "I don't think he understands, but he's a good listener."

"Very important," Tori agreed, then turned to Anya. "That doctor guy sounds like a saint."

"Oh yeah. Definitely a stand-up guy. Clearly not in the mood for bureaucratic bullshit either. Most of the hosts at Greenland seemed okay but..."

The hosts from the New Allied Territories—Asmund, Ursula, Vastukar, and Zixin—could pose a problem. But they were out in the open. What they wanted was obvious: their own country.

The ones that made Anya's stomach knot itself into a little ball of anxiety were Renn and his crew. They sounded nice, they had acted polite enough, they had helped organize the other hosts. But something about them, Renn especially, didn't sit well with Anya.

"That Renn guy sounds kinda shady," Tori said, as if reading her mind.

"I was just thinking that. He didn't do anything bad just... I dunno. I'm probably just being paranoid."

"They smelled funny," Pan said. "Especially the man with horns. Harry? Harlon?"

"Harrison," Anya said. "Yeah he seemed a little extra weird."

"Can't say I blame you," Tori said. "I got a little something to take your mind off it though. Check this out!"

Tori extended her hand. The aether focus bracelet sparkled on her wrist, and the clear gem in its center glowed.

"*Leggera*," she said, and a tiny point of light appeared above her palm. It was no bigger than a marble, and it flickered like a weak lightbulb, but it was there.

"Holy shit," Anya said and grinned. Tori closed her hand and the light vanished, and she fell back against the couch with a heavy sigh. She was breathing a bit heavier than she had been a moment before, and a few beads of sweat had appeared on her forehead. "You okay?"

"Yeah. It just feels like I jogged up a couple flights of stairs. Still, improvement. Yesterday I could barely do it at all and felt like I'd run a mile. Nothing compared to what you can do, or Samaira I'm sure, but it's not nothing!"

"I mean, I actually kinda think this is more impressive. Having the Archive is like cheating. Tori, you actually learned magic. Or aether, or whatever. You just say that word and it happens?" Anya asked and looked at her friend's hand. The focus had become dull and ordinary once more, just a piece of modest but pretty jewelry.

"Sort of. That book you gave me says it helps to have a mental focus, as well as a physical one. The bracelet thingy here lets me draw the aether to me more easily, but I still need something to kind of solidify what I want the aether to do, which requires mental focus. The most basic mental focus the book suggested were words, but not just ordinary ones. Something you associate with the outcome you want the aether to take.

"My dad's side of the family is Italian, and I know a little, but not much. Not something I ever use outside of a few very rare trips we've taken to see relatives in Italy. But I can use it to help me concentrate on what I want and act as a sort of 'trigger,' for what I'm doing."

"So 'leggera,' is light, I'm guessing?" Anya asked and Tori nodded. "Any particular reason you wanted to make a light ball for your first spell? Or whatever you call it."

"Manifestations. The instructions in that book are pretty straightforward, which is weird. I expected it to be like a dusty old Grimoire or a religious text but it's more like reading a car manual. It advised non-physical manifestations for beginners. I can do the ball of light, and a sound like echoing footsteps. That's it.

"I've kept a bunch of notes for Samaira which I'm sure she'll want to look at. Nothing too impressive but she seemed pretty interested in what I learned. I'm not exactly ready to help you fight aliens, but I'm going to have some awesome party tricks in another week or two."

Anya laughed. "You know you don't have to help me fight, right? I'd actually be pretty terrified at the thought of you facing one of the gnosiphages."

"Me too!" Pan said and curled up under the coffee table. "I haven't seen any yet but they sound scary. The fight in Greenland was really awful."

"You know I'm not thrilled with you fighting them either. This whole thing sucks," Tori said.

"I know."

"I'm also kind of worried that you seem like you're... starting to like it," Tori said and looked down. Anya was about to protest, but didn't even bother. Tori would know she was lying, and she didn't want to insult her friend like that.

"Is it that little bird thing? The Flame Dominion?" Tori asked.

"Making me want to fight? No. It's not like that," Anya said.

"How do you know?"

"How do you know the aether isn't affecting you?" Anya asked.

"I guess I don't. But if it is, I'm not capable of doing anything with it besides what you just saw. What're you capable of now? You could probably blow up this building if you wanted, right?"

Anya almost scoffed. She could probably blow up the whole block.

But she didn't want to. She had no more desire to go on a rampage than she did before the Archive hit her.

"The bird, the Dominion, whatever it is, I don't think it's bad. It just is. It's like a hammer. You could use it to build a nice bookcase or smash somebody's brain in. I think the only thing it wants, if it's capable of wanting anything, is what I want."

Tori regarded her in silence for a few moments, her concern obvious.

"Pan?" Tori asked and peeked under the coffee table.

"Yeah?" he replied.

"You've got Earth Dominion, right?"

"Yes!"

"You ever hear any voices from strange people who aren't there? Have any weird dreams?"

"Nope!"

"I don't wanna be mean but maybe Pan is a bit too simple, to make contact with a Dominion?" Anya whispered and Tori grunted.

"I mean, you're pretty simple, too," she said and smirked. Anya gave her a light shove and grinned.

The pizza arrived not long after, and Anya carried the huge stack of boxes back up to the Shadow Ray. They flew in silence for a few minutes once Anya got the location of the latest campsite from Samaira, until Tori scooted forward and leaned around Anya's shoulder.

"Promise me something," Tori said.

"Okay. I promise," Anya said.

"You don't wanna hear what it is, first?"

"I trust you, and whatever it is, I promise."

"Use the RAC store to buy me a floating island and a hunky beef-cake android."

"What?" Anya snorted.

"Kidding. For real this time: promise me that if any of your skills start to get weird, if you start to lose control, if that bird turns out to be an evil demon or something, you'll stop. Or get that respecification token thing later and change them. Okay?"

Anya sighed but nodded. "If anything starts making me become not-me, I'll change. Promise."

"Thank you."

"Can you put anything on pizza?" Pan asked as he stared at the boxes on the floor of the Shadow Ray's cabin.

"Pretty much. Still some debate going on about pineapple," Anya said.

"Can you put ants on pizza?"

"No," Anya and Tori both said at once.

"Aw," Pan moaned, and Anya chuckled as she landed the Shadow Ray and went out to see her new friends.

33

Anya and the others patrolled the rest of the East Coast over the next few days, but found nothing. For the first time since the invasion, news from around the world had become quiet. Anya kept in contact with the other hosts around the world, but none of them had found any aliens either. Amahle and Bernard from South Africa had found two other hosts, and Brody and Cooper from Australia had located three on their own as well.

That was some good news, at least.

Normally Anya would have been grateful for the quiet, but the lack of alien attacks had put her on edge. The gnosiphages had gone on an all-out murder spree of hosts during the first week after they landed. Then they had just vanished. Felix had kept up with the signal count, and stated that the number of global host and alien signals had continued to drop, but at a much reduced pace. The aliens were still out there, still killing, but had gotten better at hiding.

While Anya was relieved that hosts weren't being killed off at a steady clip, she wasn't so thrilled that the aliens had become all but impossible to find. She had been snapping awake in the middle of the night more often, usually from visions of the pharaonic cobra striking at her in her dreams and the phantom pain of its acid eating away at her Sun's Heart.

Anya took a breath of the warm ocean air wafting in from the Gulf of Mexico. She and the others had decided to take lunch on the western side of Florida, and been lucky to find a secluded beach to enjoy the view and some quiet where nobody was likely to see them or their vehicles.

Anya and Samaira sat on the nose of the Shadow Ray, while Arvo watched Pan playing in the dirt and making golems out of sand. Gary had flown his truck to a nearby scrap yard to collect more parts and expand his growing army of bots. He had built enough to necessitate attaching a trailer to his truck to keep them all in.

The trailer itself had been upgraded as well, using some of the same hovering technology as Anya's Shadow Ray, or at least as near as Gary could get it with spare parts from Earth's junkyards.

Anya munched on her sixth Cubano and watched the waves lazily unfurl across the white sand. For a moment, she could forget about everything.

Then Samaira ruined it.

"MacDougal says we're due in DC tomorrow. Hanover's going to make all of this official," Samaira said as she looked at a text message on her phone.

"Ugh," Anya said. Moment of tranquility gone.

"They're probably gonna push for you to join their new department. Officially," Samaira added.

"Double ugh," Anya replied and leaned back on the Shadow Ray. Samaira giggled and looked down at her.

"You don't think MacDougal's warranted a little trust by now?"

Anya frowned. "She has... and I think if it was just her I might be okay with it. But..."

"But Hanover. And whoever else," Samaira said and Anya nodded. "I can't say I like the idea of being under anybody's thumb. And if they force me to get them stuff from the Archive's store that's clearly made just for killing, I don't think I could do that. But I think MacDougal is smart enough to know where our boundaries are. I don't think she'll push anywhere she knows we won't give."

"You think. But you can't know."

"Can't really know anything. Gotta have a little faith in people. You had faith a bunch of total strangers would show up in Greenland and not go full psycho-killer on each other. It worked out."

"Barely. Still not convinced some of them aren't psycho killers."

"But you're working with them anyway. MacDougal and Hanover and the rest aren't much different. And I think showing them that you're willing to cooperate would go a long way in earning some goodwill and getting them to be more understanding," Samaira said.

"Maybe, all right?" Anya sighed.

"Maybe's an improvement," Samaira grinned at her and brushed her long black hair away from her face as the warm breeze made it flutter around her. "You ever think about what you wanna do after?"

"After the invasion?"

"Yeah."

"I hadn't really thought about it. Too focused on not dying and trying to make the best of probably the most insane historical event I can think of," Anya looked around her at the beach and the waves, the sky and the sun glimmering across the water.

"Something like this might be nice. A beach, somewhere. Before all this, the idea of owning a house or even a shitty little apartment was just a fantasy. But now? I could set up on some tiny island out in the middle of nowhere. The Shadow Ray could get me anywhere on the planet in a few hours, tops. This is assuming we're stuck here and the Engineers keep blocking anything from the RAC store with FTL abilities. If I can afford it and it's possible, I might get a cool ship and go explore the galaxy," Anya shrugged. "You?"

"A beach somewhere quiet with a little house does sound nice. Wouldn't have expected that from you, though."

"Oh?"

"I feel like you would get bored."

Anya laughed. "After all this, I could do with some boredom."

Samaira smiled at her and then looked down at Chandrali, who had curled up on her lap. She caressed the cat's back and she purred her appreciation. "A long boring stretch does sound pretty good right about now."

The silence stretched between them, and Samaira asked, "Still haven't told your family?"

"Ugh," Anya said and put her hands over her face. "You got a gift for ruining a perfectly nice day, y'know that?"

"Sorry, sorry. Touchy subject. I just know you mentioned your family was somewhere on the East Coast and while we're in the area…"

"No. Stop," Anya groaned. "I wouldn't even know where to begin with my mother. All this other shit is bad enough."

"Well, I don't know the specifics, and we've only known each other for about a week but… well, if you ever decide to go see your mom, and you want some moral support, I'm happy to help."

"Thank you. That means a lot, actually."

Samaira smiled at her, then glanced up as a whooshing sound filled the air. Anya followed her gaze and saw Gary's truck, trailer in tow, descending on the beach. It landed with an ungraceful thud and a squeak of suspensions and sank several inches into the sand. The old man emerged and gave them a wave.

"Build something good?" Samaira asked.

"This and that. While I appreciate the aliens giving me more time to get my factory up and running, I'm not too keen on them hiding like this," Gary said.

"We heard from MacDougal," Anya said. "She wants us in DC tomorrow."

"You kids have fun with that."

"Could you at least come with us? Maybe just meet some people?" Samaira asked.

"Nope."

"Gary…"

"I guarantee you as soon as I show up, they're gonna want to know exactly what skills I got, where my factory is, and how many bombs I can give them, or something like that. They won't be able to help themselves. Anya gets it. You're still pretty firm on not joining up with these clowns, right kid?"

"Well…" Anya said and shrugged. Gary's mustache pulled down

as he frowned. "I'm a maybe. I don't see the harm in at least meeting with them and pretending to listen."

Gary grunted.

"If things go wrong, it'd be good to have you around," Anya said. "That's all."

Gary polished his glasses and folded his arms over his chest. "Fine. I'll see what they have to say. Nothing else though."

"Really?" Samaira asked.

"I s'pose. Besides, I don't need both of you bugging me about it."

"Thank you Gary," Samaira said and hugged him.

"All right, all right," Gary said and gave her an awkward pat on the back. Arvo and Pan walked over, and the latter dismissed his golems so that they turned back into ordinary piles of sand.

"Hugs!" Pan said and joined Samaira in hugging Gary.

"Chrissakes," Gary said but patted the pangolin on the head all the same.

"Of course, I'll be coming too," Arvo said. "No harm in listening."

"We've got a few more hours of daylight," Gary said as he extricated himself from the group hug. "Might as well get in some more patrolling while we can, then settle in for the night."

"Wanna try and cover Georgia?" Anya asked.

"Don't suspect we'll find anything, but might as well," Gary said.

Anya glanced out the window of the Shadow Ray as she and the others took to the air. The beach really was lovely. Anya allowed herself a few moments to stare at the waves and think of some distant day where she had nothing to worry about except encroaching boredom.

"Anya?" Pan asked behind her.

"Yeah buddy?" she replied, snapped out of her reverie.

"Things will be okay, right? We'll meet the MacDougal lady and things won't be so scary?"

"I hope so, Pan. Whatever happens, I'll take care of you," she reached behind her, and gently held the pangolin's claw in her hand. Pan smiled at her, and Anya followed Gary's truck across the sky.

34

nya had never been to DC before. Her work schedule and lack
of funds had prevented her from doing much besides the
occasional day trip outside the city. Among the places she
would have gone if she had been in the nation's capital for pleasure,
the White House was near the bottom. She just never saw much of the
appeal when the Air and Space Museum and a dozen other more interesting places were nearby.

Still, she had to admit that it was neat to be given a behind-the-
scenes look at the place, past what the walking tours got to see. It was
a little surreal when she, Samaira, Arvo, Pan, and even Gary entered
the Oval Office. Anya had seen it in news broadcasts, and replicas of it
on TV shows and movies, but it was still a strange feeling to be in the
room itself.

President Hanover had had the place decorated with thick, pale
curtains, and furniture to match. It was functional, and of good quality,
but lacked anything notable or interesting. Some portraits of Lincoln
and Washington had been hung up, along with pictures of Hanover
and his family. It was bland and safe: an office organized by committee
and PR reps. Anya supposed she couldn't blame Hanover for playing

it safe, but once the surrealism of being in the Oval Office had worn off, she found its blandness irritating.

President Hanover himself stood behind his desk, while MacDougal sat in a plush armchair near Anya and the other hosts. General Tully of the marines stood near Hanover's desk and was flanked by the Secretary of Defense and Secretary of State. A number of other officials sat or stood around the office, along with a half-dozen members of the Secret Service, and a photographer. It was on the crowded side, but there was enough sitting room for most people.

A single piece of paper lay on Hanover's desk: the executive order that would officially create the Department of Extraterrestrial Research and Defense. All it lacked was Hanover's signature.

"So he just signs it and then that's it?" Anya whispered to MacDougal.

"As far as making the DERD exist, yes. We'll still need to set up the physical space for the department, get all the staff organized and transferred from existing organizations, but this will get the ball rolling. After this, Hanover will be making an official statement to the press in the briefing room," MacDougal said. The photographer set his camera up in front of Hanover's desk while she spoke, and Hanover settled himself into his chair.

"He's telling the press about the aliens today?" Samaira asked.

"Yes. Recent unofficial news broadcasts have necessitated we speed things along," MacDougal said and glanced meaningfully at Anya. "Which also means confirming which hosts will be joining the DERD."

"Oh boy," Samaira said.

"I thought you'd at least wait until you heard back from the hosts out west," Anya said.

"Thanks to you, Ms. Upadhyay, and Dr. Immonen, we've been able to make contact with them through the Bureau offices in California and Washington. Some of them are willing to join, some are not. For now they've agreed to stay where they are and continue to patrol the western half of the country. As things become more official and set with the DERD, we may ask them to come to DC to fill out some paperwork, but for now it's just you all," MacDougal continued.

"Just me, really," Samaira said and then glanced at Anya, a silent request in her eyes.

"Are we gonna be in front of the cameras or anything?" Anya asked.

"If you agree to sign on, yes, that would be for the best. If not, then the President may still want you to make an appearance, just to look good."

"All right. I can do that," Anya said and MacDougal nodded.

"I know where Mr. Hendricks is at regarding coming aboard the DERD," MacDougal continued and looked at Gary, who gave a barely perceptible shake of his head, "but you've continued to be coy, Dr. Immonen."

"I won't help fight anything but aliens, and I won't give you anything from the Archive except medicine and medical technology. And any medicine or tech I give to America will be made freely available to all. No charging people their life savings for the cure for cancer or anything like that. And if I learn that you've weaponized anything I give you, I will not be cooperating with your government any longer. If those terms are acceptable, then I am happy to come join your new department, so long as I am able to continue helping people around the world, and it does not cause any undue distress with the Finnish government," Arvo replied.

"I think that's very doable. President Hanover has spoken with your Prime Minister, and she is accommodating, so long as you're willing to offer her similar terms."

"I would also like to provide my assistance to the people of countries that may be hostile to America."

MacDougal frowned.

"I am intent on using my gift to help everyone, Madame Director. The only true enemies here are those aliens," Arvo added.

"I'll make it work," MacDougal said.

"Then with Samaira and myself, you have two for your group," Arvo said with a smile.

Anya bit her lip and then looked down at MacDougal, who regarded her with a gaze that was as level and unwavering as a steel beam.

"Fine. I'll sign on," Anya said and Samaira grinned at her.

"Kid…" Gary started to say, then sighed and shook his head.

"Under one condition," Anya continued.

"I'm listening," MacDougal said.

"I get to quit when I want. If Hanover is getting too pushy with wanting access to the RAC store, or one of the generals wants to turn me into their own personal WMD, I'm out. No repercussions, no bullshit."

MacDougal pursed her lips and said, "If somebody is giving you trouble, you give me a week to resolve the problem. If I can't, then yes, you may quit. Deal?"

Anya started to extend her hand and then paused. "Two conditions."

MacDougal sighed and waved her hand for Anya to continue.

"I assume the DERD will need people like accountants to manage their expenses?"

MacDougal squinted at her, confused, then blinked and nodded.

"Ah, yes. Your friend, Victoria, she's some kind of accountant according to her file, yes?" MacDougal asked.

"Yeah. Tori's stuck being a secretary at a shitty investment firm, but she's smart, and she deserves better. If she wants, can you give her a job with the DERD?"

"If she wants," MacDougal nodded.

"Wait. Three conditions. But the last one's small!" Anya said as MacDougal started to scowl. "My contact in the press was Jennifer Chang and Angel Ramierez with Brooklyn Channel 08 news. I agreed to let her interview me first. If there's any sort of news stuff, the DERD contacts her, and if you want me personally to do any sit-downs, she gets first crack at me."

"Is that all?" MacDougal arched an eyebrow.

"Yes. I think," Anya said and paused as she thought, then nodded. "Yup. No more conditions."

"That's acceptable. I'll put in a call to Channel 08 and they can be here in a few hours, tomorrow at the latest. You may need to answer some general questions in the briefing today, but Ms. Chang can conduct your first personal interview. Deal?"

"Deal," Anya said and stuck her hand out. MacDougal's hand was tiny compared to hers, but Anya took it gently and shook.

"I'm with Anya!" Pan said beside MacDougal's chair. "I wanna join the dee-ee-ar-dee thing too!"

"I'll have to look at drafting some kind of procedure for non-humans," MacDougal said, "but I see no reason why you can't stay with Ms. Nowicki."

"Yay!" Pan cheered.

"Mr. Hendricks? You're the odd man out now," MacDougal said and looked at him.

"Suits me fine. I'll help where I can, but be happy I agreed to put in an appearance at all. You keep Hanover from trying to crawl in my ass and we won't have any problems."

"Mm," MacDougal said and then turned away to look at the President. He was still fidgeting in his chair, asking one of his aides to adjust the curtains so the lighting was better.

"Thank you, Anya," Samaira whispered beside her.

"For what? Just agreeing to play nice until they piss me off," she said.

"I know. And I know it wasn't something you decided on a whim. So just… thank you for thinking about it, and helping."

"Yeah. You're welcome. Hopefully I don't regret it."

Samaira took her hand in a gentle manner, as if testing if this was all right. Anya looked at her, returned her smile, and gave her hand a soft squeeze.

"If you change your mind, you can come hang out with me. We'll be the odd folks out together," Gary said and Anya grinned at him.

"Is that good news I hear over there?" Hanover asked as he paused for a photo, his pen poised above the executive order.

"I'd say so, Mr. President," MacDougal said. "We have four willing applicants to be some of our first agents of your new department."

"Why don't we get a photo with you and our new DERD members?" Hanover asked. Anya held back a sigh, but joined everybody except Gary, who remained at the edge of the room. Pan was just visible over the edge of the desk, and Anya had to hunch down to get in the picture frame, but she managed.

"Smile and say 'Four More Years!'" Hanover said but Anya kept her expression neutral.

The photo session took several more minutes, both before and after the order was signed. When it was finally done, Anya decided she would be quite happy if she never had to stand in front of a camera again.

"The press briefing with the President is scheduled to take place in an hour," MacDougal said as she checked her watch. "President Bisset of France and Prime Minister Stark of the UK will be making similar statements a few hours after ours."

"It's really happening then," Anya said. "Everybody's gonna know. Officially."

"Gonna be hell on the stock market," Hanover said. "They'll blame me, of course. Like I decided to have aliens show up."

"Yes. The stock market," Anya said dryly.

"You'll likely be able to take credit for the inevitable resurgence once the aliens are defeated as well, sir," MacDougal said and Hanover grinned to himself.

"I'm gonna go sit in my truck," Gary said.

"Please escort him," MacDougal said to one of the Secret Service members, who shadowed Gary out of the Oval Office. "If the rest of you want to go elsewhere, please let us know. Just avoid the briefing room and any public areas. Especially Pan."

"Why me? Did I do something bad?" Pan asked.

"No, buddy. It's just that people aren't used to seeing a special pangolin like you. It might surprise them," Anya said as she knelt down next to Pan, then looked at MacDougal. "Anywhere you would suggest to get out of the way? Maybe get something to eat?"

"You can borrow the kitchen," Hanover said as he held up the executive order for another picture. Anya, Pan, and Samaira all left with a pair of Secret Service Agents while Arvo went to go join Gary.

The White House kitchen was smaller and more normal looking than what Anya had expected. It was large, but not gigantic, and most of the space was taken up by stainless steel counters and equipment. Pots and pans in the dozens hung from the ceiling, and the smooth floors were lined with rubber mats. The kitchen was empty but for

Anya and the others, and the agents informed her she could help herself to whatever was in one of the towering refrigerators, which she did with gusto.

"This all makes everything feel a lot more real for some reason," Samaira said as Anya worked her way through a stack of sandwiches.

"I guess it'll all be real for everybody after today. I'm not sure if that's for the better or worse," Anya replied.

"Better," Pan said and Anya and Samaira looked down at him. "Aliens are scary. But not knowing there are aliens when there are aliens is more scary."

"Well said, Pan. I think things are gonna get weird for a while. But it's better to know what you're dealing with," Anya said then looked at Samaira and asked, "You been online much during all this?"

Samaira shook her head. "A bit. I wasn't really on the internet much before this either, though."

"I'm not as much as I used to be, but when I am, it's pretty wild. People think the world's falling apart. All this crazy shit happening and fuck-all to explain it. Having an explanation, even a batshit crazy one, is better than being in the dark."

"Will I have to fight now?" Pan asked.

"Not if you don't want to," Anya said. "Though I think you should learn how to defend yourself in case of emergencies."

"Defend," Pan repeated, then tilted his head to the side as he pondered the word. "I can do that. Can I defend you and Samaira?"

"Of course," Samaira said. "We'll need all the help we can get. You've got some pretty good skills for it too."

"What about the news people?" Pan asked. "Do I need to fight them?"

Anya laughed. "No. No fighting the news people. You shouldn't need to defend against them either. They'll probably have a lot of questions for you later, but we can help you with those."

"I don't know very much. Why would they ask me questions?"

"Like we said earlier, nobody's ever seen a talking pangolin before. It's a novelty."

"Novelty? A book?" Pan scratched at his head.

"That's a novel. A novelty is like something new and interesting," Samaira explained and Pan nodded.

"Novelty," Pan repeated.

"Sorry, Pan. English is weird," Anya said.

"I like it. Talking is fun. I can say things like novelty, and asshole, and…"

"Yeah, uh, don't say any bad words to the news people later," Anya said and Samaira giggled. Anya debated whether or not to teach him all the bad words just so he knew which ones to avoid when her ear beeped and Felix appeared.

"Incoming message from Gary!" the AI said.

"I'm getting one too," Samaira said as she and Anya brought their communication windows up and tapped on Gary's flashing name. The old man appeared on their screens, driving his truck somewhere.

"Hey, you guys all right?" Gary asked.

"Uh, yeah, what's up?" Anya asked. Gary's mustache was pulled tight across his upper lip as he grimaced.

"Aliens," Gary replied and Anya's throat tightened.

"Aliens… plural?" Samaira asked and Gary nodded.

"Six of them."

"Oh God," Samaira said.

"Where?" Anya asked and looked between Gary and Felix.

"I was flying around with the doc, just taking a break before the press briefing started. Gizmo picked up a signal just outside DC, probably closing in as we speak," Gary said. "I'll be landing on the South Lawn in about fifteen seconds."

"I haven't picked anything up," Felix said. "They must be getting better at hiding their signals if they're that close."

"Hey, Secret Service guy!" Anya said and pointed at one of the men in suits standing at the edge of the kitchen.

"I heard," he said and then touched his earpiece and began speaking into it. The other agent in the kitchen stayed where he was.

"Aliens?" Pan asked in a quavering voice and curled into a ball.

"What should we do?" Samaira asked.

Anya's combat cognition kicked into gear.

The White House was full of people: government officials,

members of the press, staff, and tourists. She figured there were also a lot of armed personnel and built-in defenses as well, but those would only be so useful against the aliens. However, the surrounding areas weren't any better. DC was packed full of people, and the aliens could be here any moment. The White House had large expanses of lawn that were walled off from the public, while the rest of the area was packed with buildings and tourists. With as close as the aliens were, running wasn't much of an option. Better to stay here.

"We meet Gary and Arvo outside on the lawn while drawing the aliens' attention towards ourselves while the Secret Service gets everybody out," Anya said then turned to the remaining Secret Service agent. "Can you show us the way to the South Lawn?"

"I think I'm supposed to keep you here," the agent said and Anya rolled her eyes.

"You heard aliens are on the way, right? We're trying to help, here, and it'd be better if you showed us the way out," she replied.

The agent thought for a moment, but nodded and waved a hand. "Follow me, no wandering off," he said and then spoke into the radio in his sleeve to update whoever was listening on the other end.

"Pan, you should stay close," Samaira said as they hurried out of the kitchen.

"Okay," Pan said and scuttled after the two women and the agent.

When they had gone down to the kitchen, the hallways had been mostly empty but for an aide carrying papers or an agent standing guard at an intersection. Now the whole place was a flurry of activity, with armed guards escorting people out and voices echoing along the halls.

"Anya, they're close. Maybe forty-five seconds away," Felix said.

"Shit."

"That's not all. I recognize one of the gnosiphage signals," Felix said and Anya was about to ask how, but then shuddered when the realization hit her. She had only fought one alien that had gotten away.

The snake.

35

Anya heard the helicopter before she saw it appear over the roof of the White House. President Hanover emerged from the West Wing, surrounded by a small squad of Secret Service agents and made for the center of the South Lawn as the helicopter began to hover overhead. MacDougal and General Tully were also with him, and the crowd moved with purpose across the lawn and waited for the helicopter to land.

Anya ran toward Gary and Arvo when something dark shot across the sky and collided with the helicopter. It exploded in a ball of fire and shrapnel and the boom echoed across the lawn.

"Shit!" Anya said and darted toward Hanover. She soaked up the heat and fire from the explosion and created a small field of gravity around herself and the others that repulsed the shards of the helicopter. Hanover was screaming in panic, despite being completely covered by the agents surrounding him.

"The hell?" Tully shouted.

"Aliens!" Anya replied. "They just got here!"

"Marine One is down! Hostiles on the South Lawn!" one of the agents shouted into his radio. "Move the President to the North Lawn!"

"There's at least six," Anya said to General Tully, who grunted and moved with Hanover, MacDougal, and the agents back into the White House. The smoking wreckage of Marine One had fallen to the ground, and a form emerged.

It was a toilet.

The lid opened, and a bouquet of long arms emerged with a flourish. Each arm was roughly human in shape, but they had too many elbows, and no skin to speak of. The hands were too large, and each only had four overly-long fingers with five joints.

Anya launched herself at the alien toilet in a spinning kick, her foot igniting like a miniature sun, and the air around it warping as she increased the gravity behind her kick. The hands emerging from the toilet banded together, palms upward, and formed a translucent shield of pink light just as Anya's kick landed. The ground around the toilet bowed downward in a crater and the arms trembled under the attack, but held.

"Kid! Above you!" Gary shouted from behind her, and Anya dodged to one side without pausing to look.

A large fire-hydrant, almost as tall as Anya herself, crashed down where she had been a half-second before. A writhing collection of slick tentacles emerged from beneath it, and the hydrant's sides throbbed and undulated as if they were made of rubber instead of metal.

One of the sides of the hydrant opened and shot a compressed jet of water at Anya that she just managed to dodge and deflect with a shove of gravitational force. It struck the East Wing of the White House behind her and demolished the outer, then inner walls, and blasted out the other side before it stopped. A single blast had reduced one side of the East Wing to rubble in seconds.

Holy shit, Anya thought. *A tank probably couldn't have done that much with one shot.*

A bolt of blue light sped past Anya and hit the hydrant, encasing it in a large bubble that began to float into the air. Another bolt followed it and split into dozens of smaller shards and forced the toilet back, each of its hands forming a small shield to deflect them.

Samaira leaped up onto the remains of the East Wing and continued to pelt the two aliens with arrows of light while Chandrali rushed the toilet and began swiping at it with her huge diamond claws.

"I've got these two!" Samaira said. "You make sure Hanover and everybody else gets out of here, and find the other four aliens!"

"Be careful!" Anya said, then looked around for Pan as she ran after Hanover. "Pan! Stay with Gary!"

Pan squealed in terror and rolled as fast as he could to Gary's truck.

"I've got the little guy!" Gary said. "And I've got my bots escorting people out of the building. I don't know where the doc went. But kid, I saw a few shapes fly overhead a second ago. I think they might be in the White House or the North Lawn."

"Dammit!" Anya snapped and then flew up to the roof of the White House to get a better view. A few snipers had taken up position along the edges of the roof and jumped when they saw her, one of them even aiming his rifle at her.

"No! She's with us," another one said and Anya showed them her hands. It was meaningless as anything but a gesture of non-aggression, but the snipers got it. One of them pointed toward the far side of the roof, near the north side of the White House. He was pointing at a newly formed hole in the roof which something had crashed down through.

"Something went right past us a second ago!" the sniper said and Anya cursed. Hanover was down there, somewhere. She sensed the heat of the remaining humans in the building, but no aliens. One group of people was particularly clustered together and moving awkwardly through the hallways. That would likely be Hanover, MacDougal, General Tully, and their escort of guards. Anya flinched as one of the heat sources detached from the group, and remained behind. Gunshots echoed up from the hallway below and then the heat signature faded.

"Shit! Stay up here and kill the ones on the lawn if you can!" Anya said and pointed down at the toilet and hydrant just as a trio of Gary's bots jumped onto the roof after her. One of them emitted a forcefield around itself, the snipers, and the other bots, while the remaining two aimed what appeared to be automatic railguns at the aliens below and opened fire.

"I got this covered, kid. Go!" Gary's voice said from a speaker on one of the bots, and Anya jumped down through the hole in the roof and landed with a thud two stories below.

"One floor down!" Felix said in her ear. Anya slammed her feet down in a powerful stomp that collapsed the floor and sent her down again. "Next hallway!"

Anya punched a hole in the wall next to her and ripped a portion of it away that allowed her to step through. She came out just ahead of Hanover and his surviving security detail. The President, MacDougal, Tully, and the agents looked at her with expressions ranging from surprise, to terror, to confusion.

The hall behind them was thick with dust and smoke, and an inhuman shape moved within it.

"Move!" Anya said and shoved past the group, putting herself between them and whatever alien lurked ahead of her.

The dust and smoke cleared to reveal a short, squat traffic light. It was just a vertical column of three lights within a yellow cover sitting atop a stout metal pole at a casual glance. However each of the traffic lights was a glistening, twitching eyeball, and the metal pole crawled with pulsating silver veins. Its base was the same metallic gray as the pole, but was something that looked like two enormous human hands fused together. The thick fingers acted as scrabbling little legs that allowed it to dart forward and side-to-side. Anya jumped at the street light alien, and the top light of the column—or rather, the eye—glowed a bright red.

Anya froze in place. Some unseen force held her, all of her, from any movement. She couldn't even blink, or shout. She could barely breathe.

But she didn't need to do any of that to summon heat and fire.

Anya preferred the up-close-and-personal attacks because it allowed her to cause more damage for less energy. Heating the air over long distances, or hurling fire away from her, was too inefficient.

That didn't mean she couldn't do it.

Anya caused the air between her and the traffic light alien to ignite all at once. The hallway went from a simple stretch of wood, stone, and paint and turned into a kiln within moments, before the alien could unleash any sort of follow-up attack.

The wallpaper caught fire, the rug turned to ashes, and the traffic light's eye's blinked and flickered in surprise. It changed to the center light, the pupil of which flashed to a glowing yellow arrow that pointed to the alien's left. Anya shouted in surprise as the entire hallway rotated violently to her right. She became able to move again, but the sudden unnatural movement of the hallway spinning onto its side disoriented her for a precious second. Worse, her movements all felt backwards, wrong somehow. She tried to stand and only fell backwards onto her ass.

Anya made to yank it toward her with a well of gravitational force centered in front of her. However her gravity well formed to her left, and she was pulled toward it instead. The alien was tugged forward as well, but its hand-foot clung into the floor and anchored it in place. The yellow eye in the center blinked, and the glowing arrow switched to pointing in the opposite direction. Anya grunted and continued spinning as the hallway rotated to her left and she tumbled back to the floor, then the opposite wall.

Whatever force the alien was using to rotate the hallway, it wasn't gravity. Her Dominion told her that the Earth's normal center of gravity was the same as it had always been. The hallway itself hadn't actually moved either: it was intact but for her fire attacks. The alien was making her personally spin around and feel like up was sideways and down was across and everything forward was behind her. The hallway spun again, but Anya held herself in place, floating above the ceiling and below the floor as her sense of space spun again.

It was nauseating, but it wasn't actually hurting her. The impacts against the walls and floors would have shattered a normal person's bones, but her kinetic dispersal, enhanced regalia, and Cloak of the Gale absorbed the worst of the hits.

Then the traffic light switched to green, and the traffic light alien became a blur of motion as it sped at her faster than she could follow. Anya's spatial awareness flipped around back to normal, and she instinctively jumped up and over the traffic light as it zipped along the hallway beneath her and landed behind it. A pair of metallic, mantis-like limbs had emerged from the side of the metal post, each one curved into a sharp blade. It had extended the blade-arms to cover the whole of the hallway, and they had sliced through the stone walls as if they had been made of nothing more than foam. Their edges shone an acidic green and Anya scowled.

"Somebody taught you a little trick, huh?" she said.

The yellow light flashed and Anya was sent falling toward the traffic light and it switched back to green and spun in a deadly whirl-wind of blades. Anya curled into a ball, making herself as small as possible, and ignited the air for several feet around her. The spatial weirdness the traffic light caused made it almost impossible to aim a distance attack, so Anya settled for just trying to get close and hitting it with everything she had.

One of the blades stabbed into her waist. Her regalia held for a moment, then tore and the blade sunk a few inches into her side. She gritted her teeth as the acid burned her, then seized the metallic mantis arm and started to superheat the metallic appendage. The glowing yellow arrow spun and Anya screamed as the hallway and any sense of normalcy turned into a vortex of omni-directional insanity.

Anya was close enough to the alien that she didn't need to worry about what was up or down, she just needed to hold on and burn the bastard as much as she could. The alien slashed at her head with its other arm even as she melted its first and tore it away. She just managed to deflect the stab to her forehead, and detonated the air between her and the alien in an explosion that shattered the walls of the hallway and sent both her and the alien spinning away from each other.

Anya groaned as she held her bleeding side as her regeneration began to knit it back together. Her orichalcum chestplate boosted her healing and took care of the wound and the acid in short order. Her regalia also began to reknit itself, but very slowly.

She patted the ground next to her, just to make sure she was on the floor and not the ceiling or somewhere else. Her spatial awareness had normalized and she sprang to her feet as her side finished healing. The alien was two rooms away, blown back by the force of her blast, and the bottom red light/eye had cracked and was seeping some kind of crimson sludge. The eye flickered and went dark.

"One down, two to go," Anya said.

The alien glared at her with its remaining eyes, then flicked the lower one to green and fled with unnatural speed back toward the South Lawn.

Anya considered following it for a moment, but let it go. Gary, Samaira, Chandrali, the snipers, and Gary's robots were already on the South Lawn. The sounds of the fight with the hydrant and toilet echoed down the hallway to her.

There were still three gnosipahges unaccounted for, and people to evacuate. Anya soaked up any remaining heat in the hallway from her fire attacks, and then sprinted through the nearest wall in the general direction Hanover had gone. Crashing through the rooms was faster than navigating the damaged hallways, and she barely noticed herself barreling through the reinforced walls.

She burst out through a window adjacent to the North Lawn just as a convoy of armored black SUVs pulled to a stop. Hanover and his entourage emerged from a door several yards away along with each of the agents, MacDougal, and General Tully. The general and the agents had firearms drawn and were looking in every direction.

"Go!" one of the agents said and pointed at the lead SUV. No sooner did Hanover and his escort approach the armored SUV than Felix spoke up in her ear.

"Anya, another alien!" they said. Anya darted toward Hanover and the two agents protecting him, scooped all three up in a huge bear hug, and dove to the side. General Tully saw her, grabbed MacDougal, and dove after her.

There was the loud, unmistakable sound of a copy machine printing off a piece of paper, and then the SUV exploded and was sent skyward at the top of a column of fire.

"Just get out of here!" Anya said as she put the President and his agents down and spun to face whatever new threat would emerge from the smoke of the ruined SUV. Anya waved them away along with MacDougal and General Tully just as the sound of a printing machine reached her ears again.

A typical piece of printer paper floated out of the black smoke around the SUV, a few yards away from Anya. It had some kind of rune printed on it: a sharp, angular line surrounded by a circle and smaller alien glyphs. The rune glowed, and then bolts of lightning shot out from the paper and crawled along Anya's body. Her jaw was forced shut and she roared with pain as the lightning made her muscles seize up. The attack stopped after a few seconds, and the floating piece of paper disintegrated.

Smoke from the ruined SUVs cleared to reveal a copy machine like what she might see in any office building. Except this machine had random eyes blinking across its surface, and tiny centipede legs emerging from beneath it.

The machine made another noise, and unearthly red light seeped out from the edges of its scanning tray. Anya didn't wait to see what it was about to print off.

She darted in low, faster than a charging rhino, and slammed her burning fist into the copy machine alien's side with all the force she could focus into her knuckles. The air around her boomed, and the force of the impact blew the remaining smoke from the SUVs away. The machine squealed from a mouth inside one of its paper trays and went spinning across the lawn.

Anya snared it in a claw of gravity and yanked it back to her, into a flaming roundhouse kick delivered to its other side. Yellow and orange fire erupted around her. Whatever armor or carapace the machine was covered in shattered and turned to molten slag. The asphalt beneath it cracked and several of its legs snapped off. Milky white blood sprayed from its wounds and it squealed again and unleashed a flurry of papers in a white blizzard.

Anya ignited the air around her and managed to burn most of the papers before they could activate the runes printed on them, but several more escaped her wave of heat. One of the papers exploded in a sudden torrent of yellow goop that covered Anya and stuck her to the ground where she was. Another sent more lightning crackling over her skin, and a third erupted in a flash of blinding white light that forced her to close her eyes and look away.

She tried to move but whatever the goop was, it was strong, like what the refrigerator alien had used in Chicago but worse. Everything was a blur of pale colors and light when she managed to crack her eyes open.

She couldn't see.

She couldn't move.

She could sense the heat of people around her, some as far away as a quarter mile, but no aliens. Samaira, Gary, Pan, Arvo, and Chandrali were all still alive and nearby. MacDougal, Hanover, and the others must have found another ride because she couldn't sense their grouped signatures any longer.

Anya created a small field of inverted gravity around her that would repel most things that came near while she struggled to free herself from the goop. Her flames helped somewhat, causing the goop to liquefy a bit faster and slide away from her, but whatever the stuff was, it was stubborn.

"Anya! More!" Felix cried.

Anya's eyesight cleared just enough to show her a thin, rectangular shape flying toward her.

A carpet.

It stopped feet away from her, and unfurled to expose an intricate pattern of geometric shapes in diverse colors woven across its surface. The surface of the carpet alien was thick and bristly, like porcupine quills, and each one of the countless colored quills shifted their position and hue. The result was a kaleidoscopic display of colors and shapes that was unearthly in its beauty, as well as literally hypnotic.

Anya's previous thoughts of how to escape from the goop, how best to attack the copy machine, how to get Hanover and the others away and unharmed, all of it became background noise.

There was only the carpet, its shapes and its colors.

From somewhere far away, the copy machine printed another piece of paper.

More goop covered Anya, mostly her upper body and the lower part of her face. It sealed her mouth and nose, but not her eyes. Those remained locked on the carpet, entranced by its surreal and captivating display.

Anya knew, somewhere in the back of her mind that she couldn't breathe, that she could barely move.

But it was a fleeting thought. Everything was fleeting. Everything except the shifting patterns of the carpet before her.

Another form appeared just beyond the edges of the carpet, falling from the sky like a squirming comet. Anya was familiar with it, and a spike of fear registered in the back of her mind before it too was smothered by the haze of colors before her.

It was dark gray and serpentine, and it had grown back the arms Anya had torn off its side days before.

The pharaonic cobra and the other two aliens converged on Anya as she slowly suffocated and was held in helpless sway.

36

"I got this covered, kid. Go!" Gary said into his mouthpiece as Anya stood on the roof of the White House. She didn't bother to respond as she disappeared down into the hole caused by one of the other aliens.

Gary was inside his truck, flying just above the chaos on the South Lawn below. Pan lay on the floor of the passenger side, tucked into a trembling ball of scales. All the readouts across Gary's dashboard told him that the thirty-eight robots he had built were all deployed and engaged in some form or another.

Most of his robots were focused on evacuating everybody from the White House, whether they wanted to go or not. They had picked people up, encased them in temporary forcefields, and flown them out and away from the immediate area. Most of the people had been cleared without incident or injury, but a few had been killed in crossfire.

Samaira and her big tiger drew the focus of the fire hydrant and toilet aliens, and Gary's bots took shots and disrupted them where they could. It was obvious that Samaira was struggling against the two aliens, even with her tiger and Gary's help.

"Hey little guy, I don't suppose you could summon a bunch of your golems to run interference?" Gary asked and winced as the fire hydrant blasted three of his robots to scrap below them.

"Noooooo!" Pan wailed. "Can't do anything with earth while I'm in the air! And it's scary down there!"

Gary sighed but couldn't blame the critter too much. He was basically just a kid.

The draft for Vietnam hadn't much cared who wanted to fight and who didn't or couldn't. It threw thousands of dumb, scared kids into the thick of things and sent their guts home in boxes.

Can I be honest with you, Hendricks? I'm scared shitless.

The voice echoed at Gary from decades ago, from a jungle so thick and hot every breath had been a struggle. It had been such a stupid war.

The Finnish doctor had turned to some kind of smoke or shadow as soon as the aliens had appeared and taken off somewhere. That was probably the smart move, and if the doc was as good as he seemed to be, he was probably helping people escape or tending to the wounded. His signal glowed on Gary's map, moving with impressive speed in and around the White House.

The doc certainly had guts to stick around an active combat zone when he didn't have any offensive powers to speak of.

Gary tracked Anya's dot on his menu map and started to dispatch some robots to back her up when his menu screen flickered. The signals of Anya, Samaira, and the doc all jumped around the map. Gary glanced out his window at Samaira as she flipped over a lance of pink energy the toilet shot at her from its hands, then returned fire with an enormous harpoon of aetheric light. She was right below him, but Gary's map said she was on the North Lawn, then inside the Oval Office, then gone entirely, then a half mile away. After a few seconds of this, his map turned to unreadable static.

"Gizmo! What the hell is going on?" Gary demanded. His gray AI appeared on the dashboard in front of him.

"Looks like enemy interference on a scale we haven't seen before!" Gizmo said.

"That snake thing Anya mentioned," Gary grunted. "Is it just the map getting interfered with?"

"Negative! I'm currently locked out of accessing the RAC store and making any adjustments to your skills," Gizmo replied. "Long range communications are also out."

Gary grunted again. He didn't have any skill points left, and he'd spent most all of his RAC on his factory in Antarctica, so neither of those was an issue. And since Anya, Samaira, Arvo, and Pan were in the immediate vicinity, he didn't need the map to find them.

Long range comms being out was a problem though. Gary figured worst case, he could call another of the teams for back-up. There was the West Coast American team, and another three in Canada; but with the comms down, they were on their own.

"Any chance you've found the other four aliens yet?" Gary asked Gizmo.

"Negative! Before the interference started, their alien signals were overlapping heavily, which tells me that all six are within a one-mile radius," the AI replied.

Gary looked at his readouts again, and scanned the White House for life signs. It looked like Anya and the doc were the only people still in the White House. Anya's heat signature lit up like a small nova, along with a small section of hallway.

She must have found another alien.

Gary's hand flew across his dashboard, redirecting all the robots he'd had escorting people away from the White House to return and back up Samaira and Anya. A half dozen more armed battle-bots descended on the South Lawn and began firing lasers, micro-missiles, and railguns at the two aliens below, just as a third joined them.

It looked like some kind of short traffic light.

It dashed out of the White House from the blazing hot hallway Anya was in and immediately charged at Samaira with incredible swiftness. She barely managed to flip backwards out of the way, but then the traffic light alien's yellow light flashed and Samaira went flying to one side, directly into the firing line of the fire hydrant alien.

"Focus on the hydrant! Shield bots to cover Sam!" Gary shouted and a swarm of his droids unloaded a devastating salvo at the hydrant. His defensive droids on the roof abandoned the snipers there and rocketed toward Samaira, each one deploying a large kinetic force field several yards ahead of themselves and around her.

The fire hydrant was knocked to the side from the force of the joint attack, its body warping inward and tearing open from the countless projectiles slamming into its side. The brunt of its water cannon blast missed the shields, but the edge of it still hit. The forcefields around Samaira were just enough to divert the remainder of the attack, but not enough to stop it entirely.

The fields flickered, then fell and Samaira and the bots were thrown back in a torrent of water and through an already weakened wall of the White House. Chandrali snarled at the alien and hurried after Samaira, out of sight.

"Sam!" Gary shouted. The traffic light alien turned its attention to him, and its yellow light displayed a downward arrow. Gary and Pan both shouted in alarm as the truck plummeted to the ground hard enough to make the shocks creak. If Gary hadn't upgraded his truck into something much, much more, it would have shattered apart like a cheap toy from the impact.

Sensing their creator in danger, the droids entered their pre-programmed defensive protocol and converged on Gary, covering the truck in layers of forcefields and focusing their fire on the immediate threat of the traffic light. Three of them were taken out at once by a barrage of pink beams of light from the toilet alien's hands, another two by a devastating torrent of pressurized water.

"This is really scary!" Pan wailed as the truck shook and rattled under the force of attacks and the air boomed and rattled from the robots retaliatory fire.

"Well, we're on the ground little guy," Gary said and checked the truck's readouts. It was functional, but the hard drop and crash into the ground had caused the anti-grav discs in the tires to fracture. "And we're not going anywhere for a bit. Can you summon any of your golems?"

"Scared!" Pan shouted and then shrieked as the truck was hit by a focused beam of pink light that nearly broke through the forcefields. One of the defensive droids was blasted to bits and the field weakened even further.

"All right. Last resort," Gary said and flipped open a cover in the center of his steering wheel. A large red button shone beneath it. Gary pressed it, and the display on his dashboard flashed a message.

"Internal Battery at 75%. Primary cannon requires two minutes to charge. Divert power from shields to expedite charge?" the display read.

"Hell no," Gary said. The last remaining wave of his bots, another dozen or so, had arrived on the South Lawn to provide back-up. They would help, but at the rate they were going, they wouldn't last two minutes.

And there was still no sign of Samaira after the water cannon had hit her.

Gary put his hand on Pan's back, and the pangolin peered out from behind his claws.

"I don't mean to scare you little guy, but we might be in trouble," Gary said.

"Wh-what do we do?" Pan asked.

Gary didn't think just yelling at the pangolin to fight would help any. Besides, the critter was only at level 11. Gary was more than three times that level and he was barely holding on. Ditto for Samaira, assuming she wasn't dead already.

The truck rocked under another explosion and Gary winced. Several of his robots were sent flying into the air and in different directions by the traffic light alien. Gary looked at his dashboard and saw it had barely been half a minute.

He didn't need Pan to fight. He just needed him to buy them some time. Seconds.

The pangolin was just a kid.

It wasn't fair.

But it needed to be done.

"You know… if Anya were here, she'd kick these aliens' butts," Gary said. Pan uncurled himself a little and wiggled his nose.

"Y-yeah?" Pan asked and Gary nodded, trying to keep his voice calm and steady even as the truck shook under another blast.

"She's fighting right now. And I know you're scared, but so am I. So is she, probably. It's okay to be scared. But she needs your help."

"She does?"

"We all do."

"Wh-what can I do? I can't beat an alien! I can't fight!"

"Don't need you to. Can you dig?"

Pan nodded emphatically.

"Yes! I can do that lots!"

Gary took the next few precious seconds to explain what he needed the pangolin to do.

———

SAMAIRA STRUCK the side of the ruined East Wing and tumbled onto her side, dazed and reeling from the alien's attack. Her Lunar Shroud, a constantly moving piece of gossamer silver and aqua fabric pinned to one shoulder by a jeweled focus crystal, had protected her from the brunt of the damage, but she was still in bad shape. Her vision darkened at the edges, and the half-dozen or so aetheric spells she had been concentrating on began to fade along with her consciousness.

Chandrali bounded after her and stood over her in a defensive posture, but Samaira knew her cat wouldn't last long like that. Chandrali was more about running interference and distracting Samaira's opponents than dispatching them outright.

"Run," Samaira muttered and gave the tiger a shove. Chandrali growled at her and stayed put as Samaira fell back against the cracked rubble beneath her.

Something grabbed her hand, and Samaira tried to pull it away.

"Stay still, this will only take a moment," a familiar voice said.

Arvo Immonen.

There was a rush of pain in Samaira's back and side, and then it soothed at once.

"A few broken ribs, a concussion, and a fractured spine. Nothing I can't handle," Arvo said as Samaira's vision cleared. The room came back into focus around her, but the doctor was little more than a haze of shadow. Chandrali stared at him, but knew he was there to help and let him do his work.

"Ow," Samaira winced. The self-restoration runes and healing crystals on her outfit would have healed her in time, maybe a few minutes, but the doctor was doing it in seconds, and far better than what the aether would have been capable of at her level.

"Better?" Arvo asked.

"Yeah, much. Thank you," Samaira said and gave Chandrali a pat to let her know she was fine. The tiger bounded away and stood on guard near the crumbling wall. "Anya and Gary and Pan?"

"Gary and Pan are in the truck, but it's been downed. Anya isn't far, but she's in trouble. I have to go," Arvo said.

"Be careful!" Samaira said with a nod to the shadowy figure of the doctor as he all but vanished a split second later. Samaira darted to the wall and peered around the side.

Gary's truck had crashed to the South Lawn, and was surrounded by the remainder of his junk-bots, most of them focused on defense, but a handful of them giving the trio of aliens as much punishment as they could dish out.

The toilet had lost a few of its arms, and the white porcelain-like substance of its body was cracked. The hydrant's rubbery exterior appeared less stable than it had, and it had also lost a number of tentacles. The new alien, the stumpy traffic light, had one of its eyes damaged along with a mantis-like arm.

All of them were wounded, but they were still fighting, and they were winning. Four of Gary's defensive bots were destroyed by a barrage of pink energy beams from the toilet, while the traffic light zipped over to the robot with the largest railgun and managed to slice it into pieces faster than Samaira could blink.

"Draw the hydrant's attention," Samaira said to Chandrali. It was the heaviest hitter, and also the slowest to attack: whatever inhuman process it used to generate such destructive blasts of water took it roughly fifteen-to-thirty seconds to get ready, during which time it relied on its tentacles for attack and defense. Chandrali was fast, and could easily dodge the powerful but slow-to-fire water cannon blasts.

Chandrali flicked her ears, then bounded out from behind the cover of the wall and pounced at the fire hydrant immediately after it fired another powerful blast at Gary's truck. One of the forcefields around the vehicle flickered and then faded as the robot projecting it shorted out and exploded.

The toilet and the traffic light aliens both turned their attention to Chandrali just as Samaira sprinted out from behind cover and nocked an aetheric arrow into her bow.

The only thing inherent to the aether was how mutable it was. It was a purely malleable substance, nothing at all on its own, and therefore capable of being anything, doing whatever Samaira wished within the bounds of her abilities.

She had raised her intelligence stat significantly and her brain was now a multi-leveled powerhouse capable of concentrating intently on multiple tasks at once. Each aetheric manifestation, which she formed into arrows, could perform a number of functions, but each function required its own mental focus point.

Samaira could currently focus on imbuing six functions into any single arrow.

The toilet was the next heavy hitter, and it could fire much more quickly than the hydrant. It could defend as well, its long arms giving it the reach and maneuverability to defend the other two gnosiphages.

Samaira needed to get around its defenses, and then trap its arms, and damage it if she could.

Function one: Scatter. Her arrow would fly out as a single projectile, then scatter into a dozen smaller missiles upon contact with the pink energy shields the alien projected.

Function two: Ensnare. When the smaller projectiles hit their target, they would seek each other out with cords of powerful aetheric energy and anchor onto one another.

Function three: Constrict. The cords of aether would tighten and pull to each anchor point, binding the toilet's abundance of arms into a single, tangled mass.

Function four: Shock. The cords would then emit a hopefully paralyzing amount of electrical energy that would damage the toilet, or at least shock it enough into immobility or buy her a few seconds to ready another arrow and target it or the traffic light with a purely destructive shot and do some real damage.

Functions five and six would be used to reinforce functions two and three, strengthening the durability of the aetheric cords and keeping the toilet's arms bound.

It took Samaira less than a second to summon the aether to her. The invisible currents swirled to her in a surge as she formed them into the arrow she needed, pulled the glowing bowstring to her ear, and fired.

The arrow whistled as it sliced through the air between her and the toilet alien. It raised its hands in front of it to form a half-dome shield of pink light, which the arrow struck. As planned, it shattered into a dozen smaller shafts of pale blue light. Each one arced up and around the shield... and then shot straight up into the air, where they vanished. With their secondary function failed, the aetheric arrows dissipated.

The traffic light alien had focused its attention on Samaira's arrow, and the glowing yellow light/eye had transformed into an "Up," sign pointing at the sky.

"You!" Samaira shouted and flipped over a lance of pink energy the toilet shot at her. She nocked another arrow, this one designed to seek out the traffic light regardless of its location, and explode on impact. Samaira layered multiple functions to focus directly on the traffic light, and fired.

The yellow light/eye, flashed a sideways arrow symbol, but Samaira's aetheric missile continued forward regardless and exploded in a burst of azure light. The alien was thrown back, its single mantis-limb slashing at the air.

Samaira didn't waste her opening.

She nocked a third arrow, the design of which was the same as her original idea for the toilet—ensnare and shock—and fired again.

It worked.

The alien raised its shields, and Samaira's arrow shattered, burst around it, and connected with the numerous arms. Threads of light spun around the arms and snapped around them, then sent bolts of crackling electricity coursing through the toilet.

The electrical currents spread across the puddles created by the fire hydrant, shocking the traffic light alien and the hydrant itself as well.

"Chandrali!" Samaira shouted. Her tiger saw what was happening, and leaped away before she too was given a nasty jolt.

The energy in her ensnaring and shocking arrow wasn't infinite. She was only able to fill each arrow with so much of the aether. And while the toilet was struggling, it was strong enough to snap one, then two of the glowing cords that held it.

"Gary! Hurry!" Samaira said.

The last of her glowing cords snapped even as Samaira readied another arrow. She had used so much of the aether in the vicinity already, and she was having to pull more from farther and farther away, taxing herself more for less as the fight continued.

It was also taking longer to create her arrows, as the aether had to be pulled from greater distances. She had to either compromise and make weaker arrows from less aether, or wait longer until she could accumulate enough of the ephemeral substance.

The toilet aimed several of its skinless, spindly hands at her, and a half-dozen orbs of pink light condensed and prepared to fire. Chandrali was knocked aside by one of the fire hydrant's tentacles, and the alien ignored the big cat in favor of turning its deadly water cannon toward Samaira.

Huge, misshapen forms of earth and grass sprang up out of the ground and piled onto the toilet and the hydrant, at least seven of them all together. The toilet panicked as its arms were pulled in different directions and its beams of light lanced harmlessly into the sky. The hydrant's water blast missed Samaira by several feet and destroyed whatever was left of the wall behind her.

"Pan!" Samaira said and looked around, but couldn't see the pangolin. Was he still in the truck? No, he said he had to be touching the ground to use his powers.

That was when she noticed a not-so-subtle lump moving around beneath the cratered surface of the lawn. It darted back and forth and away from the aliens with surprising speed. The traffic light alien, glowing green now, ran toward Samaira and promptly fell into a large sinkhole that appeared beneath it, bashing itself against the side with its own momentum.

"Pan! I love you!" Samaira laughed.

"Sam! Just pin them down!" Gary's voice echoed from a loud-speaker on one of his few surviving drones. "Do whatever you can to keep them from running and then get clear with Pan! Ten seconds!"

"No problem," Samaira panted and then whistled at Chandrali. Her tiger sprang to her at once and she sprang onto her back as she used as much aether as she could gather to create a network of powerful aetheric anchors and chains to hold the trio of aliens.

The golems Pan had created were helping, but weak. They lasted a few seconds at most, but more were summoned as soon as they fell. There was no way the earthen figures could win against the aliens, but they were an excellent distraction.

Samaira let out a low grunt of effort as she fired her arrow, and all three aliens were bound to each other and the ground around them.

The hood of Gary's truck split down the middle, then opened to reveal something that looked like a modified jet engine and a snub-nosed battleship cannon. A white glow blossomed in the throat of the cannon's barrel, and a deafening hum of energy filled the air.

"Pan!" Samaira yelled and she and Chandrali sprang toward the moving mound of dirt and grass. She extended her hand, and a claw popped up from below as she and her tiger flew overhead. She gripped the pangolin firmly and yanked him up and out with all of her strength and Chandrali's momentum. Pan squealed in surprise and fear as the three of them bounded away at speed.

"Get off my lawn," Gary said over the loudspeaker, and then the cannon on his truck fired. Samaira didn't dare look back. Everything around her turned white, her shadow stretched out in front of her. A powerful shove at her back sent her, Chandrali, and Pan flying.

Samaira clutched Pan close to her as the pangolin curled into a defensive ball, and held onto Chandrali as best she could with her legs. The tiger flipped with the force of the explosion and landed on her feet, Samaira and Pan still secure on her back.

"Whoa," Samaira said as the white light faded and revealed a huge column of smoke and debris rising from a newly formed hole in the lawn. Calling the ruined expanse of ground in front of the White House a "lawn," anymore was something of a joke: it was nothing but a single massive crater surrounded by torn up hills of earth and scattered with the white rubble of the building itself.

Something boxy floating in the sky caught Samaira's attention and she looked up.

The cab of Gary's truck had somehow jettisoned itself from the frame of the vehicle, and was now floating down to earth on a parachute that had deployed from its roof. Gary leaned out the window and waved down at Samaira.

"I think I got 'em!" Gary said.

"No kidding," Samaira replied. A series of explosions and flashes of light from the far side of the White House drew her attention.

"Oh no, Anya!" Pan said. Gary's makeshift escape pod landed with a thud a few feet away, and he hopped out at once.

"I'm out of bots and my truck is slag. That cannon was a one-shot," he said.

"I-I'm really tired," Pan said, panting and shaking. Samaira glanced down at him and saw the pangolin was barely holding it together. He had also wet himself at some point.

"He's still only level 11, I think," Gary said. "God knows what distracting those freaks took out of him. But hey, you did really good, little guy. Damn proud of you."

"Th-thanks," Pan said, and then passed out in Samaira's arms and began to snore.

"Get him and yourself out of here," Samaira said. "Chandrali and I will go help Anya."

"There's still three left," Gary replied and he took Pan and then grunted as he had to set him down on the ground. Samaira had enhanced her strength a bit with her charms and clothes, but Gary was still just a normal man without his robots.

"Will you be okay?" she asked and he nodded.

"I'll figure something out. Just go, and try not to die."

"That's the plan!" Samaira said and then sped away with Chandrali.

37

octor Arvo Immonen had never been fond of violence.

He had performed many surgeries and operations on his patients throughout the years, which had required him to slice into their bodies and remove the maladies that plagued them. Blood did not upset him on its own, nor the sight of organs—whether whole or in pieces from some trauma—because those things on their own were only natural. The body, even injured or suffering from illness, was nothing to be repulsed by: only healed and mended and made whole once more.

But doing injury to a body, the act itself, made his stomach knot.

It's why he had been one of the few medical students operating on their first cadaver who did not vomit, but a drunken brawl at a bar later that same evening made him sick for hours afterward.

When the Archive had come, the mere idea of taking some sort of battle skill made him nauseous for the better part of an hour. He couldn't imagine the idea of taking a skill that would let him shoot lasers or punch through a human as if they were so much wet paper. When he later learned of the alien invasion, he understood how those things might be necessary, but did not regret his choices of healing skills.

If they were in a war, they would need healers and fighters both.

So when everybody met in Greenland and he met the other hosts, he decided to go with Anya and the other Americans. They all seemed rather keen on fighting the aliens (except for the pangolin), and Arvo was equally keen to keep them alive.

Except that he had spent the overwhelming majority of the invasion avoiding the gnosiphages. His one non-healing skill, living shadow, allowed him to avoid detection and slip away from danger. It was good in the short-term, good when he was alone and needed to get away, but in a fight that required he stay and tend to the wounded, it wasn't ideal.

Samaira had come flying through the air, bashing herself against a ruined section of the White House, and practically fell right in front of him.

His body scan skill told him that she had been badly injured: broken ribs and a fractured spine, as well as internal bleeding, a concussion, and a real danger of a ruptured lung if one of her broken ribs jabbed it too hard.

Living shadow made him somewhat hazy to look at under direct light, more like a smudge in the background of one's sight than anything else. Samaira jumped as his indistinct figure took her hand.

"Stay still, this will only take a moment," he said.

The body manipulation and matter generation (biological) skills were more than enough to knit Samaira back together, as well as relieve her of any initial fatigue she may have been experiencing.

The matter absorption (biological) skill removed any loose bone shards or blood that wasn't where it was supposed to be. Arvo took the wayward material into himself, and broke them down into their basic components to refill the energy he had expended restoring her bones and organs and muscles.

"A few broken ribs, a concussion, and a fractured spine. Nothing I can't handle," he said.

"Ow," Samaira replied as she sat up. While she would technically be fine, it wasn't unusual for some of the pain of the injury to linger for several seconds after the healing. As far as Arvo could theorize, it was similar to the phantom pain one might experience after losing a limb.

"Better?" Arvo asked.

"Yeah, much. Thank you," Samaira said and gave her huge tiger a pat. The tiger bounded away and took up a defensive posture near the crumbling wall. "Anya and Gary and Pan?"

"Gary and Pan are in the truck, but it's been downed. Anya isn't far, but she's in trouble."

His body scan skill was effective at a range of a couple dozen meters when he focused on it. He focused on the intense heat signature he knew to be Anya, and body scan informed him that her body temperature was fluctuating, and her adrenaline was spiking.

"I have to go," Arvo finished, and then hurried away.

"Be careful!" Samaira said after him. He hoped she, her tiger, Gary, and Pan would be all right. They had each other, but Anya had been fighting alone for several minutes already.

Arvo sped through the ruins of the White House, living shadow allowing him to move with more speed and agility than he normally would. Some doors through the expansive Presidential residence had been locked, or otherwise blocked by debris, and Arvo had to wind his way through the rubble.

He was further slowed by helping any injured stragglers he came across: White House staff that had been concussed by flying debris, or wounded by an errant alien attack. Healing them only took seconds, but every second was vital. He made sure they could find their way out before continuing toward Anya.

Anya had moved away from her initial position, and her body had equalized for a moment. Then something exploded and Arvo sensed a number of small injuries on her. She had found another alien.

He scrambled through a broken doorway, and paused. He was only a dozen meters or so from her, just out a broken window and onto the North Lawn, but his scan of her brought him up short.

Something was wrong with her brain.

Arvo couldn't read her thoughts, but body scan could read the basic functions and metabolic processes of it. It had been pumping adrenaline, like any brain would when engaged in a fight, but then it just stopped.

Now her brain was releasing an unusually high amount of

dopamine and serotonin: very odd to happen during such an intensely stressful and dangerous situation. Her heartbeat slowed down to something more appropriate for somebody in a deep sleep, and that intense heat at her center cooled.

Arvo slid over to the broken window, hoping his semi-invisible appearance would be enough to keep him hidden.

She was stuck in some kind of gel or sludge, and facing three aliens. One of them looked like a copy machine, the other was a huge floating rug with strange patterns on it, and the third was a towering snake creature that Arvo recognized from Anya's description of it.

She had mentioned it to him one night after they had spent the day patrolling, and he had been simultaneously fascinated and terrified. A gnosiphage that adapted as it fought, changed its body on the fly to meet immediate needs, and could actually talk, albeit very little.

Arvo glanced at the rug, at its swirling patterns, and then looked away. He had started to lose focus, enter something like REM sleep. He looked up at Anya, careful to keep his focus on her. She stood hunched and unmoving, held up by the hardened gel around her.

The aliens had hypnotized her or put her into a sort of fugue state, and they were seconds away from killing her. The huge serpent gnosiphage loomed over her, its pharaonic hood spread wide, the dark gray armor of it gleaming in the late afternoon sun.

All three aliens were bunched somewhat closely together, just feet away from each other and Anya. They appeared to be savoring the moment before they killed her.

Arvo had an idea.

It was risky, and certain death if it failed but he had to try.

All he needed was a second.

Maybe two.

Arvo kicked off his shoes and took off his socks.

The doctor calmed himself, forced his own adrenaline levels down to manageable levels, and then made his move.

He jumped out of the broken window, still almost entirely invisible, and was pleased to note that the aliens did not turn to face him. The snake might have twitched as if it sensed something, but kept its focus on Anya. It placed its clawed hands on her shoulders, then opened its mouth wide to bite her head and neck off.

Arvo ran at full speed, then slid on the grass between the snake and the copy machine, and underneath the floating rug.

One bare foot touched Anya's exposed hand, while the other reached up and poked the rug, while both his hands reached out as far as he could stretch them and grabbed the copy machine and snake.

While body scan did not work on the aliens at range for some reason, it did work once he was in physical contact with them. Their bodies were bizarre, protean structures made up of a staggering variety of organic materials that Arvo had no time to process, but they also had rudimentary nervous systems and a sort of brain. Curiously, their brains weren't entirely localized but spread throughout parts of their body in concentrated knots of neurons and synapses. Some parts had denser neural pathways than others, and of course they had organs and bones (except the rug) though both of these were so literally alien in composition that it made Arvo reel. However, when it came down to just the basics, they were just walking (or floating or slithering) brains.

Beyond that was something Arvo could not understand at first. It was an entirely foreign, unknown sensation to him that almost made him recoil away from it on instinct. Had he not been so intent on his course of action, and had death not been so certain otherwise, he would have.

None of the aliens were singular.

He had been thinking of the gnosiphages as a group of monsters, each one a single entity to be faced and defeated.

But they were all one single thing. They were all sharing the same consciousness, each one just a tiny fragment of the larger whole. The alien consciousness forked thousands of times over, splintering to each individual gnosiphage, but remaining linked to the whole.

Arvo felt, as the aliens felt, where the others of their kind were across the globe, just as he felt the inner workings of their individual bodies. Body scan had linked him into the entire alien network of consciousness.

The snake was different.

It too was just another part of the whole, but that wasn't all. The rug, the copy machine, they connected to each other and every other alien on the planet, which included the snake.

But the snake connected to something else.

Arvo felt the stream of its consciousness stretching up, up, up, into the sky, through the atmosphere, and away to something vast and terrible. He knew if he followed that, it might break him. Whatever the alien consciousness was, above all else, it was unmistakeably murderous.

It was like staring into the throat of a volcano, or the eye of a hurricane. There was only the primal capacity to destroy there, to unleash untold destruction.

Thankfully, whether due to the current skill level of body scan or something else, Arvo's ability to sense the connection faded once the line of alien thought left the atmosphere.

He was able to tell that the snake was connected to two other such aliens on Earth at the moment.

All of this information rushed through Arvo in less time than it took to take a breath. He felt it, absorbed it, rather than thought it. Each of the aliens took a moment to look down at the shoeless doctor, spread eagle below them, hands and legs outstretched so as to touch them.

"Hello," he said, and then caused each one of their nervous systems to seize up. The rug stiffened, the snake hissed and arched its back, and the copy machine began vomiting blank papers in a white cascade.

His particular combination of skills allowed him to heal most anything: body manipulation let him alter a body's existing structure and accelerate natural healing processes, while his biological matter generation and absorption abilities let him create new, healthy flesh and remove any damaged tissue or foreign bodies.

He had taken it to heal, not harm.

He had avoided thinking too much about how the abilities could be used to cause damage, until now.

Arvo caused multiple tumors to blossom within each of the aliens' bodies, internal cysts full of spiky bone growths that pierced and tore, an excess of acid bile that seared them from the insides, and worse. All the while he absorbed what he could from their defenses: their dense bones weakened, their armor cracked and became brittle, their arteries clogged.

And then there was Anya: she wasn't physically damaged too much, but the chemicals in her brain had been thrown out of balance by whatever hypnotic process that rug had subjected her to. The rug itself had fallen flat on the ground beside Arvo, his hand still on it as it twitched and writhed, its patterns flashing across its surface in nonsense visual noise.

"Uhhh," Anya said, drooling a bit. Arvo tried to balance her chemical output as best he could, as well as encourage the glowing, fiery heart in her chest to kindle faster. It was a curious organ, if it could even be called that. It was a biological part of Anya, but it was also made of material he could not identify: like a living crystal, maybe.

He sensed a consciousness from it as well: not necessarily hostile or friendly, merely present and eager, almost excited.

What's up, Doc? A smooth, amused voice echoed in Arvo's head as he sensed the Sun's Heart and kindled it to life.

"Anya!" Arvo said, ignoring the voice as he began to sweat. The snake hissed at him, and Arvo made all of its muscles seize up in debilitating cramps and spasms that would have caused an elephant to snap its own spine in half.

It wasn't enough. The snake was too strong. It gritted its teeth, glowing blue eyes wide and hateful as its body contorted and inexorably began to resist Arvo's attempts at controlling it.

"Anya!" Arvo said again, more of a gasp. The level of effort required to keep all three aliens under control was making his heart race. Another few seconds, maybe, and then he would pass out.

"Arvo?" Anya asked, then blinked and looked around.

"Help!" the doctor wheezed.

Anya didn't respond. Her entire body ignited in a swirling aura of flames, and Arvo winced as his foot was singed.

"Sorry, Doc! I'll take it from here!" Anya said, and some unseen force pushed and threw Arvo through the air and across the lawn. He landed on the soft grass with a gentle thump, cushioned by the same unseen force, then rolled to a stop among the bushes. He allowed himself only a moment to catch his breath and make sure Anya was all right.

It was the only time in his life he had ever been comforted by the sight of a raging inferno.

————

ANYA HAD BEEN SWIMMING inside a sea of colors, but then they had all blended together in a gray haze and she hadn't really been able to think of anything.

What was happening?

She had something important to do.

Was it studying? Did she have to study for a test?

No. Maybe it was something about her mother. Her mother was angry about something she and her little brother had done and...

That wasn't it either.

Her muddled thoughts became even more confused, until there was no thought at all. There was only a lingering anxiety that she should be doing something, and that something else very bad was about to happen.

Then a bright star of clarity shone through the enshrouding fog of confusion. Her head began to clear and she snapped back to reality.

Arvo Immonen lay on the ground beneath her, barefoot, stretched out like a starfish, and sweating heavily. He had his hand and both bare feet on each of the aliens, all of them spasming and writhing in some kind of seizure.

"Arvo?" she asked and blinked down at him.

"Help!" the doctor wheezed.

Anya didn't really understand what was happening, but she got the basics, and knew what she had to do.

She needed to light shit on fire.

Welcome back, little ember. I like your doctor friend, the voice of the bird said.

The Sun's Heart swelled as Anya came back to herself, and the air immediately around her body ignited in a swirling, pulsing aura of fire.

Arvo winced and drew away instinctively. Anya pushed and then hurled the doctor away with a surge of localized gravity, aiming him for some soft-looking bushes and grass far away from the conflict that was about to happen.

"Sorry, Doc! I'll take it from here!" Anya said and willed a swelling vortex of gravity at her feet, bringing the aliens in close as their seizures subsided. She condensed the heat and the oxygen around her into tight balls, and then ignited them like dozens of little miniature novas. The air around her became a swirling hell of crushing force and searing flames. The lawn for several yards beyond the visible fire turned to ash in an instant, and the nearby asphalt of the road took on the consistency of taffy.

Anya had a moment of concern as she remembered to make sure she didn't ignite the President of the United the States. The nearest heat source was Arvo, and he was well out of range. Anya assumed Hanover and the rest had gotten to safety while the aliens had been preoccupied with her.

The rug alien was turned to little else but crumbling black fragments of ash and dust. The copy machine wailed and tried to pull itself away, but Anya's gravity well yanked it back. Its armor, much weaker now for some reason, cracked and glowed under the heat, cooking whatever flesh and bone might lay inside.

The snake was less troubled.

It had a moment coming out of its seizure where it recoiled from the heat and tried to back away, but then glowing rings of pale blue light surrounded its wrists and encircled its head. It waved its hands, and the three circles broke, and Anya grunted with surprise as a shockingly cold wave of force hit her, threw her back, and she brought herself to a halt hovering in the air across the expanse of the North Lawn.

"What the hell was that?" Anya asked. Her fire had been dispersed in a moment, all the heat just gone, and the cyclone of gravitational talons crushing the aliens had been lost when her concentration had wavered.

The lawn around the snake was frosted over, and the air had

become cold enough that Anya's breath billowed out of her in thick clouds.

"Surprised it took you this long," Anya said. During their last fight it had managed to defend itself against her fire attacks, but not counter it directly. It had come up with other foils to her: acid to chew at her regeneration skill, incredible speed to keep up with her in the Shadow Ray, armor that repelled heat accelerants, and attacks that would keep her at range, where she was weakest.

But it had never adapted fully to counter the Flame Dominion.

Until now.

"Thief," the snake said in a rolling, rumbling hiss. "Ours. All ours. Not yours to take."

"What the hell are you?" Anya asked.

"Hunger," it said. It coiled its tail like a spring and then rocketed at her faster than a bullet train. Anya diverted the snake's course around her with a deflective field of force even as she dodged aside. The snake was too fast for her and had far too much momentum to simply stop or throw it around with gravity like she had with Arvo. The best she could do at the moment was divert it and keep herself from getting smashed.

That was when the copy machine got back into the fight. A dozen pieces of paper appeared around Anya, each with a rune printed on its surface, and each one activated before she could react.

Blinding light, freezing cold, a clap of sound, and more surrounded Anya and wracked her body with pain. Anya squeezed her eyes shut and flew up into the air, away from the aliens, blind to what was around her but knowing she needed to make some distance.

A claw, harder than steel and immeasurably sharper, grabbed her ankle. Anya screamed as the claws sliced through her armored boot and into her flesh. She still couldn't see clearly, but a familiar acidic burn told her what had ensnared her.

This was a bad move on the snake's part. Anya didn't need to see if the alien held her. She turned her focus downward, and the air gasped as all the nearby oxygen was pulled into the sudden swell of fire that exploded outward.

The claw loosened just enough for Anya to dart free as her vision came back. The snake glared at her as it lunged forward again, mouth open, and a gland in the back of its throat swelled with green bile. Anya darted to one side as a jet of pressurized acid shot past her face, then grunted as another rune from the copy machine flashed.

Cords of energy emerged from the rune, and tied Anya up as tightly as a rabbit in a snare. She squirmed against them, her muscles swelling and bulging against the cords, and she tried to burn them, but they didn't react.

Aether? Anya thought. They had a faint, familiar glow to them, just like Samaira's workings of the magical substance, though it glowed a furious red as opposed to Samaira's calming blue. The copy machine's attacks were so varied because it was using the aether, using runes like how Samaira used her bow.

Good to know, though not very useful at the moment. Anya didn't know shit about the aether or how to manipulate it. She roared and pushed against the glowing cords of energy that bound her. They cut into her skin, but they were giving way.

Not fast enough. The snake slithered to her as spines sprouted from the sides of its long tail, each one glistening with acid. If it got its tail around her, those spines would dig into her, melt her from the inside out.

She started to fly away, just to put more distance between herself and the serpent, when a huge flash of white light blossomed from behind the White House. A tremendous gasp of air blotted out all other sounds as everything—from trees to rubble to ruined SUVs to Anya and the aliens themselves—was sucked toward the explosion. Silence filled the space left by the gasp of air for a single tranquil moment, then a deafening crash and rumble obliterated it as everything that had been pulled toward the explosion of light reversed course and went flying through the air.

The snake and the copy machine both let out inhuman screeches of rage as they ignored Anya and shielded themselves against the force of the blast. Anya, still tied up with aetheric cords, tumbled across the lawn and into the bushes nearby where Arvo appeared at her side, his hand on her bicep.

The damage and exhaustion she had acquired during the battle faded in an instant.

"Thank you," Anya grunted and Arvo just nodded in response.

"Three aliens are gone!" Felix said. "Only the copy machine and the snake are left!"

"Three?" Anya gaped.

"I'm hoping that means the explosion was from our fellow hosts," Arvo said. A moment later Samaira appeared at the top of the White House (or what remained of it), glimmering hair fluttering in the wind, Chandrali beside her.

"Look out, Sam!" Anya shouted, then turned to Arvo to tell him to get clear, but the doctor had already vanished.

Samaira aimed her bow and arrow at Anya and fired. The arrow burst against Anya's chest, and the glowing cords of aetheric energy the copy machine had bound her in faded away into gossamer strands no more binding than cotton thread.

"It's just us!" Samaira said as she leaped down and twirled away from a hail of stingers the snake launched at her, then retaliated with a salvo of glowing arrows. Chandrali sprang at the copy machine and began clawing and tearing at it.

Anya didn't stop to wonder what Samaira meant. Were Pan and Gary dead? Wounded?

No time to think about it.

The copy machine glowed with light, and then it copied itself. One became two, became four, became eight. The air was a sudden whirlwind of rune-enhanced paper, dozens, maybe hundreds of them, each firing off a spell that would harm or hinder.

"No you don't!" Anya said and summoned a tidal wave of heat from within herself that she sent just a few feet ahead of her as she flew across the lawn. The ground melted or ignited beneath her as she pushed the burning wall of heat ahead of her. Any rune-enhanced paper that came near her was scorched to ash, but for every one she destroyed, there were two or three dozen more being printed off and activating their runes.

Some of the papers even seemed to be acting as heat sinks of some kind: their runes glowed when she neared and then sucked away the heat Anya pumped out.

"Behind you!" Samaira shouted and fired an arrow past Anya's shoulder. The snake bellowed as the arrow hit it in the third eye in its forehead, and a creeping crystalline growth began to spread across its face. It backed away and began to claw at the crystal growths sprouting over its face, now creeping into its mouth and stabbing it from within.

Anya ignored the snake for the moment and tackled the nearest copy machine. It felt softer than before, as if duplicating itself had weakened its structure somehow. She punched right through its outer shell, making it crack and splinter, then ripped it in half with a bellow.

"The printers are using the aether!" Samaira said as she fired more crystalline arrows at the snake while Chandrali mauled a copy machine. Samaira fired several arrows around all three of them, creating protective domes that diverted the myriad attacks coming from the copy machine's printed runes.

"Yeah, I guessed! The snake, it's got some kind of skill that's canceling out my fire attacks. I don't know how it's doing it," Anya said as she seized another copy machine in gravitational talons, then crushed it flat against the ground and delivered a flaming drop kick for good measure.

The copy machine continued to make more copies of itself, more papers unleashing deadly attacks of lightning, ice, a hail of metallic splinters, the same pink energy the toilet alien had used, and more. But the copies were now starting to visually decay as well: they began to look lumpy and misshapen, as if they were made of soft clay.

The snake bellowed as it finally broke free of Samaira's crystal attack and surged toward them. Samaira and Anya both turned to attack it, with aether and flame, but the snake gestured with its four clawed hands and the rings of negative blue light surrounded it once more.

Samaira's glowing arrow vanished in a flurry of blue sparks and Anya's fire snuffed out, and the temperature around all of them dropped another several degrees.

"Look out!" Anya said and shielded Samaira with her body and a repulsive field as the snake unleashed a storm of thin acid barbs. Anya cried out as a few of them hit her arm and shoulder.

They weren't just barbs this time.

They were some kind of worm, wriggling of their own accord and burrowing into her skin. Anya screamed and ripped one of them out, but two more managed to get under her skin and begin to inject their corrosive acid into her bloodstream.

Anya doubled over, fighting the acid as best she could. Samaira shot some kind of healing arrow at her, but its effects were minimal.

Then a hand touched her shoulder, and the acid and the worms both vanished from her system. Arvo knelt beside her and turned to flee, but the snake's head followed his movements.

The snake spun toward Arvo's general direction and lunged across the lawn, covering a span of almost half a football field in a blink.

"No!" Anya said and tried to intercept it. The snake's claws extended out toward the doctor's vague form as he threw himself away. His hazy figure coalesced into view as the claws raked his right side, slashing open his chest, ripping away the flesh and muscles, and taking his entire arm off.

Anya tackled the serpent, grappling with it as the two tumbled and spun. More acidic barbs sprouted from its body, stabbing her and making her skin sear, but she held tight. She didn't know the extent of Arvo's healing abilities, but she guessed that if the snake tore him to pieces, that would be the end of it.

Anya dodged a slash at her head from one of the snake's claws, then grabbed it by the wrist and turned her palm into a furnace that began to melt through its armor. The snake used its other arms to make a gesture and the nullifying light appeared around its wrists and head again. Anya's fire was snuffed out, and she summoned more to replace it, faster, her body becoming a conduit for the Flame Dominion.

Anya held onto the snake's arm, ducked behind it, put her other palm against the back of its shoulder, and yanked back as hard as she could. The snake hissed as she snapped one of its arms, but the other three reached behind it and slashed at her face and back and she was forced to jump backwards.

"Copy machine's down!" Samaira said behind her.

"What about Arvo?" Anya asked but kept her eyes on the snake. It was looking between her and Samaira, and its obvious lack of backup.

"Healing himself. It's bad, though."

"Can you tie this thing up for me?"

"I can try but I'm running on empty," Samaira said, and Anya heard the exhaustion in her voice. She was aware that her own resources were dwindling. The restorative crystal at her chest was half-full. If she ran out of juice now, that would be it.

And the snake looked like it was considering retreating again.

It would be easy to let it run, heal the survivors, and regroup.

But the same was true for the snake and the other gnosiphages.

They had already killed several people in the White House. Arvo was seriously wounded, nearly dead.

They might not be so lucky next time. The snake might come with even more back-up, or catch them when they were separated.

The snake glared at Anya, then turned to flee.

"Fuck that," Anya said and launched herself at it like a living cannonball. One of Samaira's arrows flew past her and struck the snake, then transformed into countless threads of blue light that trapped its arms against its sides. Anya reinforced the threads by wrapping her arms around the snake's torso as much as she could, pressing it to her with her own strength and Singularity's Grasp.

Every time she launched an external attack at the creature, it used that nullifying light to cancel it. However, her Sun's Heart never lost any of its heat, nor did Anya's body react to the warmth-erasing cold the snake put out. So Anya did not ignite the air around her, or the space between her and the snake. The Sun's Heart beat within her, faster and brighter, as she focused all of its energy within herself.

Her veins glowed through her skin, and then her skin itself became radiant. The alien tried to move its arms, but Anya and Samaira's cords held them close. It still had that halo of the nullifying light around its head, however, and Samaira's cords vanished in an instant.

The temperature around Anya dropped dramatically.

But her inner fire did not. The heat she had inside of her rushed into the cold vacuum immediately, and continued to burn the snake.

"Got you, asshole," Anya said, then winced as acidic barbs burst from its chest and stomach and stabbed her in the throat, and sides.

She held on.

"You think you're the only one that comes up with new tricks on the fly?" Anya rasped at it, the pain of the acid becoming easier to ignore as she burned, hotter and hotter. There was a thought, far back in her mind, that she must have some upper limit, and could easily turn herself into nothing but a cinder if she wasn't careful. Her skin, her muscle, all of it was tingling from the heat, and starting to hurt. Even her regalia, which was supposed to be entirely fireproof, was starting to smoke and crisp along the edges.

But being careful wasn't something she was concerned about at the moment. If it was, she wouldn't have flung herself at the snake. She wouldn't have done a lot of the things she had.

Anya kindled the fire further, and the snake and everything around her was bathed in the blazing solar glow of her. The snake writhed in agony, desperate to escape the localized inferno she had become.

Yes, little ember! More! Brighter! BRIGHTER! the voice of the Flame Dominion crowed.

"I got one other skill I've been working on, y'know?" Anya asked the snake. "I got really fucking good at hugging."

Anya grinned savagely as the snake howled and screamed, its plated armor glowing white hot. The burn of the acid was a distant memory now, evaporated from her veins as her blood boiled and became liquid fire itself. She broke the snake's back in her arms, dug her glowing fingers through its fractured armor and into its guts.

It tried to wriggle free, but she kept it close to her with her strength and the pull of her Singularity's Grasp. The air itself had become weighted, pressing herself and the snake down into a crater that grew deeper by the second.

And then Anya's arms closed together as she hugged her way through the snake's torso, crushing it in half.

It screamed.

It hissed.

It burned.

It was finished.

Anya wasn't.

She grabbed the snake's lower jaw and tore it away, then grabbed its monstrous head between her hands, and created a single point of extreme gravity between them.

The snake's head flattened between her hands like an empty soda can.

Anya didn't recall what happened next. One second she was shouting into the snake's ruined face, her Sun's Heart singing to her, the bird laughing uproariously in the back of her mind, and then she heard somebody yelling.

Samaira.

"Anya!" Samaira said from above her.

Very high above her.

Anya stood at the bottom of what was now some kind of pit, rather than a crater. The inside of it was entirely black, charred earth from top to bottom. A pile of ashes and charred remains that might once, with a lot of imagination, have been the snake lay around her.

"Stop! It's dead. I think you got it," Samaira said.

Anya looked up at Samaira, then down at the unrecognizable pile of black dust and crumbling remains beneath her.

"Fuck yeah I did," Anya said, and then face-planted into the burning dirt.

38

Anya snorted and snapped her eyes open as she sat bolt upright. Her fists were up and both ignited with whirling wreathes of fire.

"Whoa!" Samaira said and jumped away from her. "Easy! It's okay!"

"Samaira," Anya muttered, then blinked and looked around as she lowered her fists.

She sat on the ruined and blasted lawn just outside the White House, or what remained of it. Arvo lay a few feet away from her, snoring loudly. His wounds had been healed, his arm regrown and was much pinker than the rest of his skin. Fire fighters, police, and other emergency services hurried around, tending to civilians and setting up perimeters around the rubble.

"Anya!" a tiny voice said, and Pan waddled over to her, his arms wide. He fell against her side as he hugged her and she gave him a gentle squeeze back. "I did it! I fought! Kind of. It was really scary and a lot of my golem friends got smushed and I hid a lot but Gary said I did good and I helped and—"

"Easy little guy," Gary said as he sauntered up behind him and smiled down at Anya. He was covered in soot and grime and machine oil, his glasses slightly bent and one of the lenses cracked, but he looked fine otherwise.

"Everybody's alive?" Anya asked.

"Well, not quite," Samaira said and stroked Chandrali beside her. "A couple secret service agents, a tourist, and some White House staff were killed by stray alien attacks."

"God dammit," Anya said.

"Kid, it could've been a lot worse. A lot. Hundreds of people were here. Thousands more in the streets and buildings around the White House. We saved a lot of folks today," Gary said.

"I know, but…"

"But nothing. It's war. The aliens killed those people, not you, so don't start blaming yourself for what the monsters do. You did damn fine work."

Anya looked around at the ruins of the White House and the many, many, many smoking craters and patches of burnt grass and trees. She then looked up at Gary and cocked an eyebrow.

"They can rebuild the damn White House. The Canadians burned it down in 1812, so maybe it was overdue for some remodeling," Gary said. "Place still probably smelled like Lincoln's farts, anyway."

"Technically it was the British that burned it down," Samaira said.

"Whatever," Gary shrugged and Anya chuckled.

"Why is Arvo asleep?" Anya said and glanced down at the doctor.

"Guy passed out after he healed you up a minute ago. Put his hand on your shoulder and then flopped over and started sawing logs. Can't blame him. Regrew most of his whole side and arm and probably saved everybody's ass."

"Saved me for damn sure. He did something to the aliens when they had me. We'd all be dead if he hadn't done that," Anya said. "What about the President? And MacDougal?"

"I texted MacDougal and told her the aliens were dead. She messaged me before you woke up and said that she and Hanover were in a hidden bunker somewhere outside the city. They'll contact us soon enough, but we should stick around for the time being," Samaira said.

"I just want to sleep for a week," Anya groaned. Her Sun's Heart was beating steadily, but it felt drained more than ever before. She doubted if she could summon enough fire to light a candle at the moment.

"Well, just sit tight for now. I'm gonna go dismantle some of the wrecked cars and get some robots back just in case," Gary said and nodded towards a no-longer-flaming pile of random SUV parts, then left with a wave.

"I can definitely do that," Anya said and flopped onto her back, arms and legs splayed out as she looked up at the sky. Samaira sighed and laid down beside her, Chandrali curled up on her chest. Pan stood watch over them, his tiny chest puffed out with bravado.

"Oh wow," Samaira said as she brought up her menu.

"What?" Anya asked.

"Check out your main menu."

Anya brought hers up and her eyes widened.

"Holy shit! Felix can you confirm this?"

"I sure can!" Felix said as they appeared. "You gained nine levels from defeating the six aliens. Most of that came from beating the snake."

Anya's main menu now showed her at level 41.

"I'm about the same," Samaira said and pointed at her screen, which showed her at level 39.

"Me too!" Pan said and his yellow menu screen displayed his current level at 27.

"Weren't you at level 11 before the fight?" Samaira asked and Pan nodded. "So why did you jump up so many more levels than Anya or I?"

"The Archive dispenses experience for defeated enemies to hosts within a given range. You were all pretty close by, so even though Pan didn't directly kill any aliens himself, he was close enough to get experience regardless. Also, it requires more experience to level-up the higher the level is, so Pan got a lot more of a boost since he was already pretty low."

"Makes sense, I suppose," Samaira said.

"Pretty standard in games and stuff," Anya confirmed. "Incentivizes a player to keep going after tougher and tougher challenges."

"Is that why the Engineers designed it this way? To make us want to fight meaner and stronger aliens?" Samaira wondered and Anya just shrugged.

"Who knows what those assholes think."

Her ear beeped.

"Felix?" she asked.

"Uh, it's them," the AI replied.

"Them? Them who? The Engineers?"

"Yeah. They—theeeyyyysssssshhhkhhhhhb," Felix's reply distorted into nonsense and his rose-shaped head turned into a jittering mess of static as he floated before her. Samaira's and Pan's AIs both appeared in similar states, without them being summoned. Arvo's AI, colored white, also appeared floating above his head even though the doctor remained sound asleep.

"Greetings Earth forms. Please confirm: is this one addressing Hosts Sol-3022, Sol-11405, Sol-2380, Sol-9331 and Sol-17652, local designation Anya Nowicki, Samaira Upadhyay, Pan, Arvo Immonen, and Gary Hendricks, respectively?" a somewhat familiar voice asked. Anya had heard it once before, in an empty lot in Jersey when all the shit had well and truly hit the fan.

"You're the Engineer. Or one of them, anyway," Anya said.

"Correct. This one is Initiate Engineer Red-507. Please confirm identities before further inquiries. Time of current communication window is uncertain."

"Identities confirmed. Arvo Immonen is currently unconscious and Gary Hendricks is... oh, hey Gary," Samaira said, then looked up as Gary jogged over. His gray AI floated at a steady distance in front of him, its head also converted to static.

"Please confirm expiration of gnosiphage local administrative overseer," Red-507 said.

"Of what?" Anya demanded.

"This gnosiphage," the Engineer replied and then each of their AIs converted to a rotating hologram of the snake alien. Anya shuddered.

"Yeah, it's fucking dead."

"It's coal dust is what it is," Gary said and laughed.

"This one has confirmed overseer expiration. Thank you."

"Don't you dare run off again!" Samaira snapped and Anya flinched at the sudden anger in her voice.

"Communication window is narrowing by the moment. Gnosiphage interference continues, but is disrupted by the loss of local overseer form. This one cannot control when—"

"Then be quiet and listen," Samaira said. "Can you unlock more points for us in the Archive? Anything that would let us be stronger and put the gnosiphages down for good?"

"Negative. Archive protocol forbids unlimited access. Further, too much skill data relayed to a single lifeform at once could have catastrophic effects to biological and psychological stability. The points and levels are a safety measure to ensure gradual, safe progression."

"Bullshit," Anya said.

"Translator error. Bovine fecal matter not relevant to previous statement. Please reiterate?"

"Forget it. You're saying that we can die if we use too many points at once? How many is too many?"

"The current maximum amount of levels gained at one time should not exceed 30 for host comfort and safety. There is also an upper limit of data a given lifeform can sustain. Current level cap for Earth lifeforms is 50. Currently, Engineer overseers are debating raising the cap to 100. This one is not privy to the current status of the debate."

"Great," Gary said. "I'm just about at the current cap. Got a truckload of levels from the fight."

"Can you do anything else to help us? Please. Most of the hosts here are dead," Samaira said.

"This one and several other Engineers are using the current communications window to alter the Archive's signal. This will effectively scramble it, and deny the gnosiphages the ability to track you easily."

"Thank God for that," Anya said. "Hey, can you unlock the redacted skills too? That one Dominion skill and the faster-than-light tech, things like that?"

"Negative. Security protocols in-place from Engineer Prime due to threat value of humanity exceeding normal Archive classifications for distriiii-bu-bu-sshhuuuun. Communication windo-kkkkkkh—error.

Gnosiphaaaaa—" Red-507's voice stuttered, was reduced to white noise, and then silence.

All of their AIs vanished at once.

"God dammit," Anya swore. "Fucking aliens."

"It's not all bad. It's actually pretty good. If what that Engineer said was true, the gnosiphages won't be able to pick us off so easily anymore," Samaira said.

"Still would've liked another few minutes to grill the bastard," Gary grunted and then spat. All of their AIs reappeared, back to their normal, flower-headed selves.

"Hey, Felix. You okay?" Anya asked.

"Yeah. Just checking the logs. Wow, lots of data," they said.

"Speaking of, if that snake was such a big deal, did we get any special information from it?" Samaira asked her blue AI.

"Uh, ye-yes, but it's heavily encoded," Boo muttered. "I'm sorry I'm so bad at this."

"It will take at least several days to a week to decode, but I'm already on it," Felix said.

"Thanks you guys," Anya said.

"Ugh," Arvo grunted next to them. He blinked and looked between the AIs and everyone else. "Uh, what did I miss?"

———

GARY CAUGHT Arvo up on what had happened while Samaira left to go try and contact MacDougal again about the Engineers. Anya sat on the bumper of a fire truck next to a broken refrigerator that had been blown free of the White House at some point, and was stuffing her face with anything remotely edible.

Her ear beeped and she almost choked on a sandwich as she brought her menu up.

"It's not the Engineers," Felix said as Anya's communications window flashed. She tapped on it without looking and finally managed to swallow her food as Renn's helmeted head appeared before her.

"Am I interrupting?" he asked.

"Yes," Anya wheezed.

"Are you injured?"

"No, I'm eating. What's up?"

"Myself and the rest of the Western European team were just attacked by eight gnosiphages. We have one fatality. I tried connecting with you a while ago but my AI informed me your communications were being blocked. The same was true for the New Allied Territories team," Renn said.

"Holy shit," Anya whispered. "They coordinated three big strikes? All at once?"

"Possibly more. I haven't tried the others yet."

"Jesus. Uh, we're fine. Six aliens. One of which was some kind of overseer. We got a call from the Engineers too."

"As did we. They mentioned some kind of gnosiphage boss going down and disrupting their relay network or some such thing. We have you to thank for that?"

"I guess."

"I see. Did... one moment," Renn said and then glanced to one side and touched something on his screen and then spoke to somebody Anya could neither see nor hear. *"Bonjour.* Yes. Yes. I'm glad. I've got one of the American hosts on-line now. Yes. Anya."

Anya's ear beeped and a name flashed in her window. Ursula: the polar bear from the New Allied Territories. Anya tapped the name and the polar bear's armored face appeared, her black nose unnervingly close to her screen.

"They get you too?" Ursula asked, her voice a rough growl. Her white fur had blood splattered across it, and her black metal armor was cut and dented in several places. Anya and Renn both repeated to Ursula what they had told each other.

"How many aliens targeted yourself and the others?" Renn asked.

"Twenty-three," Ursula growled and looked behind her at distant pillars of smoke.

"Holy shit!" Anya nearly choked. "Is everybody okay?"

"No. Four dead hosts, probably a hundred regular humans, for whatever they're worth."

Anya scowled at that remark. If Renn had any issue with it, his reflective faceplate concealed his expression and he remained silent.

"How many hosts do you have left?" Anya asked.

"Why? So you can come fight us again?" Ursula asked. Anya glared at the polar bear and started to snap something back before Renn interrupted.

"No. So we may send reinforcements and possibly to aid with any injured you may have," he said. Ursula curled a lip at him and exposed a few silvery fangs.

"We're fine. We have plenty of hosts left to hold down our defenses and rebuild what little damage they did. Vastukar will probably have the place up and running twice as strong as before by tomorrow afternoon."

"Glad to hear it," Renn said.

"You said you fought some kind of overseer?" Ursula asked and Anya nodded. "So did we."

Anya raised her eyebrows. She had subconsciously figured that if there was one special alien on Earth there might be more, but it was disturbing to hear it confirmed.

"What did it look like? A snake?" she asked.

"No. Vastukar called it a crab. Sort of. Black armor, glowing blue eyes. It was big. The size of a house, maybe."

"*Merde*," Renn said.

Aside from the alien looking like a crab, its basic description matched the snake. They were the only gnosiphages that had anything in common, appearance-wise. Anya thought back to the night of the battle with the fridge in Chicago. Afterwards, Felix, Boo, and Gizmo had shown her and the others a map tracking the aliens and how many hosts each had killed. The snake had the second highest kill-count. The other one had been in China and working its way toward India.

"Did you kill it?" Anya asked.

"No. We hurt it a little and then it took off. Coward," Ursula said and spat. Anya tried to hide a smirk. She had never seen a polar bear spit before and it was an odd sight.

"Dr. Immonen's kind of out of it right now, but if you need a healer I can fly him over in a few hours, tops," she said.

"Thank you, but we're all right. The aliens do not seem interested in leaving any wounded behind, only the dead," Renn said.

"We've got our own healers," Ursula said.

"I'm going to continue to check in with the other hosts. I'll be available if you need anything," Renn added, and then nodded his head in a farewell before his window closed.

"I'm gonna go, too. Gotta lift a building out of a road," Ursula said. "Before I do: how's that little pangolin doing?"

"Pan? He's fine. Why?" Anya asked.

"Not too impressed with humans since I got smart. You all seem like a bunch of bastards. But him and the whale, they seem all right. You better watch out for him."

"I will."

Ursula made a noise in her throat like a growl and a purr, then ended the call. Anya sighed and leaned back against the firetruck as she closed her menu.

"What a day," she said to the empty and smoke-filled sky above her, then continued to enjoy her meal in silence while she could.

39

MacDougal requested that Anya and the other hosts depart for Dover Air Force Base in Delaware following the attack, and report to Colonel Perkins. Riley went with them, and informed them they were to wait here until MacDougal contacted them again.

MacDougal wanted the hosts kept a fair distance away from President Hanover, in case the aliens tried another attack on them. Better to keep their targets at an armed and alert military base than close to the leader of the country.

Anya decided to allocate her level-ups and points during the quick ride back to Dover. While still not as dramatic a bump as when she had taken her class, she had gotten some nice bonuses for passing level 40 in addition to the standard progression from leveling up so much, as well as several natural points from the fight itself.

ANYA NOWICKI: LEVEL 41 PHOENIX MONK
Statistics

- Awareness-10
- Dexterity-21 (+10 from gear)
- Fortitude-43 (+13 from gear)

- Intelligence-10
- Strength-23 (+5 from gear)
- Willpower-10

Skills

- Flame Dominion-43 (+16 from gear)(+5 from Artifact)
- Kinetic Dispersal-21 (+6 from gear)
- Combat Cognition-18
- Regeneration-37 (+14 from gear)
- Xhama Thul-16 (+4 from gear)
- Gravity Dominion-23 (+6 from gear)

There was also a huge chunk of RAC she had received from the aliens, the levels, and Archive contributions. After everything was totaled up, she had 1,363,731 RAC. She could have afforded to upgrade almost all of her gear at least once, but decided against it for the moment. She would need to go over the exact amounts needed to upgrade her gear with Felix, as well as look at any good alternatives now that she had some serious cash to throw around.

She leaned back in the pilot's seat, and endured the pain of the upgrade as the Shadow Ray flew itself to Dover.

"We've set several dorms aside for you all for the moment," Colonel Perkins said when Anya and the rest arrived just as night was falling. Perkins, a dozen airmen, and Riley escorted the hosts toward Dover's main cluster of buildings and away from their collection of vehicles.

"Wherever, as long as you let me at the dining hall again first," Anya said.

"I could definitely eat," Gary said.

"Me too," Samaira said.

"I'll join you," Arvo added.

"They have good ants here," Pan said.

"Dining hall it is," Perkins said and left them at the large, mostly empty cafeteria with Riley and their escort. The airmen stationed themselves around the edges of the hall, while a few directed Anya and others to where food was stored. It was a bit too late to get anything fresh, but there were plenty of leftovers.

Anya sat at a table with her usual pile of food. Everybody else had a much more sensible amount, except perhaps for Chandrali, who was working her way through multiple tins of tuna.

"They should be making the announcement soon," Riley said as he turned to a huge flatscreen TV on the wall nearby and began to flick through channels. Every channel was the same: aerial footage of the White House in smoking ruins, intermixed with blurry photos and chaotic video footage of the attack that afternoon.

"Here we go," Riley said and turned the volume up. The picture had changed from more footage of the attack to a podium with the Presidential Seal on it. Hanover stepped behind the podium from just out of frame. Unlike when the President usually took center stage at any announcement, there was no flashing of cameras, no rushed salvo of questions from reporters. Wherever Hanover was, it was somewhere private.

"My fellow Americans," Hanover began.

"Today, the White House came under attack from a force that has been confirmed to be of extraterrestrial origin. Many strange and destructive incidents that have occurred across America—and the world at large—have been directly caused by these same hostile alien forces that have invaded our planet.

"We only recently began to suspect the impossible: that Earth had become the target of aggressive alien life. We confirmed it days ago, and have been working with other world governments to contain the threat and protect our people. The creatures that attacked the White House this afternoon have been eliminated. Many of the creatures that have caused so much death and destruction over the past week have also been neutralized, but many remain on our world, and within our borders.

"We have not been idle during this time. I, along with members of Congress, have approved the formation of the Department of Extraterrestrial Research and Defense. This new department has already made great strides in combating the alien hostiles, protecting our people, and coordinating with foreign governments to save our planet.

"Agents of the DERD have come into contact with advanced alien technology that has enhanced them in ways that are highly beneficial to stopping the alien invaders. It is thanks to their bravery, alongside the hard-working and courageous members of the government and armed forces, that we have neutralized so many of the creatures that would seek to harm us.

"I understand that this news is alarming to hear, that many may consider it an elaborate prank, or a mistake. I assure you, it is neither. It is very real. We are sending out more detailed information to federal, state, and local law enforcement offices. Please be alert for any announcements to come in your area, and cooperate to the best of your abilities.

"This has become a war, but unlike any we've been in before. It isn't for land, or an ideology. It's for us: all of us. The invaders have proved to be non-communicative, only interested in violence, and our destruction. We will resist, and we will win.

"God bless you all, and God bless America."

The shot of President Hanover faded until only the Presidential Seal was left, and then it cut back to the newsroom, and the stunned faces of a pair of news anchors.

"One of his better speeches," Gary muttered. "Almost made him seem Presidential for a second there."

Anya only grunted. She'd seen enough of Hanover to know it was an act. He was probably grinning about how the invasion would help his popularity numbers or whatever.

Still.

If Anya had been just another normal person, it would have been comforting in a weird way. It would have been good to see a stern-faced authority figure telling everybody they were solving the problem and everything would be okay.

Anya thought of the snake.

Thief, it had said. Not yours to take.

The invaders were not entirely non-communicative.

She knew a lot more than any normal person, and none of it was comforting.

"I'm gonna head to bed, I think," Anya said, suddenly very tired.

"You okay?" Samaira asked. "Aside from nearly dying several times this afternoon."

Anya laughed at that.

"Yeah I'm good. Just want to turn my brain off for a while."

"Can I come with you?" Pan asked.

"Of course, buddy. You need any ants?" Anya asked.

"Yes please!"

"Airman, if you would escort the lady and pangolin outside and then to their room?" Riley asked and a pair of female airmen nodded and took Anya and Pan outside. Pan had enough time to uproot some ants from a nearby lawn, and then they were shown to a cordoned off section of the dorms.

"All of you will be staying here. You're free to move around inside this building, use the bathrooms as need be, but please don't try to leave without one of us," the airman said to her and Anya and Pan both agreed.

This dorm was much nicer than the last one Anya had stayed in at the base. Each room was private, and had its own tiny bathroom. Nothing fancy, but at least as nice as Anya's apartment back in Brooklyn. After so long spent flying from place to place and camping out in shifts, it was heaven.

There was a part of her brain that worried about staying in one place, about endangering the airmen of Dover just by being here.

But she was also very, very tired.

And the thought of just one night in a real bed, even if it wasn't hers, and a hot shower was enough to make her swoon. Besides, if the Engineers were to be believed, they'd made it a lot harder for the gnosiphages to find the hosts.

Pan, Felix, and Bee-Eff all chatted with each other while Anya cleaned herself off, and then searched the nearby closet for any spare clothes to sleep in. She found a t-shirt and some cotton exercise shorts that were a bit snug on her, but still fit.

"Good night, Pan. You did really great today. Very brave," Anya said as she stretched out as best she could on the bed. Pan had curled up on a folded blanket on the floor and wriggled his nose at her.

"Thank you, Anya. It was really, really scary but I'm glad I did it. I'm glad I could help my friends," Pan replied.

"Me too, buddy," Anya yawned and was asleep before she realized it.

———

ANYA OPENED her eyes to find herself, expectedly, in the Flame Dominion.

The bird was also there but, unexpectedly, it had changed. It had been a tiny, glowing sparrow before, but now it was much larger. It looked like a cross between an eagle and a peacock, with long flowing tail feathers and a sharp beak. It spread its wings and flapped them in greeting.

"Nicely done on roasting that snake-looking freak, little ember," the bird said.

"Thanks. You got a makeover?" she asked.

"Not quite. But you've grown, your connection to the Dominion has grown, and so I've also gotten a bit of an upgrade."

"I'm stronger now? Because I beat that snake?"

"Still a bit too linear with your thinking, though. You're better. 'Strength,' is part of that, yes. You also resolved whether or not to join MacDougal, and did so in a way that is true to you and the Dominion. You initially assumed it was binary: join under her terms and be a drone or refuse and remain free. You changed the situation: you joined but on your terms, and you helped get your friend a pretty cushy gig to boot, and kept your promise to the reporter. You're learning. Hug-exploding the snake alien was pretty awesome, though."

"Yeah," Anya grinned.

"So, what's the plan now?" the bird asked.

Anya blinked at it. Its eyes glowed an unflinching white, and a flurry of embers rose up around it as it ruffled its feathers.

"Finish killing the aliens?" Anya asked. The bird huffed and then flew up and pecked Anya on the head a couple of times and she swatted at it.

"Ow! Ow! Fuck off!" she said.

"That's a goal, not a plan!" the bird said as it flapped away and landed in front of her.

"All right, geez," Anya said and rubbed her head. "Hey, if I'm asleep in bed, why does my head hurt when you peck it? I'm not really here, am I?"

"That's some metaphysical stuff that, no offense, you aren't smart enough to unpack."

"Hey!"

"The short version is that your 'essence,' is here, and you think it should hurt when I peck you on the head for being a doofus, so therefore it does," the bird said. "Your physical body is still in the bed. Now stop changing the subject."

Anya crossed her legs beneath her and her arms over her chest as she floated in the soothing, amber-colored vastness of the Flame Dominion. Her first thought about what to do was just to train somehow, grow closer to the Flame Dominion and her other powers through dedicated use.

"Short term solution," the bird said. "Also only focusing on half the problem."

"Stop reading my mind and let me think!" Anya snapped. The bird huffed but waved a wing at her to continue.

Anya's eyebrows drew together as she focused. Destroying the aliens was the goal, but if the bird's talk about her and the duality of the Flame Dominion was to be believed, it was only one part of it. She'd been mostly focused on fighting: fighting the aliens physically, and fighting against MacDougal's efforts to bring her into the government. She'd cooperated a bit with MacDougal now, but she could do more. She had to.

If all Anya relied on was herself and the hosts finding and killing the aliens, it was a risk. So many hosts had died already, and if they lost too many—or all of them—then Earth would be largely defenseless.

Game over.

"There you go," the bird said and nodded. "You can't just destroy your enemies. You have to build up your allies."

Anya immediately thought of Tori and the aether.

"And maybe that means sharing the Archive, like what I did with Tori, or what Samaira wants to do with an aetheric university," Anya replied.

"It's one idea."

"That Vastukar guy is maybe already doing it with the New Allied Territories. He's making a whole new country around hosts. But he pretty much admitted to destroying an existing government to do it."

"Forest fires are part of nature. Burn away the old to make room for the new," the bird said.

"Is everything a fire metaphor with you?" Anya asked.

"I mean," the bird said and gestured at the unending fiery void around the both of them, "kinda."

"I'm not going to destroy the government."

"I'm not saying you have to. Again, no offense, but you don't really have the, ah, temperament or the attention span to be a nation-builder. But maybe start kindling abilities in others, like Tori."

"I'm just worried what it could mean for everybody if this power gets out of control. A lot of people could get hurt if the wrong person learns how to chuck a fireball."

"And a lot of people could get hurt if the aliens wipe all the hosts out. Nuclear power was a gamble, so was electricity, planes, gunpowder, medicine, space flight, every advancement. It's all a gamble. This is one more."

Anya ran her hands through her hair and sighed. She thought of Tori again, and what she had promised.

"I think I need to clear something up before we go any further," Anya said.

"Sounds serious."

"I like this. The Flame Dominion, I mean. And talking to you is weird, but nice. But if this is all some trick to turn me into a pyromaniac, or possess me, or whatever, I'm out. If you turn out to be some evil fire demon, you can kiss my ass."

The bird cocked its head at her, then laughed.

"What's so funny?" Anya demanded and the bird just regarded her again. Its avian visage shifted for a second, becoming more human, feminine, and familiar before shifting back.

It was Anya's face.

Her eyes widened.

The bird had said it spoke like it did because that was what she wanted. It had also said she had been bringing herself here, and not the other way around.

The bird was her.

"Oh shit," she said.

"Figured it out?" the bird asked.

"Maybe? You're me? I think?"

"Well, yes and no. The Flame Dominion isn't a person. It's not exactly a place either. It's an idea, a force, a feeling. Same with all the primeval Dominions. Something like that can't interact with people on its own. So, it becomes those people. If you were an evil fuckhead, I would be too.

"I have memories of other people who have been here, knowledge of what the Dominion really is and how it's been used well beyond your scope of understanding, but all of that gets filtered through you, and makes me. I'm not *just* you, but I'm not *just* the Flame Dominion either."

"I have a headache," Anya said.

The bird laughed again.

"Then I'll make this simple: I want what you want. Sometimes you might not consciously know it, but your heart does, and so, then, do I. If you're worried about going crazy with power, or changing too much, that's a *you* problem. The fire can refine or destroy. It might transform whatever's in it, but only to the extent that it's already capable of. That help?"

"Kinda? But maybe—"

"Maybe that's exactly the sort of thing an evil transdimensional fire demon might say to get you to lower your guard," the bird shrugged its wings and Anya nodded. "What's your heart say?"

Anya bit her lip and stared at the bird.

All the people that had wanted to control her, from her mother to her boss to President Hanover, they'd all wanted something. A picture-perfect daughter to be quiet and be a little dress-up doll, a stoic work-horse to meet quotas, or a source of power to guarantee re-election.

The bird had only wanted Anya to be herself.

"It says you're probably right," Anya replied. The bird nodded and puffed out its chest.

"I usually am."

"Also that you're a smug jackass."

"I got it from watching you."

Anya snorted.

"I need a vacation," she said.

"You don't have to solve every problem at once. We'll talk later, little ember," the bird said. "Although, I do have a favor to ask."

"Go ahead."

"It's a bit obvious that you're kindling a little fire of your own for that Samaira gal. Maybe try asking her out? I think it'd be good for both of you."

"Have I said how much I hate that you can just read my mind?"

"This particular fire isn't exactly in your mind, if you catch my drift."

"Please stop."

"It's in your pants."

"Cut it out!" Anya snapped and swatted at the bird. It crowed with delight and soared away.

"See you again sometime," it cawed, and vanished into a flurry of sparks.

Anya huffed and glared after it, then settled back into the void. She didn't wake up right away as she had done before. Instead, the warm hues of the Flame Dominion faded away, and Anya sank back into dreamless sleep.

FROM EARTH #5

From Rutherford International News Network:

UNITED NATIONS MEET FOLLOWING CONFIRMATION OF ALIEN PRESENCE

Chaos and hysteria continue around the globe following the announcements of multiple world leaders—including Prime Minister Stark of the UK, President Hannover of the United States, President Bisset of France, and Prime Minister Miura of Japan—that hostile aliens have landed on Earth.

Government-sanctioned documents have appeared online that describe the aliens as "mimics," that have taken the shape of household appliances, cars, statues, and other objects. Video footage of multiple sightings of such creatures have also surfaced and been confirmed by the American, British, Japanese, Brazilian, and Saudi Arabian governments, among many others.

The revelations have caused panic across most major cities around the globe. Public demonstrations have broken out in Tokyo, Hong Kong, Paris, New York, Toronto, Cairo, London, Cape Town, Sydney, and at least twenty other cities in the last day alone.

Members of the United Nations gathered in New York City following the attack on the White House to discuss the ongoing crisis.

Secretary General Al-Balawi and the leaders of several other nations have agreed to officially share resources and provide disaster relief to any and all countries that may require it.

"Now, more than ever, we must live up to our name: to unite and come together," the Secretary General said.

Representatives from India were notably absent from the assembly. Drawing concerns over what some diplomats at the UN are referring to as a rogue nation.

———

From the public chatlogs of *World of GuildCraft*, an MMORPG:

BartyMcBly: Did you see the President? Was that real?

Orka_ThragSkull: Pretty sure everybody saw that, or some version of it. Kinda hard to miss news like that.

Lady LeFay: Crazy stuff

BartyMcBly: Did you see that tall red-haired lady in one of the videos of the White House fighting? Is she an alien? I'm still not entirely clear on the details.

Arbiter Dane: Hell yeah I saw her. Muscle girls are the best. Think she likes short fat dudes who play paladin?

BartyMcBly: Jesus. Dude, it's the end of the world, the White House is trashed, aliens have invaded, and your only response is "Muscle girls hot."

Arbiter Dane: It may be the end of the world but I'm not dead yet. Just saying I'd let her step on me.

Lady LeFay: Gross.

Arbiter Dane: no u tho

Orka_Thragskull: I think Dane is like 12 or something.

BartyMcBly: Anybody else who isn't in the throes of pre-adolescence worried about the literal alien invasion?

Fairy_Poppins: It sounds like things are progressing as best as they can. Hanover and other governments are doing stuff. At least flying saucers aren't blowing cities up. Yet.

BartyMcBly: If you don't count that city in India getting nuked. Bangalore or whatever.

Lady LeFay: I'd be okay if my town blew up. It sucks here.

Orka_ThragSkull: I just want to see an actual alien. What the heck do they look like? All I saw on the news was some video of something that might have been a snake? Are they snake aliens?

Arbiter Dane: I hope they're sexy. Hot aliens. Muscle aliens.

Lady LeFay: Dude, shut up

Arbiter Dane: Probe me! My body is ready!

Arbiter Dane started dancing

Fairy_Poppins: I also volunteer Dane to be probed

———

From *Oni-Chan* (鬼ちゃん), an online message and image board, sub-board /WN/ (World News):

Anon-01: Pres Handlover confirms aliens. Where were you when you learned humanity is not alone?

Anon-01: *Hanover, dammit

Anon-02: Phone poster spotted

Anon-03: He will forever be Pres HandLover.

Anon-04: Anon was that an autocorrect? What kinda shit are you typing that replaces Hanover with Handlover?

Anon-01: Seriously? My phone's autocorrect is more worthy of discussion than literal aliens? Let it go already.

Anon-05: Answer the question, Phone Anon. Why did your autocorrect go to Handlover? I've texted about our bland-as-balls president before and never once had my phone autocorrect to Handlover.

Anon-04: Phone Anon confirmed for hand fetishist.

Anon-06: Maybe the aliens are handlovers too. They tire of tentacles and require sweet Earthling digits.

Anon-01: I can't believe you assholes

Anon-03: Wait, do the aliens have tentacles? Other anons are posting videos of killer stop signs with lobster claws and shit

Anon-04: Is that a thing? Are there actually fucking lobster stop signs killing people?

Anon-03: I'll find the video

Anon-03: lobstersign.webm

Anon-04: No way is that real. Some found footage shit

Anon-06: It's been confirmed by the Canadian government. It was in Montreal a few days ago.

Anon-04: Jesus

Anon-05: This is all terrifying and wild but can we please get back to the topic at hand(lover) RE: the autocorrect incident

40

I t had been two days since the aliens' attack on the White House.

Anya stood beside Gary, Samaira, Pan, Arvo, Riley, MacDougal, and other government officials in the ruins of what had once been the White House's Rose Garden. It had been partially replanted, and the White House itself was currently undergoing repairs.

President Hanover stood in front of them, at a podium crowded with a bouquet of microphones, and addressed an enormous crowd of reporters and cameras.

"May I present the first field agents of the Department of Extraterrestrial Research and Defense," President Hanover said and gestured to the assembled hosts and officials to either side of him.

"Hm," Gary grunted.

"It's just for show. He knows you're not actually an agent," Anya said and joined the rest of the crowd in clapping as countless cameras flashed from within the crowd.

"This is nice," Pan said as he waved at the crowd. "This is famous? Are we famous?"

"Oh yeah," Anya chuckled. She had spoken to Tori and knew her friend was watching in New York, but it also occurred to her that her mother and brothers might be tuned in as well. They probably wouldn't recognize her as she was now: tall and muscular and with bright red hair and slightly glowing yellow eyes.

The thought made her wince.

She needed to talk to them.

That could come later.

The press began shouting at Hanover as he opened the gathering up for questions.

"Why are these aliens here?"

"How many of these creatures are on the planet?"

"If the White House can be attacked like this, is anywhere really safe?"

"Is the pangolin some kind of science experiment?"

"What will the DERD and its agents be doing to prevent such attacks in the future?"

And a dozen others, more every second until Hanover held up his hands for quiet and began to call on reporters individually. He answered them as much as he could, though Anya noticed he kept the details of the Archive secret.

MacDougal had briefed them before the press meeting that any details of their skills were to be kept classified, and they needed to keep their AIs out of sight. If they were asked any direct questions about their powers, simply refer to "advanced technology," and any other information beyond that was classified.

"This is for the tall lady with the red hair," one reporter said as he stood up. "You were the one who hijacked the Rutherford International News broadcast several days ago, correct?"

"I cooperated with an inside source at the news network, but yes, that was me," Anya said.

"Were you working with the DERD or the government at that time, or was that a decision you made on your own?"

"I—" Anya started to reply before MacDougal stepped forward.

"She was in contact with us at the time and I was aware of her actions," the older woman said. While it was technically true and made it sound like MacDougal had given her the greenlight to broadcast, it didn't really answer the reporter's question.

Anya frowned.

Was she going to have to start thinking like MacDougal? How to manipulate everyone, give half-truth answers to every question?

"...call you?" another reporter's question butted into her thoughts and Anya blinked.

"Uh," she said.

"Wants to know what to call you," Samaira whispered behind her.

Hanover was the one to come to her rescue this time.

"Given that the DERD field agents are in a very unique position, we're keeping their exact details private for the time being. However, we'll be working on call-signs that we will make available to the press," the President said.

"I'm gonna get a superhero name?" Anya muttered, and MacDougal glanced at her from the side.

"Call-signs," she corrected under her breath.

"Do I get to pick?" Anya asked. MacDougal smirked.

"We'll see."

"Better not give me a bad superhero name," Anya crossed her arms and Samaira covered a smile behind her hand.

When the press briefing was over, Anya had a call with Jennifer Chang and Angel Ramierez from Channel 08 news. The interview MacDougal had scheduled had been postponed due to the attack, but she was working on rescheduling it.

"Just remember: I got dibs on that interview," Jennifer said over the phone.

"I know. I promised," Anya said and smirked.

"We'll be in touch, Ms. Chang," MacDougal said and hung up.

All of them, except Gary, had to stick around for a debriefing at the Pentagon with MacDougal and Riley. It was mostly just a basic restating of known information: what the Engineers had told Anya after the attack, what the other host groups were doing, and how other countries were forming their own alien defense organizations.

"There is one more thing," MacDougal said. "We need to figure out where to put all of you, long term."

"I figured I'd just go back to my apartment unless I was patrolling or something. Now that the Engineers have scrambled our signals, I'd like to go back to my own bed," Anya said.

"I understand, but you're all very high-value, now. You're also a potential danger."

"I would never hurt anybody!" Pan said. "That's mean!"

"I'm glad to hear it, but it's not what I meant. What if the Engineers scrambler fails, or the gnosiphages find a way around it, or something else happens?" MacDougal asked. Anya, Samaira, and Arvo all exchanged glances while Pan curled up into a ball at the mere mention of the gnosiphages.

"New York ain't exactly secluded, Anya," Riley said. "I get wanting to be in your own space, but it's better for everybody if we could make sure you're all somewhere away from normal people. No offense."

"I get it," Anya sighed. It sucked, but it made sense. She was also very aware that this meant it would be easier for MacDougal to keep tabs on them, but the risk of innocent people getting hurt wasn't worth it just to sleep in her own bed.

"I take it you have a suggestion already?" Arvo asked.

"We do. There's a base up in Alaska we were thinking about," MacDougal said.

"Alaska?" Anya said.

"What's an Alaska?" Pan asked.

"A frozen wasteland."

"Cold weather is yucky."

"Oh, please. You could be in Florida if you wanted to be in a couple hours or less," MacDougal said.

"Won't you need us to patrol, though? Not much of America up north," Samaira said.

"It's been deemed a waste of time and resources. You're all at a zero success rate for your patrols, so no, that won't be a regular part of your duties. For now, we'd like you secluded, and to study the Archive. To an extent you all will allow," MacDougal said.

"I'm amenable to that," Arvo said.

"I'm a-man-table too if Anya is," Pan said and Anya snorted.

"Fine," she said. "Fucking Alaska."

"We'll make it as cozy as we can," Riley said.

"We appreciate it," Samaira replied, and then they were all

dismissed for the night, and told to report back to the Pentagon bright and early tomorrow morning.

Gary waited for them outside next to his new truck, which looked a lot like his old truck, parked beside Anya's Shadow Ray and Arvo's flying egg.

"How'd it go?" Gary asked.

"We got assigned to Alaska," Anya grumbled. Gary let out a bellow of laughter and patted her on the shoulder. "What's so funny?"

"Well, I'd say you could come visit me, but it'd be a helluva flight and the weather would be even colder," Gary said.

Anya thought about what could be farthest away from Alaska and have colder weather.

"You built your factory in Antarctica?" Samaira asked and Gary chuckled and nodded.

"Remote and plenty of unclaimed land. Pain in the ass to get everything set up down there, but it's really gonna pay off," Gary said.

"I take it we should keep this information to ourselves?" Arvo asked and Gary waved a hand.

"When it was under construction? Yeah, didn't want anybody knowing. Now that it's basically finished and all the defensive systems are in place, it doesn't matter much to me. You'd have to drop a damn asteroid on the thing to make a dent. I made sure of that," he said. "Would rather you not bring any suits with you if you come visit. Maybe Riley, if he behaves himself. Otherwise, come see me anytime. I'm sure I'll pop back up here whenever I'm needed. Or bored. Or want a decent hot dog."

He paused for a second and smirked.

"Or to see you kids, I guess."

"Aw, what a big softy," Samaira said and Gary grunted.

"Don't push it," he said, but smiled at her all the same.

"Well if you're going to Antarctica tomorrow, and we're probably going to Alaska, we should go have dinner together," Anya said. "I know a good place in New York."

———

ANYA PICKED UP TORI, of course, and the six of them went to a rooftop Mexican bar and grill on the edge of Brooklyn. The place had been about to close for the night, but then the owner had recognized Anya and the others from the news and insisted on serving them a meal, free of charge.

"No, no, we're paying," Anya insisted and patted her rock-hard stomach. "I eat a lot."

Anya paid with the card MacDougal had given them specifically for this purpose, and ate through the grill's remaining supply of fajita meat, nachos, and guacamole, while the others had comparatively sensible meals. She also got through eight margaritas before she realized with a sigh that her regeneration was making it impossible for her to get drunk.

"Alaska, huh?" Tori asked as they both stood at the balcony and looked out across the city. A chill wind blew by, but Anya was passively releasing enough heat to warm the entire rooftop.

"Yup," she said.

"They need accountants up in Alaska?"

Anya laughed.

"I'm sure MacDougal would be fine if I asked you to come along but do you want to? It sounds like it's gonna be pretty dull."

"All the more reason for me to come. Besides, if I stay here they might actually make me work. If I come with you I can probably get away with more goofing off," Tori said. Anya smirked and then looked back at the others. The idea of spending more time with Pan, Arvo, and Samaira definitely didn't sound bad. She would miss her apartment, but if Tori could come too, then it didn't matter as much.

Home was people, after all, not just a place.

Tori followed Anya's gaze to Samaira.

"Oh. Oooooh. Maybe I could stay here after all. I wouldn't want to be a third wheel," Tori said.

Anya looked between her friend and Samaira and shook her head.

"It isn't like that... yet," she said.

"Yet? Are you crazy? She's super cute. And the world could end tomorrow, so why wait?"

"Geez. You and the bird. What is it with people butting into my love life?"

"Wait. The bird? As in the bird from the Flame Dominion?"

"Yup."

"An interdimensional fire entity has given you dating advice?"

Anya rolled her eyes.

"I don't know if that's impressive or just sad," Tori said and Anya gave her a gentle shove. "Well, if you're not going to hit on the cute doctor, then I definitely am."

Tori gave her a wink and then sauntered back to the table where Arvo and Pan were talking about dirt versus rocks. Anya turned back to look out at the city again, and almost jumped when Samaira appeared at her side.

"Sorry," Samaira said. "Didn't mean to startle you. Tori said you wanted something?"

Anya looked back at Tori, who gave her a sly grin and a wink, and then turned to speak with Arvo.

"Nothing important. Just thinking about stuff, wanted your take."

"Plenty to think about. The DERD, the aliens, the Archive, the Engineers, the New Allied Territories."

"Yeah. There's a lot," Anya said and then took a breath. "I was also thinking about what kind of places they'll have to eat in Alaska. I've gotten a bit spoiled for choice living in New York. Maybe... maybe we could go find a nice place. Together?"

"Well, Pan just eats ants, but I'm sure Arvo would..." Samaira said and then trailed off. She looked at Anya, and Anya sensed the warmth in her cheeks growing as she blushed. "Oh. You're asking me out."

"Yeah, that was the idea."

Samaira grinned and tucked her hair behind her ear.

"I'd like that."

Anya smiled, and both her regular and Sun's Heart skipped a beat.

"Me too."

"Well, I think our schedule is gonna be up in the air once we get to wherever they're sending us, but when we get a free weekend, yes," Samaira said.

"It's a date," Anya replied.

The two of them chatted about what kinds of restaurants they liked, and rejoined the group. When dinner was finished and they'd taken a few pictures with the owner at his request, they each went to their own homes, with good-byes and assurances they'd see each other at the Pentagon tomorrow, except for Gary.

"Factory should be totally finished in another week, tops. When it's done, I'll come see you all. Promise," he said as he climbed into his truck.

"You better," Anya said as she, Pan, and Tori got into the Shadow Ray. Anya dropped Tori off at her place, and then returned with Pan to her apartment. The pangolin climbed onto her ratty sofa and was almost immediately asleep.

Anya almost felt like a stranger in her own apartment as she looked around. The window that the Archive had crashed through over two weeks ago was still only covered by tape and a delivery bag.

Had it really only been two weeks?

Two weeks since her life had been irrevocably altered, along with the entire planet and the course of the human race.

Two weeks.

"Helluva thing," she said as she changed into some pajamas and lay in her bed, staring at the ceiling.

Samaira had been right. There was plenty to think about. Things had only accelerated since the Archive had struck her in the chest, and they didn't look to be slowing down any time soon.

But for the first time, Anya felt like it was starting to get better. Plans were being made, people were coming together. The hosts weren't isolated anymore, people knew what was happening, and the world still had not ended.

Situation changed.

Plus, she had a date.

Anya smiled to herself in the darkness, stopped worrying about everything bad that could happen, and started hoping for the good that might.

FROM SPACE #1

From a public galactic announcement via the Luorian Galactic Union(Translated from Luorian Basic):
SECURITY UPDATES FOR UNION SECTORS

To all citizens of the Luorian Galactic Union:

The rogue group of scientists and information terrorists known as "The Engineers" remains at large and their mobile enclave has been spotted simultaneously in Sectors 13 and 14. Any civilian or commercial crafts that see evidence of the Engineer's Enclave are to alert the nearest Luorian security outpost and not approach the Enclave under any circumstances.

Those who come into direct contact with the Engineers will be under suspicion of possession of CLASS 1-1 CONTRABAND and escorted to a maximum security holding site for inspection and detainment. Please do not attempt to engage with the Engineers in any way.

As a result of this, the aforementioned systems have been temporarily quarantined until the situation is resolved. We apologize for the inconvenience and distress this may cause, but know that it is necessary to the larger serenity and safety of our unified systems.

456 FROM SPACE #1

456 FROM SPACE #1

456 FROM SPACE #1

456 FROM SPACE #1

Additionally, the systems of Buat, Harthiel, and Noto-Kono in Sector 63 are now locked down due to the arrival of a gnosiphage splinter-swarm. All traffic to these systems has been diverted accordingly, and evacuation procedures are underway. Prime Minister Axun has secured the assistance of seven of the Cosmic Wardens, but our own Luorian Rescue Corps is still in need of volunteers to assist our fellow citizens in their escape from their besieged homeworlds.

The Vet-Har Empire has also made incursions into Luorian space near the Tuhd system in Sector 42. Civilian and commercial craft will be closely monitored if they enter these areas, and some may be turned away if the situation worsens. Please have all papers and licenses ready to present to any Luorian security teams that may request them.

There is a general advisory warning for commercial craft and luxury civilian craft with any intention of traveling through Sectors 86, 87, 88, and 89. There has been a noted increase in pirate activity, with some surviving witnesses claiming it is the infamous Henahkten Marauders. Defense Minister Feuxellian has increased the amount of security patrols in these sectors, but it is advised that they be avoided for now, only entered if absolutely necessary, and to be done with extreme caution.

We will triumph over these hardships, and emerge stronger than before.

Stay vigilant.

Stay the course.

The Union prevails.

From the recorded minutes of the weekly Minister meeting of the Luorian Galactic Union (Translated from Luorian Basic):

Prime Minister Axun: Recording to begin. I call the meeting to order. This meeting has a 2-3 informational rating and will remain classified for two standard months, at which point it will enter into public record under the Declaration of Informational Access. So say I.

Defense Minister Feuxellian: Acknowledged and seconded. This meeting is so ordered.

Finance Minister Colya: The Henahkten Marauders are becoming a real problem. They've effectively cut off four of our busiest sectors, and the security forces are occupied with the Empire and the gnosiphage swarms and not in any shape to deal with them.

Defense Minister Feuxellian: Maybe if somebody would increase the Defense Ministry's resources?

Finance Minister Colya: You claim enough already. Earn your keep.

Energy Minister Gregar: The Solar Sphere around the Tuhd star in Sector 42 has been compromised, along with eighty percent of the resource mines along the system's primary asteroid belt. It's knocked out our defenses in that system and given the Empire a foothold. They do not appear to be idly testing our defenses this time. I've already ordered energy from the neighboring spheres be diverted to the Tuhd system, but it may take a while, and my workers tell me they've already encountered some Imperial scouting craft.

Defense Minister Feuxellian: I know I'm in the minority here, but perhaps it's time to extend a peace offering to the Engineers? They have our best weapon, after all.

Justice Minister Uktop: They have violated far too many of our laws to allow that.

Intelligence Minister Qohara: And it's only gotten worse, I'm afraid. I received a report this morning regarding another shipment of the Archive.

Defense Minister Feuxellian: The one the Engineers tried to send to Melarus-III? It failed. The gnosiphages wiped the entire planet out along with the Archive.

Intelligence Minister Qohara: No. The Archive never reached Melarus-III. The Engineers diverted it at the last moment to space much farther outside the Union, almost to the edge of the galaxy.

Defense Minister Feuxellian: Where?

Intelligence Minister Qohara: The Sol System. Earth. Humans.

Defense Minister Feuxellian: What? Is that a joke?

Justice Minister Uktop: Madness.

Finance Minister Colya: Oh good gods, if they make it off-world it'll be a disaster. It'll be like before, when—

Prime Minister Axun: Further discussion of that topic is classified beyond the bounds of this meeting, Minister Colya.

Defense Minister Feuxellian: They're fucking animals. Beasts. And the Engineers gave the whole planet the Archive?

Intelligence Minister Qohara: A little over a thousand members of the population, currently, yes. I have confirmed it myself. As of now, the Engineers have had the foresight to deny them subspace travel and any other FTL options we're aware of, as well as access to any tech or ability that permits teleportation, and redacted the Ninth Dominion and related skills entirely. However, most everything else is accessible within the standard limitations of the Archive.

Finance Minister Colya: Small comfort.

Prime Minister Axun: I want that gods-damned Enclave found now. If that many humans get off their primitive rock with the Archive… I can't imagine.

Feuxellian, contact some of the Wardens operating in Sector 63. See if they'd be willing to help us with this. I'm sure keeping such a violent and chaotic race grounded on their homeworld will fit into that self-righteous code of theirs somewhere.

Qohara, I want the Sol system under constant surveillance. Reports on my desk daily, and hourly if there are any major changes.

Intelligence Minister Qohara: It will be done. I have agents that have tapped into an Enclave communication line as we speak.

Prime Minister Axun: Good. We'll discuss more of this tomorrow. For now: Energy Minister Gregar, let's see what we can do about reactivating our defenses around the Tuhd system.

———

From an intercepted communication between the Engineers via Luorian Intelligence Ministry (LIM) (Translated from Luorian Basic):

Initiate Engineer Red-507: Confirm Earth Archive Hosts have destroyed one gnosiphage network overseer. Two remain on-world. Current gnosiphase on-world numbers at roughly 25% of initial force.

Elder Engineer Green-28: Acknowledged. New survival parameters for humans?

Initiate Engineer Red-507: 14% survival rate, up from initial estimate of 11%. Down from previous estimate of 16% given rise of possibly combative factions within Earth host ranks that may prove problematic post-invasion.

Elder Engineer Green-28: Acknowledged. Status of re-establishing reliable communication line with Earth hosts?

Initiate Engineer Red-507: Progress on re-establishing communication has been stalled due to moving Engineer Enclave. Luorian Intelligence had observed previous location and locked its status from 157 possible outcomes to twelve across two systems we are projecting into. Engineer Council advised immediate relocation.

Elder Engineer Green-28: Acknowledged. Re-establishing communications moved to secondary priority. Confirm Archive irregularity with host Sol-3022, local designation Anya Nowicki.

Initiate Engineer Red-507: Confirmed. Breach of Archive protocol was regarding Flame Dominion skill. Dimensional irregularities detected around host. Possible influence of trans-dimensional force responsible. Artifact classification: Sun's Heart, shows signs of unauthorized alteration and enhancement. Unable to revert to Archive-approved quality.

Elder Engineer Green-28: Probability of outside influence on Archive parameters and safeguards is 0.004%. This outcome is highly improbable. Elaborate.

Initiate Engineer Red-507: Probable oversight or error due to unexpected re-calibration of Archive for Earth life from previously planned integration with life on Melarus-III. Records show irregular integration with non-human life on Earth, along with other unforeseen problems. Current probability of outside influence on Archive parameters and safeguards has increased to 2.1%.

This one has received update from Initiate Engineer Yellow-740 that host Sol-4507, local designation Renn, has also caused an Archive irregularity.

Elder Engineer Green-28: Undesirable.

Initiate Engineer Red-507: Agreed.

Elder Engineer Green-28: Explain plan to curtail future Archive protocol breaches.

Initiate Engineer Red-507: Clarification needed: plan?

Elder Engineer Green-28: Host Sol-3022 is within your purview. You are responsible for Archive protocol breaches the host may cause. Elaborate on plan to curtail future breaches.

Initiate Engineer Red-507: Oh. Oops.

Elder Engineer Green-28: Unacceptable response. You are responsible for Archive breaches by hosts within your purview.

Initiate Engineer Red-507: This one was unfamiliar with that responsibility.

Elder Engineer Green-28: Unacceptable response. How have you allowed this?

Initiate Engineer Red-507: Primary priority is relocation of Engineer enclave. Secondary priority is re-establishing stable communication with Earth hosts. Tertiary priority is tracking of main gnosiphage swarm. Quaternary priority is monitoring gnosiphage dimensional rifts and splinter-swarms in sectors 60-through-80. Quinary priority is organizing meal delivery for Elder Engineer Green-28. Senary priority is—

Elder Engineer Green-28: Statement understood. Please cease elaboration of priorities.

Initiate Engineer Red-507: This one is only a single consciousness. This one is also partially responsible for securing enclave transmissions from outside interception by Luorian Intelligence following the expiration of Initiate Engineer Blue-122. This one has many priorities and cannot tolerate any more without others suffering in quality.

Elder Engineer Green-28: Understood. Monitor host Sol-3022 for now in case of future breaches and compile reports for review by Engineer Council. Additionally, explain: what is this communications irregularity?

Initiate Engineer Red-507: Irregularity? Oh. Oops.

Elder Engineer Green-28: Unacceptable response.

Initiate Engineer Red-507: This one's previous statement is proven: communications irregularity is likely Luorian Intelligence comm spike that was only permitted while this one was attending to multiple other priorities. Re-routing communication line through back-up security matrix. Please hold.

—SIGNAL LOST—

ACKNOWLEDGMENTS

No book is written alone, though it can frequently be lonely work. This book simply wouldn't exist without the support of a lot of people. First and always: my wife and parents. Their material and emotional support has been nothing less than essential and I owe them more than I can say.

I started a Patreon back in 2019, and anybody who donated and helped, you have my thanks. But once again I must make specific note of Noelle and Scott, who have remained steadfast through almost two years of largely non-existent updates. It always made me happy to see you both were, for whatever reason, still there. It meant, and continues to mean, a lot. Thank you both.

No book is ever really complete without its cover. For my own cover (which I think is outstanding) I have the immensely talented, patient, professional, and incredible Enzo Fernandez to thank. Your work is almost as wonderful as you.

The RoyalRoad community was very helpful in pointing out the weak spots, flaws, and shortcomings in my story. It wasn't always nice to read, but it was usually helpful. Except for that guy who kept PMing me wanting to know the exact measurements of all the female characters' breasts. C'mon dude. Chill out.

The Reddit communities—specifically r/writing, r/LitRPG, and r/ProgressionFantasy—were all sources of inspiration, support, laughs, and a lot more. LitRPG and its overlapping genres are still pretty niche compared to the larger genres out there, and it's great to interact with what feels like a much more tightly knit and encouraging network of like-minded readers and writers.

And of course, you, Fellow Reader. If you're here, if you made it to the end, I appreciate it. Time is limited, stories are many, and it means a lot that you chose to spend your time reading this story. I can only hope that you enjoyed it, and that we'll see each other again next time.

Until then, take care of yourselves, and each other.

All the Best,
Justin "JayAck" Ackerknecht

LITRPG GROUP

To learn more about LitRPG, talk to authors including myself, and just have an awesome time, please join the LitRPG Group.

FACEBOOK GROUPS

<u>Facebook Groups for LitRPG, Gamelit, Progression Fantasy, and more</u>

A lot of these groups help authors like me, and readers like you find other great books in the growing LitRPG/Gamelit/Progression Fantasy genre. If you liked this book, there's a very good chance you'll like some other books that are frequently talked about in these groups. Also, they're generally full of nice people who post funny memes.

Gamelit Society

LitRPG Books

LitRPG Forum

LitRPG Releases

Fantasy Nation

Science Fiction and Fantasy Book Fans

ABOUT THE AUTHOR

Hello there! I know these are usually done in third-person or something, but that feels weird to write about myself like that.

First, I've been writing since before I properly knew the alphabet. I'd get my parents to write for me while I dictated. Once I was able to, I spent most of my waking moments drawing and writing stories of my own, or inhaling the stories of others through books, comics, video games, and later anime and manga.

I was born in Arizona, raised in California, and then moved back to Arizona for college. I definitely preferred California. Post-college, I moved to South Korea, where I spent about a decade living between the cities of Ulsan, Suwon, and Seogwipo. I'm currently living next to several large, pastoral sheep fields in the UK.

I've had a lot of jobs over my life: a snake handler, a janitor, a busboy, an accountant, a cashier, a car-washer, an associate professor, and a few others. Presently, I'm working as a writer. Hopefully this'll be a permanent gig, as it's my favorite one by far, and I've been doing it for free for years anyway. Fingers crossed it works out!

STAY IN TOUCH

One last thing:

If you'd like to get updates about anything I'm working on (including the sequels to this very story) you can find me on-line at www.jjackerknecht.com and sign up for my newsletter there (assuming I've gotten it up and running).

If you have business or other inquiries, you can e-mail me at jayack@jjackerknecht.com

Previews of upcoming work, including advanced chapters of my current projects, are at https://www.patreon.com/jayack which is also a great way to support me between releases if you're so inclined.

On Twitter, I'm likely retweeting cool artwork very talented artists have done along with absurd shitposts if you'd like to follow me at https://twitter.com/jjackerknecht or just search for @jjackerknecht.

There's also a Discord that you can come by to chat at https://discord.gg/un2wVMf

Hope to see you there!

www.ingramcontent.com/pod-product-compliance
Lightning Source LLC
Chambersburg PA
CBHW061507020726
47502CB00006B/1969